THE SASSY SUBMISSIVE

Book 1 of Stronghold Doms

GOLDEN ANGEL

Cover art by Wicked Smart Designs
Cover Photo by CJC Photography
Cover Models: Gideon Connelly and Rachael Baltes
Edited by MJ Edits and Raisa Graywood

Thank you so much for picking up my book!

Would you like to receive a free story from me as well? Join the Angel Legion and sign up for my newsletter!

THANK YOU

Thank you so much to my readers who encouraged me to write the *Venus Rising Quartet*. I'm glad you fell in love with the characters as much as I did, because that's where the *Stronghold* series was born.

An extra special thank you to Katherine, Amanda and Fifi, who have helped keep me motivated and made this book into what it is.

As always, love and appreciation to my ever-supportive husband, to whom I dedicate this book. Any similarities between him and the hero are purely coincidental, I swear. Even though they have the same name. And look exactly alike. And I've used actual things he's said to me for dialogue.

Total coincidence.

ANGEL

Walking into the club was the hardest thing Angel Jones had ever done in her life.

She'd deliberately chosen Chained because it was a new club and it was in Virginia, much farther away from her home than the club she actually wanted to join—Stronghold, in DC. It was doubtful regulars to Stronghold would search out a new club; they were comfortable in their space at Stronghold and trusted the people there. Why would they drive such a distance to check out a new place?

Easy answer: they wouldn't.

This was the second time Angel had ever been to a BDSM club. The first time had been years ago, in New York City, when she was still in college. Since then, she'd realized she was submissive, but she didn't have any friends currently living in Maryland who were in the scene. Even worse, other than her best friend Leigh, she didn't have any *close* friends who were female and contemplating the idea of trying to convince one of her guy friends to come with her made her want to whimper, so she was making this difficult journey alone. Which was absolutely terrifying.

Getting out of her car, Angel smoothed her hands over the long, embroidered jacket she was wearing. She'd dressed very carefully tonight because she was going to be doing something wrong—she was going into a club as a Mistress rather than a submissive. It was dishonest, which rankled her, but all of her 'experience' was research and reading. Not at all the same as real life experience or having someone there with her who knew what they were doing.

As a self-defense instructor, she taught her students that the first step to keeping themselves safe was to stay out of dangerous situations. To her, putting herself in a position to be tied up and at the mercy of a stranger was pretty much the textbook description of a dangerous situation, yet she couldn't stay away. The one night she'd experienced in New York, she had been entranced but did nothing more than watch. Once she was more comfortable in the club and felt more confident about knowing the scene and her ability to keep herself safe, without backup, she would go to Stronghold as a submissive. No harm done to anyone and she'd have a nice and easy introduction into the world she'd been fantasizing about ever since she first heard about it.

Of course, she wished she had a friend she could do this with. She might have felt safer jumping straight in as a submissive if she had a buddy by her side. Unfortunately, she didn't have anyone she felt comfortable asking to go with her. Even though Leigh would probably have come if Angel had asked, because she was a good friend, Leigh's boyfriend, Michael, would never have approved of the outing.

At twenty-five years old, Angel had only ever had two serious relationships; the second one had ended over a year ago and since then she hadn't dated anyone seriously. Neither of her previous boyfriends had been able to give her what she craved, neither had been able to make her feel the excitement she got reading BDSM erotica stories. Sure, she'd had orgasms during sex, but it always felt like there was something missing, and eventually that had led to the end of each relationship. And it didn't help when most of her closest friends were guys, which tended to cause some jealousy and misunderstandings with her boyfriends, but she figured someone confident enough to be a

Dom would have to be secure and confident enough not to mind she had a lot of guy friends, right?

She wanted a man with the confidence, the self-assurance to be uncaring about her male friendships. Also, a man who was sexually controlling in the bedroom... at the very least she needed to try it out, to see firsthand whether or not this was a lifestyle for her. And if it was, then maybe she could find someone into the lifestyle she could have a real relationship with.

Tonight she was dressed in thigh high leather boots with six inch heels, leather shorts, and a brocaded green skin tight top boned like a corset but had an Asian inspired mandarin collar and little capped sleeves. It covered her upper body completely except for a wide swath between the neck of the collar and her bust; a keyhole opening which showed a generous amount of cleavage. She'd straightened her hair and worn it loose, letting it flow over her shoulders to swing halfway down her back—almost two inches longer than when she let her naturally curly hair fly free. Black lace gloves and the embroidered jacket completed her look, although she'd take her jacket off when she got inside. It was a damn sexy outfit and she was pretty sure it fairly screamed 'in charge.' Because that's exactly how she wanted to appear tonight. How she'd been practicing to appear.

Tilting her chin up haughtily, she strode towards the door of the club. It was a plain wooden door with a discreet sign above it said "Chained." There were no lights or anything else to draw attention to itself. She liked that.

When she signed in at the front desk (pseudonyms were allowed, although when she'd filled out her form for the guest pass she'd had to give her real name and the pseudonym she planned on using) she put her name down as Mistress Angela before handing her coat over to the girl behind the desk, a sexy blonde wearing a naughty secretary outfit. The irony wasn't lost on Angel and she gave the girl an approving smile, which made the receptionist flush happily as she took Angel's coat.

"Welcome to Chained, Mistress Angela," she said.

"Thank you, dear," said Angel, sliding into the role she'd assigned herself. She'd never wanted to pursue theater as a career (monetary pressure took all the fun out of it) but that hadn't stopped her from pursuing it as a hobby in her free time. Even though she'd only started auditioning in the area a few months ago, she'd already been cast in a show at a community theater. Tonight was going to be the performance of her life because she wasn't onstage. Acting was so much easier with cues and lines.

Still, she could feel her nerves humming the way they did when she was standing in the wings, waiting for the curtain to go up. And that's exactly where she was right now; this lobby was the wings and as soon as she stepped past the hulking (and kind of hunky) bouncer through the door to the club then she'd be center stage. Well, not quite. She'd be surrounded by the other players, but she assumed many of them would be very good at reading body language. At least that was always how it seemed in the books she read.

Hopefully her acting training would be enough to cover up her nerves, inexperience, guilt at the deception, and the little voice inside of her insisting she'd never pass as a Domme.

The lobby was tastefully decorated in dark reds and grays with hardwood floors, giving it the feeling of a boudoir. When she walked into the main area of the club, she was surprised she found it rather overwhelming, almost tacky, in comparison to the lobby. The space was bigger than she'd expected, with a dance floor to her left, a bar straight ahead of her, and a wall lined with little alcoves for scening on the right. Chandeliers flickering with multi-hued lights hung from the ceiling, red velvet curtains were tied back at the edges of the alcoves— obviously they could be used to create a more private area if desired— and the dance floor had neon lights blazing over it, creating interesting patterns on the floor. Everywhere she looked, the walls were covered with either bondage equipment or artwork (and there didn't seem to be a theme to the photographs and paintings, or any attempt at arranging them in a way that would be pleasing to the eye). The bar in front of her was decorated to look almost like a tiki bar, clashing sharply with the rest of the decor. Seriously?

There were people walking around, some of them involved in

scenes, some on the dance floor, and some at the bar, wearing all sorts of interesting and revealing clothing. Angel found herself examining a small group of men at one of the bar tables, four of them, all extremely attractive and wearing various amounts of leather.

Dominants, definitely. She could feel the wash of heat straight through her body as she saw their self-assured movements, their predatory gazes flicking around the room. But she didn't show any of her reaction to them on her face, keeping her expression carefully blank. All four of them were attractive, but it was the blond one—who looked half-Viking, half-pirate, with facial hair making a neat frame around a sensuous mouth—that caught her attention. Or, rather, he caught her gaze in his and she found herself struggling not to lower her eyes immediately from the sheer force of his presence.

That's what a submissive would do, she reminded herself. Lowering her gaze was what she instinctively wanted to do, but that's not what she was tonight. Struggling to maintain her expression, Angel gave him a careful nod, very slight and without taking her eyes away from him, acknowledging him as an equal. He gave her a nod back and smiled.

The hard look in his eyes made her want to melt. Or get down on her knees and beg him to tie her up, spank her and fuck her. Instead she straightened her spine and curved her lips in a small smile back.

Remember, you're a Domme tonight and keep it together!

ADAM

Adam Rawn was not impressed by Chained. He was only here because his good friend, Rick Winter, had been hoping his friends might be willing to make the longer drive to Virginia every so often, in trade for him usually being the one to make the commute. Fortunately, it didn't look like Rick was very impressed either. Normally Rick only made it to Stronghold once a month or once every other month, because it was about a two-hour drive for him to get there. Chained was only an hour's drive from Rick and an hour away from the rest of them. It would have been the perfect compromise, except none of them were happy here.

Not that they would ever abandon Stronghold completely, since they were also good friends with the owner, Patrick Murphy, but they would have been able to see Rick more often—the temptation of new submissives they hadn't seen before had been intriguing.

"Sorry Rick, I don't think I'll be coming back," said Chris. He had come purely to hang out with Rick and had no interest in checking out new submissives, since he was currently in an exclusive relationship with his best friend, Justin, and their girlfriend, a sweet, curvy brunette named Jessica. "Or recommending to Justin we bring Jessica here."

Rick looked around the room, his disappointment written clearly on his face. "I know, it's not what I was hoping either. Maybe it's too new."

That was part of the problem. The decorations were too eclectic and whoever owned it hadn't quite found their stride yet. Rather than a tasteful mix of eroticism, bondage, and bar feeling, all the elements had been spattered like spaghetti on a wall. The other problem was there didn't seem to be many unattached subs. That factor was important to Rick and, to a lesser extent, Adam and Andrew, the fourth man in their little reconnaissance force this evening. Rick wanted to find a meaningful relationship like Justin and Chris' with Jessica, just without the sharing, and Adam was starting to think he might be ready to stop playing and get serious about a submissive too. If he could find the right submissive. Andrew wasn't interested in any kind of relationship after his last one had ended so badly; he'd been single for years now.

The lack of unattached subs at Chained tonight was a problem because it left them with nothing to do but sit and drink and talk. Which they could have done anywhere. And Adam wanted to play. It had been awhile since he'd found someone he wanted to scene with, although he'd indulged once or twice in the past couple of months when asked to do an introduction or teaching scene at Stronghold. But it was ultimately unsatisfying.

At thirty-one years old he was surprised to find himself yearning for permanence in a relationship, he'd always thought he'd be a confirmed bachelor until at least his mid-thirties, but seeing the love and devotion between Chris, Justin, and Jessica, the way they came together to make their tripod relationship work, had made him surprisingly envious. Their relationship had ended up creating another one between Liam, another Stronghold Dom, and Jessica's best friend, Hilary. Since then, Adam had started considering a real relationship, something Rick had already been looking for.

Something neither of them were going to find at Chained, apparently.

"Well, that's interesting," said Rick, perking up a little. All of the men turned to see where he was looking, at the door leading to the lobby.

A stunning woman had just walked in by herself. A long fall of dark brown hair caressed her shoulders, framing a roundish face which wasn't quite conventionally beautiful, with almond shaped eyes hinting at Asian heritage. She also had the most incredible lips Adam had ever seen, small but somehow plumply bow-shaped to the extent they almost looked like they'd been created for sex appeal, the way Betty Boop or Jessica Rabbit's lips would appear in real life. Made for kissing or wrapping around a man's shaft. The tiny shorts she was wearing hugged curvy hips, hinting at a fantastic rear view. The unique top she was wearing interested him immediately, despite the fact it covered most of her. The curves of her breasts in the top's opening were full and creamy, pressing the soft mounds upwards into almost a shelf. She was at least a D cup. Maybe more. The thigh high leather boots with the fuck-me heels were skin tight on her legs, showing them to be long and lean.

Looking at her made his dick stir.

"Damn, she's a Domme," said Rick, deflating as he took in her attire, the tilt of her chin and the aggressive way she looked around the room. Moodily he took a swig of his beer.

"What, you don't want to try out being a switch?" Andrew asked, nudging his friend in the ribs. The other three men laughed as Adam continued to study the woman. Not once in his entire life had he ever been attracted to a Domme, no matter how physically attractive they were, but this woman had his complete attention and his groin was already tightening. Why?

He watched her look around, observed the slight distaste on her face as she took in the decor before she covered up the expression. Something about her was slightly off, although he couldn't quite figure it out. When her eyes swept around the room, examining the people, he was still looking at her. The minute their eyes met she had some kind of reaction, but he was too far away to see it clearly. The nod she gave him was careful, entirely appropriate, but something about her body language was *off*. As if she was unsure of herself. A new Domme maybe? Inexperienced? He smiled at her, to see how she would respond. She smiled back when she met his eyes before looking away again to continue her examination of the room.

"What's up?" Chris asked, leaning over to see where Adam was looking. "Why are you looking at the Domme?"

"I'm not sure," Adam confessed, taking a sip of his own beer to cover his frown. "There's something about her..."

"Think she's a switch?"

Hm. "Maybe. Or maybe very new."

Now all of his friends were looking at her again, watching her as she studied the small room. Chained wasn't even a third as big as Stronghold, but then again Stronghold hadn't started out very big either. It had expanded and renovated as it became more popular and successful. The woman they were all watching seemed to feel their eyes on them. Turning her head she stared right back at them. Some men might have looked away or pretended they weren't looking at her at all. Not this group. She seemed a little startled at first as they all stared back at her, and she was the first one to look away.

"We won," said Chris, laughing.

Adam was still watching the woman, when she glanced back at them there was a small, rueful smile on her pouty lips, and then she started walking toward them. The rolling gait her high boots required made her hips move in a manner that was both sensuous and graceful.

A lot of women would have trouble walking in heels that high. He'd seen them on the sidewalk shuffling along, looking like they were walking on stilts. Despite the height of her heels this woman walked easily, with a slight swaying motion that made his already hardening cock stand straight up.

As soon as they realized she was heading toward them, the men all started watching her again, appreciating the beauty of her movements.

ANGEL

Angel felt completely out of her element. The club itself wasn't as intimidating as she'd expected, but the four men in front of her were. Which, perversely, had drawn her to them, even though she was supposed to be a Domme tonight, not a sub. She figured it would be okay though because as a Domme she shouldn't be scared, right? So when they'd all stared her down, going for a power play, she'd stared back for as long as she could stand it. Eventually she'd had to look away, sure they could see her heart pounding in her chest. When she'd turned back the handsome blond one was still watching her. She felt drawn to them. Him. Initially she'd wondered why there weren't subs flocking to their table, but after a quick look around she'd noticed there didn't seem to be many singles other than the men at the table. Most people were there as part of a couple.

She envied those couples. Especially the woman tied to the St. Andrew's Cross who was being very lightly flogged, warming her up for a more strenuous workout. Her Dom was completely focused on her, murmuring encouragement as he turned her skin a light pink. It made all of Angel's girly bits throb to watch them. The rise and fall of the flogger had her fantasizing about being in the sub's place—at least until she realized there were a couple other people watching her watch the scene, and she started to worry they might realize she was more interested in being the one receiving the whipping than in wielding the flogger. So she decided to approach the small group of men instead, justifying it to herself by hoping they could give her some information about the club and BDSM in general.

Their collective, appreciative gaze as she walked toward them made her quiver inside a little, but she knew nothing showed on the exterior as she smiled warmly. Acting 101 for the win!

"It's not nice to stare," she said mock-sternly, as soon as she got within hearing distance, wanting to see their reactions. The blond with facial hair who kept watching her smiled appreciatively at her scolding; the look of approval in his blue eyes made her want to melt right down into her boots. Up this close she got a hint of his well-defined muscles under the crisp white button down shirt he was wearing. Strange to see a Viking in what she considered a dress shirt. Strange to see a Dom at a BDSM club in one too, now that she thought of it, even if he was wearing it with black leather pants.

Tall, dark, and handsome wearing a black cotton shirt and jeans threw back his head and laughed. The other blond, who had no facial hair, grinned and shook his head almost apologetically. Since he was on the other side of the table all she could see of his outfit was the black leather vest he was wearing, but she assumed he had the leather pants to match. The last man had naturally tanned, caramel skin, black hair, and was wearing nothing but leather pants to show off his admittedly spectacular upper body; he arched his eyebrow at her. The one in the black shirt was casually dressed but the other three together looked like a bondage ad for Studs'R'Us. Eye candy at its finest.

"May I get you something to drink, Mistress?" As soon as she approached the table, a scantily dressed young man popped up at her elbow, looking up at her worshipfully. Wow. He was cute, only two inches shorter than her in her boots which meant he'd be taller than her if she had been wearing any other shoes. Too bad she *wasn't* looking for a sub.

"No, thank you," she said. It didn't seem polite to assume she could join their table. Looking disappointed, the server walked away.

"No, thank you?" asked the gorgeous blonde pirate-y man, sounding kind of judgmental. He was studying her like she was some kind of insect pinned to a board. The scrutiny made her uncomfortable, especially because those bright blue eyes looked like they could see deep inside of her, sorting through her secrets. Approaching these men had probably been a mistake, but she'd been drawn like a moth to the flame. Even though tall, dark, and handsome was her usual type, she found herself feeling more interested in the blond. Maybe it was the way he seemed interested in her. Not in a sexual way, but he seemed curious and speculative, as if she'd done something wrong or unexpected.

Oops. Apparently Dommes don't say thank you?

"Didn't your mother teach you manners?" she asked back dryly.

"Must have had a strict mother," observed tall, dark, and handsome.

"I take after her," quipped Angel with a wink, making them laugh. Okay, time for introductions. They weren't taking the lead so she would. That's what a Domme would do, right? "I'm Angela." She left off the 'Mistress.' None of these men would ever use the honorific for her, just as she wouldn't use any for them while she was pretending to be a Domme.

"Chris," said tall, dark, and handsome. "Nice to meet you." He winked at her. There was nothing seriously flirtatious in his face, he was naturally flirtatious and friendly.

"Andrew," said the other dark-haired man, reaching out to shake her hand. Angel smiled and responded with her most professional handshake; the one she used whenever she was making a sales pitch. Firm, confident, poised.

"Rick," said the blond without facial hair. He shook her hand too.

"Well now I feel left out. I'm Chris." Shouldering Andrew aside, he claimed her hand and shook it as Angel laughed. Chris was fun.

Turning to the gorgeous blond with the well-trimmed mustache and goatee, Angel held out her hand, arching her eyebrow. He took it slowly, deliberately, almost as if he was testing her. The easy confidence of his movements took her breath away, and the warmth of his hand wrapped around hers was almost enough to make her knees buckle. All of them were deliciously authoritative, but unlike the other men there was something about the way he was looking at her, touching her, it wasn't quite flirtatious but was definitely sexual.

Covering her immediate response, which was melting arousal, Angel raised her eyebrows at him and pulled her hand away.

"Adam," he said, after she'd removed her hand from his. He rubbed at the sides of his mustache with his thumb and forefinger, observing her so intently that for a moment she worried he knew he'd made her wet, just from his handshake. Jesus, he was extremely alpha and she was a little shaken by how much he affected her.

It would probably blow her cover to drop to her knees and beg him to teach her everything he knew, right? *Might be worth it.*

"Ignore him," Chris said, fortunately taking her attention before she did something stupid, like confess she was a submissive to a whole group of men she didn't know or have any reason to trust. "He's been in a bad mood all night."

Adam glared at him. "Would you like to join us?" he asked, as if trying to prove his friend wrong.

"Um." She glanced around. Yeah at first she had come over because she was hoping to ask them questions but now that she'd met them she was starting to feel a little unnerved. Especially by Mr. Grouchy, whose intense blue eyes seemed to search her own, as if he could see into her head. Which, considering the situation, was more than a little unnerving. "This is my first time here, I was thinking about taking a look around."

They all nodded understandingly. "Feel free to come find us later," said Chris. "And ask any questions you want. None of us are new to public scening."

Angel smiled and thanked them—since that had been her excuse for approaching them in the first place—before heading off to see what else the club had to offer. Too bad she hadn't come in as a sub; she felt like she would have been able to trust one of them pretty quickly. Especially Mr. Grouchy... but maybe that was because of the intense spark of attraction she'd felt, and attraction was a bad bet to place trust in. There were plenty of attractive guys who were total assholes.

But they seemed to have bought her Domme act and they all seemed experienced, even though none of them had subs with them. Maybe she would swing back around to get some good information off of them after she'd explored. Part of her brain thought that was a great idea, the other part of her brain was already trying to talk her out of it.

ADAM

Watching Angela walk off through the club, Adam couldn't help but notice what a fantastic ass she had. Not only curvy, but the kind of J-Lo bubble butt a man wanted to cup with his hands. The kind of cheeks a man could get a solid grip on as he pounded into her.

Shifting a bit uncomfortably in his seat, he turned his attention back to his friends to find they were all staring at him.

"What?"

"What was with the power play man?" Rick asked, looking at Adam a little askance. "You don't usually pull tricks like that. I would have expected it from Chris but not from you."

"Hey," said Chris. "I was perfectly polite to the lady."

Rick rolled his eyes. "Mostly."

All three of them looked at Adam, even Andrew who normally didn't get involved in the interrogate-your-friends sessions. Since he didn't like to talk about his own issues, he rarely got involved in trying to talk about others'. The fact that Adam's actions had aroused even Andrew's curiosity meant he'd been less subtle than he'd thought.

"I wanted to see what she would do," he said simply. It was the truth, but not the whole truth. The whole truth was he'd been hoping, from the moment he saw her, that she was submissive. The attraction he felt for her was undeniable, but not tenable if she was a Domme. Not even a switch, because he'd never be able to satisfy her dominant needs, but he'd be willing to try and work something out if she had any submissive tendencies. Even if it wasn't a lasting thing, because it had been far too long since he'd felt such real attraction and curiosity towards a woman like he immediately had towards Angela. For a moment he'd even thought he'd felt her respond to him, but the moment was so fleeting he wasn't sure he hadn't imagined it because he wanted something to be there.

When it became obvious he wasn't going to give them the answers they wanted, his friends turned to other more interesting subjects. By the time Angela came back, her cheeks slightly flushed with arousal, Adam was the only one left at the table. Chris and Andrew had left together, although Rick was still hanging on, hoping the club might get better as the night went on. He'd gone to the bathroom, leaving Adam alone.

Touring the club had obviously intrigued her. Her breasts were heaving a little bit in the tight confines of her top and the flush on her cheeks emphasized the sparkle in her unusually bright hazel eyes and the pretty pink bow of her lips. When her tongue flicked out and licked her lower lip, it did absolutely nothing to help calm the images he had in his head of pressing the head of his cock to her gorgeous mouth.

Disrespectful thoughts. *If* she was a Domme. Not that he would question her if that's what she said she was, but there was something... *off*... unless it was his imagination or plain old wishful thinking getting the better of him. He wasn't sure, which was not a situation he was used to and not one he enjoyed. He wanted to sit her down and hash it out until he *could* be sure, but it wasn't exactly something he could order her to do.

"What do you think of Chained?" he asked, curious about her impressions. She couldn't answer immediately because almost as soon as she sat down the young sub who had approached her earlier came up again. This time she ordered a Jack and ginger. Adam watched the interaction closely. Although she seemed to appreciate the young man's obvious charms, there didn't seem to be any true interest there.

Maybe the server wasn't her type.

Maybe subs in general weren't her type, maybe she only thought they were.

Maybe Adam was a big, overanalyzing idiot. That seemed like a pretty good possibility.

"It's fascinating," she said brightly. Energy flowed from her, she practically quivered in her seat with it. The bouncy quality of her personality seemed almost at odds with the in-control Domme she'd introduced herself as before, her teasing had been careful but pointed, now she seemed more natural. "I'm not a big fan of the decor, but I love being able to see everything going on. Some of the scenes are..." She shivered a little, a reaction she obviously wasn't able to suppress. "And I do love a good tiki-bar, even if it's not outside." She beamed playfully at him, tugging at something instinctive deep within him that he couldn't quite decipher.

If she'd been his sub he would have asked her to expound on what she found so fascinating about the activities of the club. As it was, he held the question in, still watching her carefully.

"What do you think?" she asked in return, shooting a quick smile at the sub who brought her drink. The young man nearly fell over himself with happiness at her notice of him, but she turned back to Adam quickly enough, leaving the young man to sigh with regret and trot off again.

"About the same as you," he said. "Except I wish there were more single female subs around." Angela's eyes darted away around the room as she brought up the drink to her mouth. Internally, Adam frowned. Had she done so to hide her expression? Taking a sip of drink or a bite of food was a good way of changing the way your face looked. Or was he reading way too much into everything? *Stop it.* "Our server seems to have taken a liking to you."

Angela's lips curved into a sweet smile as she put her drink down. "He's cute, but not my type."

Immediately he wondered again what her type was, the thoughts whizzing past him with no brakes. Did she even know?

"How did you hear about Chained?" he asked, even though what he really wanted to know was how she decided she was a Domme.

"Oh, theater people," she said. "I got into a community theater show recently, one of the crew and I were talking and she mentioned Chained. I thought I'd come check it out."

"What show?" This time he wasn't making small talk, he was genuinely curious. He'd done a lot of theater in high school and college, although he hadn't pursued it since then. Some of his friends from theater had gone on to New York or LA, or were working the circuit in DC, and a few of them did community theater, although he almost never went to see the shows.

"*The Rivals*. Eighteenth century comedy of errors type thing, only this production they've set at an island resort in the 1960s." Angela laughed, a cheerful and forthright sound, loud and clear. He could see her doing theater. Despite the noisiness of the club, he hadn't had trouble hearing one word she said. She was obviously very good at projecting her voice to exactly the right degree to make herself heard but not include the entire room in their conversation. "So what about you? How did you end up here tonight? I'm assuming since this place just opened it doesn't have 'regulars' yet."

Adam was trying to decide whether or not to tell her about Stronghold (it seemed a little gauche to advertise another place while still in the club) when Rick came back up to the table.

"Alright, I give in," he said with a groan. "There are no submissives I'm interested in here tonight. Unless you're a switch?" The question was said with a complete lack of hope, making it a joke, to Angela.

"Switch?" she asked, looking momentarily confused and highlighting her newness to the scene, even if she obviously had done some research.

"Someone who enjoys being both dominant and submissive," Adam explained, watching her reaction carefully.

Did she catch her breath a little? If she did it wasn't much, and she immediately lifted her drink to her mouth again.

"Um, no," she said. "Definitely a Domme." Well that last part was said with complete conviction. Still, Adam couldn't shake the feeling he was missing something about her. There had been some hesitation, unless he was fooling himself. Maybe she was scared of admitting to a submissive side? Or maybe his wishful thinking was getting out of hand. He really needed to find a sub to scene with if he was going to start lusting after Dommes.

"That's what I thought," Rick said with another mournful sigh. "I think I'm going to be getting out of here." He switched his gaze to Adam. "Want to come back to my place for a beer?"

"Sure," said Adam easily. What he wanted to do was untangle the mystery of Angela, but that might be easier done in a more private location. He flashed a quick look at Rick, giving a slight tilt of his head towards the beautiful Domme. Fortunately, Rick was quick on the uptake.

"Join us?" asked Rick. Bless him.

"Oh, uh..." Angela looked completely taken aback.

ANGEL

Join them? Good grief... no. She couldn't possibly do that. Being in the club and talking to Mr. Grouchy, who had become decidedly less grouchy and even more sexy as they'd chatted, was making her feel all melty inside. She was having more and more trouble pretending she didn't want to beg one of them to show her the ropes. Literally.

Going back to a private place with two dominant men, one of whom she was very attracted to, sounded like a recipe for disaster if she wanted to keep up appearances. And she knew they wouldn't appreciate being lied to. BDSM was all about honesty and communication, not exactly something she was excelling at every time she lied to them about her predilections. Plus, heading off with two men she'd just met wasn't safe either, no matter how trustworthy they seemed.

Especially since she'd lied to them *again*. Why hadn't she said she was a switch? That could have solved so many problems in one fell swoop. They knew she was new to the scene. Instead, she'd panicked and insisted she was a Domme.

Self-preservation maybe. After all, even if she was going to experiment with this, did she really want to start off with someone as intimidatingly alpha as Adam? Rick wasn't quite as scary, but she wasn't as attracted to him either. Also, no matter what her instincts about their trustworthiness were, she didn't *know* either of them. Insisting she was a Domme was the best tactic.

Before she could decide whether or not to accept their invitation there was a small commotion to the side, Dungeon Monitors converging on one of the scenes to her right. Rick and Adam turned in their seats to see what was going on as an angry Dom punched one of the DMs who was dragging him away from the bound sub. Two of them were unhooking her from the St. Andrew's cross and she was obviously crying. Angel bit her lip. That kind of scene was exactly why she was experimenting at Chained, getting her bearings before going to the club she wanted to join. The scene must have gotten out of control and either the sub didn't have a safe word, didn't say it, or the Dom ignored it.

No, she shouldn't be trusting strange men, not even if her instincts told her they were okay. And not even if they were both staring at the scene with contained violence, like they wanted to jump in and help the DMs drag the recalcitrant Dom from the club. The gist of what he was saying seemed to indicate he was more of an abuser than a Dom or maybe a sadist. She only caught a glimpse of his sub as they wrapped her in a blanket, undoing the ball gag from around her head before hustling her off to a private room.

"They'll take care of her," she heard Adam say, and felt his soft touch on her hand. Very gently. That was when she realized she was trembling. The feel of his hand on hers sent a shiver of lust straight through her, despite the upsetting scene she'd witnessed. Time to go. She wasn't trying the lifestyle out tonight, on her first visit, no matter how good looking and tempting Master Adam might be. He'd probably hate her if he knew she was lying, only pretending to be a Domme, and who could blame him?

Pulling her hand away from Adam she gave him a nod, her face carefully blank to control the emotions roiling underneath.

"I think I've had enough for tonight," she said firmly, even though there was still a little bit of drink left in her glass. "It was very nice to meet you."

He frowned at her and she got the feeling he was disappointed she wasn't going to accept Rick's offer to join them. Why? While she was very attracted to him, he couldn't possibly be interested in her considering he thought she was a Domme. Unless maybe *he* was a switch but she didn't believe that for one second. He had an incredible aura of power and confidence around him, just from his personality. Although being over six feet tall and muscled like a professional athlete probably didn't hurt either. It was an aura she could project when she needed to, but with her it was an act. Apparently an effective one, but still make believe.

The look of disappointment and disapproval on his face made her squirm internally, testing her ability to keep her expression under control. *I am a Domme*, she reminded herself. For tonight at least. But somehow Adam made her want to stop pretending, drop to her knees, and beg to be punished for her deception.

In fact, she was probably going to masturbate fantasizing about him the second she got home.

Unlike Adam, Rick didn't look at all disappointed or perturbed. He gave her a friendly smile and held out his hand. "It was nice meeting you, Angela."

"You too," she smiled back at him, taking his hand and giving it a firm shake. Turning to Adam she offered him her hand as well. "It was nice to meet you."

His intent gaze on her face caused her smile to slip a little as he reached for her hand and shook it, his thumb practically caressing her skin. Angel's breath caught in her throat, although she did her best to hide it, and she tugged her hand away. For a moment he didn't let her and heat flared through her body. Had he found her out? Then he released her and she had to use all of her willpower to keep her traitorous knees firmly locked. He had that kind of effect.

"Good night," she said, noting with pleasure that there wasn't the slightest hint of a tremor in her voice. Just because she'd never wanted to be a professional actress didn't mean she was without abilities. With a firm and steady step, forcing herself not to rush, she headed to the entrance to collect her coat before escaping outside. Getting into her car, she groaned a little over the late hour and the long ride home. Where there would be a warm bed and her vibrator waiting, and she could lose herself in a fantasy of knowing blue eyes dominating her completely. It was too bad that would never come true, since he obviously belonged to Chained and she wasn't going to be coming here as a sub. Although she'd be back next week, to check things out again. See if there were any more situations like that awful Dom and the poor girl tonight. Mostly it looked like everyone was keeping it safe, sane, and consensual, and she found that very reassuring.

And it didn't have anything to do with the possibility she might run into Mr. Grouchy and his icy, demanding eyes again.

෨෧෨

ADAM

"Okay, what is with you tonight?" Rick asked, frowning at Adam. "I've never seen you act like that around a Domme before."

Adam rubbed the fore and middle fingers of his right hand over the sides of his goatee, and then smoothed it all down as he sighed. He knew the movement was one of his tells, which meant he could control it if he was paying attention, but right now he was a little too worked up. Especially in the groin region. Something inside of Angela had responded when they said goodbye, responded in the way a sub would, not a Domme.

"I think she might be a switch and not know it," he said, which was only partially true. Another part of him was wondering if she only thought she was a Domme. She was obviously new to the scene and sometimes people came in thinking they were one thing when really their desires went in a completely different direction. While she'd done some research and had the right clothes, that didn't equate to the knowledge which came from actually exploring desires. His groin tightened again as he remembered how beautiful her skin looked against her curling dark hair and the forest green of her top.

She's not for you. Even if she is a switch, she thinks she's a Domme. And even if she is a switch, you want a sub, *not someone who has needs to be on top as well as bottom, remember?*

Grimacing, he downed the last of his drink.

"You mean you hope she's a switch so you can play with her," said Rick, looking amused. It wasn't often anyone got to see Adam thrown off kilter and he was obviously enjoying seeing it happen. "I didn't notice anything to indicate that, but I wasn't watching closely either. Unlike some people, apparently."

"Did you see the way she responded when I didn't let go of her hand right away?"

"Maybe she didn't like being challenged but didn't feel like she could say anything."

Well that was a possibility too. The enigma that was Angela was going to haunt Adam all night, he could already tell. He didn't like mysteries but he couldn't stop running through his mind all of the interactions with her he'd had over the evening, trying to figure her out.

"Let's go," he said. Maybe if they got out of here he would be able to focus on something else.

🌿 2 🌿

ANGEL

A ngel was in the middle of baking a new recipe off from Pinterest—salted caramel butter bars (one entire pound of butter, good grief)—when her doorbell rang. Setting down her hand mixer and the bowl she hurried to answer it.

"Leigh," she said, feeling her heart sink as soon as she took in the sorry sight of her best friend. "Come in, are you okay?"

Looking forlorn in her flannel pants and Wonder Woman t-shirt, Leigh walked past Angel into the apartment. Her waist length straight brown hair with its dark blonde highlights was up in a messy bun. Normally, Leigh wore nothing but classy little suits and stylish outfits, helping her present a certain 'image' to the world. It was all for the good of her long-term boyfriend, Michael Rocke, whom she'd been dating since their freshman year of college.

Now, whenever she came over looking like this it meant there was trouble in 'paradise' again.

"Leigh?" Angel asked, closing the front door as her friend didn't answer. Whatever it was it couldn't be too bad because Leigh didn't look like she'd been crying.

"I don't know," said her friend with a sigh. Her mismatched eyes looked miserable as she met Angel's gaze, one greenish hazel and the other hazel, framed by some of the longest lashes Angel had ever seen. There were times when she'd joked about finding a way to steal them from her. "Michael's acting weird again and I'm... Annoyed. Frustrated. Antsy."

"Come into the kitchen and tell me about it," Angel said, giving her friend a big hug. Leigh clung to her for a moment before letting go and they went into the kitchen.

"Where are the guys?" Leigh asked, referring Angel's housemates. Angel had responded to a Craig's list ad three years ago and ended up getting along so well with the guys when she first met them that they'd accepted her application immediately and they were all still living together in the same house three years later. Leigh liked them too, although she preferred not to talk about her Michael-issues when they were around because they'd get all defensively protective, despite the fact that they weren't exactly poster boys for male aggression.

Angel snorted. "They're at a LAN party so they've been gone all weekend. I don't expect them back until late tonight."

About six times a year her housemates would go to a friend's, hook up their computers with about five other guys, and play whatever new gaming release had recently come out. Or they'd have friends over to do so at the house. They were always trying to get her to start gaming with them, especially World of Warcraft, but she already knew she didn't have the time for the kind of commitment they gave to their characters. She also knew if she started, she probably wouldn't be able to stop, so it was better to never start.

Grabbing the hand mixer off the counter and returning her recipe, she flipped the mixer on again, cupping her hand around the edge of the bowl to keep the dough from flying out.

"What are you making?" Leigh asked, speaking extra loudly to be heard over the whirring.

"Salted caramel butter bars. I need to run the mixer for another minute and then we can talk."

Pulling over one of the chairs from the table in the breakfast nook, Leigh scooted it closer to Angel as she watched the mixing process.

The kitchen was a little warm, thanks to the pre-heating oven, but Angel had the window open to let in some of the icy winter air to counteract how warm the kitchen got when she was baking. Once the batter was evenly mixed, Angel put the hand mixer to the side and divided half of the dough to go into the bottom of the greased pan.

"Okay, speak."

"I mean... I can't pin anything down. He's being distant. And every time he gets distant I get paranoid."

"Isn't he in the middle of some big project right now?" Angel didn't entirely understand what Michael did. Something to do with business consulting about... something. She had the bad habit of letting people run on and on about work and letting it go in one ear and fly out the other. There was a reason she didn't have an office job.

"Yeah, the one in London. They're looking to start trying to branch out to the international market and possibly open an office over there, and he's in the thick of things."

"So maybe he's busy with work stuff. That sounds like a lot of pressure."

While Angel didn't like Michael, she often found herself playing Devil's Advocate for him ever since he'd broken Leigh's heart the first time. Leigh's heart had healed enough to give him another chance, but Leigh also still worried sometimes that he was going to do it again. Especially since he hadn't gotten any experience in dating other women, which he'd claimed had been why he'd broken up with Leigh.

Pouring the melted caramel layer on top of par-baked dough, Angel sprinkled a little bit of champagne sea salt she'd gotten from a specialty store over the caramel before crumbling the remaining dough to make the top layer of the bars. Glancing at her friend she could see the worry still on Leigh's face and her stomach clenched. Leigh's instincts might be all messed up since last year when it came to Michael, but she usually saw reason once Angel reassured her. The fact that she was obviously still anxious made Angel even more anxious.

"He hasn't wanted to have sex this week."

"That happens sometimes," said Angel soothingly, although she knew the truth was it rarely happened with Michael. Leigh didn't believe in TMI, not when it came to her best friend, and so Angel was well aware Michael and Leigh's sex life was pretty regular. As in once a day regular, or at least every other day; sometimes more if Michael was stressed or under pressure and needed an outlet. Privately she'd sometimes wondered if that was the real reason Michael had come crawling back to Leigh after a mere three weeks, because he'd realized he couldn't get steady, reliable, safe sex as a single man. Especially a single man just out of a six-year relationship who didn't have the time to build a new one due to work.

"Not with us," Leigh said, shooting her a look which said she knew Angel knew better.

Angel pursed her lips. There wasn't much she could say on the topic she hadn't already said before and she didn't think Leigh needed to hear more on Angel's theory that Michael used her for sex. Well, and because Angel believed he truly did care about Leigh, although she didn't believe for a second he cared more about Leigh than he cared about himself. But the remnant of love he carried was enough for Leigh to survive on. Of course, that was Angel's opinion and she also knew she couldn't see what happened when it was Leigh and Michael alone. She *could* see he treated her well for the most part. Angel couldn't get over the callous way he'd treated their short separation and the reasons he claimed he'd come back after his failure at dating someone new. Angel felt protective over her friend, even though she knew her opinion on their relationship didn't matter in the long run. Leigh sighed and rubbed her hands over her face as Angel popped the pan into the oven.

"Let's watch *The Tudors* and have some wine, we still haven't finished watching the fourth season."

It was their standard downtime activity. They'd lived together for a while during college, before Michael and Leigh moved in together, and had often indulged in days of sitting around marathoning various television shows while eating junk food. Pretty standard girl stuff.

Leigh brightened a little. "Got any tater tots?"

"Better, smiley fries." Angel grinned as she pulled them out of the freezer. They'd take a little longer because the caramel bars needed a lower temperature than the smiley fries, but that didn't matter. They could wait. "They're so happy to be eaten!" The girls giggled as Angel dumped the fries onto a tray and Leigh got out the wine and wine glasses, already looking a little better at the thought of having some Angel and Leigh time.

About an hour later they were ignoring the smiley fries and gorging on the salted caramel butter bars, which had to be the best freaking thing Angel had ever tasted in her life.

"We can't eat *all* of these," she said for about the tenth time as she picked up her fourth one. "There's a pound of butter in them. Don't let me forget that." She was pretty sure she could feel her arteries clogging with every bite, and yet she couldn't stop.

"That's only half a pound each if we share the whole thing," said Leigh rubbing her stomach. She was on her fifth one. They'd eaten about a third of the pan already. They were warm, crumbly, caramel perfection, with a little bit of salt to balance out the sweet and tingle their taste buds, and wonderfully gooey, melty yumminess. "What else are you going to do with them?"

"What I do with all my leftovers, leave them out for when the guys come home." Angel smiled smugly. During the past year she'd picked up on the perfect way to try out her recipes without gaining a hundred pounds: bake when the guys weren't home, eat what she wanted while it was still warm from the oven, and feed the rest to the human garbage disposals she lived with.

"This is the perfect pick-me-up food. Mmmmmm. Oooooo that's good." Leigh let out a moan better suited to sex than food. They'd both been doing that all morning. Fortunately, the weather was way too cold in January for the windows to be open so the neighbors couldn't hear them or they'd probably think there was an orgy going on. Of course, that made Angel think of all the incredibly sexy, authoritative men she'd met last night. Mmm... Dom orgy. Maybe one in particular. Remembering the way Adam's eyes had seemed to burrow into her, demanding all of her secrets, made her insides clench.

"What's that look for?" Leigh asked, her own eyes looking rather demanding. They'd known each other for long enough she could read Angel like a book. She sat up, looking excited. "You got all far away and dreamy looking. It's about a guy, isn't it?"

Angel moaned and picked up a pillow, burying her face in it for a moment. Her friend knew her way too well. "I met a guy yes, and he's super-hot and incredibly sexy and no I'm not seeing him again. I met him at a club."

"When?"

She hesitated. "Last night."

"I thought you were staying in last night." Leigh was looking at her expectantly. Angel felt like burying her face in the pillow again. Even though they were seated on opposite sides of the couch she knew Leigh wasn't going to give this a rest, and if Angel took too long about answering she'd find Leigh invading her side of the couch and probably poking Angel's side with her finger. First came the begging though. "Come on Angel, I need to live vicariously through my single friends. It will make me feel better and distract me from all my woes."

She gave Angel a comically miserable face with her lower lip pouted out, but Angel could still see the real hurt in her friend's eyes, the desire to forget about her problems with Michael.

"Okay but you can't tell anyone."

Leigh rolled her eyes. "You know I won't."

"I know, but I'm just saying. Like, seriously. This is kind of embarrassing."

"You? Embarrassed about something?" Leigh raised one of her eyebrows, looking surprised. "This must be good."

Angel stuck her tongue out at her friend. But it was true, she was rarely embarrassed about anything anymore. Too much time as a nerd and a klutz growing up that she'd become immune to the feeling. "Um... so do you know what BDSM is?"

"Yes..." It was obvious from the way Leigh dragged out the word and her tone of voice that she wasn't sure where Angel was going with this. "We've talked about it before, remember? Stop stalling."

"Well I went to a BDSM club last night."

Leigh shot up like a rocket and bounced closer to Angel on the couch, her eyes alight with interest and curiosity. "No way! Wait... alone?"

"Yeah, don't worry. I was pretending to be a Domme so no one messed with me."

"Domme?" Leigh knew what the word meant but she obviously

wanted it explicitly spelled out since it was now a word pertaining to her best friend and she wanted to make sure she wasn't misinterpreting.

"As in Dominatrix. Woman with a whip. That kind of thing."

Leigh's brow furrowed. "Wait, pretending to be? Why would you do that? Why didn't you be yourself?"

"I didn't want to put myself in a dangerous situation so I pretended for a night at this club that recently opened up down in Virginia. I wanted to see what a club was like before I put myself out there."

"So you're going to go back as a... as a submissive?" Leigh looked confused. Not her fault. The entire situation was confusing to Angel too.

If only she could go back as a submissive and see Master Adam again... but then she'd have to admit she'd lied about being a Domme. Telling Leigh was a little bit different, of course. They'd been friends for so long, and out of all of her friends Leigh was probably the only one who could keep it entirely a secret and who wouldn't judge her. Plus, she knew some of the terminology thanks to the new BDSM book craze.

"No, not back there. There's a club in DC I want to go to, called Stronghold, but I didn't want to start out there because I was too scared to go into a fetish club for the first time as a submissive. I don't know what I'm doing, I don't have anyone to go with, and there are too many bad things that can happen."

"I can get that," said Leigh, nodding her understanding. "Especially alone. Why didn't you call me?"

"You can't come," said Angel immediately, looking at her friend aghast. "Michael would flip out! Not to mention it's not something you're interested in... Is it?"

Her friend hesitated and then shrugged. "I probably could be if Michael was. I like it when he ties my hands to the bed but we haven't done anything other than that. It's fun to read about. But you're right, he wouldn't want me there." She sighed and then brightened again. "So tell me about the guy."

"There was a whole group of guys," Angel said, keeping her tone casual. She knew Leigh wouldn't entirely buy it, she was the one person who almost always managed to see through any of Angel's acts. "They were all very attractive. Very alpha-male. And very friendly. It almost made me wish I *had* gone there as a submissive."

"But you can't go back there as a submissive cuz then they'd know you were lying. That sucks."

"Yeah," Angel shrugged. "But there will be other Doms at Stronghold." Would any of them have the surprising attraction for her that Adam did? She hoped so. Otherwise she was going to regret this plan. But she found herself not wanting to tell Leigh about her attraction to the one man in particular, because it wasn't something which could ever lead somewhere. After all he must live somewhere down in Virginia to be at Chained rather than at Stronghold—and she'd lied to him. The former might not be a huge deal but the latter probably was.

"Good. Well I'm glad you're getting out there and looking."

Angel had to laugh. Leigh was always trying to hook her up with guys, not that Angel felt like she needed it. None of her relationships had worked out because she hadn't been admitting what she truly needed. Now she was finally admitting to what she wanted and she was going to get it. Going to Chained had been the first step.

For the rest of the afternoon she and Leigh finished the fourth season of *The Tudors* and she told Leigh all about Chained. By the time she left, Leigh was in a much better mood and feeling much more optimistic about her relationship and life in general. Angel was feeling a lot better too. The impromptu girl time had been something they both needed.

Smiling to herself, she cleaned up the kitchen, left the bars out for the guys in case they came home while she was up in her bedroom, and went to study her lines.

ADAM

Despite the chaos of his work week, a certain hazel-eyed Domme kept popping up in Adam's thoughts. He owned a temp agency and had been extra busy thanks to hiring his friend Justin to handle the social media marketing. For the first few days Adam pushed the image of Angela aside—*was Angela her real name or was she one of the ones who had assumed a name for the club?*—and found projects to distract himself with. Then, on Wednesday, he found himself looking up the play, *The Rivals,* online. Just out of curiosity. His excuse being that he enjoyed theater and it wasn't a show he was familiar with. The description of the character of Lydia made him grin. He could see Angela playing a part like that; bouncy, seductive, a little manipulative in a comedic and enticing way, and overly dramatic, the queen of all she surveyed. Telling himself he'd been curious about the play, he turned his mind back to work.

During his lunch break on Thursday he searched the internet to see what community theaters in the area were doing a production of *The Rivals.* There weren't any in Virginia, but there was one in Maryland. Not too far away from him, by a group called The County Players. The theater they performed at was only about a twenty-minute drive from his house and the show opened in two weeks. *Interesting.* So what was Angela doing performing in a community theater show an hour and twenty minutes away from Chained? Did people travel that far to do community theater? Or maybe she was traveling in order to be in this particular show?

Frowning he grabbed his cell phone and pulled up Rick on his contact list.

"Hey Adam, what's up?"

"Are you going back to Chained this weekend?" Adam hated talking on the phone so his friends knew not to bother with small talk when he called and he knew Rick wouldn't take offense at his lack of greeting.

"I was thinking about heading up to Stronghold, why? Wanting to see if you run into Mistress Angela again?" Rick emphasized Angela's title a little, as if reminding his friend that he needed to give up on this. They'd talked about it Saturday night when he'd gone back to Rick's place, and even though his friend agreed Angela might have submissive tendencies she wasn't aware of, he thought Adam needed to let her explore and come to the conclusion on her own without outside interference. After all, with all of his experience and his naturally dominant personality, it was possible he could end up pushing her into something she didn't want just because it was what *he* wanted.

"Maybe." He decided not to tell Rick about his internet searches. Somehow it seemed a little too much like stalking. *Seems? Keep telling yourself that.* "I won't push her Rick, I promise. I want to see if she's there again. And maybe there will be other available subs this weekend."

Rick chuckled. "You don't believe that any more than I do. Alright man, I'll take one for the team. Watching you moon over a Domme is worth it in entertainment value and it'll save me some gas money."

"Thanks," said Adam dryly. "I'll see you Saturday at nine?"

"Works for me. See you then."

Adam put his phone down.

"Was that about the Domme Chris told me about?" Justin drawled from the doorway of Adam's office. He was leaning against the frame, arms crossed over the broad expanse of his chest. While Adam and Rick looked alike enough superficially because of their hair and build, Chris and Justin really did look like they could be brothers or possibly even twins. Even their facial features were somewhat similar, and the more time they'd spent together in their threesome relationship with Jessica, the more their behaviors had rubbed off on each other as well. Two years ago Justin might not have even asked the question, and if he had it wouldn't have been with amusement in his eyes or the slight teasing note in his voice. Although he was glad to see his friend more relaxed, thanks to Chris and Jessica's influence, Adam missed those days sometimes. Like now.

"Yes." There was no point in denying it, Rick would tell on him anyway. Sometimes their group of friends could be as bad as teenage girls when it came to gossip, sad to say. "What do you need?"

Fortunately, Justin retained most of the "get down to business" aspects of his personality. Chris would never have let the subject go so easily, but Justin walked forward into the office to stand by his desk. One of the reasons he and Adam got along so well was because neither of them minced words. Whatever Justin needed he obviously didn't think it was going to take a long discussion because he didn't sit down.

"I'm going to need some help soon," he said. "Everything's expanding so quickly, I'm going to start running behind eventually with everything that needs to be done. Especially since Linda's going to on maternity leave soon." Linda was Adam's main marketing person, she worked closely with Justin, and while the original plan had been for him to pick up the slack while she was out, the truth was the entire department was getting busier the more successful the company became. Adam also wanted to open up the possibility of consulting services in the near future and he was going to need a whole new marketing angle.

"Okay," Adam said. "Talk to Victor and let him know what you need. If we're lucky maybe one of our temps will be interested, otherwise he can start the ball rolling on looking." It wouldn't take him long, he was one of the most efficient HR people Adam had ever met.

"Thanks." Justin turned to go and then stopped once he got to the doorway again. "Maybe I'll come down with you on Saturday and bring Jessica."

"Chris told me he didn't think you would be interested."

"In Chained? No. In meeting Mistress Angela? Absolutely. I bet Olivia will want to come too."

Adam growled at him but Justin laughed and walked away. Maybe he should rethink Saturday. He'd finally decided he wanted a serious relationship. Decided he was ready for commitment. He should be out looking for a sub who was interested in that too. But he knew he wouldn't. The mystery of Mistress Angela was bugging him too much at the moment.

ANGEL

"Saturday?" Angel asked, feeling her heart sinking.

"Please, please, you have to," begged Leigh. "I know it's last minute, but I can't be there alone. I can't. Michael's acting so weird lately and I'm likely to fall apart if I don't have a friend there to keep me sane."

Angel groaned. It was Thursday morning and her plans for returning to Chained on Saturday again were falling apart. So much for her secret hopes of seeing Mr. Grouchy. Now she was the grouchy one. Leigh had called while Angel was teaching one of her self-defense classes and Angel had answered her cell phone thinking it must be some kind of emergency. Well, according to Leigh it was.

Some big benefit dinner was happening on Saturday and Leigh was attending with Michael, of course. They were supposed to be going with another couple, one of Michael's friends from college, who was a former reality television star, and his wife. Unfortunately, his wife had recently been diagnosed with mono and wasn't going to be making any kind of public appearances for a while. Owen needed a date and Leigh needed a back-up friend.

"I hope he's okay with the fact that I've never seen his stupid show," she muttered, feeling a large amount of resentment toward a man she'd never met. Not that Master Adam had said he'd be back at Chained this Saturday, but people tended to follow habits. Although, to put it in another perspective, maybe this was fate's way of telling her to stay away from Mr. Grouchy. It was probably for the best. After all, it wasn't as if she could pursue the guy. He thought she was a Domme and she hadn't given herself much wiggle room there.

"I'm sure it will be fine," said Leigh, excited now that she had her victim well ensnared. "Thank you, thank you so much. You won't—"

"Please don't say I won't regret this," interrupted Angel, although she had a smile on her face. "We both know that's probably not true."

Not only would she be missing out on seeing sexy dominant men, she was going to be paired up with someone who wanted to put their personal life out on television. Ugh. She would never understand the appeal.

"He's a nice guy, I promise." Relief and gratitude filled Leigh's voice, making up for whatever disappointment Angel was feeling. When Leigh needed her, she would be there, and vice versa.

"You owe me. Email me the details, I've got to get back to my class."

Not the best way to finish out her class since her concentration was completely shot after that, but she struggled through.

The students were already practicing the hits Angel had showed them, taking turns back and forth with their pads. The room echoed with the word "NO!" being shouted over and over again.

"Yell it as loud as you can, every time," Angel reminded Priscilla—one of the women who often got so into hitting the pads that she would forget to yell—before moving on to watch the next pair.

Her mind kept wandering though. She still wanted to go back to Chained. At least one more time before she turned around and went to Stronghold. She'd go this Friday instead. Next weekend her show opened and if she went Chained she'd have to stay until two in the morning to make the drive worth it.

Sighing, she reminded herself she hadn't wanted to run into Mr. Grouchy again anyway. Right?

ANGEL

Friday night at Chained wasn't as bad as last Saturday night—it was worse. There were no major interruptions to the evening, thank goodness, the Dungeon Monitors didn't need to do anything other than walk around and keep an eye on things, but none of the men she'd met last Saturday were there either. She wandered around and watched the various scenes, even met a few other Doms and Dommes who were very nice although none of them were as friendly as Chris, Andrew, Rick, and Mr. Grouchy. As she explored, she found herself feeling disappointed rather than interested. Bored rather than intrigued. The only big difference between this week and last week was no Mr. Grouchy. She found herself sitting back at the table she'd sat at with him last week when everything had seemed shiny and new, thinking about Adam. *Master Adam.*

Looking around the club, Angel decided there was nothing for her here. Being in the club made her want to shed the Domme persona she was hiding behind and be who she truly was. She felt like she could be brave enough to do so now. Especially, if she went on a Thursday and did an Introduction Scene, the way the club recommended.

With one last regretful sigh, Angel glanced at the clock on the wall and headed for the door, trying not to feel like she'd wasted gas by coming down here. She wouldn't be back. After this weekend she had dress rehearsal Thursday nights and then shows on the weekends for the next three weeks.

After closing night of her show, she'd finally go to Stronghold and get what she really needed.

On Saturday, Angel met Michael, Leigh, and their friend Owen at the benefit dinner, glad of the opportunity to dress up in her favorite red silk floor-length dress she hardly ever had an occasion to wear. She got to spend some time with Leigh, eat good food, and her date, Owen Michaels, was very charming and fun.

"Your wife is a riot," Angel said, handing the phone back to Owen after reassuring his wife that he was behaving himself.

"I can't believe you haven't seen my show," he said as they wound their way through the crowd to meet up with Leigh and Michael.

"Nope. I hardly ever watch television. I wait for the shows I'm interested in to come out on DVD."

Owen rolled his eyes at Leigh as they joined her orbit. "This crazy woman in red has never seen my show, can you believe it?"

"That's because reality television is made up of a bunch of attention whores," Leigh said teasingly, laughing loudly.

"Leigh!" Michael's voice interrupted the conversation and Leigh winced, smoothing her face over in a bland mask as she turned to the businessmen Michael had been talking to. One of them looked appalled, the other amused, and Michael looked infuriated. Angel's lip curled. Okay, maybe Leigh had been a little loud when she'd said 'attention whore' but that didn't mean Michael had to use that tone of voice with her. And his uptight colleague could suck it.

"I'm sorry, gentlemen," Leigh said. Although she was in complete control of herself, Angel knew very well Leigh only went expressionless when she was covering up emotion. They'd done theater together so Angel knew Leigh was more of a singer than an actress, and when it came to situations where she was feeling upset she shut down rather than being able to pretend everything was truly alright. "I didn't mean to be so crass."

"We'll talk about it later," Michael said to her in a low undertone the businessmen couldn't hear. Owen looked rather uncomfortable at the entire situation and Angel had to exert all her self-control not to toss her drink on the patronizing ass. When had Michael turned into such a jerk?

"Come on, Leigh," Angel said, grabbing her friend's hand. "Let's go to the bathroom so these men can finish their super important discussion." It was an effort not to let any sarcasm drip from her voice but she managed. Lacking the sarcasm made the remark sound even more biting. She could practically feel Michael's eyes glaring daggers into her back as she pulled Leigh away, but she didn't care. What an asshole. When had he started acting like this? Was this why Leigh had been so upset lately?

She managed to calm Leigh down, and they returned to the party, yet the mood had changed. Although Angel was glad to be there for her friend, she wondered if she'd have been better off going to Chained.

❧ 3 ❧

ADAM

They'd ended up taking a van down to Chained because Chris, Justin, Jessica, Liam, and Hilary had all decided to come with Adam to "see Rick." Although it was obvious the main goal was to see the Domme Chris, Andrew, and Rick had told everyone else about. All in all, Adam was almost surprised it wasn't a larger party. Despite the many questions his friends kept asking about Angela, Adam kept replying she was nice and she was not the reason he was going there again.

Liar.

Although the look on the others' faces when they got their first good look at the tacky decor inside Chained was almost worth the drive in and of itself. Chris sighed as he looked around.

"I kept thinking maybe I was remembering wrong when I thought about the decor, but it's worse than I remembered," Chris said, his fingers wound firmly through Jessica's hand as she looked around the space with an expression caught between horror and amusement as she took in her surroundings. Hilary was snuggled up under Liam's arm, giggling to herself with wide eyes. She'd come a long way from being the terrified little tourist who had practically run for the hills after her first night at Stronghold. Liam was a lucky man.

"Where's Mistress Angela?" Justin asked, scanning the people rather than the decor. His interest was in seeing "Adam's Mistress," as he'd been calling her all week, not in seeing the club. Adam had a feeling Justin had picked up the nickname for Angela from Chris, but Chris would never use it in front of Adam because he knew he probably wouldn't be able to get away with it. Since Justin worked for Adam, he had to show a little more restraint. Beating up his employees didn't exactly do much for morale, even if they deserved it.

"I don't see her," Chris said, scanning the room now for the same thing. "I do see Rick though. Hey man!"

They all turned to the direction Chris indicated as Rick walked up to them, looking rather surprised at the large group. Of course, it didn't take him long to figure out why.

"Well if I'd known a Domme was all I needed to get you guys down to Virginia I would have found one a long time ago," he joked as they headed to a table near the bar. Well, some of them. Justin and Chris split off to play with Jessica since Angela wasn't there yet, leaving him, Liam, Hilary, and Rick to sit at the table. Liam pulled Hilary onto his lap, stroking her silky blonde hair as she settled into him. Both Rick and Adam watched enviously.

It had been way too long since he'd had a relationship. The last one had been Brooke, after college, and had lasted a little over a year. They'd both been interested in BDSM but it hadn't worked out because the more they'd learned, the more they'd realized they weren't compatible. Brooke was more of a masochist than Adam was a sadist. While he liked to see a pretty butt reddened from spanking as much as the next Dom, Brooke wanted hard whippings and canings along with a little bit of needle play. Which was too much for him. When Brooke had gotten a job across the country and had to move away, it had been a relief to end a relationship which had already been on its way out.

Now he wanted to settle down, but he was stuck on Mistress Angela. Why? It couldn't be pure physical attraction. There were plenty of women who were physically attractive. But there was something about her. The confusing responses she gave him had intrigued him to the point where he had trouble thinking about anyone else. He'd enjoyed seeing her light up with excitement last week after taking a tour of the club. Seeing her excitement, her joy. He'd been fantasizing about seeing the same expression in much more intimate circumstances.

The young male submissive serving them caught his eye. It was the same one as last week.

"Excuse me," he said, catching his attention.

"Yes, Sir?" he asked, keeping his eyes cast downwards in the proper manner. Well trained. Attractive. So why hadn't Angela been interested? Especially after the young man seemed more than willing to bend over backwards for her?

"The woman who was with us last week, have you seen her here tonight?"

"No, Sir. Mistress Angela was here last night."

"Thank you," Adam said in dismissal, trying to stem the wave of disappointment he felt. Why had she come last night instead of tonight? Chance? Or was she avoiding seeing him in the same way he was trying to see her? As he turned back to his friends, he realized the conversation had stopped and Rick, Liam, and Hilary were all grinning at him, obviously listening in on his questioning of the server.

"What are you going to do if she shows up?" Rick asked, his eyes dancing with laughter. Adam sighed and rubbed his goatee.

"I don't know," he admitted.

"But you had to ask," said Liam. "Man have you got it bad."

"Be nice," Hilary said, looking up at Liam who raised his eyebrow reprovingly at her. "Please be nice, *Master*." All of the Doms smiled, hearing the gentle reproof in her voice. Their relationship didn't include the Master honorific and Hilary only called him that when she thought he was being overbearing. Liam's mouth quirked in the ghost of a smile and he gave her ass a slap, although not an overly harsh one, earning a stunning smile from her.

"Thank you, Hilary," said Adam, glaring at his friends. "At least someone at this table likes me."

"We like you, which is why we don't want to see you get involved with someone inappropriate again," Liam said. He'd been at Stronghold when Adam and Brooke had first started going so he knew why their relationship hadn't worked out. And had seen all the women Adam had dated since, which he'd ended up rejecting for one reason or another along the way. "Why are you so hooked on this Domme anyway?"

Adam groaned. Like he hadn't been asking himself that same question over and over again.

"I don't know," he muttered. He seemed to be saying that a lot about Angela. "Don't worry about. We won't be coming back here again."

"I'll say," said Liam. "Sorry Rick."

"No problem," Rick said easily. "I like Stronghold better anyway. I'm thinking about moving—not because of the club. I've already put in a job application to some of the school districts in Maryland."

Well that news quickly turned the conversation. Everyone was glad to hear Rick was moving closer, although Adam found himself distracted as he looked around the room, thinking about Angela. Trying to pretend like he wasn't looking around in hopes she might come back again tonight. Not that he had any idea what he would say if she did show up.

No one commented on his distraction and he contributed to the conversation as best he could.

Once it was late enough he felt sure Angela wouldn't be coming, he started to feel even more frustrated. The night had been a complete waste of time, for both him and his friends. Firmly he squashed down his irritation with her. It was his own damn fault for deciding to come here anyway. And for getting hung up over a Domme. Even a gorgeous, mysterious one. Besides, if he wanted to see her again, all he had to do was go see her show.

A smile spread across his face. Now why hadn't he thought of that before? The show was much closer to home than Chained.

Feeling much better about the night in general, Adam took another swig of his beer and rejoined the conversation.

ANGEL

Hanging up the last of her costume pieces, Angel sighed. Her face felt raw from scrubbing—the stage-make up was always harder to remove than regular make-up, but it was important to get it all off or she'd have acne like none other.

"Can you believe we open in one more day?" asked Karen softly, sounding rather awed.

"Open in one more day and then it's two weekends before it's all over," Angel said with a sigh.

Opening weekend always made her feel a little melancholy, because after the months of work and rehearsals and memorization and soul-searching, it was the beginning of the end.

"But they're going to be great weekends."

"They're going to be *amazing* weekends," Angel replied, grinning as she forced her spirits back up. There was no point in wallowing, especially since the actual shows hadn't even started yet. And she did love doing the actual shows, although unlike some actors she loved the rehearsal process as much as she loved the performances.

"I'll see you tomorrow!" Karen gave her a quick hug and a wave before heading out the door. Angel's smile faded, but she reminded herself that she still had something to look forward to once the show was over.

Stronghold.

There was no point in going all the way back to Chained and teasing herself with Doms whom she couldn't try anything with because she'd lied to them. Better to go to Stronghold and start something she could finish. Plus, she'd talked with Mike last night and he'd reassured her that she would be fine; he hadn't been to Stronghold in a while, but he knew the owner was well known for looking out for people who were new to the scene, especially unattached subs. Too bad Mike was in California or she'd be making him take her to the club.

Grabbing her purse, Angel opened up her phone, she always checked her calls and texts before heading out to her car. She was usually the last one out of the dressing room because she preferred to take off her make-up at rehearsal rather than driving home with it. Getting pulled over for speeding while in full stage make-up had only happened to her once, but that had been enough. Nothing as embarrassing as talking to a police officer when you had giant freckles drawn on your face.

Checking her missed calls, she frowned when she saw she had one from Michael. Leigh's Michael, not her Mike. Michael hadn't called her since before he and Leigh had "separated." A little wave of panic went through her as she hit the call button—had something happened to Leigh?

"Hello, this is Michael."

At the standard greeting Angel rolled her eyes. It was his cell phone number, he knew who was calling him, but he pretended he didn't know as if that was somehow more polite than acknowledging the Caller ID. Still, her panic subsided. He would have never answered the phone that way if there was something wrong. "Hey, it's Angel. You called?"

"Hey Angel," he said as she left the dressing room and waved down the hallway at some of the crew members before heading toward the parking lot. "I ah... was hoping to ask you for a favor."

"You can always ask," she retorted cheerfully. It was her standard answer because far too many people had realized over the years she was a sucker for helping people out. She used to say "whatever you need" and then Leigh had pointed out people were taking advantage of her and had told her to stop being such a doormat. Which was funny, considering how often Leigh played the doormat for Michael.

"I want to take Leigh away for our anniversary in a couple of weeks and I was hoping you could help me surprise her with it... I found a B&B with all sorts of activities and spa treatments and I'd appreciate it if you could look over the choices I've picked out and let me know if you think I made the right ones. You two like the same things and I think I've done a good job but I'd like a second opinion." Angel raised her eyebrows, Michael sounded almost hesitant, as if he was nervous about his decisions. "And I wanted to surprise her with it so I was hoping you could come over and pack for her the Friday we're going to leave, maybe if you have time in between classes or something."

"Wow... Michael that's so sweet!" She grinned. Good, this was exactly what Leigh needed from him! And he was sounding more like the Michael she'd first met, less like the jerk he'd been the weekend before. "Of course, I'll help out! And I can come and pack for her on Friday, I don't have any classes scheduled for Fridays right now. Usually I spend them sewing, but I can put it aside for an hour to pack a bag for her."

"Thank you," he said, sounding truly relieved. "I'll email you the link to the B&B along with the list of activities and spa treatments I picked out so you can look that over."

"That works, do you still have my email address?"

"Still angeleyes?"

"Yep, that's me."

"Great, thank you so much Angel."

"Not a problem," she said enthusiastically. "Anything to help you and Leigh have a great weekend together."

"I appreciate it." Something about his tone of voice and the high level of gratitude in it said that he knew she wasn't his biggest fan and he really did appreciate her putting aside her own judgment of him in order to help him out.

What he didn't get was that Angel would do almost anything to make Leigh happy.

ANGEL

Walking in the front door of the house, Angel was greeted by pure mayhem. The main room of the house was always chaotic, especially in the evenings, because that's where the television, gaming systems and computers were, but tonight was particularly bad. Her roommates Q, Mark, and Sam were all pretty insular, but they had a wide group of friends from World of Warcraft and other online games.

Someone must have forgotten to tell her they'd be having a bit of a convention at the house. There were several more computers than usual, along with several more guys in various states of dress hunkered down around them, barking out orders, insults, and suggestions into their headsets, and chugging Red Bulls.

"Oh, dear God..." Angel muttered as she took in the scene.

Quickly she looked around for Q, who tended to take the lead when it came to organizing events—he was also head of the Guild the guys were all involved with in the game. He was also the easiest to find because he was the biggest at about six feet tall. With dark brown skin and enough lean muscles that most people looked at him and thought "jock" rather than "gamer." His real name was Quinton, but she was the only one who ever called him that; Sam and Mark only attempted it at their own peril.

"Quinton..." she said, standing with her hands on her hips as she glared around the room at them.

"Uh oh... mommy's home," murmured Sam, not even taking his eyes off the screen. His real name was Sampson, but he looked more like a Sam. Unlike Q, he was basically the epitome of the gamer stereotype: skinny, geeky white kid with glasses. Even though he was twenty-five, he was still basically a kid. He worked at the Apple store, was constantly bringing home various electronics to take apart and play with, and was thoroughly convinced that one day (possibly soon) robots were going to become too intelligent and end up battling humankind for supremacy. The worst part was, the longer she talked to him and the more she learned about technology, the more some of his theories started to make sense.

"Uh... hey... SHIT! Hey Angel." Q didn't take his eyes off his computer screen either. "Uh..."

"Did you forget to tell me something?" she prompted. The three guys whose names she didn't know were now eyeing her warily as if they recognized the dangerous tone of voice and weren't sure if they should run from the room now or wait and watch the fireworks.

Mark, the last of her roommates, started to come into the room from their kitchen, took one look at her standing in fighting stance with her hands on her hips and flipped right back around and back into the kitchen. Avoidance at its best.

Her lips quirked.

"Sorry Ang," Sam said, giving her a rueful shrug.

"Yeah, sorry," Q echoed although it was obvious he wasn't giving her his full attention. "We kinda uh... decided to continue the LAN party from the weekend... here... I forgot to let you know..."

With a sigh, Angel kicked off her shoes and nodded a greeting at their company. No point in yelling at the guys now, they wouldn't pay attention to her anyway. Maybe later, although probably not. They weren't bad guys or bad housemates, even if they were a little forgetful sometimes.

It was a good thing she didn't have the standard office job though, or she'd be a lot angrier. She knew from experience that the guys were going to be up all night, chances were they'd called out from work tomorrow already, and they wouldn't *mean* to be loud, but they wouldn't be quiet exactly. Which was why she had the room furthest away from the main room.

Her bedroom was her refuge. Unlike the guys she didn't spread out all over the house, although her sewing machine was down in the main room. She usually enjoyed being surrounded by the guys while she worked on her latest project or order, but not when they were doing a LAN party. Then they were way too involved in their game to be able to talk with her at all and they didn't want the TV on because it was too distracting. At least she had some stuff that needed to be stitched by hand she could work on tomorrow.

Sitting down at her desk, she flipped on her laptop so she could go through her nightly routine. She had three email addresses, one for personal emails, one for women who took her self-defense classes, and one for her Etsy store. It was easier to keep it all separated so she didn't lose track of things.

Unsurprisingly, Michael had already sent her the email. A little smile played on her lips as she scanned through it. Couples massage, body wrap, mani-pedi, horseback riding, and a wine tasting. It was going to be cold, but Leigh loved horseback riding even though she'd never had lessons, so she'd appreciate the gesture. It looked like a good combination of things both Leigh and Michael enjoyed, but it was obvious Michael had put a lot of thought into pampering Leigh with the spa treatments.

Lucky girl.

Angel sighed. Michael could be an ass, but he was good at grand gestures. He might suck at the small stuff and the day-to-day stuff, but what girl wouldn't like celebrating her anniversary with a guy who planned out an entire romantic weekend? And the B&B was gorgeous. Just looking at the website and the description of the restaurant made her wish she had someone who would do that.

Typing out a quick email to Michael telling him he'd done a great job and Leigh was going to love it, Angel decided it was time to do a little something for herself.

She clicked on the button she'd created on her Favorites bar which took her straight to the Stronghold website. Their application process was more involved than Chained's. Hopefully she'd be accepted as a member by the time *The Rivals* closed. Then closing weekend might not be so depressing, since she'd have something to look forward to the next weekend.

The first bit of the application was the standard personal information, including asking if she wanted to use a pseudonym in the club. She chose Angie. Again, close enough to her real name, but softer. Checked the box indicating she was new to the scene. Filled out a little blurb about what interested her in BDSM, why she wanted to try it.

And then a page came up with a list of kinks and dirty deeds, asking her to indicate her interest on a scale of one to ten. One being "hell no absolutely not" and ten being "yes please!" At least that's how she interpreted it.

There weren't too many things she said no absolutely not to. Needles, knives, and blood. Full hoods—she was too claustrophobic for that. Same thing with mummification. Shiver. Piercings. Anything to do with excrement or golden showers.

A couple of the more severe toys scored a two. Especially the scarier looking whips. So did sex with a member of the same gender. While she didn't think she was entirely opposed to it, she didn't have an interest in it either. She wanted to be open minded, so she figured a two was probably the way to go. After all, it was almost a "hell no."

In the middle were things like group sex (which she'd always been curious about but felt kinda slutty for indicating an interest) and double penetration, Shibari, electricity, and some of the heavy toys which didn't seem quite so scary. Clamps, paddles, a cane that didn't look *too* threatening, etc.

Bondage restraints, spanking, the Saint Andrew's Cross, most of the anal toys (none of which were too big or frightening), anal sex, vibrators, verbal orders, etc. were all on the "yes please!" side. In fact, checking those things off was getting her hot and bothered.

Feeling very daring, she clicked the 'submit' button (giggling a little to herself as she thought "yes please!" again). A little notification popped up saying she'd hear back from them within the week about her application.

"Woo," she said, grinning.

Okay, time to get off the computer. She needed to get some rest so she could concentrate on sewing tomorrow. Maybe write a few proposals for some new locations for self-defense classes. Q had given her a pretty good template for churning those out, since he was a proposal writer when he wasn't gaming, and she only turned to him for edits now once she was done with a proposal. And she liked to try and keep a regular schedule or she'd end up sleeping too late. It was too easy to waste time sleeping in.

Grabbing the book she was reading, a steamy Cari Silverwood book, she tossed it onto the bed before stripping down and putting on her nightshirt. The sounds of the guys talking and laughing were faint enough that she could snuggle into her bed and shut them out, diving into a world of alternate Victorian history with automatons, wild inventions, and vampires.

❦ 4 ❦

ADAM

Strumming his guitar, Adam absently went through the fingering he'd memorized in high school for Scarborough Fair. It was his go-to song for when he wanted to sit and think; it was a soothing song to listen to and he'd played it so many times that his fingers went through the motions without him having to pay attention to what he was doing.

His brother had been the one to teach him how to play guitar. Brian had been incredibly musically gifted. Adam knew his friends were impressed with his ear for music and his apparent ease with stringed instruments, but he was nothing compared to how Brian had been. As he played, his eyes wandered around the den and over to the one family picture he kept up there. That picture was the reason he hardly ever went into this room.

It had been taken when he was seven and his brother was ten, the year before their parents' bitter divorce. At the time he hadn't understood why his mother had left so abruptly, although he'd completely understood his father's anger. Eventually he realized he'd rarely seen his parents together during the last two years of their marriage. His father had always remained shut up in the basement working while his mother did her best to pretend she wasn't lonely and didn't feel neglected. But the worst part of the divorce hadn't been the separation, it had been the way both parents had used him and Brian as weapons against each other after the marriage had ended.

For a long time after his brother had overdosed on drugs, he'd blamed both of his parents for Brian's descent into oblivion. It was during that time he'd started refusing to choose between them for holidays. In high school and college he'd gone to friends' houses, and once he'd gotten old enough he'd started having his own celebrations. Ever since his brother had spiraled wildly out of control, Adam's life had been focused on maintaining control. In and out of bed.

Sometimes he wondered if his parents' influence was the reason he'd held off on having a real relationship for so long. Well, that wasn't entirely true. He had cared about Brooke, the closest he'd ever come to falling in love with someone, and it wasn't because of his parents the relationship hadn't worked out. It had been almost a relief to know a relationship could end on good terms, that he wasn't necessarily destined to crash and burn like his parents had. Then again, he and Brooke had both been honest enough to know they weren't meeting each other's needs. Last he'd heard she was very happy in a relationship with an accomplished sadist.

And his parents weren't doing so badly themselves anymore. His dad had started dating a woman named Claire while Adam was in high school and they had been living together since then, although they didn't seem inclined to actually marry. Last year his mother had remarried, an Englishman named Sam who worshiped the ground she walked on and made her blissfully happy.

Maybe his parents' ability to move on was why he was finally feeling ready to have another go at a real relationship.

So why the obsession with Mistress Angela? A woman who obviously wasn't right for him. All week he'd been debating whether or not to go see the show she was in. Last weekend at Chained the answer had seemed obvious, but the more he thought about it the more he waffled.

And waffling was not something Adam was used to.

There was a strange sound threaded through the delicate fingering of the guitar and it took him a moment to realize he was grinding his teeth. With a sigh he leaned his head back, resting his hand on the body of the guitar. He was losing it over a *Domme*. How had his life come to this?

Opening his eyes, he looked up at the clock.

Damn. He needed to get ready to go to Stronghold.

Sighing, he set the guitar on its stand next to the chair he was sitting in. Patrick had decided the club needed more unattached subs and was accepting applications from a few newbies to the scene, which meant they needed Introduction Scenes. Subs with more experience in the lifestyle weren't required to do the Introduction Scenes, although they were offered to get them used to the space and give them a Dom to relate to, but the newbies needed careful handling. It was something all of his group of friends had occasionally done, but since Justin, Chris, and Liam were now all in serious relationships and Rick never came to Stronghold during the week and Jared and Marissa were back together, the duties were mostly falling to Andrew, Olivia, and Adam.

Tonight was his night.

With a groan he got to his feet, trying to convince himself this was a good thing. A good way to meet new subs to the club and see if he had any chemistry with any of them. In fact, he was getting a jump start on the other Doms by doing the Introduction Scenes.

He needed to be meeting and thinking about submissives. Not about Angela.

ADAM

The club was pretty quiet when he first got there, which is why Patrick chose Thursday nights for the Introduction Scenes. There were less people, even less were dressed scandalously, and overall it would be less intimidating for newbies. Allison was at the front desk, Jared at the door.

"Intro scene tonight?" Jared asked after they greeted each other.

"Yeah."

Adam had read over the email Patrick had sent him before leaving his house; the sub was apparently interested in doing *everything*. She'd indicated she thought she was both a masochist and submissive but she had never tried anything so she was going based off of what she had read in books. Something must have made Patrick think she was more than a tourist though—the club had gotten a lot of those when BDSM erotica had first become big, but Patrick had weeded through them easily. Just in case, he still did interviews with each applicant before giving them over to a Dom for an Intro Scene. To tell the truth, Adam felt as though he would have preferred to introduce another Dom to the club tonight than a sub, then he could have stepped back and monitored, maybe done a little bit of teaching.

"She's cute," Jared offered, obviously seeing Adam was less than thrilled about his duties for the evening.

"She won't be my type."

"You don't know that."

"Yeah I do, she thinks she's a masochist."

Jared shrugged his big shoulders, before both he and Adam nodded a greeting to a passing couple. "She might be wrong."

This time Adam slanted a look at the big man. He expected Jared to grin at him, but Jared was looking in the other direction, watching the main room of the club before the door closed after the couple who had just entered. Adam raised his eyebrow.

"Is Marissa here?"

The expression on Jared's face went stony. "Yeah."

"Do you want me to check on her?"

"No. She'll do whatever it is she wants to do." The bitterness in his friend's voice made Adam wince.

He didn't completely understand how Marissa continued to have such a hold on Jared, and he wished he knew how to break it. It was Jared's life though and so far everyone except Olivia had pretty much stayed out of it. Marissa was the neediest and greediest woman Adam had ever met. She'd latched onto Jared and was slowly sucking the life out of him. And she had a bad habit of flirting with his friends, which was why Adam had been avoiding her.

"I'd better get in there before Patrick thinks I've blown him off," he said. If he went in there and Marissa was flirting with another Dom, he wasn't sure he'd be able to stay out of it.

Jared waved him through and he could feel the big man's eyes following him as he entered. Fortunately for all of them Marissa was in the lounge area with the one unattached submissive currently in the club, chatting. No wonder Jared was on edge though; by being in the Lounge area Marissa made herself approachable to other Doms. It was a very Marissa-move, enough to make Jared anxious and upset while not pushing the line so far that neither he nor anyone else could do anything about it. If questioned she'd insist she was keeping the other sub company and become affronted at anyone suggesting she shouldn't be there.

As her Dom, Jared could insist on it, but they all knew it wouldn't work because Marissa would lay on the guilt if he tried to enforce it. And anyone else trying to interfere would have to deal with Jared's displeasure since no one but him had the right to give orders to his sub. Patrick might be able to get away with it, but Patrick was busy with the sub Adam was going to be working with.

For a moment he thought about going over and looming over the two of them, to make his own displeasure with the situation known, but he was supposed to be in Patrick's office by now. Waving to Andrew behind the bar, he headed over to Patrick's office and knocked on the door.

ADAM

"RED! RED!"

Adam sighed. That was the fourth time in the past hour Stephanie had yelled out her safe word. Immediately he let the paddle drop to his side and knelt by her head where it was resting on the spanking bench, cupping her face in his hand and lifting it slightly to look at him. Her eyes were wide and horrified, not at all turned on.

"Stephanie, I don't think you're a masochist," he said in the most patient tone he could, considering it was the sixth time he'd made the statement since they'd started playing with equipment.

The initial meeting had gone well enough. The pretty blonde was attractive and obviously eager to try things out, but almost as soon as they'd gotten to the Dungeon it had gone downhill from there. She spent as much time trying to top from the bottom and control the scene as she did trying something out. At first she'd wanted to try some bondage, so he'd used a Saint Andrew's cross to string her up, but then she'd wanted to be let out of the bondage before trying anything else. Frowning, Adam had told her she needed to let go and submit if she was going to be a submissive and gave her bottom a sharp slap.

Which had initiated the first time she'd said the safe word. Apparently, she hadn't been ready to be spanked.

It was quite possibly the most frustrating Introduction Scene he'd ever done in his life because she kept insisting on trying painful things and yet she couldn't take the slightest amount of pain. Eventually he'd taken complete control of the scene, put her down on the spanking bench—although they'd compromised and he had only bound her legs to it and not her arms—and smacked her with the paddle. About as hard as he'd done the first spank. This time she'd gotten through three sharp smacks before saying her safe word, but he could see the disappointment in her eyes that her fantasy wasn't living up to reality.

"But... I like it so much when I read about it," she said, looking completely confused. "That's what gets me the hottest. But this doesn't feel like pleasure-pain, it feels like *pain* pain."

Adam couldn't help but chuckle. Though she seemed submissive and she'd responded very well when he'd stopped letting her top from the bottom, she was also very sensitive and barely had a medium tolerance for pain. Not the qualities a masochist was made of. Real pain didn't turn her on at all.

"We're not all made the same," he said. " I can give you a spanking that *will* feel like pleasure pain, but I have to recommend you absolutely not advertise to any Doms that you're a masochist. We have several Sadists here at Stronghold who are looking for partners and would probably love to try you out, but I can guarantee you wouldn't enjoy it." He pressed his thumb against her lip as she opened her mouth to give another protest. "That doesn't mean you won't continue to enjoy your fantasies, but I think you'll find a lot more pleasure in submission than in attempting to force your fantasies onto yourself."

The woman made a face which said she didn't want to give up yet, but she was reluctant to let him near her tender backside with another implement of pain. "Can we try the spanking you think I'll enjoy?"

"Absolutely," Adam said, grinning wickedly at her. He ran his hand over her hair approvingly, watching her face light up and her pupils dilate. Clearly submissive. Not for him, but he could already think of several Doms around the club who would be interested in her. She was adventurous and eager to please, not everyone wanted a brat. He certainly didn't. If he was looking for a play partner instead of a real connection he might have suggested to Stephanie they do a few more scenes together, but he could tell she was the kind of woman who would want a deeper connection pretty quickly and he already knew she wasn't quite a match for what he wanted.

Angela's wide-eyed excitement after she'd toured Chained popped into his head before he forced it back down. Dammit. Why was the best chemistry he'd had in years with a Domme? It made absolutely no sense and yet there it was. Which pretty much explained his preoccupation with her and his very deeply hidden hope that maybe she had her inclinations wrong. That did happen, especially with people who were new to the scene. Just look at Stephanie and her insistence she was a masochist when she was the farthest thing from.

Trying to overcome his distraction, he finished out the Introduction scene with a light spanking for Stephanie and giving her an orgasm with a vibrator. He was somewhat aroused, but more because he kept fantasizing rather than focusing on the woman at hand. They didn't have the kind of connection he wanted, even when it came to a play partner for more than one night.

So when she tried to flirt with him before leaving, he gently but firmly let her know while he was happy to be a Dominant for her as she explored her boundaries, he'd be introducing her to other Doms who would suit her. The disappointment on her face wasn't very deep, but he still made a mental note to make sure to introduce her around the club before she could get too attached to him. There was always the risk of inexperienced players misinterpreting the intensity of the scene for intensity of emotion.

As he was seeing Stephanie out he saw Olivia at the bar and motioned to her that he'd be there to talk in a moment.

"Tough night?" The sultry redhead asked when he sat down on the barstool next to her with a heavy sigh.

For a moment he looked his friend over. She was gorgeous, with her flaming red hair and eyes which shifted from grey to blue, flawless skin a Dom who didn't know better might dream about whipping, and had all the requirements he'd want in a woman (other than being submissive in the bedroom) and yet he'd never had a lick of attraction to her. Because they didn't mesh that way, so the issue of sexual attraction never came up. So why with Mistress Angela?

"That bad?"

"No," he said, shaking his head and pushing his recent obsession away. He needed to get a grip on himself. "It wasn't terrible, but she didn't want to admit she wasn't a masochist."

Olivia snorted, glaring at him as she grabbed for napkins. "Don't say things like that while I'm drinking. What finally convinced her?"

He smiled. "I gave her a bit of a 'come to Jesus' lecture, she was pretty determined."

"Lucky she didn't end up with Andrew or me then." Amusement quirked Olivia's full lips. Andrew might have taken Stephanie at her word and gone right into something painful before realizing his mistake, Olivia would have done something similar to Adam but without the lecture. She was a big believer in letting people come to their own conclusions and considering how stubborn Stephanie had been...

Ouch.

"Is Jared still here?" he asked. The big Dom had been replaced at his post at the door by Patrick, who had looked so surly that Adam had bothered to do more than nod at him while he'd sent Stephanie on her way.

"No." Olivia's voice was sour as she took another sip of her drink. "Truckstop decided to tell him she's going on yet another whirl-wind adventure to find herself, which resulted in them having an argument, which resulted in Patrick sending Jared home so they could 'work things out.'"

"Ah."

Not much to work out there. Marissa didn't seem to like staying in one place and was constantly taking short-term out of state and out of country jobs to try and 'find herself.' A task which apparently usually involved having an open relationship with Jared so she could try to 'make sure' he was the right man for her—which obviously she couldn't do unless she tested out other men.

A little smile played on Olivia's face, surprising Adam. He raised his eyebrow at her.

"That's not why Patrick's so grumpy though."

"It's not?" He was surprised, the circumstances surrounding Jared and Marissa's relationship (if it could even be called that) was normally more than enough to make any of their group pissy. Olivia's statement and amusement intrigued him.

Her smile broadened, her eyes sparkling blue with good humor. "Nope. Lexie called in to get Amy's number to see if she could cover for Lexie this Saturday."

"So?"

"Apparently Lexie has a date."

Adam was about to ask "so?" again before a number of factors suddenly collided in his mind with several observations he'd made over the past few months. His mouth opened, closed and then a little smile curved his lips as well. "Interesting."

"I certainly thought so."

"Do you think anything's going on there?"

"No, Patrick promised Jake he'd take care of Lexie. And so he will." Olivia's lips quirked. "Even if it kills him. And I don't think he'd be open to alternate interpretations of 'take care of' even if part of him wants to be."

"Should be interesting to watch."

"Nearly as interesting as watching you pine away over a Domme?"

Adam groaned and then glared. He'd almost managed to forget about Mistress Angela for a few minutes. "I'm not pining away."

"You're not acting like yourself either. What happened to being more open-minded about the submissives in the club? You know Patrick's trying to play match-maker, putting you, Andrew, and me in charge of the majority of the Introduction Scenes, but you barely glanced at the sub you had tonight. What was wrong with her?"

"Andrew's never going to go for a newbie." Not after what happened when he tried to introduce his now ex-girlfriend to the scene. The scars from it were still affecting him today.

"You know it, I know it, even Patrick knows it, but I think he's hoping that pushing Andrew will at least force him to confront his issues. Now stop avoiding the question."

"We didn't have any connection. Chemistry. Whatever you want to call it." Stephanie had been perfectly nice, but he hadn't felt any interest. He glowered at Olivia, not particularly enjoying having his own issues questioned. He knew very well his friends considered him too picky, but he was actively looking now. Really.

"Sometimes you have to let that grow."

And sometimes it was instant. The way it had been with Mistress Angela.

Dammit. Maybe he should go see her show this weekend. See if the chemistry was still there or if he had imagined it. Maybe he was building it up to something bigger than it was in his head.

"Ouch!" He glared at Olivia as he rubbed his side where she'd poked him. Hard.

"What were you thinking about?" she demanded.

"My plans for the weekend," he snapped back.

Olivia rolled her eyes. The sparkling blue was slowly fading to a more neutral grey. "Please tell me you are not going back to Chained."

"No," he said. They sat in silence for a moment because she knew him well enough to know there was more he wasn't saying. Adam sighed. Out of all of his friends he was most comfortable talking about women with Olivia. Not just because she was one, but because if he asked her not to tell anyone about their conversation she wouldn't.

"Angela told me about a play she's in at a community theater. It opens this weekend."

"You're going to drive to Virginia to see community theater?"

"Nope. The theater is about twenty minutes away from where I live."

"Hmmm." Olivia put her empty glass down on the bar and shook her head when Lisa came by and asked if she wanted another one. Adam continued to nurse his drink. "Why do you want to see her again so badly? I'm not going to condone you pushing a possible Domme into trying out being a submissive because she's new to the scene and you're a lot more overpowering than you realize."

If Olivia had been anyone else, Adam would never admit his conflicted feelings. But when Olivia wasn't being a pain in the ass and mocking him, she was one of the most comforting and emotionally astute people he knew. "I want to know if the chemistry I felt with her is real. I want to know why I'm attracted to a Domme. I want to know if she *is* a Domme or if she's attracted to the scene and isn't aware of her true inclinations."

"And you're hoping she's wrong about her inclinations and is submissive," Olivia said drily. He didn't respond, knowing she was going to be a little pissy about that aspect of it. While she knew none of their group of friends were the type who thought women should automatically be submissive, men like that did exist and Olivia'd had to deal with a few jackasses in the past. It made her rather touchy on the subject. He let her think things over until she was ready to say something. "Tell you what. Don't go this weekend. Come here, talk to some of the subs. If, next week, you are still hung up on *Mistress* Angela, then I will go see her play with you."

"And you won't tell any of the guys?" He knew he sounded insecure and needy asking, but he had to confirm.

"I won't tell any of the guys."

"Thank you."

"I do, however, reserve the right to mock you relentlessly in private."

Adam sighed.

ADAM

T he lobby where the audience gathered after the show to greet the actors they knew was surprisingly full. Adam and Olivia hung around on the outskirts, in one of the nooks. He'd purposefully placed them near a trio he'd heard mention Angel's name when he'd walked by them.

It was nice to know her real name, and interesting she'd used a version of it for Chained.

"That was... not what I expected," Olivia said, looking rather thoughtful. She'd enjoyed the show as much as Adam had, it had been funny and surprisingly easy to follow, despite the dated language.

"Me either," he admitted.

Partly because he'd expected the vivacious and confident Mistress Angela to be playing Lydia, the vivaciously confident and spoiled heroine. Until she'd appeared onstage, he'd assumed the Angel listed in the program had nothing to do with Mistress Angela. Instead, when she appeared, it was as Julia. A sweet, quiet, wistful Julia who did everything she could to please her love, Tommy, and when he was unable to give her what she needed, broke up with him in a quietly passionate and tearful monologue, setting him up to redeem himself and win her back. In fact, her character could almost have been called submissive.

"She was very good."

He nodded, trying not to look like he was trying to overhear what the trio nearby was saying. The man was quiet while the two women chattered. Probably mother and daughter, they looked a lot alike, and they were talking about how well Angel had done with her part.

Then his attention was drawn, rather obviously away from Olivia, when the pretty brunette started jumping up and down yelling Angel's name and waving. Instinctively he drew back a bit, wanting to observe without being seen himself. He almost didn't notice Olivia as she coughed and hid a smile, subtly moving herself so it would look like they were talking but he could still look past her to where Angel and the brunette were colliding like two trucks.

She looked... very different. Most of her stage make-up was still on, but it was more and less than that. With her curls ruthlessly pulled back into a pony-tail they were obviously trying to escape, a few wisps hanging around her face, and a bright, open expression on her face she seemed somehow younger. More vulnerable. Or maybe that was the impression he was getting after seeing her play Julia... but Julia wasn't Angela—Angel.

Bouncy. He'd noticed that at the club. Only now she was even bouncier, and she and her friend were talking a mile a minute while the older woman nodded and occasionally inserted a comment. The man stood off to the side looking slightly pained by the high rate and volume of the conversation, until Angel finally turned to him and gave him a hug. Not a romantic prospect, since as soon as she released him, he sidled closer to the unknown brunette and put his hand on her back.

Dressed in figure hugging jeans and a button-down shirt with a ruffle and a high collar with some kind of pin at the throat, she looked like some weird cross between historical and modern. But it was an interesting look. Not one that he'd seen before. It made him want to look at her longer, study her more.

Or that was the excuse he gave himself.

"Is she everything you remembered and more?"

He looked down to see Olivia's grey eyes laughing up at him. They were more blue than grey right now which meant she was highly amused.

"I'm not sure," he said honestly. Angel was different than he remembered, but this was a very different setting.

"Do I get to look now?"

Sighing, Adam obligingly moved so they circled each other naturally, allowing Olivia to peer around him without making it obvious they were staring. The redhead watched for a few moments, her face thoughtful.

A wry smile curved her lips. "They rather remind me of Jessica and Hilary."

Adam had to smile at the observation.

"Do you think she's submissive then?" He cleared his throat as Olivia laughed again, realizing how damned hopeful he'd sounded.

"I'm not going to be able to figure that out from watching her like this," she said, shaking her head, grinning. "Man, you have got it bad, don't you?"

He scowled. "She's a mystery and I don't like mysteries."

"Oh, she's answering her phone... I think she's saying goodbye to them... oops she's headed this way!"

Well of course she was, they were standing right on the way out. Adam's back was to her but he could still swear he could feel her approach. And after a couple hours of watching her on stage he recognized her voice as she walked by him.

"Hey pretty-boy, give me another second to get outside... it's crowded in here and I can't hear a word you're saying—no stop trying to talk to me!"

Then she was gone and past. He glanced over to watch her walk away. Even without the super high heels she had a nice little swing to her walk that did delightful things to her ass. The jeans cupped and hugged her body, emphasizing the bubble of her bottom in a way that made it hard for him to tear his eyes away, even knowing Olivia was watching and laughing at him again.

Hey, he couldn't help being an ass-man.

"Sorry boy-o but I think you're out of luck," Olivia said when he turned back to her.

"I thought you couldn't tell." He certainly couldn't. Something about her called to him and he wanted to explore it. Especially after seeing how sweetly submissive she could be onstage. Part of him insisted that was an act—*but what if it wasn't?*—a little voice in his head whispered.

The Domme snorted. "You did hear her call whoever it was on the phone 'pretty boy,' right? If I didn't know she was into the scene I wouldn't think anything of it, but since Mistress Angela was at Chained, I'd guess she has at least one submissive and that was him. Stop scowling at me, it's not my fault."

Damn. He was scowling. Rearranging his features, he tried to ignore the stab of disappointment slicing through him. Olivia was right.

"Well at least now you know," she said pragmatically.

"Right." Adam rubbed his hand over his face and through his goatee before looking around the room. "Let's get out of here. Through a different door."

ANGEL

"Hey pretty boy, give me another second to get outside... it's crowded in here and I can't hear a word you're saying—no stop trying to talk to me!"

Wow, for a moment Angel thought she saw Mr. Grouchy from Chained...but it wouldn't have been the first time she thought she'd spotted him and had been wrong. Any tall male with sandy blonde hair made her heart leap a bit before she'd look at his face and realize it wasn't him.

Putting one finger in her ear, Angel tried to hear what Mike was saying as she practically bolted out the door.

"Okay, now I can hear you, what?"

"We need to work on your respect, darling," Mike said in an exaggerated Southern drawl. He usually only had a tiny twang, but when he was talking to her—especially when he called her darling—he would lean on it. Cuz he knew she loved it.

"Kind of hard to give me a spanking from the other side of the country," she teased. Not that Mike ever had. Their relationship wasn't like that. Unfortunately. But she had a lot to thank him for, including pushing her into exploring BDSM. He was the one to take her to her first club, to encourage her to apply to Stronghold, and he gave her a sounding board when she needed it.

"Ah, but I'm not going to be on this side of the country for very much longer," he said, and she could hear the wicked grin in his voice.

"You're coming back to D.C.?!"

"Yeah, I'm not enjoying California as much as I thought I would."

"I thought you were doing well."

"I am. But I was doing as well in D.C. and I miss my family and friends and having all four seasons. I also miss doing the stage stuff. I don't think television or film is for me."

"Didn't you just get cast in something?"

"I turned it down."

He said without any regret, even though Angel was pretty sure she remembered him saying it was a fairly decent role in an actual movie. Then again, Mike had always been decisive when he'd put his mind to something.

"Well I'm so flattered!" she said. "I had no idea you missed me so much."

"Pest. Anyway, I'm calling cuz Kirk has someone who's willing to take over my lease here, but he wants to do it in two weeks, not a month, so I need to get out of here and my place in D.C. isn't available yet because I didn't realize I wouldn't have a month..."

"So you need a place to stay." Angel grinned. "Are you sure you want to invade the nerd castle? You remember what happened the last time."

The last time Mike had visited he'd spent the weekend sleeping on Angel's couch and had gotten absolutely no rest because he'd somehow gotten involved in one of her housemates' marathon Halo games. They'd connected two televisions and two X-boxes and eight of them had battled it out the entire weekend. Mike had left more exhausted than he'd arrived and hadn't left her house the entire time.

"Well Amy and I broke up last week when I told her I want to move back to D.C. so unless something's changed with you since we last talked, I won't have to sleep on the couch anyway."

"Nope, still single, although I'm going to Stronghold next week for my Introduction Scene, so no promises," she said teasingly.

"You're going to Stronghold?"

"Yeah, they accepted my application! I could have gone this week if it wasn't for the show."

Mike chuckled. "Well I'm looking forward to hearing about it. When I get in town we'll have to go together."

"Sounds good."

"Alright darling, I have to go. I'll call you later and we'll hash out the details." Like many things Mike said, it came out as an order rather than a question. Angel didn't mind, she'd always been easy going and honestly, that part of Mike's personality had been what attracted her to him. It was part of what told her she was submissive. Of course, that didn't mean she didn't poke at him, because that was part of *her* personality.

"Okay, pretty boy."

"Pest." The insult was said affectionately.

Angel sighed as she hung up the phone. She hoped she did meet someone at Stronghold she could connect to. Master Adam's face floated through her head again, but she pushed it away. She wasn't going back to Chained.

⚜ 6 ⚜

ADAM

Adam had invaded Justin's office and was eating lunch with him when his phone rang. Pulling it from the case permanently attached to his hip, he checked the caller ID and flipped it open.

"No."

"Come on, you don't even know what I'm going to ask!" Andrew sounded more resigned than offended though.

"Yes, I do, and the answer is no."

From across the desk, Justin held back laughter as he watched Adam talk.

"I need the night off, my sister's ride to the airport fell through."

"Tell her to take a cab."

Andrew sighed. "You know she never asks me for anything. I don't want to tell her no, and Olivia can't because she's gonna be at some conference. Please, Adam."

He groaned, knowing already he was going to say yes. Andrew's complicated relationship with his younger sister Iris was something all of them were well aware of. If she'd asked Andrew for help, then Adam couldn't be the bad guy and stand in his way.

"Fine, but you owe me."

"Thanks, man."

Hanging up the phone, Adam let out a huff of air and glared at Justin, who was obviously amused. This was already not the best Monday he'd ever had and it had already gotten worse because he was not interested in dealing with an Introduction Scene this week.

"I blame you," he said, glaring at Justin. The other man raised one dark eyebrow. "If you and Chris hadn't gotten together with Jessica then Liam would have never met Hilary and all three of you would still be helping out with the Introduction Scenes."

"And if you were trying to find a sub instead of talking about trying, then you might not be helping out with them anymore either," Justin said, completely unfazed by Adam's bad temper.

"You and your logic."

"Gets you every time."

But it was true and Adam knew it was. Normally that would be enough to help him get back on an even keel, but he'd been decidedly off kilter for weeks now and the weekend hadn't helped the way it was supposed to.

Dammit. He'd still been attracted to Angel, mistress or not, and he'd found himself more intrigued rather than less. Last night he'd had a dream about her. Sadly, not an erotic one. No, it was all too obviously a correlation for his life; he'd spent the entire dream chasing her, never quite catching her. She'd been wearing one of the costumes from the first act of the play, a soft pink sundress which matched her lips and made her look like innocence ready for debauching.

Once he'd woken up, he hadn't been able to get back to sleep and it had put him in a pretty bad mood first thing in the morning.

He studied Justin. In some ways he'd always considered them to be fairly alike. Despite that they managed to get along well and even work together. "How did you know?"

"Know what?"

"About Jessica."

"What about her?" Justin looked at him with exasperation, not an expression normally seen on the intimidating Dom's face. Subs would probably cower at the almost threatening tone to his voice.

"You and Chris... you two barely knew her but you were drooling over her long before you followed her to the Venus School. How did you know she'd be right for you?"

"We didn't," Justin said simply. He looked at Adam and sighed, clearly seeing that such a concise explanation wasn't going to cut it. A little smile played on his face, but he didn't mention Mistress Angela. Adam decided he liked Justin even more than he'd thought. "We were both attracted to her. We both liked what we saw, and even though she never gave us the chance to talk to her, we had observed her talking with the people she was more comfortable with. We went to the school because we wanted to get to know her and we wanted to see if either of us would connect with her."

"And you both did."

"Yes." The smile on Justin's face belonged to a happy, smitten, and smug man. "But we couldn't have known so in the beginning." He paused, obviously thinking back to the time before his last stint at the Venus School. "And Olivia thought she was probably a submissive, and she was friends with Jessica so we trusted her judgment."

Inwardly Adam groaned. Olivia again. Except Olivia thought he should leave Angel alone.

He rubbed his hand over his face again. He'd been doing that a lot lately. Because, deep down, he knew Olivia was right. It was time to get his head out of his ass.

ANGEL

Breathe. You can do this.

Easier said than done. Breathing in a corset was never easy in the first place. Breathing in a corset when she was sitting down was even more difficult. Although this one was at least slightly less constrictive than some of her others; it was one she'd made special—basically a waist cincher with a shelf for her breasts to rest on. She'd put on a filmy shirt that gave the illusion of possibly being translucent underneath it; the high neck and long sleeves were edged with lace and looked faintly Victorian. All of it was pure white, as was her skirt, her fishnets, and the incredibly high heels she was wearing.

Tapping her fingers on her steering wheel, Angel stared at the behemoth of a warehouse that was Stronghold.

It reminded her strongly of how she'd felt when she'd gone to Chained weeks before. Except this was so much harder because she'd been there to observe; tonight she was going to have an encounter with a real, live Dom. Who was going to touch her and more. Spank her. Tie her up. Let her try all the things she'd been fantasizing about.

The fabric of her shirt rubbed against her nipples and she blushed when she realized how hard they'd become.

Glancing at the clock she decided to go inside. Testament to her nerves, she'd gotten ready early and then couldn't stand sitting around the house so she'd come to the club twenty minutes too soon. Now she was sitting in her car because there had been no traffic and she couldn't stand sitting here either.

Might as well go into the club. Maybe they'd let her poke around for a few minutes. At any rate, there had to be more to look at than the inside of her car.

Normally she had no problem walking in high heels, in fact the higher the better, but her knees were wobbly as she made her way to the front door. She double checked the address, because this didn't look like a sex club... but it was correct.

Taking a deep breath, she pushed open the door and was immediately coaxed inside by the warmth seeping out of the building.

Okay, not as much to look at as she might have thought. Chained's first room had been a lot more impressive. This was obviously an entryway lobby, meant to give you the option to turn around and run screaming if you'd somehow happened into it by chance. A bored looking pixie-ish girl with black hair was sitting behind a desk in front of what looked like a closet; the only other person in the room was standing in the doorway to what Angel assumed was the club.

He was huge; possibly the tallest person she'd ever seen in real life. Gorgeous, with dark skin and short bristles of black hair hugging his skull. If he ever got a bald spot, no one would know; they'd have to be a pro basketball player to be tall enough to see the top of his head. Of course, he'd never be able to sit down again. The thought made her grin, and then blush as she realized he was smiling back at her, his dark eyes studying her almost as intensely as she was studying him.

Ducking her head at his scrutinizing gaze, Angel turned her attention to the girl behind the desk, assuming that's where she was supposed to go. The girl was studying her too, but she wasn't nearly as scary as the big guy.

"Hi, I'm Ang—Angie," she said, remembering the club name she'd chosen. "I'm here for an Introduction Scene."

The girl's face lit up. She had bright blue eyes with long black lashes, startling with her pale skin and black hair. It was pretty though. Angel had always wished she had some kind of exotic combination like that, although she'd eventually grown to love the amberish cast to her own hazel eyes. Dressed in definite Goth clothing with a black fishnet shirt, black bra, and black skirt, she made Angel wonder if she should have gone with a more 'traditional' fetish outfit. But her white cincher was the only one she had which left her breasts free... all her other corsets completely covered them and would have had to be taken off if the Dom wanted to play with her boobs—she wasn't sure that would prohibit it.

Kind of slutty reasoning, on one level, but she didn't want to miss out on any experiences and yet she didn't relish the idea of being entirely unclothed.

"Welcome to Stronghold, I'm Lexie," she chirped back, grinning in a warm and friendly fashion. Angel found herself relaxing immediately. "Can I take your coat?"

"Yes please... do I need my ID and things?"

"Yeah, you'll want that kind of stuff to give to Patrick. He'll hold onto them while you do your scene, although normally you'll turn stuff in here. Leave your cell phone here though, they're not allowed in the club unless you're a doctor or police officer or something like that." Lexie looked at her questioningly and Angel shook her head.

Taking the small clutch out of her pocket, Angel shrugged off her coat and held it out to Lexie.

"Oh my god... I love your outfit!" Lexie was staring in frank admiration. "I've never seen an all-white get-up... where did you get the corset?"

"I made it."

"Holy crap... it's gorgeous!" Lexie's eyes traveled all over Angel, taking in the way her breasts were propped up and accessible, and how tiny her waist had been pulled in. "Do you think you could make one for me?"

Angel grinned. "I have a shop on Etsy, although if you let me measure you I can make you one for free." She figured it didn't hurt to get in good with the front desk if she was going to be coming to Stronghold on a regular basis.

"Oh no, if you have a shop I'll order one. Although, I wouldn't say no to a discount."

"You'd better order one of the shirts too," a deep masculine voice chimed in. "In fact one of those shirts would be perfect. Any kind of shirt at all would be welcome."

Lexie glared and Angel giggled as she turned. The big man had come up behind her and had obviously been listening to the conversation. "Angie, this is Jared... one of my many self-appointed big brothers. Jared, this is Angie."

"Hello Angie."

"Nice to meet you... Sir." Angel tacked the honorific on to the end, assuming by his size and the strength of his presence that he was a Dom. Even if he wasn't, couldn't hurt to be careful.

"If you could make Lexie some shirts, nice and high necked like this one, we'd all appreciate it." He grinned down at her, obviously teasing Lexie and yet entirely serious about the suggestion as well.

The young woman bristled. "There are plenty of women who wear a lot less than I do when they come to the club, Jared."

"Um..." Angel didn't want to get involved in this, but she did want to know where she was supposed to go next.

Just then a side door banged open; it was almost concealed as part of the wall so she hadn't noticed it immediately. Lexie jumped and spun around as Jared seemed to stand a little straighter.

The newcomer was shorter than Jared but not by much. His skin was several shades darker than Jared's, his head completely bald and he had a wicked looking scar running down the side of his face. The kind women might swoon over as being dangerous. And speaking of not being dressed in much, he was wearing nothing more than a pair of leather pants. Not that Angel was going to complain, because the scenery was delightful.

He fixed Lexie with a look that could have killed. "Why is it you haven't let me know Angie arrived yet? And why are you keeping her out here instead of sending her into my office?"

"Because we were talking and I was getting to know her. She got here early so it's not like she's late yet. Sir." The tone of Lexie's voice was distinctly bratty and Angel stared at the back of her head with something like awe. She didn't know if she'd have the balls to talk like that to this man. Beside her she could feel Jared moving away, returning to his post, leaving her and Lexie alone with Mr. Wrathful.

Dark eyes like onyx skimmed over Lexie's attire. "Why aren't you wearing more clothes? I told you to stop dressing like this."

"This is more than I wore last week and I'm within dress code for the club. Deal with it."

"The dress code is for the floor, not for employees."

"Well I'm not allowed on the floor, remember? I should be able to dress however I want." Now Lexie's tone was distinctly mocking, and the storm clouds on the man's face were growing. Obviously he was some kind of boss—and maybe even lover—to Lexie. He sounded like a jealous lover. And Lexie was poking the bear, trying to get some kind of reaction. Angel was ready to give her a medal for bravery. She didn't want to draw any attention to herself while the man was glaring like that.

"You'll be on the floor for your damn Valentine's Day party."

Lexie snorted. "That's not in return for my outfits, that's because you don't want me going away for a weekend with Tyler."

"Damned right I don't. I'll let you throw the damned party but I'm not going to act happy about it. And you'd better not try to sneak out early with the little bastard."

Even though her back was to Angel, she could tell Lexie was rolling her eyes as her fists found their way to her hips. "Who died and made you king?"

"Your brother left me in charge."

"He sure as hell did not."

"As good as."

Angel sneezed. Which she regretted on several levels. Watching Lexie and Mr. Scary battle was as good as a soap opera. The sexual tension levels were out of this world, although Lexie was obviously seeing someone else. The dark eyes that had been glaring at Lexie were focused on her and he still looked pissed as hell.

"I'm sorry," she muttered as Lexie handed her a tissue.

"Don't worry about it," Lexie said. She jerked her thumb over her shoulder. "This is Stronghold's owner, Master Patrick. He's in a mood right now. Don't let it bother you. I don't."

A growling noise sounded from behind her but Lexie ignored it, flipping up her skirt before she sat back down. Angel was pretty sure she'd given Master Patrick a pretty good view of what was under it. The look on Lexie's face was part defiant, part fearful, and part expectant.

"Come on back, Angie."

Patrick strode away through the door he'd popped out of, leaving it open behind him.

"Sorry about that. He's my older brother's best friend," Lexie said with a sigh. Now she looked both disappointed and resigned. If Angel had a guess, she'd bet Lexie was deliberately poking at Patrick. The girl had a crush, even if she was dating someone else, and Mr. Scary was resisting. "Stop by on your way out and let me know how your scene goes?"

"Definitely." Angel smiled. She didn't always make new friends with girls easily, but Lexie was impossible to resist and she didn't have any of the cattiness or reserve Angel tended to associate with her own gender.

Going into Master Patrick's office was a little scary, but though he seemed kind of riled up it wasn't like he had laid a hand on Lexie. Even though she'd been pushing for it. And he'd obviously wanted to.

The entirety of the office seemed to be designed for both comfort and intimidation. Everything was made out of either maple wood or black leather, implements for spanking lined one wall, another was covered in some of the most beautiful and erotic bondage photographs Angel had ever seen.

The desk Master Patrick sat down at was huge, it made her feel like a dwarf by comparison. A man smaller than him would have looked overwhelmed by it, but it suited him perfectly.

"Have a seat."

Yeah, no mistaking this man for anything other than "in charge." The authoritarian tone of voice had her moving before she even thought about it to one of the cushy black leather chairs in front of the desk. It was incredibly comfortable. The kind of chair she'd like to curl up and wallow in, read a book on a rainy day... it would have worked as well in front of a fire as it did in this office.

But with the scary man behind the desk, his hard gaze fixed on her, she couldn't relax. Instead she shifted her weight, taking tiny peeks at him because for some reason she couldn't bring herself to directly meet his eyes for more than a moment or two.

"I'm sorry about my ah... altercation with Lexie," he said in clipped tones. Clearly not a man used to apologizing. "You shouldn't have had to see that."

"It's okay." Angel met his dark eyes for a moment and then dropped her head again. "Sir."

When she peeked at him this time he had the faint traces of a smile around his lips, which made him seem a lot less intimidating.

"Did you read over the contract I sent you?"

"Yes Sir." About fifty times. It had included all the rules and regulations which governed Stronghold.

"Good girl."

Something inside of Angel warmed as he reached into his desk and pulled out a stapled stack of papers. Yeah, she wasn't attracted to

Patrick, even though she could acknowledge he was extremely attractive, but she still liked being called a good girl by him. There was something about it which satisfied a need deep inside of her and made her feel all happy and glow-y.

"This is the same thing, in paper form. You can look it over if you want. And then you need to sign it." He glanced at the clock. "Your Dom for the evening should be here any minute."

She felt awkward looking over it in front of him, because part of her said to trust his word, but the more cynical part of her said always be sure. She skimmed it, familiar enough with the sentences by now to know they were identical to the one he'd sent her online.

As she picked up a pen to sign, Patrick's phone rang.

"Hello?" There was a long pause. "Shit. Alright, I'll be right down."

Putting down the phone with enough force that Angel jumped (okay, she might be a little bit jittery considering she'd signed a release to have all sorts of dirty and debauched things done to her), Patrick sighed and gave her a reassuring sort of smile. It warmed his face and enabled her to meet his eyes.

"I have a situation I have to see to... I don't want to have to leave you here alone though. Hold on a moment." Getting up, he went back to the door they'd come in from, the one connected to the lobby. Angel clasped her hands together. A situation? What did that mean? Was a sub hurt? Someone's scene gotten out of control? Why would the owner of the club be needed unless it was something bad?

As her panic started to well, Patrick stuck his head out of the door. "Jared.... oh hey, good you're here. Never mind, Jared." He shifted so more of his body was out of the door, muffling what he was saying. Something about a Tom and an Ellie. Then he turned slightly, and she could hear every word again.

"Anyway, Angie's in here, so you can chat with her before choosing a room for the scene. Interrogation, jail, and school are all open."

"Okay, thanks." Her ears must be playing tricks on her because that voice sounded vaguely familiar, but who would she know at Stronghold?

Then Master Patrick was moving away and another man was entering. Angel was starting to stand, feeling she should get up and intro-

74

duce herself, but as soon as she caught his crystal blue gaze her knees and lungs locked up and she found herself sinking back into the chair.

Very tall, very attractive, with very blue eyes, blonde hair and a goatee... and he looked more than grouchy as recognition flashed across his face.

He looked downright pissed.

7

ADAM

Adam had studied the survey and information Patrick had sent him on Angie and hoped the Introduction Scene wouldn't be as frustrating as his one with Stephanie. From the survey, as long as she had filled it out truthfully, it seemed like it should be an enjoyable scene for him. And from the amount of question marks and indications of "never tried, would like to" answers she'd given, he assumed she was being truthful. Stephanie's survey had been full of confidence that she would like her fantasies, Angie obviously didn't have much experience but wanted to try a whole lot.

He was okay with that.

Especially because going by the survey, she was interested in trying a lot of his favorite things. There was nothing more Adam liked than playing with a woman's ass and Angie had indicated she was familiar with and enjoyed anal play and sex. From the survey she looked a lot more compatible to him than Stephanie, so he'd tried building up his anticipation on the drive over.

It almost worked. At least he wasn't dreading the evening. When he stepped into the club Jared grinned at him in an encouraging way, which was good. Lexie was behind the desk, her expression rather grumpy. She looked at him in surprise as he approached.

"I thought Andrew was doing the Intro scene tonight."

"He had to take Iris to the airport."

Lexie scowled. "Nice of Patrick to let me know."

"You two need to learn how to play nicely," he teased.

"I will if he will," she retorted. Adam grinned. He wasn't one hundred percent proof positive Lexie had feelings for Patrick that went well beyond sisterly, and Patrick was fighting his own feelings when it came to her, but lately it seemed more and more likely.

Which was a hell of a lot of fun to watch.

Just then, Patrick stuck his head out the door. "Jared..." His eyes swept around the room and landed on Adam. "Oh hey, good you're here. Never mind Jared."

Adam walked around the desk, heading for Patrick.

"I've got a situation downstairs... Tom offered Ellie a club contract last week but she refused."

"Of course she did. Ellie never signs club contracts." In fact she was almost as well-known as Andrew around the club for her refusal to participate in anything even resembling any kind of relationship. Which was why they most often partnered each other to play, especially since Ellie was a masochist and Andrew was a sadist. They could satisfy themselves without making any move towards something more. Even Adam had had some short club contracts since Brooke, usually not lasting more than a month and he'd never been interested in taking them outside of the club or extending them. But he had them.

Club contracts were for people who wanted to play inside the club, exclusively with each other, for a certain amount of time. Some could last up to a year or more if the participants felt they had the right chemistry. The contracts clearly outlined what was expected of each party, but they only existed for inside the club. It was for those people who wanted stability in their play but weren't interested in a relationship outside of the scene.

"Yeah but she's been scening with him a lot lately, I think he got his hopes up."

Adam snorted. To his knowledge, Andrew and Ellie were rather unique in that they never signed club contracts. They only scened.

"Anyway, she turned him down for a scene tonight and accepted an offer from Will, so now I've got to get downstairs because Tom's throwing a hissy fit, Ellie is making it worse by ignoring him, and Will is pissed."

"As he should be, if Tom's interfering with a scene over a sub he has no claim to."

"Yes, thank you for telling me what I already know." Patrick gave him a look, but Adam shrugged. "Anyway, Angie's in here, so you can chat with her before choosing a room for the scene. Interrogation, jail, and school are all open."

"Okay, thanks." Maybe school. He hadn't been there in a while and that was always a good scene for an Introduction.

Patrick moved out of the doorway heading for the club and Adam entered the office, a room he was very familiar with. Angie, the submissive, was sitting in one of the chairs in front of his desk, and she started to rise as he walked in.

With her brown hair piled on top of her head to show off her unadorned neck, she was a vision in white. The corset pushed up plump breasts, offering them up despite the thin, high-necked top she wore underneath. In fact, her top only invited someone to rip it away and reveal the lush curves underneath. A short white skirt flirted around her thighs, white fishnets clinging to her long legs, and white high heels that would dig into a man's back when she wrapped her legs around him.

She was innocence and sin, wrapped together with a sensuality that couldn't be denied. She was a fallen angel.

Adam's fists clenched as adrenaline and anger rushed through him in equal measure, a roaring sound filling his ears as he sucked in a deep, shocked breath.

"*You.*"

Tottering on those thin, high heels, Angel sank back down, her eyes incredibly wide as she stared up at him. Those pouty lips opened in shock, temptingly pink and inviting. All too easy to remember how he'd fantasized about sliding his cock between them on the very first night he'd met her.

"Oh my god..." Her voice was breathy and high, nothing like he'd ever heard her sound before. Not at Chained or in *The Rivals*. "What are you doing here?"

Slamming the door shut behind him, Adam stalked forward to tower over her. He could see the pulse fluttering in her neck, her hands grasping the arms of her chair and her fingers wrapping around them so tightly her knuckles turned white, and her pupils dilated as he moved closer. Shock, fear, and arousal all in equal measures. Usually the emotions he enjoyed eliciting in a sub, right now he was too overwhelmed by his own raging emotions.

Part of him was thrilled to see her. Another part was feeling completely blindsided. What was she playing at, coming to Stronghold as a submissive when she'd been so very clear in telling him at Chained that she was a Domme? And what about "pretty boy?"

"My name is Master Adam," he said, crossing his arms over his chest and glaring down at her. "I'm supposed to be giving a submissive named Angie her introduction scene. What are *you* doing here, Mistress Angela?"

The bite in his voice made her shiver, she seemed to shrink in on herself, exactly the way a submissive caught in bad behavior would. Her hands left the chair and curled in on each other on her lap, as if she wanted to wrap her arms around herself. It was hard to ignore her obvious discomfort with the way he was looming over her.

He purposefully didn't tell her that he knew her real name. Or that he'd seen her show last weekend. Already he felt like the control had been knocked from his hands. Keeping something from her, when she'd obviously kept things from him, helped his equilibrium a bit.

At least she looked as shocked as he felt, but then again, she was an actress. How would he know? She'd certainly fooled all of them at Chained.

"I'm Angie."

Her voice was so low he almost didn't hear it.

"I'm sorry, what was that?"

Sitting up a little bit straighter now the initial shock was over,

Angel raised her eyes almost defiantly to his. They were even prettier than he'd realized with her head tipped back like this, and the black and gold liner accentuating their almond shape and bringing out flecks of gold in the bright amber color.

"I'm Angie. That's my... it's my name for this club."

She eyed him warily, as if she expected to need to run at any moment, which didn't help his temper.

"I see. And what happened to Mistress Angela?"

Angel took a deep breath, which drew his attention to her breasts. Not where it needed to be if he was going to stay in control of this situation. She was staring at his crossed arms.

"She never existed. I just... I'm new to this and I... I went to Chained as a Domme because that seemed like a good way to find out what the clubs were like. I always intended on coming to Stronghold later." She met his eyes again, briefly, warily. "I didn't expect anyone else to go to both... they're far enough away from each other I thought I'd be safe. And I couldn't imagine why anyone would go to a new club like Chained if they were already a member here."

The look in her eyes was almost accusatory.

"I was visiting a friend who lives down there," he said, even though he didn't owe her an explanation. He had a much better reason for being down there than she had, as far as he was concerned. Especially since he hadn't been masquerading as anything. The dishonesty rankled. Trust and honesty was integral to BDSM and if she wasn't willing to trust then she couldn't be trusted. "So you played at being a Domme at Chained and now you want to play at being a sub here at Stronghold?"

She sat up straight, obviously indignant at his sarcastic tone.

"I'm not playing at anything," she said sharply, glaring back. One of her hands rubbed along her upper thigh. On purpose to distract him by making him look at her short skirt, or a nervous movement? "I *am* submissive... I was—"

"Experimenting." His tone was clipped, abrupt, cutting her off.

Was she someone who got her kicks by visiting the clubs in various guises and doing whatever she felt like? Toying with the people there?

"Scared. Sir." She said it like she was correcting him, tilting her chin up in challenge. Yeah, she looked terrified. *Not*.

He raised his eyebrow at her. Leaning over her in a slow and deliberate manner, he placed his hands on the arms of her chair as she scooted back. Her head tipped back further and further, eyes wide as her breathing accelerated. A submissive response. Maybe she was a switch?

"Are you a switch?" If she was, they could still do a scene, but he wanted the truth from her. He was attracted to her but he didn't like deceptions.

"No, I'm a sub," she said stubbornly.

"I'm not in the mood for games tonight, little one," he growled, coming close enough she would feel like he was invading her space. She was pressed up against the back of the chair and if his legs hadn't been against the seat, in between hers, he was pretty sure she would have been sinking down as well. "If you aren't really a submissive then you need to get out. Now."

ANGEL

Jesus... the man was practically threatening her and all she could do was cream her panties. If she ever needed proof she was submissive, surely this had to be it!

She could understand he was a little upset, even angry, although she thought his reaction was a tad over-dramatic... but part of her felt like she should at least be pissed back at him. After all, she'd told him why she'd pretended to be a Domme at Chained and he acted like it didn't matter why, even though it was a good reason. Instead he tried to intimidate her into leaving.

Well joke was on him, all he was doing was turning her on.

She flicked her tongue across her lower lip before dragging her teeth across it, a nervous habit she'd never quite been able to get rid of, she noticed his eyes dropped to her mouth. Mr. Very Grouchy wasn't quite as immune to her as he acted. That was something at least.

"I'm *submissive*. I want to be here. Sir." Her voice was back to the high, breathy squeak she hated. It only came out when she was feeling particularly shy or vulnerable.

Then again, with six feet something and who knows how many pounds of sexy, muscular, *pissed* male leaning over her, how could she feel anything other than vulnerable?

And damn her body for finding it so freaking hot.

A muscle in his jaw clenched as she stared up at him, fascinated. "All right."

The way he gathered himself and stood up straight was as controlled as his descent had been. She wondered if he did any dancing. He must be doing something physical on a regular basis to have so much deliberate muscle control. Maybe not dancing. Probably some super-masculine sport.

"I've read your survey. It seems like there are a lot of things you haven't tried. My plan was to have you try some of those things tonight. How does that sound to you?"

She swallowed convulsively. "Good. That sounds good."

Hell, if it sounded any better she might orgasm on the spot. Her nipples were already trying to drill holes through her shirt and she was more than a little thankful she'd chosen to wear a white thong *and* lacy white boy shorts underneath her skirt. Otherwise, she'd be leaving a mess behind on Master Patrick's chair.

"Sir." He gave her another look.

"Right, sorry Sir." Good grief she was a mess. She'd fantasized about this man more than once over the past couple of weeks, but she'd never thought she'd be in this position with *him*. If she'd known what she would be walking into, she never would have come.

But she had to admit she was glad she had. So far at least.

"And it indicated you're comfortable with the demonstration involving toys and hands?"

"Yes, Sir."

"Good. Alright, Angie, let's go." He stressed her name and Angel felt something inside of her stomach twist.

"Angel. My real name is Angel."

The look he gave her was both sardonic and approving. Almost as if he already knew Angie had also been a false name and appreciated her honesty.

ADAM

As he led Angel down through the main room and the upstairs, giving her the tour, he was quickly revising his game plan for the evening. No private rooms, that was for sure. He was too angry to completely trust himself with her privately. And part of him wanted to expose her publicly.

It was difficult to hold onto his anger as she stared at the private rooms with a kind of awe, the same little bounce in her step he'd noticed at Chained. His body, in particular, was less interested in being pissed and a lot more interested in the glimpses of lace he saw when her skirt flounced up or the way her breasts jiggled on the shelf of her corset. The slutty-innocent look of all white in such revealing clothing appealed to him in a way he would have never guessed.

He saved the downstairs for last. The Dungeon was the best place to deal with her, right in the center of the room where the spanking benches were. They were one of his favorite pieces of equipment anyway, and if anyone deserved a spanking, Angel did.

Once he'd shown her the doctor's office, jail, and the interrogation room, he led her to one of the many open benches. Since it was Thursday there weren't as many people here, especially since it was fairly early in the evening. Off to the side he saw Will had Ellie tied up to a Saint Andrew's cross and he was using a single tail on her buttocks. Tom was nowhere to be seen.

Noticing Angel was watching the display as well, he decided to give her a few minutes to soak it in. By the way she flinched every time the whip landed, leaving another welt across Ellie's ass, it wasn't something she'd be interested in trying. Which was fine with him, he preferred to stay away from the whips anyway. Floggers on the other hand...

Suddenly her attention jerked back to him and she flushed as she realized he was studying her.

"Sorry... Sir."

"See anything you like?" he asked, gesturing at the cross. Angel shook her head, winding her fingers around each other as she lowered her gaze to the ground. Not entirely unexpected, going by her survey.

Seeing that she was eyeing the bench he was standing next to, Adam gestured to it. "This is a spanking bench. Have you ever been on one of these before?" She shook her head again and he sighed. "Answer verbally, Angel. I need to hear your responses and you need to get used to giving them. Clear communication is quite possibly the most important part of scening."

"No, Sir, I have never been on a spanking bench."

"Have you ever been spanked?" He asked, trying to ignore the way her low voice was making his cock throb in his pants. Considering he'd been hard since he'd started showing her around the club and thinking about all the dirty things he could do with her, the fact that she could arouse him even further with her voice was more than a little disconcerting.

She shifted her weight on her feet, color heightening her cheeks. Embarrassed? It was impossible to fake a blush, right? "A couple times. I asked one of my ex-boyfriends to and he did it but it... it wasn't like what I thought it would be."

"And you think I'll be able to do better?" He wasn't able to completely keep the amusement out of his voice.

Angel peeked at him in a shy little way which made him almost forget she was a liar. "I think you have a better chance of knowing what you're doing."

Okay, that made the side of his lips twitch, but he smothered the grin which was trying to sneak out.

"Very likely. I'd like to start off by putting you over this bench and seeing how you respond to being restrained. From there we'll move on to toys and then a spanking, my hand first and then possibly a paddle or a flogger and see how you feel after that. How does that sound?"

From the way her eyes had practically glazed over as he'd spoke, he would bet it sounded damn good. She certainly reacted the way a submissive would. A flick of her tongue across her lower lip, followed by a quick drag of her teeth—a reaction he was starting to think was instinctual rather than learned, not to mention enticing as hell—and she took a deep breath.

"That sounds good, Sir."

"Do you have a safe word?"

"Uncle."

"Uncle?" His voice came out half-strangled. Good god, did he want to know the reasoning behind that one?

A sneaky little half-smile crossed her lips as she tipped her head to the side, the loose curls in her hair flopping sideways. "As in 'Say Uncle.' Didn't you ever wrestle when you were a little kid?"

"Right." That grin was trying to sneak out again. He stamped on it. No need to let her know he found her entertaining and adorable as well as sexy. "You can also use the club safe word which is 'red.' Although if the Dungeon Monitors hear anything that sounds like it's outside of a scene then they come running and you absolutely shouldn't need it during your Introduction Scene, but things happen." Like Stephanie who had thought her pain tolerance was much higher than it had been. And he certainly wasn't planning on going easy on Angel. If she was a little wannabe or playing games then she was going to regret coming into the club tonight.

He might not be a sadist like Andrew, but he wasn't going to tolerate any bullshit either.

ANGEL

Watching Master Adam and trying to figure out his thoughts could be a full-time job, Angel thought. His facial expressions were mostly neutral, but his eyes betrayed him. Any time he was amused, she could see it in the little crinkling around his blue eyes and the way their glacial depths warmed. But he could flash back to cold and hard in seconds, for seemingly no reason at all. More than once she saw him looking at her as if he was attracted to her but didn't want to be.

And that downright sucked because she was damn sure attracted to him. Hell, she'd been attracted to him at Chained and having him order her around and being all alpha-male and kind of pissed was fanning the flames. She couldn't tell how pissed he was about her deception. Somehow, she thought it was a lot more than he was showing on his face.

Nothing she could do about it though.

"Yes, Sir," she said, in response to his lecture on safe words. She'd purposefully chosen one she found amusing, and she was used to yelling out anyway (legacy of growing up a tomboy), and she thought she'd seen the glimmer of a smile before he'd gone all mean and distant again.

"Good. Now strip."

The command was so authoritative that her hands were going to her blouse before she could even think. Damn! How did these men do that?! As her fingers fumbled with the buttons at her neck, she glanced around the room again and realized more than one person was watching.

Heat and ice warred within her. Okay, so she'd kind of fantasized about getting down and dirty in front of people before but she'd never done it.

"Um... how far?"

Adam raised his eyebrow, a stern glare igniting in his eyes.

"Sir," she quickly tacked on. "How far should I strip down?"

"All of it." The look he gave her was pure challenge. His voice practically purred. "You didn't indicate you would have a problem with public nudity on your survey."

No, but she hadn't expected to have to completely strip down on her first night here. That had been the point of wearing the special corset. But the look in his eyes said he didn't think she'd do it. That she'd say her safe word and pussy out. It was the same look she'd gotten when she was younger and she wanted to play football or shoot hoops with the guys, the one that said she should turn around now and go home or put her money where her mouth was.

Angel had never been one for going home.

The same stubbornness that had served her well when she was

younger came roaring back. But she didn't say anything. She started unbuttoning her shirt and doing her best to pretend it didn't bother her. Heck, she was used to getting undressed in front of people, she reminded herself. Half of theater was stripping down as fast as you could for a costume change and it didn't matter who was standing next to you or in front of you.

Of course there hadn't been anyone so blatantly watching as Master Adam was. And none of them had been nearly as devastatingly attractive. With his arms crossed over his chest, his crisp white shirt tucked into dark leather pants, and the black dress shoes he was wearing, he looked like some kind of bondage GQ model.

Doing her best to ignore Mr. Serious and Sexy (not to mention Grouchy), Angel focused on stripping down. She felt her cheeks turning red as she noticed some of the glances she was getting from other parts of the room and the various people walking by. But she wasn't going to let embarrassment stop her. Heck, some part of her liked it. By the time her shirt and corset were off and piled neatly on the floor beside her, that was obvious by the rigidly hard points of her nipples.

And her panties were soaked through, although no one could see that. Yet.

If she wasn't imagining things, Master Adam's breathing had picked up a bit as she let her skirt drop to reveal the lacy boy shorts she was wearing. As well as the fact the white fishnets were not tights, they were thigh highs. The lacy tops of these particular stockings were only an inch or so below her ass cheeks.

Angel hesitated and then began to step out of her shoes.

"Leave the shoes and the stockings."

Was it her imagination, or did his voice sound a little bit hoarse? Taking another peek, Angel nearly turned and ran just looking at the hungry expression on his face. Master Adam didn't look like Mr. Grouchy or even Mr. Serious anymore. No, he looked like he wanted to devour her whole. Her body responded with a tingling warmth she'd never felt from stripping down. Hell he hadn't even touched her yet!

It was her body's response that was making her want to run. She so didn't feel ready for this. But she was already more than halfway there, plus she'd have to get re-dressed again, so she stayed in place and pulled down the lacy shorts followed by the g-string.

Angel didn't look at the very obviously wet piece of fabric as she laid it on top of the pile. It was too embarrassing.

"Hands at your sides," he barked out as they started to drift in front of her. Angel snapped them back to either side of her hips.

She felt decidedly vulnerable, completely naked save for her thigh highs and heels, in a room slowly filling up with people as she stripped. It wasn't full by any means, but there were more people than when she'd first arrived, and she didn't know any of them. The sensation was both exciting and unnerving.

As was the way Master Adam's eyes were slowly perusing over her, drinking her in. His face didn't show anything, but going by the bulge at the front of his pants he was at least enjoying something about the sight. She wished she didn't feel so desperate for some sign of approval from him. Then again, what woman wouldn't want approval from a sexy man who was studying her so intently?

His eyes came back up to her face and her breath stuttered to a stop. Those icy blue eyes had a tendency to do that to her. Who needed air, anyway?

"You have your safe word, but sometimes I'm going to want to ask how you're doing. If you're good and you want to keep going, say green. If you're nervous or want to slow down, say yellow." He studied her face. "How are you feeling right now?"

"Green," she said, with as much bravado as she could muster.

It wasn't entirely true. She was feeling anxious and out of her element, but she also didn't want to leave and she didn't want to slow down. In fact, the faster they could move on to the next part of this, the better.

ADAM

Does she know she has her fists clenched at her sides? he wondered. With any other new submissive he'd say she was anxious but excited, eager to continue but also tempered with an understandable amount of fear of the unknown. With Angel he wasn't sure how much he could trust his instincts. Sometimes he would give submissives the color scheme if they seemed nervous or like they were having trouble giving up control.

Angel did seem like she was having a little bit of trouble giving up control, but in a way that made a Dominant's pulse beat faster because this strong personality was following his commands, fitting herself to his will. The kind of struggle he loved to be a voyeur to. He'd given her the colors because he was feeling a bit unsure of himself, unsure of his ability to read her.

And he really, really hated that.

"Alright then, little one," he grinned at her, enjoying watching her face heat as his eyes traveled over those delicious curves again. "On the bench."

With her teetering heels he had to help her a little, providing a hand to hold for balance as she got her knees in place. Touching her sent little sizzles of heat up his skin, which he tried to ignore.

Good god, those stockings. Just inches away from her pussy lips— which were completely bare—and now he could see how they came up so very close to the rounded curve of her ass. No hidden surprises here; Angel was as roundly curved underneath her clothes as she looked. Fake padding not needed for this hourglass figure.

Unable to help himself, he rubbed his hand over her back where the corset boning had dug into her skin and left red marks. She sighed happily as his hand smoothed over her skin. He could feel Angel relaxing under his hand as he touched her. Hell, she was practically purring.

It took everything he had to move his hand away rather than letting it travel down her body to cup the now lifted curves of her ass. He had to keep a grip on himself and remind himself not to take her reactions for granted. They could be faked.

Almost angrily he snapped cuffs around her ankles and wrists. All the spanking benches were equipped with them, although of course you could bring your own from home too. Tightening them around her limbs, he made sure she could still move all her fingers and toes.

"I need you to tell me immediately if anything starts to tingle or hurt."

"Okay."

Adam reached up and smacked her bottom.

"Ouch! I mean... yes Sir." Her voice sounded properly contrite, as if she hadn't remembered. Maybe she hadn't.

Standing up, he left her there for a moment to get used to the restraints as he fetched a couple of toys from the communal chest Patrick kept available. For an Introduction Scene she wouldn't be charged, unless she requested something super fancy. But Adam was sticking with the basics.

8

ANGEL

Wriggling on the spanking bench, Angel found herself feeling both claustrophobic and excited. She knew people could see her and she was more on display than ever. But the restraints also made her feel enclosed, constrained which was their job, but she'd forgotten how much she hated not being able to move her legs. Still, she was determined to show Master Adam she could do this. She hated how he looked at her like he thought she couldn't handle anything he was dishing out.

And, even if they were making her claustrophobic, she was excited by them. It made being naked easier since she didn't have a choice now. Taking off her clothes had been much harder than lying on this bench, even if she was showing off all her goodies to anyone who walked behind her.

Now that she was all tied up, she had to trust Master Adam not to give her more than what she wanted. Obviously, he'd read her survey and she had to believe he would stick to that and he would take care of her. Unless she said her safe word, but even that was an exercise in trust because she had to believe he would stop. There were Dungeon Monitors, but how much could go wrong before they arrived?

Angel's livelihood came from helping women to know what a dangerous situation was and how to avoid them. She'd thought she would feel safe, but bent over and restrained she didn't feel so safe anymore, but instead of screaming and struggling she wanted to moan with how hot and horny she felt.

Movement approached and Angel turned her head to see dark leather pants and dress shoes before Master Adam was crouching down beside her and studying her face.

"How are you doing, Angel?"

"Green, Sir. Very green." If she was any greener she'd already be begging him to touch her. It was shameless he could make her so hot and wet when he hadn't even done anything yet.

He held something up in between them. "Do you know what these are?"

It took her a moment to focus her eyes on the small silver, rubber tipped toys he was holding.

"Nipple clamps. Sir."

"Have you ever tried them before?"

Heat rose in her face and she knew she was blushing again. "I've tried them on myself before, Sir."

"Good, then no need for explanations."

Angel moaned as he cupped the breast hanging down on that side of the bench; she couldn't help it. His hand was warm, large, and it felt darn good cupping her flesh. A smug little smile traveled over his lips and she couldn't even hate him for it, she wanted him to keep touching her.

Pain flared in her nipple and her back arched. Oh fuck it felt good. The sensations burst and popped in her breast, her pussy clenching as she panted through the initial sharp bite. She was barely aware of him moving around to her other side until the hot pinch flared on that side as well.

Making a mewling sound, she rubbed her lower body against the bench as best she could. Her body knew nipple clamps were usually followed by an orgasm. She only wore them when she was going to be playing with herself and she was feeling rough. They left her nipples sore and aching afterwards but it was always worth it.

Having someone else put them on her was so incredibly different she almost couldn't believe it. The loss of control, knowing she'd given herself over to him, added an entirely new element she'd never experienced before. And the fact a man she'd fantasized about doing very similar things with was the one making her feel this way only intensified everything.

"Angel, how are you?"

"Green... oh so very green."

The deep chuckle seemed to shiver up her spine and her pussy clenched again. Yes, this was what she wanted. What she'd been missing. Her fingers spasmed and curled around the hand holds. A smacking sound erupted in her ears before she even felt the pain in her bottom.

"Green what, sub?"

"Green, *Sir.*"

"Good girl."

The same hand smoothed over the cheek he'd spanked, and Angel moaned again.

"That feels nice, Sir," she murmured, rocking her hips again.

The hand stilled on her bottom, no longer caressing and Angel wriggled enticingly, earning herself another smack.

"Stay still."

ADAM

The little moan of protest had his cock throbbing, especially when she immediately stilled under his hand. She seemed so open and honest in her reactions, it was becoming harder and harder for him to remember she'd faked being a Domme only a few weeks ago. Successfully enough to fool everyone she'd interacted with.

Gripping her cheek tighter, he dug his fingers into the soft flesh and elicited another moan as she shivered and panted. Angel liked having her ass played with. Damn.

As if he wasn't already having enough issues with how attracted he was to her.

"I'm going to plug you, Angel. And then I'm going to give you the spanking you so richly deserve."

Unlike some scenes, that last part wasn't only to help her get into the role. Both of them knew she did deserve a spanking.

All she did was moan again as his finger slid down the soft mound of her bottom and circled around the roseate of her anus. Sometimes it could be a little awkward touching a woman he'd just met this intimately, even if they were attracted to each other. With Angel, he was having trouble keeping himself from doing even more.

Reluctantly he pulled his hands away from her before he lost even more control. She made a little mew of protest and wriggled a bit but otherwise stayed in position, so he didn't say anything as he coated a thin layer of lube on the plug he'd gotten. Since she'd done some anal play before he'd chosen a medium sized one. If she'd lied about that then she deserved the extra stretching and discomfort which would come with having to accommodate the plug.

But when he placed it against her small rosebud, all she did was moan and lift her hips as he began to slide it in. Carefully he worked it back and forth as he reached the wider part, watching her body. Everything said she was loving every single thing he was doing to her. It took all he had not to reach down and rub his cock as the plug slid snugly into its new home, much easier than it would have if she wasn't used to some kind of anal play.

She hadn't been lying.

In fact, she'd reacted as if he'd been touching her pussy rather than her ass. The pink folds below where the plug peeked out between her cheeks were glistening with cream, sweet and hot, filling his nose with the musky scent of her arousal.

Couldn't fake that. He hoped. His rock-hard erection certainly was real enough.

"How are you doing, Angel?" he asked, twirling the plug. Not that he needed the confirmation at the moment, he wanted to hear her say it.

"Green as an Irishman, Sir."

Since she couldn't see him, he allowed himself to smile. She wasn't exactly what he could call bratty, just snippy. Spirited. Fiery. Everything he'd ever said he wanted in a sub. His smile faded.

If she really was a submissive and not playing head games.

Turning his attention back to the enticing curves of her bottom, he raised his hand and brought it down on one cheek. Enough to make her cry out, but not too hard for a beginning spanking. That was all the warning he gave her before he began to pepper her bottom with short, hard smacks. Just enough to begin to pinken her cheeks, warming up her skin.

ANGEL

She moaned and rocked, her muscles clenching as best they could when she was in restraints, and then relaxing again, over and over as he spanked her from the very top curve of her ass down to her sit-spot. It hurt. There was no denying that.

But it hurt so *good*.

The growing burn licked along her senses, mingling with the throbbing tingling left in her breasts from the clamps. Her pussy clenched with every slap, her inner muscles spasming around the plug. Having her ass filled was making her desperate for an orgasm, even more so than the clamps had. Angel loved having her anus stimulated, loved being filled with a plug, and now she was discovering she loved being spanked.

This was the kind of spanking she'd wanted when she'd asked her ex to try. He'd been far too tentative and then when she'd asked for it harder, he'd gone too rough without warming her up. She could tell the blows were becoming harder as Master Adam continued the spanking, but she liked it was getting harder. She needed it to be harder.

It was a crescendo, a beautiful build of pain and pleasure that had her insides convulsing and her body aching for more.

Closing her eyes, she sank into the rising bliss, giving herself over to feeling and letting go of all of her thoughts.

❦

ADAM

From her whimpers and moans, Adam could tell Angel was enjoying the spanking. He watching as the pink and red bloomed on her ass cheeks, the flesh jiggling every time he struck. Juices were literally dripping down from her pussy to her thighs and onto the bench, which she rubbed against every time her hips pressed downward.

There was no point in telling her to stop. It was an automatic response for anyone on the bench. He was enjoying watching the movements of her body far too much anyway.

A little voice in the back of his mind, the last of his self-control, was all that kept him from taking her right there. Her ass was a hot cherry red, the plug winking as her muscles squeezed it, and all he wanted to do was pound into her from behind and watch her reddened flesh jiggle as he fucked her hard. Maybe twist the plug and simultaneously fuck her with it.

He reached down with his fingers and slid them into the molten sheath of her pussy instead. Tight, soaking wet, and spasming around his fingers. Normally during an Introduction Scene he'd be more inclined to use a toy than his actual fingers, even if the submissive had indicated she was amenable to it, but he wanted to touch her too badly. Needed to feel her climaxing around him, in some manner, even if it wasn't around his dick.

The plunge of his fingers inside of her, a stroke of his thumb against her swollen clit, and he twisted the plug in a slow circle as Angel screamed out her orgasm. Her pussy clamped down on him, rippling in a way that would have milked his cock if he'd had it in her.

Pleasure surged, burst, and he groaned, his free hand braced on her bottom as his fingers dug in and he fought not to completely embarrass himself by cumming in his pants. The way he was squeezing her ass only seemed to intensify her pleasure and he couldn't help but think of how damn satisfying it would be to be inside her for a moment like this.

She was perfect.

Beautiful, attractive, mouthy without being bratty, hell she'd even made him want to laugh when he was angry. Going by her survey she even had the same kink preferences he did.

If the survey was real.

Resentment welled up inside of him. He'd spent the past weeks thinking maybe she was confused, thinking maybe she was a submissive and didn't know it, thinking maybe she was a switch. Whenever he'd thought maybe she *was* a submissive, he'd always assigned the best of intentions to her. He'd truly believed *she* thought she was a Domme.

Instead, it turned out she'd been deliberately lying. One of the biggest red flags, in his opinion.

Pushing down his attraction, shoving away the parts of his brain that wanted to argue with him, Adam gently eased the plug from her asshole and began to undo the restraints. Angel softly murmured and then whimpered as he removed the clamps. He rubbed her breasts, ignoring the way his cock jerked as he helped the circulation return to her nipples.

He didn't want to be turned on by what he was doing. He wanted to finish the scene as quickly as possible and get out of there before he started ignoring the red flags and started indulging in his attraction to her.

Helping her up off of the bench, he picked up her pile of clothes and handed them to her. "Here. You can get dressed again here or I can take you to the locker room to get dressed there."

Swaying slightly on her feet, her heels wobbly, Angel blinked at him. The clothes hung between them in his hand. Shit. She was more spacey than he'd realized.

"What are you doing?" The sharp voice behind him was all too familiar.

Adam groaned. When the hell had Olivia gotten there? He spun around. "What are you doing here? I thought you were at a conference."

"It ended early. What the hell are you doing?" The Domme glared at him, moving past him to Angel's side where she wrapped her arm around the wobbly woman. He knew the moment Olivia recognized her, but that didn't stop the outraged Domme from cuddling Angel and giving him another dirty look. "She can't get dressed. She's completely overwhelmed."

Yeah, and he'd been about to help Angel, but now that Olivia was here he could hand that duty off to her. Take advantage of Olivia mistaking his intentions. She'd taken care of Angel and *not* get caught up in an attraction that couldn't lead to anywhere. While she might chew him out later, it'd be worth it.

Olivia glared at him. The ultimate mother hen. Olivia was well known for treating all the unattached subs as her own, match-making as she went. Before she could retort back to him however, Jared was bounding down the steps and coming up next to her.

It was amazing how fast all of them reacted to Olivia's call, without even thinking about it.

"What's going on?" he asked, immediately sensing the tension in the air. He eyed Angel's shell-shocked expression with concern.

"Here, Angel, go with Jared," Olivia said, steering Angel to the big man. Instinctively Jared reached out, scooping her up into his arms. "Master Adam and I need to have a talk." Something inside Adam's chest growled as he watched Angel snuggled into Jared's arms, closing her eyes. That was bad. He was already feeling attached.

He didn't even realize he was staring after Angel and Jared as the big man carried her over to the aftercare corner until Olivia grabbed his arm and forcibly turned him around. Every muscle tensed, a precursor to violence, before he remembered himself and she released his bicep, frowning.

"Jesus, you are on edge," she muttered before her glare came back into full force. "What the hell is wrong with you? You've been obsessing about this woman for *weeks* now, she shows up, she's obviously submissive... it's everything you were hoping for. I didn't see the full scene, but what I did see was hot as hell. What the hell happened?"

"I wasn't obsessed. And she *lied*." His initial indignation and anger welled up again, overtaking his other emotions. "She's known all along she's submissive, she was faking being a Domme at Chained. At least that's what she claims. How can I even tell? You saw last weekend what a good actress she is. She could be playing all of us."

Aggravation had him fisting his hands. He wanted to turn and look to see what was going on behind him. In fact, he was pretty sure Olivia had deliberately placed him so he wouldn't be able to see the aftercare corner. Of course, he knew Jared wouldn't do anything inappropriate. He liked after care and cuddling and taking care of a blissed out submissive. Hell, Adam liked that part too and it was now killing him to have voluntarily given it over to someone else.

As if she knew his attention had wavered, Olivia stepped forward and grabbed the front of his shirt, right around the collar. Her eyes were bright silver with anger.

"Look asshole. You don't like surprises and you don't like not knowing things, because you don't like being out of control. After the way your mom up and left your Dad and you and your brother without any warning, I get it. But this is *not the same*."

"That has nothing to do with this," he growled, glaring back at her. "I can handle surprises. I didn't know Brooke was a masochist and I handled that break-up fine." It was something he reassured himself with on a regular basis.

"Again, not the same," Olivia insisted. "You two discovered that together. You got blindsided tonight when Angel showed up as a submissive and you found out she'd been hiding it from you. I don't know her reasons for doing what she did, but I know you're taking out your own issues on her. You still decided to do a scene with her tonight and you owe it to her to take care of her through the end of it. And that includes taking care of her afterwards. Especially when she put *her* trust in you tonight and you're not repaying her trust. You should be the one taking care of her right now, not Jared."

It burned when she was right.

"Fine," he snapped out as she let go of his shirt. He knew she was standing, fists planted on her hips, and watching as he headed over to the aftercare corner. Jared glared at him as he approached.

Standing in front of Jared, looking down at the soft bundle of woman in his arms, now securely wrapped in a blanket, Adam sighed and felt the anger leaking away.

"Are you okay now?" Jared asked.

"Yeah. I'm sorry you had to come down and do my job for me."

"No problem." Smiling almost fondly, Jared looked down at the sleepy brunette. "She's a sweetheart."

Something very like jealousy stirred in Adam's chest, making his voice gruff as he answered. "I'll take her now."

"You going to take care of her?"

He bristled. "Yes."

After a moment Jared stood, easily despite the fact that he was carrying Angel's entire weight, and passed her over to Adam. She fit nicely in his arms, and didn't even seem to be aware she was being passed around. Immediately after the transfer she snuggled into him as happily as she'd been snuggled into Jared.

Either she was the world's greatest actress or the scene had been as intense and mind-blowing for her as it had been for him.

Leaning back in the couch, he thought over what Olivia had said. Scening was all about trust, and how could he trust her when she'd lied to him from the moment he'd met her?

And Olivia's accusation about his mom... So what if he didn't like surprises? He hadn't liked them before his mom left either. Sure, she'd left without any warning, but it wasn't like he had any hang-ups thinking she hadn't wanted him or Brian. The reasons his parents divorced had nothing to do with their kids and their subsequent dealings with each other had been so bitter because both of them had wanted the kids and weren't above trying to make them take sides.

The year after his mom had left he'd immediately chosen his dad because he'd been so angry with her. She'd spent so much time lying to all of them, pretending she was happy and then she up and left... so yeah, okay, he could see how Olivia might think some of his anger tonight could possibly be an overreaction due to his past. Adam couldn't be sure it wasn't.

Angel shifted in his arms, murmuring. Soft, warm woman, wriggling against his dick, which apparently didn't care he shouldn't be lusting after her. Thinking over the scene, he wanted to believe she hadn't acted or pretended for any of. It had all seemed like honest, instinctive, open reactions. The kind of giving responses a Dom dreamed about.

Looking down at the woman in his arms, he tipped her back and she smiled rather dreamily up at him. The cloudy, hazy look in her eyes said she wasn't all there. Again, the kind of thing he liked to believe couldn't be faked.

"Angel, how are you doing?"

She sighed and turned her head into his chest, snuggling into him again. Shifting her weight, he held her closer, pulling her head into his shoulder and enjoyed the sensation. Most of his anger had drifted away, although he still hated the uncertainty about whether or not he was reading her correctly.

As was becoming almost habitual around Angel, Adam felt unsure of himself. And he didn't like it at all.

ANGEL

He hadn't kissed her. Not once. That's what was bothering her. She made a face. There were a million other things which *should* be bothering her—like the fact she'd gotten naked in a room full of people and then let what was basically a complete stranger put his hands all over her body—but what was really getting to her was the fact he hadn't kissed her.

Not once.

After she'd come out of her pleasure induced stupor—which had been more than a little embarrassing—he'd helped her get dressed, gotten her water and chocolate, and took her back upstairs to Patrick's office so she could talk to the big man on campus. Kind of like an exit interview.

She hated to admit how much it bothered her the next day when she thought over the encounter and realized he hadn't kissed her. Angel liked kissing. She liked it a lot. And with her body still tingling and thrumming every time she thought about all the other things he'd done with her, she hated to have missed out on it.

Maybe it was a *Pretty Woman* kind of thing. No kissing because it was too intimate. After all, he hadn't chosen to do a scene with her. He'd been chosen for her. Just because she'd had the most amazing sexual experience of her life, that didn't mean he felt the same way.

Hell, maybe it was because it was her first time with a man doing the things she'd always fantasized about and he'd known exactly what he was doing. Maybe she'd have the same reaction to any strong dominant man who was experienced in the things she craved. All day she'd been wondering.

All she knew was she had to find out.

Good thing she hadn't made any plans for tonight, although she normally had something going on Fridays. She was going back to Stronghold.

9

ADAM

"Knock, knock." Justin matched the deed to the words, standing halfway in the doorway of Adam's office. Adam scowled. He'd purposefully avoided lunch with the other man today. "Can I come in?"

"Depends on what you want to talk about."

After being lectured by Patrick last night and receiving a blistering e-mail from Olivia after he ignored her call, he wasn't in the mood to be lectured by anyone else. Not that he was sure Justin knew, but the way gossip went around their group of friends they seriously resembled a bunch of giggling high school girls sometimes. When Justin shut the door behind him, Adam scowled even more, knowing Justin would only do it if he wanted to talk to him about something serious.

Since he knew there wasn't anything going on with the company, that meant it had to be personal.

"So." Justin sat down in one of the chairs, stretching his long legs out in front of him to lounge comfortably. "Thank God it's Friday, huh?"

Tapping the base of one of his pens, Adam stared across the desk at him. The smile on Justin's face widened to a grin which made him look even more like Chris than he usually did. Silence stretched between them, but it was obvious Adam's reluctance to speak was amusing Justin more than anything else.

"What do you want?" he asked, a little sourly. He was not in the mood for chit chat. Even after he'd gone home last night, he hadn't been able to sort out his conflicting emotions.

Discovering Angel's deception, followed almost immediately by one of the most intense scenes of his life, and then a lecture about his own failings from Patrick had not left him in the best state of mind. A good night's sleep would have been helpful, if only he'd been able to fall asleep. Instead, he found himself picking apart the scene over and over again, trying to remember every movement, every word, and every facial expression.

"I heard you had an interesting scene at the club last night."

Adam stopped tapping the pen and gripped it tightly in his fist. "I hate our group of friends sometimes."

"They wouldn't have known anything was up if you hadn't blown it at the end," Justin pointed out. "Jared texted me last night, he wanted me to check in on you this morning. Make sure you were okay. Any reason he should have been worried about that?"

Well at least it wasn't Olivia. She knew far more about what had happened than Jared did, and if Justin was in here questioning him then it meant she probably hadn't shared any of it. Thank God. Adam hadn't exactly explained himself to Patrick last night either.

"I'm fine."

"Yeah, and you look it too."

Adam opened his mouth and then closed it again, frowning. He was about to ask Justin what he would do if he found out Jessica had lied to him or misled him about something important, when he remembered both Justin and Chris had done that to Jessica. They'd not only known who she was when she went to the Venus School, they'd used their connections to ensure they'd be there at the same time as her. And they'd known the entire time she was there that they'd be seeing her when they went home, since they all worked at the same company.

At the time, he'd thought their tactics amusing. But he'd known them for a long time, he knew Justin and Chris were trustworthy and they weren't habitual liars.

Which was Angel? A liar who was possibly crazy, or a woman who had lied because she felt she had a good reason to but was usually honest?

Maybe he should be talking to Jessica.

"Why do you think Jessica forgave you?" he asked, finally. "For the Venus School."

Justin's brows rose. "Probably because she's a heck of a lot nicer than I am." He grinned. "Honestly, I was always surprised she didn't make us crawl for it. But maybe that's because she felt like she'd gotten to know us, and she'd put her trust in us enough times at the school that it was kind of like second nature. Also, once we started pursuing her in real life, we didn't give her another reason to distrust us."

The pen tapping started up again. Unfortunately, none of that helped him. He didn't know Angel. The first time they'd met she'd lied. But he'd thought her responses last night were real. Honest.

"How much did Jared tell you?"

"I know that 'Angie' is really Mistress Angela."

"Her real name is Angel." Adam sighed. "She says she's new to everything and she didn't want to come to a club alone, so she pretended to be a Domme at Chained, thinking no one at Stronghold would ever know."

"She knew she was submissive all along."

"Yes. She flat out lied to me about it when I..."

"When you what?" Justin arched his brow as Adam's voice trailed off.

He grimaced. "When I asked if she was a switch at Chained."

"You tried to proposition her at Chained?" Chuckling, Justin shook his head. "No wonder you're so pissy. We've been making fun of you for weeks now and it turns out you were right."

Crap. He hadn't even thought about it that way. Was part of his resentment towards Angel because of that?

"I didn't proposition her, exactly." Adam sighed, but the corner of his mouth turned up in a little smile. What Justin had said was true—

he had been right at Chained. Something had been off and he'd realized it. So maybe he could trust his instincts after all. At any rate, Justin's observation made him feel a little better.

"She was scared?" Justin said, although Adam could tell he wasn't actually asking the question, he was repeating what Adam had said as he thought it over. Leaning back in his chair, Justin rubbed his fingers along his jaw and then through his thick, dark hair.

"Or she's playing some game," Adam felt compelled to point out. He wasn't sure he believed that anymore, but it had been on his mind last night. Although, even if she was scared, he hated dishonesty and hidden motives.

Hm. Olivia might have a point about his issues over the way his mother left after all.

To his surprise, Justin grinned again. "You have it bad, don't you?" He laughed. "Stop fighting it or you'll end up like Liam was when he was trying to scare Hilary away, stressed and cranky. Although I'm not saying you shouldn't punish her. I sure as hell wouldn't tolerate Jessica lying, no matter her reasons. But Angel could still be worth getting to know." Standing up he headed for the door, only stopping once he had his hand on the knob. "Are you coming to Stronghold tonight?"

"No, I'll be there tomorrow."

He needed a night away from the club and his friends to get his head on straight. Giving him a nod, Justin exited leaving Adam with even more things to think about than he'd had before.

ANGEL

Tonight's theme was red.

It was a big departure from last night when she'd been decked out in all white, but that was the point. Angel needed armor in the form of a power color. She'd had to work herself up to get out of the house and headed toward Stronghold at all. Her corset covered her breasts completely and was made of a black and red brocade that went well with the short, pleated red faux leather skirt she was wearing. A red thong was under the skirt and her red crotchless fishnets slid into black pumps with a three-inch heel. A wider, much sturdier heel than the stilettos she'd been wearing the night before.

The bright red lipstick might have been a little much, but it made her feel confident. Something she'd been sorely lacking since yesterday.

Usually she liked to spend Fridays working on new projects to put online for Etsy or working on orders. Today she'd barely been able to concentrate. Yeah, she wanted to go back to Stronghold to explore more, but she had to admit to herself that a big part of the reason was because she wanted to see Master Adam again. He had seemed so... angry with her last night. Even after he'd started being nicer, he'd been stand offish and distant.

But in the middle of the scene he'd been hot, hot, hot.

Angel didn't like people being mad at her. It made her feel itchy and jumpy all over with the need to fix things and make them right. Of course, there were times when she could convince herself she didn't care, usually if she was also mad at the other person. But she didn't want Mr. Grouchy to be mad at her. She wanted to fit in at Stronghold and he obviously had a lot of influence there if he was trusted enough to be doing Introduction Scenes.

Okay, if she was being honest she didn't want him to be mad because of more personal reasons too.

While last night's scene might have been amazing because it was her first time exploring her fantasies, she had a feeling a big part of it was who she'd been exploring her fantasies with. The same man who had been starring in them lately. Was it the scene or him drawing her back to Stronghold now?

Chemistry was an ineffable, inexplicable force.

Walking into Stronghold again was a little easier than last night, although her stomach was still churning with tension. Just for a different reason.

Lexie was behind the front desk again, a chipper, friendly face that eased some of the bubbly twisting in her stomach. A new face was guarding the door, not nearly as intimidating as Jared had been the night before. Tall and muscular with spiked brown hair.

"Hey Angie! Welcome back," Lexie said, beaming as Angel approached.

"It's Angel," she said, feeling a little weird about giving a new name. But she'd told Master Adam last night so she might as well keep it up. "I decided to go by my real name."

"Hey, Angie's pretty close anyway. That's cute. Did you have a good scene last night?"

"Yeah," Angel said, a little surprised. For some reason she'd thought Lexie would have heard about it already. It was obvious she was close to the members of the club, and usually the front desk was a good place to overhear gossip. "My butt was a little sore this morning though."

Looking rather envious, Lexie gave a little sigh. "From what I've heard that shouldn't last very long unless it was a really hard spanking."

Feeling a surge of sympathy, Angel leaned against the desk. She wasn't in a hurry to get into the club anyway and she liked Lexie. It wouldn't hurt to stop and talk for a bit, especially since Angel wouldn't know anyone once she walked in.

"Why do you work here? Wouldn't you rather join the club?" It had to be hard to be on the outside looking in, especially when Lexie very obviously wanted to be in and was close with the people who were.

"I would, but Patrick won't let me. I threatened to go to another club, where he wouldn't be able to watch over my shoulder all the time, so he gave me this job. I think he thought by now I'd be frightened off by the people who come in and the very little bit I get to see being out here." The little smirk on her face said the big man had thought wrong. Angel grinned. Dressed in another fishnet shirt, this one the same color blue as her eyes, Lexie's lacy bra left very little to the imagination. As did the skintight shorts she was wearing. "Supposedly I'm doing this job until I decide the scene is what I really want."

"You seem like you already know."

Rolling her big baby blues, Lexie let out a little derisive snort. "I do. But Patrick's adamant I don't know enough yet to decide." A smug smile curved her lips. "I'm looking forward to getting in for Valentine's Day. Even if it's the main room. I figure baby steps are best. Give the guys time to get used to the fact I'm not a little girl anymore." She glanced down at her attire. "Although you'd think they would have figured it out by now."

"What's this Valentine's Day party?"

At the question, Lexie perked up. "I've been after Patrick to do some theme nights and holiday parties. Especially for things like Valentine's Day. Get attendance up during those times and make them a little more fun rather than having it be a regular night. He finally gave in on the Valentine's Day thing when he heard about the plans the guy I'm seeing was making." The gleeful smugness in her voice said Lexie had known exactly how Patrick would react and she had made sure he heard. "Now we're having a party and he's insistent since it was my idea, I have to be here to help him run it. I said no until he agreed to let me onto the main floor."

"You might be kind of disappointed," Angel warned. "There's not a whole lot on this floor. All the interesting stuff is upstairs and downstairs."

"Yeah, but it's a step in the right direction. I've been working here for months now and this is the first time Patrick has agreed to let me step beyond this room." Lexie rolled her eyes again. "You wouldn't believe how stubborn these guys can be. It's a small step for the man, but a giant leap for me."

Angel giggled at the moon landing reference. Yeah, she could see how that would be true.

"Well I'll have to come and hang out on the dance floor with you."

"Oh, I'm sure you'll get to do more than that," Lexie said, with a bit of wistful envy. "I had more than one dominant stop by my desk after you left to ask if you were new and available."

A flush of pleasure heated Angel's body, considering at least some of them had probably seen the scene and the tense aftermath. Nice to know someone wanted her. Even if she wasn't sure she wanted any of them yet.

"Hey guys!" Lexie called out, looking past her. Angel turned to see three very large men and two women walking in, a brunette and a blonde. Two of the guys were tall, dark and handsome, the other had auburn hair and was a little bit shorter than them but built with some major muscle and he moved with a kind of lethal grace that belied his boyish looks. Both of the women hurried up to say hello to Lexie.

Shifting to the side, feeling a little shy now that there was a large group moving in, Angel realized one of the tall, dark and handsomes was looking at her. He looked kind of familiar but where—

Aw shit. She'd met him before. At Chained.

For a moment she felt like running, but the second he recognized her his face lit up like it was Christmas. His big grin was so friendly and contagious she found herself smiling back at him.

"Well, well, well, if it isn't 'Mistress' Angela." The way he said it made it sound like it was some kind of joke, rather than the personal affront Master Adam had taken it as.

Still, she shrugged a little uncomfortably. "It's Angel. And not Mistress."

Out of the corner of her eye she saw both of the women gaping at her.

"Wait, *you're* the one?" the blonde squealed, reaching out to grab Angel's hand. She was rather bouncy, dressed in hot pink and black, and incredibly friendly. The slightly curvier brunette standing behind her smiled at Angel, looking a little shyer than the more overtly friendly blonde. "Oh my god, you have no idea how excited I am to meet you!"

"You are?" Now Angel was really confused. She glanced around the circle of new faces. Chris—she thought she remembered it being his name—was the only one smiling overtly at her. The one who looked like he could be Chris' brother was studying her like she was an amoeba under a microscope, and the redhead was looking at the blonde woman in front of her with a mixture of amusement and exasperation.

"Give her a chance to breathe before you bury her with questions," Chris said, laughing. "Angel, this is Hilary, Jessica, Liam, and Justin. Everyone, this is Angel, formerly known as Mistress Angela. And I'm Chris, in case you didn't remember my name."

"I did, but I wasn't sure I had it right," she replied with a smile. Her eyes flickered around all of them again. "It's nice to meet you all."

"What's with the 'Mistress Angela' thing?" Lexie wanted to know.

She was the only one who was out of the loop. Angel explained what she'd done at Chained, how she'd wanted to get some insight into going to a club before she went in as a submissive and some of the things she'd heard online had made her feel like she needed a better handle on things. Everyone listened attentively. All three of the women nodded sympathetically which made her feel better. Chris snickered now and then as if it was all a big joke, Liam looked intrigued but not condemning, and Justin's face was so blank he might as well have been Master Adam. She couldn't tell what he was thinking at all.

"Oh you poor thing," Hilary said when she was done, reaching out and grabbing Angel's hand again to give it a squeeze. "I can't imagine how hard it must have been to go in by yourself... if Jessica hadn't dragged me out here, I never would have had the guts to come."

Which was a startling sentence in and of itself, because Hilary seemed like the much more confident person between them. She was not as shy, which told Angel that Jessica probably had hidden depths.

"And I wouldn't have had the courage to come on my own," Jessica said with a little giggle, looking up at Justin and then Chris.

"You went to the Venus School on your own," Hilary countered.

"Venus School?" Angel had never heard of it.

The door to the outside opened, admitting more patrons of Stronghold along with an icy blast of cold wind. The women all shivered, which wasn't surprising since Lexie had already taken their coats which meant they were substantially less dressed than the men.

"Ok, time to go in the club," Justin said, reaching out to snuggle a shivering Jessica under his arm, as Liam did the same with Hilary. "You can tell Angel all about the Venus School in there."

"Yes, please come sit with us," Hilary said enthusiastically, her big brown eyes shining. They were like Bambi eyes. Angel felt like saying no would be akin to kicking a puppy.

"Okay," she said, gathering her confidence. It wasn't quite the same as stepping into the club with friends, since she didn't really know any of them. Except Chris had been with Mr. Grouchy at Chained so they must be friends... but *he* didn't seem like he was mad at her. "Thank you."

After saying goodbye to Lexie and feeling bad about having to leave her at the front desk, even though she put on a good show of not being envious, Angel went with the group into the club. The music was loud, but not loud enough to stifle conversation.

They sat around one of the tables by the bar, dragging up a couple of extra chairs so everyone could fit. The dynamics between them were fascinating; Liam was obviously with Hilary and she and Jessica were obviously very close, but Jessica seemed to be dividing her attention between both Justin and Chris. There was something between the two men as well, a connection almost sexual but not quite.

After they'd gotten their drinks and Jessica started explaining what the Venus School was and how she'd ended up there, with occasional interjections from Justin and Chris, Angel understood a little better. She'd never met anyone in a real ménage relationship before. It always seemed like the kind of thing that worked better in fiction than reality, but somehow it seemed to fit the three of them.

As much as they looked alike, Justin and Chris acted very differently. Justin was much quieter and more standoffish—not unfriendly, but not quite friendly either—while Chris was a bit of a jokester, very outgoing, and provided a good foil for his friend and partner. She noticed Justin seemed to tend to take the lead in the relationship, and everything else too. Whenever someone came by the table to say hi, he was the one to make sure she was introduced to them. When Jessica and Hilary's drinks got low, he was the one to catch the bartender's eye and get them water.

And after Hilary and Liam left to go to one of the playrooms, he was the one to stay behind while Jessica and Chris went to get their own playroom set up after one of the Dungeon Monitors came by to tell them the room they'd reserved was available. Angel got the distinct feeling he was watching over her, as if she'd somehow entered his sphere of responsibility by sitting down at the table with them.

"You don't have to stay," she said, feeling bad his lovers had left the area without him. "I'll go hang out in the lounge with the other unattached submissives."

For a long moment, he studied her again, as if thinking over what he wanted to say. It was a little unnerving being under his dark, steady gaze. "I'd feel better if I stayed."

"You can't hang out with me all night when you're supposed to be with Jessica and Chris," she said, with a hint of exasperation. She started to get up.

"Sit."

Her butt hit the seat and she stared at him, startled. For the first time, she saw him smile at her obvious surprise. How the heck had he done that? Last night she'd responded to Adam's orders almost from the very beginning, but she hadn't felt the same compulsion with Justin until now. It was like his voice had deepened, hardened and become a heck of a lot more commanding. It didn't turn her on, but it sure as hell got her attention and sent a little shiver through her.

"I won't stay here all night," he said calmly, as if he hadn't commanded her like a dog and she hadn't obeyed without hesitation. "Someone else should be along soon."

"Do you mean Master Adam?" she asked, nervously running her fingers over the condensation on her glass. She'd gotten a bourbon and diet for her one drink but it had dwindled down to mostly ice. If she decided not to play tonight then she could have more. And if Master Adam was going to show up then she didn't know which she wanted. "Because I'm not sure I'm his favorite person right now. I don't think he wants to see me."

Justin smiled. A slow, knowing smile that made her fidget and want to ask exactly what it was he was thinking. Stupid know-it-all Doms. "He's not coming tonight."

"Oh." Her shoulders slumped for a moment before she pushed them back up. Disappointment warred with relief.

"He'll be here tomorrow." The tone of his voice was casual, the penetrating way he was looking at her was not.

"I won't be. I have plans." A game night with her housemates, but she didn't mind the implication that perhaps she had a date. With someone who wasn't big, blond, and pissy.

"Mmm, too bad." Before Angel could ask what he meant, his expression lightened a bit. "Ah good, Olivia's here."

Turning to see who he was looking at, Angel saw a woman with flaming red hair approaching. She was a Domme, what Angel had pretended to be at Chained, wearing skin tight black latex bodysuit covering her almost completely except for a keyhole opening showing off a generous amount of pale skin and cleavage. The utter confidence she walked with was exactly what Angel had tried to emulate at Chained.

She was also vaguely familiar, and as she came closer Angel realized Olivia was the one who had stepped in last night at the end of her scene with Adam. Heat rose in her cheeks and her gaze skittered away from those clear, grey eyes.

"Olivia, I believe you've met Angel," Justin said, getting to his feet. "If you'll excuse me, I'm going to go join Chris and Jessica at school."

"Good, shoo," Olivia said, without even turning her head to look at him. All of her attention was on Angel, which was making Angel shift uncomfortably in her seat. The big male Dom paused for a moment, as if he now wanted to show Olivia couldn't order him around, but then he shrugged and walked off toward the stairways. Angel sneaked a peek at Olivia, who was now smiling at her. "Jessica's good for him."

"What?"

"A year ago, if I'd told him to shoo, he would have stuck around to make a point. Now he doesn't care, because he's happy and he'd rather go be with Jessica and Chris then stay here arguing with me," Olivia explained as she slid into the chair next to Angel.

"I told him he didn't have to stay here with me," Angel said, feeling a bit guilty and wondering if Olivia was obliquely referring to the fact Justin had been sitting with her rather than off with his partners. "I can take care of myself. I was going to go over there." She nodded at the lounge.

"No, stay here." Even though it was phrased as an order, there was something in Olivia's tone making it a request instead. Just a very strongly worded request. A server came up and Olivia ordered a drink before turning back to Angel. "I wanted to talk to you anyway. How are you after last night?"

Angel shifted in her seat. After Lexie, no one else had asked how her first scene had gone. Conversation had flowed easily enough while they'd been getting to know each other, but that hadn't come up. It wasn't until now she realized that was kind of strange. Then again, she wouldn't have felt comfortable telling them much because it was obvious from the things they'd said they were good friends with Adam and she wouldn't have wanted to say anything that could be construed as negative. With Olivia she was more comfortable because the other woman had been there.

In fact, she'd scolded Adam, although Angel couldn't remember any of the specifics of what had been said. She'd been far too out of it.

"I'm okay," she said, fiddling with her drink. "A little confused I guess." She eyed Olivia, but the other woman wasn't looking at her with any kind of judgment. Interest and a tinge of concern, but nothing that said she thought Angel had done anything wrong. "He was so angry at first... the scene was amazing, but then he was so cold and uncaring afterwards until you talked to him."

"Adam has some... trust issues, we'll call them. Finding out you were a submissive was a bit of a shock to him and he doesn't like surprises. He's not usually caught unawares." To Angel's surprise, Olivia grinned rather cheerfully. "It's good for him."

"I don't usually lie," said Angel, not wanting this woman to get the wrong impression. "I... it's scary doing this on my own. Coming here... I didn't feel safe right away. I wanted to know what I was walking into before I came in as a submissive and put myself in someone else's hands."

"I can understand, although I also understand why Adam was so upset. Honestly and communication are incredibly important, especially here. It's something that can't be stressed enough," Olivia said as the server returned with her drink. Taking it, she brought it to her lips for a short sip as she studied Angel thoughtfully. "We went to see your show, you know. You're a very good actress."

"We... you... my show?" Angel stuttered out. Olivia's lightning changes in conversation were not exactly easy to keep up with.

"Adam and me. Last Saturday. I have no doubt you pulled off being a Domme very well," Olivia went on calmly. "Rick, Chris, and Andrew had no idea and they're usually pretty observant, although Adam and Patrick are the best at reading body language. Which is why it threw Adam for a loop when he couldn't quite figure you out and then you showed up here as something different than he'd first seen you. Things that are unexpected and out of his control throw him, so he'll probably need a couple days to get over it before he's back to normal."

He wasn't the only one. Angel felt shell shocked by the knowledge he and Olivia had come to see her show. She remembered mentioning it at Chained, but she would never have thought he would remember, much less look it up and then come.

"Oh," she finally said when she realized Olivia seemed to be waiting for some sort of response. There was too much to think about and too many emotions to sort through. She had no idea how she felt about all these revelations, piling on top of each other.

Olivia smiled gently. "Come on, sweetie. I'll walk you out to the lobby. Are you coming back here tomorrow?"

"No," Angel shook her head as she got up. "I can't, I have plans. I'll be back next weekend though."

"Boyfriend?"

"No, I promised my housemates some hang out time."

Olivia smiled again as she escorted Angel into the lobby. "Then we'll see you next week. Lexie, get Angel's coat for her please."

The entire operation was done so smoothly, with Olivia ushering Angel to the front door after she'd said another goodbye to Lexie and given the girl the web address for her Etsy store since she'd forgotten to the night before, that Angel was in her car and driving before she realized she hadn't done what she'd gone to the club for. The plan had been to do another scene, whether or not Mr. Grouchy was there, because she wanted to learn.

And just because she was attracted to him and they'd shared an amazing scene, that didn't mean she couldn't scene with other people. In fact, she probably should scene with other people so she didn't spend all her time thinking about him when it was obvious he wasn't interested in her.

Except, if he wasn't interested in her, then why had he gone to her show?

❧ 10 ❧

ADAM

Something was up.

Every hair on the back of Adam's neck was tingling, as if they were doing more than standing up straight, it was like they wanted to spring right off of his skin. The feeling had grown, from the moment he'd walked in and Lexie had given him a little smile that was somehow different from her usual. Then he'd walked into the club to see his friends all gathered around the bar. Granted, Andrew was standing behind it so that might have been why, but considering Adam had come a little later in the evening than usual he would have expected at least some of them to be off scening. Especially the couples.

Instead, every single one of them was standing around chatting. Jared and even Patrick, which wasn't entirely unusual in and of itself, but combined with everything else...

Yeah something was up.

And he'd bet his favorite guitar it had something to do with Angel. Pasting a neutral expression on his face he walked over to his friends, who were all casually not looking at him. So casually they might as well have screamed that one of them had spotted him and told the others he was coming.

He figured it was better to confront whatever this was head on. Scanning his eyes over the group, he ignored the pang of disappointment he felt when he realized Angel wasn't among them. That had been his first guess, after all.

"Hey Adam, want a drink?" Andrew asked loudly as soon as he was within hearing distance. Which, of course, gave everyone the excuse they needed to eyeball him and say hi. Adam asked for a scotch, neat. Normally he would have had a beer but he had a feeling that tonight he was going to want something stronger. Patrick was downright smirking at him. Bastard.

Adam was pretty sure he could wipe the smile off of Patrick's face by bringing Lexie into the club for an evening, but he'd be risking life and limb and not just from Patrick. Besides which, the idea made him far too uncomfortable to consider as anything other than a way to irritate the big Dom.

"I hear you had a scene with your girl the other night," Liam said, sidling up to him, Hilary tucked under his arm.

The conversation around them paused, not even trying to hide they were all waiting for Adam's reaction.

"Wasn't aware I have a girl."

"Then why—" Liam's hand clapped around Hilary's mouth before she could continue her question. The pretty blonde glared at him over his fingers but didn't try to struggle or push his hand away. Nice. Adam sighed, a little enviously.

"You know we're talking about Mistress Angela," Chris jumped in, leaning against the table he was standing next to. Like Liam he was smart enough to avail himself of a submissive shield; he'd arranged his position so Jessica was between him and Adam. Hard to smack your friend when an innocent woman was standing in the way. Especially when she was looking up at you with big brown, curious eyes.

"That's not her name," he snapped back, hating the reminder of her deception. Chris grinned. Idiot.

Jessica placed a hand on Adam's arm, her features serious as she looked up at him. "We thought Angel was cool."

"We?" Something inside of his stomach sank. Angel had been here last night and at least some of his friends who had missed out on Thursday's debacle had met her. He wasn't sure what made him jumpier, the fact she'd been here without him and hooked up with who knows what Dom or the fact she'd met his friends without him. Again, events had spiraled out of his control and he didn't like it at all. He'd thought she'd take a night off, most submissives wanted a night to assimilate things after their first scene. How very like her to be so much less predictable and so much more frustrating.

She nodded. "She was talking with Lexie when we got here, and then Lexie introduced us and Chris recognized her... and then she ended up hanging out with us for a little bit."

"Who's us?"

"Me, Liam, Jessica, Chris, and Justin," Hilary jumped in, once Liam finally removed his hand from her mouth and whispered a few words in her ear. Probably warning her not to talk about whatever gossip was being said about Adam and Angel around the group.

Which was fine by Adam. He didn't want to know.

"Great." He wasn't going to ask, he wasn't going to ask... "Do you know who she scened with?"

"No one," Olivia said, making him jump a bit. That went to show how distracted he was, he hadn't even noticed her coming up beside him, he'd been so focused on questioning Hilary and Jessica. Their boyfriends were all amusing themselves by playing the part of an audience, knowing he'd be much nicer talking to their submissives than he would be to them. "Justin kept an eye on her until I got here and then she and I chatted for a bit before I showed her out of the club."

A knot of tension inside his stomach relaxed. He hadn't even known it was there until the damn thing unraveled. Adam gritted his teeth. Part of him wanted to take out some of his ire on Olivia, but he couldn't. Not only had she stopped him from being a complete ass on Thursday, but he had to inwardly acknowledge he was grateful she'd kept Angel from scening with someone other than him. Even though his gratitude made him feel even more temperamental since he was getting all possessive over a woman he barely knew and who had lied to him from the moment she met him.

"What did you two talk about?" asked Hilary, with every evidence of surprise. Adam mentally blessed her impetuous nature, since he desperately wanted to know but just as desperately didn't want to have to ask.

Olivia shrugged and looked away. "Oh, this and that."

Jessica and Hilary looked as disappointed as Adam felt, obviously realizing their friend wasn't going to expound any further. Both Chris and Andrew looked like they were about to bust up laughing, even Patrick was smiling. Only Justin and Jared were managing to keep reasonably smooth faces, although in Jared's case that might have also been because he was apparently rather distracted. Every couple of minutes his eyes would slip back to the door of the club. Marissa was probably supposed to be meeting him here; Adam could only be grateful the disruptive sub hadn't shown up yet, even if it was causing his friend some angst.

"I'm sorry I missed it," said Rick, giving Adam a sidelong look. "She was a gorgeous Domme, I bet she looked even better as a submissive."

Even knowing Rick was trying to get a rise out of him, Adam couldn't help but growl a little bit under his breath. He took a sip of scotch to hide his bristling.

"I liked her," Hilary announced.

"Me too," Jessica said. Both of them looked expectantly at Adam. He met their gazes blandly. Jessica scowled at him and turned to Rick. "She's going to be back next weekend. You're looking for a sub, right? Maybe you should try a scene with her."

"No." Adam bit out the word, an automatic reaction which had him cursing internally the moment he said it, leaving Jessica looking smug and some of his friends looking at him with speculation in their eyes. Clearly, they'd all been on board for teasing him, not all of them had realized how interested he was in Angel.

Heck, he hadn't realized how interested he was in Angel until this very moment when he thought about her being with one of his friends. Doing a scene with another Dom in the club would be bad enough, but if she did a scene with Rick and Rick decided he wanted her, then Adam would feel honor bound to keep his hands off. The idea made him feel even more out of control, verging on panicky.

Damn Jessica anyway. He glared at Justin, already knowing Chris was going to be of no help when it came to keeping their girlfriend in line, not on this subject. Her other boyfriend was barely holding in his laughter, exchanging knowing glances with Andrew.

"Come here, sweetheart, time to stop teasing Master Adam," Justin murmured, reaching out and yanking his girlfriend against his body. Twisting her head around, she looked up at him and then sighed, slumping against him. The honorific had been included specifically to remind her of where she was. In the club, she could—and would—be punished for bratty behavior. Justin gave him a long look, the hint of a smile on his face. "I think we're going to go find a place to play."

The group started to break up. Jared headed out to the lobby, probably to call Marissa and find out where she was, Patrick headed back to his office, and those in relationships disappeared downstairs. That left Olivia, Rick, and Adam to keep Andrew company at the bar.

"Are you interested in Angel?" Rick asked, drumming his fingers on the table. The muscular blonde's face had gone serious. "Because if you're not... I wouldn't mind scening with her. But not if I'm stepping on your toes."

"I don't know... doesn't it bother you she lied about being a Domme?" The fact everyone else seemed to accept her immediately was making him feel like he was being unreasonable.

Rick shrugged. "Not really. I mean, it did at first, but we were talking about it a bit before you got here. Chris thinks of it as a huge practical joke, but Jessica and Hilary both pointed out we don't exactly understand how scary it was for them. Putting yourself out there as a submissive, especially when you don't have anyone around to show you the ropes—so to speak—or answer questions and soothe doubts... we were all pretty lucky. We're all naturally take-charge kind of people and we all knew each other. But Jessica went to the school, rather than the club to explore, where she knew other people would be there expressly for the purpose of trying new things, and she wouldn't have even done that if Olivia hadn't pushed her. And Hilary would have never gone anywhere near BDSM without Jessica."

"She naturally defers to others," Olivia put in. "Even though she obviously thought she was being a burden to Justin before I showed up, and on me once he passed her off, she couldn't bring herself to remove the 'burden' once we told her no. I think she's the type to take a mile if you give her an inch, but the whole way she'll be wishing you'd pull on the reins."

"I liked her at Chained," Rick said. "She probably had her reasons for wanting to explore the scene and see what a club was like before going into one and entrusting someone else. Especially since she had no one to watch her back or to introduce her. But you seem more possessive of her than you seem angry about the fact she misled us, so if you want her..."

"I—" Adam cleared his throat. He felt his friends' eyes on him like heavy weights. "I thought you didn't want to do a long-distance thing." Why was it still so hard to say he was interested in her? Maybe because, in some ways, he didn't want to be. He didn't like the way she upset his equilibrium, but the chemistry between them had been so strong he didn't want to give that up without exploring it either.

"I've started submitting my application to some of the school systems up here," Rick said easily. "If things go the way I want them to I'll be moving over the summer."

Great.

"Yeah," he finally muttered. "I'm interested in getting to know her better. I don't know if it's going to go anywhere though."

Rick nodded and Olivia smiled. A knowing, smug kind of smile. "Good," she said. "So that's settled. I'm going to find someone to go play with. Rick?"

He watched his friends walk off. Sure, he could go find an available submissive. Do a scene. Keep his hands off but still get some kind of satisfaction out of the evening by giving a submissive some pleasure.

Instead he said goodnight to Andrew and headed out, passing Jared and Marissa on his way as they came into the club. The big, genial Dom had a frown on his face and his sub was somehow managing to pout and look gleeful at the same time. Great. Trouble was brewing again in that area, but there was nothing he could do about it for the moment.

He needed to go home and think about his own trouble.

ADAM

By the time the middle of the week rolled around, Adam was more than a little amped up. Fortunately, Wednesday was his usual day for going into Liam's Kung-Fu studio for more than classes. He tried to make it to class at least a couple of times a week, although he ran through his forms every evening at home as well, but Wednesdays were special; they were the days for individual attention and, quite often, sparring.

Adam was the only one of their group who made it nearly every week. Justin and Patrick came some of the time, and the rest of their friends attended rarely.

Adam liked the mental and physical discipline involved. He liked the flow of his body and the way it felt when he was completely in tune with himself. There wasn't a substitute for a good, physical fight with an evenly matched opponent. A bit primitive, but he always felt better after Wednesday night.

Heck, he felt like he'd been waiting for this Wednesday ever since last Thursday.

Liam knew it too.

The redheaded Dom took one look at him when he walked in and pointed at the mat. "Stretch and then we'll get to it."

By which Adam knew he meant spar, not the regular forms and exercises they normally did before sparring. As he began to loosen his muscles, he felt his tension uncoiling, like wire coming undone from around a spring, just from the anticipation of a good fight. Liam was already loosened up from teaching classes, so he went through some of his forms while Adam stretched.

"Okay, I'm ready."

Which got him a look, because he hadn't really warmed himself up, only loosened his muscles, but Liam didn't argue. Obviously he had some idea of how much inner turmoil Adam had to work off this evening.

"Weapons or hand?"

"Hand." He wanted the feel of actual physical contact, the meaty satisfaction that came when a hit landed and the flash of pain when he received one in turn.

Smiling ruefully, looking more boyish than ever as he bounced slightly on the balls of his feet, Liam raised an eyebrow at him. "You know Hilary's going to be upset if you send me home with bruises."

"Don't worry, I won't mar your pretty face," Adam retorted.

Since there was no one to referee they needed to be slightly more careful anyway. Adam craved a reaffirmation of his self-control and a reassertion of his mental peace.

Grinning, Liam bounced toward him, his lower body tensing as if he was going for a kick when suddenly his weight and movement changed and a fist went flashing towards Adam's chest. It caught in a glancing blow as Adam barely managed to pull himself out of the way, thrown off-balance enough so he wasn't able to return the hit before Liam followed up with the kick he'd been expecting.

Pain exploded as Liam's heel hit squarely on the meaty part of his thigh, and focused concentration as adrenaline and endorphins rushed through him. Ignoring the throbbing in his leg, Adam swung around, his foot snaking out in a move designed to take Liam down. As usual, the move didn't work but it did force Liam back, giving Adam enough time to recover and renew his stance. They circled for a moment before Liam came at him in a flash of movement aimed at his shoulder.

Catching Liam's arm, Adam used the other man's momentum to pull him forward, jutting out his hip and throwing Liam over it. The move was one of his favorites, something he could do in his sleep, and he'd practiced it enough that he managed to use it against Liam about fifty percent of the time. Against his other friends the percentage was much higher.

He went down on one knee, twisting around to follow up on his advantage, but Liam was already breaking his hold and grabbing his wrist. Momentum diverted, Adam flew head over heels to land with a soft thunk on the mat. Growling, he kipped up to his feet and spun to face Liam again.

Fifteen minutes later they both sat, panting, and nursing their wounds. Adam had managed to keep from marring Liam's pretty face, as he'd promised, but now had an ice pack pressed against his shoulder. Adam had one against his thigh. But he felt great.

"Angel said she'd be back this weekend."

Adam eyed his friend. He'd already heard that opening line to a conversation several times over the course of the past week.

"I've heard."

"Are you going to scene with her?"

It was stupid to be reluctant to answering, considering everyone would be able to see anyway. But it made him feel strangely vulnerable, not exactly something he enjoyed. "I'm going to ask her if she wants to."

"She'll say yes."

For a moment Adam hesitated, and then he asked the question he hadn't quite dared to ask anyone else. Not even Justin. But here, in the dojo, where they were all alone, he knew Liam wouldn't tease him. Not his style. "Did she talk about me at all?"

"No," Liam replied with a sympathetic smile. His grey eyes glinted. "I can just tell."

ANGEL

"Angel!" Mark's voice was strangely strangled and high-pitched. Kind of panicky. It wasn't the first time her roommate had freaked out over something and expected her to come running to the rescue.

"What?"

"COME HERE!"

Yep, panicked.

Rolling her eyes, Angel started down the stairs, frowning when the soft sound of crying reached her. Picking up her pace she peered around the corner of the stairwell as she came down.

"Leigh!"

It sounded like thunder as she pounded down the rest of the stairs and Leigh turned, her face streaked with tears and pulled away from Mark's arms to throw herself into Angel's. Relief and concern warred on Mark's face as he hesitated, obviously wanting to run away from the crying woman but also unable to ignore the instinct to try and fix whatever was making her cry. Mark was a sweetheart. Angel jerked her head at him, indicating permission to flee. While Leigh knew all of her roommates, she wasn't particularly close to them, and whatever had made her this upset called for girl time.

"Come on sweetheart," she said, pulling her around to the front of the couch in the main room.

Tugging her stumbling friend over to one of the couches, Angel pulled her down and held on tightly. Mark flitted into the room with a box of Kleenex in his hand and Angel mouthed a silent 'thank you' to him before he fled again. Pushing a tissue into Leigh's hand, she wrapped both of her arms back around the shaking woman as she let her cry it out.

Impatient as she was to know what had upset her friend, she was sure it had something to do with Michael. Anger and upset surged through her as she imagined the various scenarios which could have reduced Leigh to this.

"I'm going to kill him," she muttered as she hugged Leigh closer to her.

"No, no it's my fault."

"How can you say that?!" Angel would have thrown her hands up in the air in exasperation if she hadn't been hugging Leigh.

"Because it is. I broke up with him."

And she broke into fresh sobs.

It took another ten minutes of cuddling, crying, and nonsensical soothing words before Leigh started gulping and hiccupping, her shaking shoulders finally slowing from the almost violent shuddering they'd been doing. She forced herself to sit up, although Angel's arm remained around her shoulders, blowing her nose and wiping her eyes until there was a small pile of Kleenex on her lap.

"So what happened?" Angel asked, examining her friend. Leigh was not a pretty crier; her eyes and nose were swollen and pink, even her lips looked kind of swollen, and her cheeks were puffy and patchy red. "I thought last weekend went well."

"It did but... I mean... he didn't propose." Leigh had already told her that, so Angel nodded. "It started bothering me and I kept thinking about what you said, about how I should talk to him about what I want instead of waiting around for him. So I mentioned over dinner that before we went away this weekend I'd thought he might propose." She sniffed and Angel cuddled her closer again. "He got kind of irritated and told me he's not going to propose yet, because he's not ready."

"Again?! That bastard."

"Then he said I was pushing him and marriage isn't on his timeline yet. And I said we've been together long enough that it should be, and it devolved into this awful fight. I was getting pretty upset and then I said maybe we needed to take a break and think about this whole timeline thing... I meant a break from the fight, but as soon as I said it, he asked if we could see other people if we went on a break... I thought I was going to strangle him."

"You should have," Angel muttered. Wouldn't have been much of a loss.

Ignoring her, which was probably the best policy, Leigh went on. "I asked him if he really wanted to see other people and he said yes, and so I said I couldn't stay in a relationship with someone who wasn't completely sure he wanted to be with me when I already knew I wanted to spend the rest of my life with him. It's... not... fair... to me..."

Angel squeezed her friend, a few tears leaking from her own eyes in sympathy to ragged edges of pain in Leigh's voice as she broke down again.

"Oh sweetheart, I'm so proud of you... that's exactly what you should have said because it's so very true." Angel murmured, comforting Leigh as best she could. Sure some of what she was saying was cliché, but in this case it was all true.

Eventually, Leigh pulled herself back together, pushing back up to a sitting position.

"Sorry," she said, looking guiltily at the water spots she'd left behind on Angel's shirt.

"Not a problem." Angel stroked Leigh's hair as her friend wiped her eyes again. "What else are friends for?"

"Hopefully for letting me crash with them until I figure out where I'm going to live?" Leigh said, looking a little guilty.

"Of course, absolutely," Angel said firmly. A thought popped up in her mind. "Ah, you'll have to fight with Mike over who gets to sleep in my bed with me and who gets one of the couches. He gets here on Saturday."

"Mike's visiting?"

"Mike's coming back to live," Angel corrected, and explained his situation. While Leigh and Mike were friendly, they weren't friends the way Angel and Mike were, but it was a nice safe topic which distracted Leigh and allowed her to pull herself together even more.

Angel hoped her roommates would be okay with the extra guest.

Once Leigh had gone out to her car to grab the suitcase she'd packed, Angel went down to the basement to explain the situation to the guys. To their credit, each one of them immediately pledged their support for Leigh and said she could stay there as long as she wanted.

"Is she okay?" Sam asked. "Should we be paying Michael a visit?"

"You've been watching too many mafia movies," she told him.

"SAMPSON!" shouted Q and Mark at the same time, making her laugh as Sam rolled his eyes. He hated his full name.

"You gonna pull out some whoop-ass, Sampson?" Q asked, his eyes on the screen where he and Sam were currently brawling on Smash-Brothers. "Cuz you could use some right now."

"Shut it, asshole," Sam muttered, furiously pushing buttons to go on the attack.

Deciding she could leave the guys to their own devices, Angel went back upstairs to help Leigh get settled in. She'd forgotten she'd pulled out some of the clothes she'd been thinking about wearing to Stronghold and found Leigh examining one of her corsets.

"Did I interrupt something?" Leigh asked, holding it out as Angel entered her bedroom.

"Oh... no. I was thinking about going back to Stronghold tonight."

"I thought you were going to wait until tomorrow."

"I was. I am. It was just a thought. That's okay though, I don't have to go this weekend."

"What? No, of course you're going, don't be silly." The mulish expression on Leigh's face was much preferable to the devastated one she'd been wearing earlier, but Angel still wasn't going to be convinced Leigh was okay enough to be left alone.

"I'm not going to ditch you tomorrow night," Angel said flatly.

"We'll both go. I want to meet this Adam guy anyway," Leigh said. "I want to go out and do something I wouldn't normally do."

Angel opened her mouth and then closed it. Who was she to argue? Maybe Leigh would see something she liked and then she wouldn't get back together with Michael again.

"Fine. But I'm not ditching you to go do a scene while we're there."

Leigh smiled wanly. "Sounds good to me." She took a deep breath, looking anywhere but at her suitcase which was propped next to Angel's closet. "Got anything to eat? I'm starving."

"We can order Chinese, and I've got some Ben and Jerry's while we wait."

"God, I love you."

﹩ I I ﹩

ANGEL

Getting Leigh dressed for Stronghold was fun. She looked incredible in a black lace shirt over a black tank top with a fluttering navy-blue chiffon skirt and very high black heels. Fortunately, she and Angel fit into a lot of same clothing; even though Leigh was much less busty than Angel, they had the same curvy hips. It did mean Leigh didn't fit into any of Angel's corsets, and she'd never allowed Angel to make her any, but the black lace shirt worked well enough. And it meant Leigh was more comfortable, because she was basically completely covered.

Angel grinned, wondering what Leigh would think of Lexie, since the last two times she'd seen the younger woman she'd been wearing similar tops to what Leigh had on now, but without the covering undershirt.

At least the clothing and getting dressed was keeping Leigh firmly distracted. She'd had small bouts of crying throughout the day. Sometimes her eyes filling up with tears over something completely random—like the turkey sandwich she had for lunch—and sometimes because she'd start fretting about what Michael was doing. She didn't say 'and with whom,' but the unspoken sentiment always hovered in the air.

"Are you sure this skirt isn't too short?" Leigh asked, tugging at the hem as she turned to try and see her backside in the mirror. "I feel like my butt's hanging out."

"It's not, it just looks like it's *about* to be," Angel reassured her.

Leigh made a face. "That's not nearly as comforting as you think it is."

"Stop it, you look fantastic." Angel raked her gaze over her friend and gave a sigh of envy. While she loved her curves, sometimes she looked at Leigh's completely flat stomach and wished she was maybe a little bit less curvy. "Maybe I should re-think this whole bringing you thing..."

"Shut it, you look like sex on heels."

"Yeah, thank God for corsets sucking in my stomach for me."

Her friend held up her forefinger and made a face at her. "That's one... you get to three and I'll give you a spanking!"

"Sweet Jesus, what is going on in here?" The deeper masculine voice broke into the room, making both of them jump.

"Dammit," Angel muttered when she realized all three of her housemates were crowded into her doorway. She'd left the door open a crack—a *crack!*—and one of them must have peeked in to see what was going on. She sighed. "We're going to a club."

"Looking like that?" Sam's voice squeaked a little. His style was 'stylish geek' as he liked to call it and he was often taken aback by some of the more outrageous things Angel wore, but he'd never seen her looking like this before. Every time she'd gone to Stronghold she'd put on her coat before going downstairs.

She put one of her hands on her hips and used the other to gesture from her breasts up to her face. "Up here boys."

Wow, a communal blush as all their eyes flicked upwards. Even Q with his darker skin was blushing. "Do we need to have the 'you don't get to tell me how to dress' discussion again?"

"Aren't you the one who always preaches about not putting yourself into a situation where you might be in danger?" Mark said, his eyes flicking over to Leigh. Sometimes Angel thought he might have a crush on her, but she didn't think anything was going to come of it, even if things between Leigh and Michael had finally crashed and burned. "Those outfits look *dangerous.*"

"Nice to know you listened," she said. "But the place where we're going, we will fit right in. In fact, we're a little overdressed." She grinned at the skeptical looks on their faces before turning and grabbing her coat. Leigh did the same.

As she and Leigh headed down the hall towards the stairs, she heard the guys muttering behind her.

"There's a guy."

"There must be a guy."

"Did she say anything to you?"

"No, you?"

"She's been way too quiet lately."

"Maybe we should—"

Angel purposefully blocked them out of her hearing and headed down the stairs.

⚜

ADAM

The club was starting to fill up. Adam had gotten there early because he wanted to make sure he didn't miss Angel. Yesterday he'd come for a while as well but she'd never shown up. Since Thursday was a much quieter night around the club, he'd wanted to cover all his bases. He'd decided Olivia was right, he'd been too hard on Angel. The fact that his mom had called this morning and chatted with him in her usual airy, breezy, but loving way drove home to him how he did sometimes still hold onto his resentment over the sudden way she'd left them. She'd been unhappy and she hadn't spoken up about it, not until the day she'd left.

Angel was the first woman he'd been attracted to in more than a 'let's do a scene' way in a long time. He'd enjoyed talking with her at Chained, add in his attraction and it was no wonder he'd been obsessed with trying to figure her out. It had started with the mystery, but by the time they'd scened together he'd also found something more.

He figured he owed it to himself, and to her, to at least scene with her again and see if the chemistry was still there or if it was a byproduct of mystery, discovery, and anger. That, and despite knowing she'd presented herself as something she wasn't, he still hadn't been able to get her out of his head all week.

Patrick stalked in through the main door, past Will who was standing guard that evening, and immediately came over to where Adam was sitting.

"Bourbon shot," he barked at Lisa. She raised her eyebrow at him, tapped her fingers on the bar, and waited. Patrick growled. "Please."

"Don't piss off the Dommes," Adam said mildly.

"You'd think eventually someone would worry about pissing *me* off," the big man grumbled. He looked as stressed as Adam had ever seen him. For the first time, in a long time, some stubble had dared make an appearance on his normally bald head. Patrick ran his hands over it, his head bowing for a moment before Lisa returned with the shot of bourbon.

Deciding the best policy was to remain silent, because pointing out the obvious—that ninety-nine percent of the people in the club were never going to risk pissing Patrick off—wasn't going to help right now.

"What does she see in that little twit anyway?" Patrick was staring at the small glass in front of him rather than drinking it. "If Jake knew I was letting her run around with a little bastard like him, he'd come back home and kick my ass."

"I think he'd realize you can't control every aspect of Lexie's life," Adam said dryly. He studied Patrick's bleak expression. "Unless, of course, you made her your slave." Out of their group of friends Patrick was the only one who wanted anything close to resembling a full-time Master/slave relationship.

Instead of responding, Patrick picked up the shot of bourbon and studied it for a moment before lifting it to his lips and throwing his head back.

Nonchalantly, Adam let his gaze drift over to the lounge area, which was slowly filling up with the subs who wanted to play and didn't have a current partner. "You could always work out some of your tension. Plenty of subs available tonight."

"Is that what you're planning on doing?" Patrick asked, deflecting the issue back rather than acknowledging he hadn't done a scene in the club since Lexie had started working there.

"I'm waiting for a particular sub."

"Oh really?" A little half-smile lifted Patrick's face. "Does this mean you're not going to be doing Introduction Scenes anymore?"

"Don't get ahead of yourself."

The only reason Liam, Justin, and Chris were no longer doing Introduction Scenes was because they were in committed relationships. He wasn't anywhere near that with Angel. Wasn't even sure it was what he wanted with her or whether she'd have anything to do with him after last week, and he wasn't going to shirk his responsibilities to the club unless it was for something serious. Especially since that would leave Patrick shorthanded, although he knew the owner was already looking at some Doms to take over some of the duties.

"Well, next week there isn't one because of the damn party Lexie talked me into throwing, and then Andrew said he'd cover your next session since you covered his, so after he and Olivia take their turns again it'll be about a month from now before you have one again."

"Right."

They sat in silence for a few minutes, watching the subtle dance between patrons of the club. Ellie was in the Lounge again, Tom was watching her from the bar before he went over and propositioned Vicki for a scene. Although he glanced at Ellie to see her reaction, she wasn't even paying attention. His gaze hardened, then he looked away and smiled at Vicki.

One of the older couples in the club, Walter and Marianne came in. They were both in their sixties and had been married for over thirty years. While they weren't the only retirees who belonged to the club, and they weren't even the oldest, they were the longest running couple. They occasionally made use of one of the private rooms, which they kept private by drawing the shades over the windows, but mostly seemed to enjoy being around people who indulged in the same kink they did. Marianne saw Patrick and Adam and smiled and waved. Seeing his Mistress' attention, Walter peeked upwards and smiled at them as well before ducking his head back down as Marianne tugged on his leash. The stately gentleman—because that's what he was—trotted meekly along behind her.

That was what Adam and his friends aspired to. The relationship, not meekly trotting behind some woman. Although he'd noticed all three of his friends who were now in relationships had gotten... not softer exactly, but more indulgent of their submissives than they had been in any of their shorter relationships. He supposed it was a symptom of being in a relationship with a possible future.

Not all of them wanted a relationship yet, but the group dynamics were shifting. Rick was actively looking, Jared was still trying to make things work with Marissa and even Olivia seemed a little wistful when she looked at the couples lately. Of course, Patrick was resisting, but Adam was pretty sure that was because the woman he was most attracted to was off-limits.

The only real holdout was Andrew, and Adam sometimes thought Andrew would be a holdout until the end of time. The crash and burn of his first and last relationship had left layers of emotional scars on the man. Somehow, he'd managed to keep his sense of humor, but there was a darkness to him which had never lifted. During scenes he could be almost cruel, and while that left some of the submissives panting after him, none had ever managed to break through the wall he'd put up around himself.

Patrick nudged his elbow into Adam's side and he looked up to see a large group of their friends walking past Will at the door, accompanied by Angel and another woman he didn't recognize. She was drop dead gorgeous, with long flowing brown hair swinging freely down her back, slim, leggy, and big eyes that dominated her face. Yet he barely took a moment to appreciate her beauty and how intriguing she looked in her (comparatively) modest outfit before his eyes locked onto Angel.

She was wearing another one of those corsets which offered up her breasts, although the shirt she wore underneath it this time was much lower cut, showing a hint of cleavage. The corset was a deep violet, as was the shirt, worn with a black skirt and black high heels. The look of sultry innocence was completely absent from her attire, replaced with an inviting sensuality that had his blood thrumming through his veins.

They were surrounded by Jessica, Justin, Chris, Olivia, and Rick, apparently all having arrived at the same time. When Justin and Olivia headed in their direction, Angel finally looked his way and their eyes caught... and held.

❦

ANGEL

What good was being in the middle of a herd when the wolf singled you out?

Master Adam's eyes were practically drilling into hers and she yanked her gaze away, looking down and then peeking back at him. His hard gaze hadn't wavered one iota. Was he still mad that she'd lied about being a Domme? He didn't look particularly happy to see her. Again. But he didn't *look* pissed this time either.

And it apparently didn't matter to her body that he didn't look particularly pleased, her heart had started beating in triple time the moment she spotted him.

It seemed to take forever to get across the room to where he was sitting with Master Patrick. Being in the center of such a group was kind of fascinating because she noticed Justin and Olivia immediately took point, leading them in the direction they wanted to go, whereas Chris and Rick sort of hung behind, as if they were going to rope in any stragglers. It did kind of feel like being in the middle of a herd.

When they got there Angel introduced Leigh to Master Patrick and Master Adam as everyone ordered their drinks, by which time Liam and Hilary had joined them as well and were chatting with Jessica and her boys. Mr. Serious But Not Yet Grouchy listened and watched Angel as Master Patrick welcomed Leigh to the club and ensured she'd read and signed the appropriate forms with Lexie when she'd come in. Master Adam looked over Leigh appreciatively for a few moments, but then his gaze returned to Angel.

She wasn't sure if she felt relieved about that or not. If he'd switched his interest from her to Leigh, it wouldn't be the first time a guy had done so. But it would have hurt a lot more than she liked to admit. Still, his unwavering focus on her was more than a little unnerving.

"What do you think?" Hilary asked Leigh, coming up beside them, her pretty brown eyes sparkling. "Do you want to see the private rooms?" Liam had one hand on the small of her back although he had to stretch to do it, since he was currently talking with Justin and Olivia. Chris and Jessica had moved to the bar, having a whispered conversation with Andrew as Rick looked on without contributing. Angel thought Liam's desire for continuous contact with his girlfriend was incredibly sweet. In fact, it made her a little wistful.

Even though she was pretty sure a Dom would claim it was only about control, it was obvious he didn't like Hilary being too far away from him.

"Um... I'm not sure..." Leigh confessed, her eyes drifting up to some of the black and white photos behind the bar. The one directly in front of where they were sitting was of a woman kneeling facing the camera, her hands were behind her back and a man standing beside her. The woman was completely naked, the man could only be seen from the waist down but he was obviously fully clothed since he was wearing a suit and the jacket could be seen in the photograph. His hand was cupped under her chin and she was looking up at him with such an expression of trust and desire it was breathtaking. "I'm mostly here because I didn't want to keep Angel at home while I'm staying with her."

"Oh, are you from out of town?"

"No," Leigh grimaced, obviously not sure how much of her personal drama to throw down in the middle of this group.

"Us girls have to band together in times of men being assholes," Angel said solemnly, throwing a supportive arm around Leigh's waist. Her friend gave her a relieved smile. Hilary nodded knowingly as Patrick and Adam gave each other a look.

"Cheers to that," Hilary said, holding out her glass. Angel and Leigh grinned and clinked theirs with hers. Out of the corner of her eye, she saw Master Adam roll his eyes.

He was starting to look grouchier but she didn't know why. After all, it wasn't like she'd done anything.

❧

ADAM

Trying to rein in his patience as Angel and Hilary started informing Leigh about the various rooms in the club, as well as pointing out some of the areas and more interesting aspects to the decor in the main room, Adam kept quiet while he debated with himself. Angel bringing her friend tonight had thrown a kink in his plans. After all, he didn't think Angel would ditch her friend to go participate in a scene.

Especially not since her friend was apparently having relationship trouble. That kind of thing broke girl-code. He wasn't an expert on girl-code, but some things were universally understood.

Which left him in a bit of a quandary. Angel was unlikely to want to be separated from her friend while they were supporting each other, but he desperately wanted to have at least a few private moments with her. He'd wanted to apologize for the way her Introduction Scene ended. And if he couldn't scene with her tonight, he could at least plant the idea of doing a future scene together in her mind.

Jessica and Olivia drifted over to join in the girl talk, making it even harder for him to interject and ask for a moment with Angel alone. Who could break through all the giggling?

Out of the corner of his eye he saw Chris and Andrew watching him with amusement, as if they could sense his frustration and were enjoying it. They probably were, the assholes. Justin and Patrick were both watching over the entire group with a benign eye, although Patrick's attention wasn't entirely focused on the group, but more on the club in general. And his gaze wandered to the door to the lobby every time it opened, as if he could see into there too. Olivia had positioned herself next to Leigh, although she was obviously keeping an eye on Angel as well.

Mother-henning, as usual. Now that Jessica and Hilary were safely taken care of, in the sense they were Justin, Chris, and Liam's to deal with, she was obviously turning her attention elsewhere.

And Liam, as usual, was behind Hilary, with his hand stretched out to keep contact with her. Rick stood beside him, his eyes flicking back and forth between Angel and Leigh. Adam had to keep himself from shifting closer to Angel. He had absolutely no reason or right to feel possessive over her. Even if he had told Rick he was interested to keep his friend from propositioning her.

"You dominate men?" Leigh seemed fascinated by Olivia, which made Adam smirk. She was obviously, to him, submissive. Even more so than Angel, because she automatically positioned herself to follow Angel's lead.

Unless of course Angel wasn't really submissive, in which case Leigh's deferral to her would make a lot of sense.

Stop that.

His instincts said Angel was and he needed to stop over thinking it. Just because she'd misled him the first time they'd met, that didn't mean she would again. At the time, she felt like she'd had reason to.

Which wasn't entirely reassuring, but he pushed back his own issues.

"Usually men, sometimes women," Olivia said with a smile, giving Leigh a little wink. She blushed prettily, although it didn't seem to make her uncomfortable. "I do tend to prefer men though. Especially the ones that are more... challenging." Her smile was almost predatory and it made all of the men shift uncomfortably. None of them had a problem with a woman dominating a man, as long as the man enjoyed it, but by the same token, none of them could be completely comfortable with Olivia when she had that look in her eye. It was the same one she got right before she trussed a submissive up and tortured his cock and balls.

Adam didn't care if it made the sub hard, he couldn't watch without cringing. Or think about it without cringing. None of them could.

"But aren't they stronger than you?" Leigh's hand clapped to her mouth as she realized in some ways, what she had said could be construed as an insult. "Oh, I'm sorry... that's not the point is it?"

"No, it's not," Olivia said, giving her a reassuring smile. For all her fierceness when dealing with experienced submissives, especially naughty or bratty ones, Olivia could be incredibly gentle and patient with the newbs. "They submit because they want to. But yes, there are some who enjoy the sensation of being forced to submit. It's not something I've ever had a problem with." She said it without conceit, although Adam had seen some of the subs she'd had to physically enforce her orders with.

They wanted it of course, although it was harder for a large, muscular male to play the brat and then be physically pushed into position. There were a very, very few who wanted to challenge and then be slapped down by a woman and those were the subs Olivia honestly preferred.

She didn't come to Liam's dojo often, because her workouts consisted of kickboxing and Krav Maga, although he'd also seen her take down more than one sub with one of the nerve holds Liam had taught them.

"You're not worried about..." Angel's voice trailed off as she looked worriedly at her friend. "I mean, you don't need to come to one of my classes for a refresher course do you?"

"Oh, no, of course not!" Leigh looked shocked at the very idea and Angel relaxed and smiled at her.

"Okay, good, just checking."

"What kind of class?" Jessica wanted to know.

Angel's cheeks darkened a bit in a blush. "Um, I teach women's self-defense classes."

Both she and Leigh looked a little uncomfortable and Adam suddenly realized Angel must have worried Leigh's "guy troubles" had become physical. He could have told her not to worry. From his reading of Leigh's interest in Olivia, he would say it was a fascination a new submissive had with someone who was obviously dominate and yet approachable. A lot of new subs went to Olivia with their questions, finding her less intimidating than the other Dommes and Doms roaming the club.

"That's so cool! Where do you teach them?" Hilary asked.

Immediately she was yanked backwards and into Liam's arms. Angel and Leigh looked surprised and almost a little alarmed before they realized everyone else was either chuckling or observing the couple with amusement.

"You don't need self-defense classes, honey-girl," Liam said, frowning down at his girlfriend. "And if you do, you can come to the dojo."

"Women's self-defense is different from martial arts," Angel said, interrupting whatever response Hilary was about to give. She gave Liam a hard look, not at all submissive. "It's about learning how to avoid situations where you'll be at risk and about getting away once you're in them. It's not the same as fighting, because the goal isn't to win, it's to escape. *Every* woman should take self-defense at some point in her life, because you never know when you might need it and it's not like you can be right next to Hilary every second of every day. And a woman needs to know she can make herself safe."

She said it so fiercely, Adam realized her forceful demeanor came from passion about the subject. Something angry and protective rose up in his chest as he wondered if there was a reason from her past she was so fervent. He completely understood Liam's reaction. A Dom considered it his duty to care for his sub, and that included protecting her.

But Angel's argument was also indisputable.

In fact, Angel's little speech had roused both Chris and Justin's protective instincts as well. Both were frowning and had shifted closer to Jessica, their too-alert stances indicating they were suddenly searching for any threats they might need to eradicate for her. Patrick was suddenly eyeing the door to the lobby as if questioning the wisdom of leaving Lexie out there without his personal protection, never mind the bouncer who was always guarding the door.

The feisty brunette looked around at the emotional havoc she'd created among the Doms and laughed. "Wow... sorry guys, I didn't mean to put everyone on alert."

Realizing his hand had tensed around the drink he was holding, Adam relaxed his grip. If someone had hurt Angel it was in the past and there wasn't anything he could do about it. As for the urge to make sure she was never hurt again... well that wasn't his job. Although he was starting to consider making it his.

Hilary tapped Liam's forearm and twisted her head around to look up at him. "If I want to take self-defense classes, you aren't going to stop me."

"I know." He kissed her forehead gently. "I don't like the idea you might need them."

"Well neither do I," she teased, rolling her eyes. They both laughed and the tension around the group started to break. Adam looked back at Angel and saw she was looking at the couple wistfully.

Off to the side Chris and Justin had both closed in around Jessica, who was smiling up at them reassuringly. She looked over at Angel. "I'd love to take some too, you'll have to let me know where and when you have a class."

"Right now I'm mid-session for all of them, but I can let you know the next time one starts. I'm always looking for new places to hold them, it's not the steadiest work except for the college courses I teach."

Liam shifted and Hilary looked up at him with a demanding look. Covering his smile with his hand, Adam didn't give away that he'd seen the little blonde pinch her Dom. "You could hold one at my dojo," he said. "Advertise to the subs here, I bet a lot of them would be interested."

"Hell, we could have one here," Patrick said, gesturing at the stage. "Usually I rent the club out Sunday through Wednesday for other groups, but I can co-op one of those nights for classes. Especially since it's something which would help the subs."

Looking absolutely thrilled, Angel was practically bouncing on her feet. "That would be amazing! I'll have to think about ways to tweak the curriculum to apply it directly for people who are involved in the scene. Although it's usually best to do something like this twice a week, once a week doesn't give people the time they need, although outside practice is encouraged as well."

"Mondays and Wednesdays then. It can't hurt to have extra emphasis on how to be safe in the scene," Patrick said agreeably. "We try to have a class about that at least once a month, for both the Doms and the subs. Now, does it have to be only women's self-defense? We have a lot of male subs here who I think would also benefit from having some kind of self-defense class."

Angel hesitated, her tongue flicking out over her lower lip before her teeth dragged across it. Knowing what they were talking about was serious, Adam tried not to find the gesture erotic. "It does change the dynamic to have any men there at all... especially when it comes to discussions. Maybe I could do two sessions? One all women, for those who feel more comfortable in that setting, and one mixed? They'd run for about an hour each, so two hours total each night."

And in the meantime, she'd have secured two full sessions of classes for herself rather than one. Adam had to admire her business sense along with her logic. Patrick nodded, apparently willing to concede the point—and an extra night.

"So, no men at the one session at all?" asked Justin, looking a little displeased. Having already been the object of censure, Liam looked relieved he hadn't been the one to have to ask the question.

"None," Angel said emphatically. "There are some things women can't talk about when men are around." Then she smiled and batted her eyes at Justin. "But we could certainly use some male assistance for the practical exams."

The big man looked at her suspiciously but there was no way he and the other Doms weren't going to butt in wherever they could. "You'll have it."

"Great!" She bounced on her feet a little bit, looking adorable. Adam wondered if he could convince her to go apart with him for a few minutes now that she was in such a good mood. Leigh and Hilary were talking quietly about the classes already and surely Angel wouldn't feel like she was completely abandoning the other woman if she went to have a private conversation with him for a few minutes.

But then Olivia asked if Dommes could come and Angel immediately said yes, which led to Justin looking disgruntled again about not being able to be included, which started a debate about whether or not the Dommes would inhibit the submissives even if they were fellow women. Adam wasn't sure why Olivia wanted to go, unless it was to play mother hen some more, since she could already kick ass when she wanted to, but that was her prerogative.

Justin eventually pulled Jessica away, he'd been so focused on Angel he hadn't even noticed when Chris had disappeared to go set up a room. Rick was gone too, apparently having picked a sub out of the lounge.

For once Liam didn't seem inclined to drag Hilary off to a room, probably because she was having too good of a time making new friends. Adam knew some of the friendships she and Jessica had had become strained after Jessica started living with two men at the same time, since Hilary was very vocal about her support for the unconventional relationship.

Adam realized his friends were already integrating Angel into their group as if she belonged. Or was she naturally working her way in there? It was hard to tell, because she was naturally friendly. But he knew his friends wouldn't have taken as much interest in her if it wasn't for his own interest, despite what their girlfriends did.

He needed to get her alone to talk for a bit. Apologize. Ask if he could see her again. Scene with her again. Get to know her better.

Just as he was shifting to move closer to her, to ask her to step aside more privately with him, she looked up towards the lobby door as it swung open. Her expression brightened, like the sun had risen in her eyes as the biggest smile he'd ever seen lit up her face. And it wasn't at him. Jealousy sliced through him as he turned to see who could possibly have put that expression on her face.

"Pretty boy!" she squealed, at a high enough pitch that everyone next to her winced, before she was pelting head-long across the club.

Adam stared. Olivia stared. Chris rubbed his ears, cringing dramatically. Leigh laughed.

"*That's* 'pretty boy?'" Adam asked in a strangled voice.

While he had longish straight brown hair, the ends of which brushed the sides of his square chin, there was nothing at all feminine about the man. He was tall, over six feet and possibly approaching Jared's height although without the bulk of the other man; lanky but muscular, in the way constant swimmers had long, lean muscles. Which was very evident when Angel literally launched herself at him from about two feet away and threw herself into his waiting arms. She wrapped her legs and arms around him, hugging him with her entire body. Dressed in black leather pants and a button down black shirt and with an aura of authority in his every movement, he was obviously a Dom.

Jealous fury rose, only to be smashed down by more anger. Was this another way in which she'd lied? Did she already have a boyfriend? A Dom? He and Olivia had assumed 'pretty boy' was her submissive when they thought she was a Domme. While he couldn't imagine a Dom willingly going by such a sobriquet, maybe Angel was a brat who said it to get herself in trouble.

"Well he is very pretty," Olivia murmured admiringly under her breath. Adam shot a glare at her. His temper was already dangerously roiling, he didn't need Olivia to feed the flames.

Cool fingers touched his hand, surprising him, and he whipped his head around to look down at Angel's friend. For the first time he noticed Leigh had mismatched eyes; not immediately obvious when you first looked at her because one was hazel brown and the other was hazel green, blending enough that only someone standing very close to her could see they tended towards different hues.

"It's not what you think," she said in a soft voice, barely audible over the music.

"What do you mean?"

She gave him a little smile and glanced down at his hands. Dammit. He unclenched his fists for the umpteenth time that night.

"It's not what you think," she repeated, and nodded towards Angel and Pretty Boy. Pretty Boy had set her down, although his hands were still on her waist and her head was tilted up towards him as if asking for a kiss, her hands gesticulating wildly between them as she chattered up at him. "They've never been an item. They never will be."

Adam raised his eyebrow at her naiveté.

"I'm not saying they never wanted to be an item in the past," she said. "But Angel had a boyfriend when she first met Mike. He ended up dating another friend of ours." Leigh's lips pursed. "Monica was our other best friend, until she decided she didn't like Mike being so close to Angel, even though there was no tension between them once he started dating Monica."

"What do you mean?"

"It goes away. I don't know how or why, but it does. The second Mike started dating Monica, it was like Angel lost interest in him that way while they were together. The next time she got a boyfriend it was the same thing. They're only like this when they're both single, but it's never going to happen because of Monica." She scowled at the skeptical look on Adam's face. "Look, I don't know if you can understand this, because I've heard it's different for guys, but Monica, Angel, and I were like sisters. Once a guy's been inside your sister, you don't want him inside you."

He had no idea what the look on his face was, but it must have been hilarious because Olivia took one look at him and burst out laughing.

"How long ago was that?" he managed to ask, rather than continuing to gape like a total idiot. Besides, if Angel did happen to glance over here, he wanted her to see him involved in conversation. Not staring jealously.

"Years ago," Leigh said and shrugged. "But she and Mike sleep in the same bed all the time while he's visiting and nothing ever happens."

"And how do you know that for sure?" he asked, trying not to growl. Did that mean Mike was going to be sleeping in Angel's bed for this visit? No, wait, Leigh was staying with her... dammit, the woman was getting him all turned around again! Just when he thought he had a grip on his emotions, when he thought he had a plan on how to go forward, the woman shot them all to hell without even trying. The abrupt loss of control, again, made him feel panicky. No one had made him feel like this in years, maybe not ever. Not since his mother left. He was a wreck, and she hadn't even meant to do it.

"You have it bad, don't you?" Leigh asked, leaning in a bit and studying his face as if looking for confirmation. "Good, because I think she likes you a lot too."

Now what the hell was he supposed to do with that?

ANGEL

"Come on, pretty boy, I want to introduce you to everyone," Angel said, grabbing Mike's hand. She had been so relieved to see him walking in the door. Any extra support seemed beneficial at the moment.

No matter what the topic of conversation had been or who was talking, she hadn't been able to shake the feeling Master Adam's full attention was on her. And he was slowly turning into Mr. Grouchy. It unnerved her as much as it excited her, but she didn't think it should excite her. Chances were, he was mad she'd invaded his friend group, but she couldn't help it—they were so friendly! And they seemed to think there was something going on between her and Adam, but while she might like the idea, she thought it was wishful thinking when it came to him.

Unless he always looked pissy when he was interested in someone?

Somehow, she doubted it. At any rate, she'd been overjoyed to see Mike walking in the club, a day earlier than he said he'd arrive, as a distraction for her nerves. Especially because if Master Adam did ask her to do a scene she knew she would want to say yes but she couldn't ditch Leigh. With Mike here, maybe Leigh wouldn't mind as much...

"Angel, you can't drag me around here," Mike said, refusing to be tugged along. Angel stopped pulling and looked up at him, confused. He laughed and ruffled her hair, ignoring her scowl as she pulled away, her hands automatically going to make sure he hadn't messed it up. "We're in a club, pest, one which I plan on coming to on a regular basis now that I'm back in the area. Which means I can't have you undermining me in front of everyone."

"Oh..." Well that made sense. After all, submissives weren't 'sup- posed' to act the way she often did with him. She knew it amused Mike, which was the only reason he put up with it. That, and she wasn't *his* submissive. She looked up at him, arranging her face into a solemn expression of reverence. "Would you like to come meet my new friends, Sir?"

"Brat," he said, chuckling, as he began to walk beside her towards the group. "If you were mine, I'd beat you."

Laughing, she turned and had to force herself to keep the smile on her face when she saw Master Adam and Leigh leaning close in to each other, engaged in what was obviously a private conversation. If she'd fooled herself into thinking she was okay with Master Adam not being interested in her, the lurch in her stomach told her otherwise. Still, she'd done the whole "guy I'm interested in ends up dating one of my friends" and she'd eventually ended up losing a friend over it. She couldn't lose Leigh... she'd go insane. Leigh was her rock and she was Leigh's.

"Is that Leigh? That's not Michael next to her."

"No, that's Master Adam. And yes, that's Leigh. She and Michael are having some issues." Angel looked up at him. "She's staying with me too right now."

Mike sighed and put the back of his hand to his head in fake distress. "I guess this means I won't be sleeping on a bed tonight."

Stifling her giggle, Angel bumped him with her hip and nearly knocked him off balance. "Oops, sorry. Forgot."

"I should spank you," he muttered, loud enough Olivia obviously overheard him as she turned to greet them. "Often."

"Mistress Olivia, this is Master Mike," Angel said loudly, ignoring his threat.

"Michael, please," he said, looking pained. Angel made a face; she knew he preferred to be called Michael by other people but she never called him that. Too confusing with Leigh's Michael.

"And this is Master Patrick, Master Liam, and his girlfriend Hilary, and Master Adam."

Introductions all around, everyone but Mr. Grouchy smiled at Michael. Seeming to ignore the dark look he was getting from the big blond, Mike turned and gave Leigh a big hug. "Hey beautiful. You're looking better than ever. Never thought I'd see you in one of these places."

"I didn't know we had any new Doms coming in," Adam said. His expression was closed and hard to read, but he didn't seem very welcoming.

"Michael came with a recommendation from Brent," Patrick said easily. He grinned at Michael, who was looking at Adam with something almost like amusement. "He's a Master Sadist and has been in the scene for years now. And you know I've been looking for more single Doms to help with ah... club responsibilities."

If anything, Adam scowled even more, as though there were hidden undercurrents to Patrick's bland statement that she wasn't understanding. What was wrong with looking for more people to help out around the club if Patrick needed help? Angel was feeling increasingly out of her element.

"When I showed up at Angel's tonight, her housemates told me she'd gone out to a club. I figured they meant here and followed along," Mike said, sliding his arm around her shoulders. She looked up at him, slightly confused. While they'd always been physically affectionate, because that's the way she was, it almost seemed like the gesture was something other than casual for him. And he wasn't looking at her, he was looking at Adam. She looked at Master Adam too, but he wasn't looking at either of them. He was looking at the lounge area.

Thinking about getting a sub to play with?

Her stomach clenched. If he did, she was so leaving. While he might not be interested in her, she was way too attracted to him and way too emotionally tender after her Introduction Scene last week. She didn't feel like being in the same building if he was playing with someone else. Give her a couple more weeks to get over her crush and she'd be fine. In fact, knowing he was playing with others would help with that, but tonight she'd leave rather than be in the same building where it was happening.

Deliberately she looked up at Mike, trying to ignore the big, blonde grouchy man who was taking up far too much of her focus.

"Are you going to play tonight?"

"No, pest, I only came here to catch up with you and get my bearings. That and I know what happens when I'm unchaperoned with your housemates," he teased. Angel laughed, although she couldn't blame him for not wanting to get sucked into video game land again. It was so hard to get back out again! Especially when the opponents were as engaging and skilled as her housemates. "You can go play if you want to."

Angel hesitated for a moment and then shook her head. The only man she was currently interested in playing with was still eyeing the Lounge area and she didn't feel like joining the women over there. If she were to go to the lounge and he ended up picking out a different sub to play with, it would be obvious the reason she was leaving was because of Adam. "No. I'm not going to ditch Leigh."

Smiling, she reached out to grasp her best friend's hand. Her best friend rolled her eyes. "I told you I'm fine. Especially if Mike's going to hang out for a bit."

"Maybe tomorrow. If we come back."

"In that case, I'm going to get a real drink," Mike said, sliding his arm off of Angel's shoulders and turning towards the bar.

The rest of the night went surprisingly well. Andrew and Mike hit it off right away, talking about their preferences for various whips with Patrick's occasional interjections, making Angel shiver a little. She and Leigh sat on two bar stools next to each other, chatting with Olivia and Mr. Grouchy. He didn't say much, but he didn't leave to go play with anyone either. And he ended up being not so grouchy. He and Olivia were a little bit like brother and sister, constantly poking at and teasing each other. Eventually those who had gone off to do scenes came back, at which point Olivia headed over to the Lounge area to pick out a sub.

By the end of the evening, she and Leigh were no longer sitting together. Instead, Leigh was chatting with Rick, Hilary, and Liam, while Angel was seated between Adam and Justin, arguing with them and Chris about whether the old Batman movies were better than the new ones. She and Chris both liked the newer ones better, but Adam and Justin were holdouts for the originals—although even Chris turned on her when she said her favorite old one was the Adam West version.

"Come on! Bruce Wayne and Catwoman, tied up with their hands behind their backs, having a super sexy moment where he promises he'll protect her? That was hot!"

"You have issues," Chris said, shaking his head. "And you can't claim that as your initial interest in BDSM, because he was tied up too."

"Just because I'm submissive doesn't mean I can't appreciate a hot man all tied up. I like to look, I'm not saying I'd know what to *do* with him. And yes, I do think that's where my interest in bondage started. Or at least, when I realized what might get me all hot and bothered."

"With Adam West?" Master Adam groaned. "It kills me that he and I share a name."

"Oh, come on, you had to like the show when you were growing up."

"When I was growing up? Yes. Now? Maybe if I'm really drunk."

Angel giggled at the face he made. He'd already had a couple of drinks at this point and it had loosened him up. "Seriously though, the movie was brilliant! Shark repellant? The penguin submarine?"

"Don't forget the sky riddles," Justin said. They all looked at him in surprise and he shrugged. "What? The Riddler was always my favorite."

When it was finally time to leave, Angel was a little disappointed. She'd been having fun. Especially once Mr. Grouchy stopped being so grouchy and had started talking to her. She'd enjoyed their conversation. While he wasn't as lighthearted as Chris, that made it even more of a triumph when she managed to make him laugh. And he seemed like he needed more laughter in his life, he was way too serious.

All in all, even though she didn't get a chance to do any of the things she'd initially set out to do that evening... she couldn't help but feel like it had been a success.

Tomorrow, though? She was going to go to the Lounge area and offer herself up as an available sub. While she liked the new friends she was making, she was going to Stronghold to explore her sexuality not to make new friends.

And if she was really lucky, maybe Mr. Grouchy would continue to be her tour guide.

12

ADAM

So Angel had a very close guy friend she had been sexually attracted to in the past. Who was staying with her for the next two weeks.

What it came down to was trust.

As did so many other things. How much could he trust Angel? He couldn't know without getting to know her better. He'd started that last night, although he'd never gotten around to asking her if she'd want to do another scene with him at some point. Or apologizing. After "Pretty Boy" had shown up, he hadn't been entirely sure he wanted to jump right into doing that.

But he'd liked talking to her. It had also helped that Michael had spent more time getting to know the others in the group than he had catching up with Angel. Adam hated to think the other Dom had picked up on the wave of jealousy that had engulfed him when he'd seen how easily Michael and Angel were physically affectionate with each other, but he was pretty sure the other man had caught his glare and that's why he'd finally moved away from her.

Someone who was interested in Angel wouldn't do that, would he?

Angel hadn't seemed upset Michael wasn't spending any time with her. Then again, he was staying with her, so would she be?

The discordant sounds of his guitar strings as his fingers hit the wrong chord for the umpteenth time made him grit his teeth. He couldn't get it together today, couldn't find peace of mind even in music and he knew exactly why. The woman had him all out of sorts, because for the first time in years he didn't know exactly what to do about a situation.

Every time he made a decision, something would happen and he would be forced to reevaluate.

His pocket began to vibrate and Nat King Cole started to sing to him. Although he didn't feel like talking, at least he knew his mother would distract him from his current chaotic thoughts. Hell, she'd probably give him some new chaotic ones.

"Hey mom."

"Hi honey! You picked up! How are you?" The surprise and pleasure in her voice that he hadn't let the call go to voicemail made him feel a little ashamed. While they talked on the phone on a pretty regular basis, it was always when he called her. He rarely picked up when she called. Having been so recently confronted with his issues, he wondered if it was a control thing with him or an emotional lashing out about keeping his relationship with her completely on his terms.

"I'm good. How are you?" With anyone else he would have asked why they were calling, but he knew it would hurt his mom's feelings. Especially with her all the way across the ocean, he tried to follow the social niceties which made her feel like he wasn't giving her the brush off. She'd gotten enough of that from his dad while they were still married. Not that she'd complained, which was the other part of the problem, but it didn't mean she didn't feel it.

"I'm wonderful, Samuel and I just got home from the river cruise we went on, which was marvelous. We'd been a little worried because we heard sometimes all you can see from the boat is the trash in the river, but there wasn't anything like that on our cruise..." And she was off and running, not requiring anything more from him than a few non-committal responses. He could hear the joy in her voice as she described the various activities and excursions she and Samuel had indulged in on their cruise.

When he'd first met Samuel, he'd resented the Englishman had taken his mother away to another country, especially as it made the choice of which parent to spend the holidays with even more stressful. Then he'd realized what a blessing it was, not only because his mother was more understanding when he didn't spend every holiday with her now, but because of how happy Samuel made her.

"That's great, Mom," he said when she finally finished her recap. "I'm glad you had such a good trip."

"We're thinking about coming out your way soon," she said brightly. "Can you believe Samuel's never seen the cherry blossoms in DC? Or been to the Natural History Museum?"

"Do you need a place to stay?" he asked, trying to keep the cringe out of his voice. The last time his mother and step-father had come to town it had only been for a weekend, but they'd flitted around his house like two honeymooners. Some things, a child did not want to know about his parents. Even if he was an adult.

"Oh, I don't think so this time," she said breezily. "We wouldn't want to impose on you for an entire week, especially when you'll be having to work. But I want to spend some time with you."

"And I want to spend some time with you. I can take off a day or two for sight-seeing." The relief of knowing they'd find somewhere else to stay made it easy for him to make the offer.

"That'd be wonderful!" his mother gushed. "And uh... you should feel free to bring someone along, if you *have* a someone to bring along."

"Subtle, Mom."

She made an exasperated sound. "Well I was trying to be."

Laughing, Adam shook his head, even though she couldn't see him. For some reason his mom had always had trouble coming right out and saying what she felt or wanted or asking what she wanted to know. It was the reason she and his Dad had ultimately not worked out. But at times like this, it was almost cute.

"There's... there's no one at the moment."

"Well you can always change your mind," she said, a hint of curiosity in her voice. Likely she was wondering about the sudden hesitation, although she wouldn't ask. Which was good because he wasn't sure how he would have answered.

He was suddenly wondering whether or not Angel and his mom would get along. It wasn't such an incongruous thought since he'd been thinking about Angel before his mom had called, and they were the only two women he'd ever met who were capable of throwing him for a loop on a regular basis.

ANGEL

Going by the way Mike was adapting to the club, Angel was pretty sure her friend wasn't going to be content with hanging out at the bar in the main room for long. She'd seen him looking over at the available subs more than once, although at the moment he seemed involved in his conversation with Adam, Andrew and, Patrick. Tonight he'd said he'd come along so she could play if she wanted to, without ditching Leigh, but she was still working up the courage to go over to the Lounge.

To be honest, she was waiting to see if Master Adam showed any indication of wanting to talk to her before she went over there.

She, Leigh, and Mike had arrived pretty early tonight and set themselves up at one of the bar tables; she'd wanted to give Leigh plenty of time to get settled in before she went over to the lounge. Her friend swore up and down she was okay with Angel doing a scene and leaving her for a bit as long as Mike was willing to hang out and watch over her. And Mike swore up and down he was fine with that as well.

Unfortunately, her number one choice for Dom and the man she was most attracted to seemed more interested in talking to Mike than in talking to her.

"Didn't you say you were going to play tonight?"

"I am," Angel said, refocusing a little guiltily on Leigh. "I'm... you know. Still deciding if it's what I want."

Leigh gave her a look. "And it doesn't have anything to do with the fact you keep looking at Adam every couple of minutes?"

"Mmmmm."

"Uh huh. You could ask *him* you know."

"I'm not totally up on BDSM etiquette, but no, I'm pretty sure the sub isn't supposed to approach the Dom."

"Go over to the Lounge and wait for him to come to you."

"In a minute."

"Oh my God." Leigh looked almost awed.

"What?"

"You're scared."

"Am not."

"Are too. You're scared you'll ruin your chances with him if you go over to the Lounge. You're scared he won't follow you over there."

"You get the weirdest ideas when you've been drinking."

"One, I've had one drink. And don't try to change the subject. I bet he'll follow if you go over there."

Angel rolled her eyes. "And on what evidence do you base that?"

"The fact that when you're not looking at him, he keeps looking over at you."

She glanced over at him, unable to help it. As usual, he wasn't looking at her. "Liar."

"Only one way to find out if I'm right."

"Who made you an expert on men?"

Leigh's face fell and Angel immediately felt like complete and utter shit. Like she didn't already know Leigh was having a hard enough time with the whole separation from Michael thing. Not only had she taken yesterday off work, and spent most of it trying to distract herself from crying, she'd barely been better off today. "I'm sorry, I didn't mean it like that. I was joking and it was stupid and insensitive and I'm sorry."

Reaching out, Leigh placed her hand over Angel's. "It's okay, I know you didn't mean it that way." She smiled and her eyes regained a little bit of their sparkle. "But I still bet I'm right."

Angel peeked at the guys again. "Five minutes. I'll go over there in five minutes."

ADAM

For the first time, he'd come to the club without knowing what he was going to be doing. Normally he knew exactly what he wanted to do at the club, whether it was a scene with a sub or spend time with his friends. Tonight he'd decided to leave it open to a spur of the moment decision. It was not a comfortable feeling for him, but since he couldn't decide what he wanted before he left the house he figured it was best to stay flexible.

So far all he'd done was observe.

Observe Angel. Observe Angel with Michael. Observe Angel with Leigh. Observe Angel as she sat with Leigh, separated from Michael.

Somehow, they'd ended up in gender groups, him, Patrick, and Michael in one conversation at the bar while Angel and Leigh sat at a table only a few feet away having their own separate conversation. And Adam still didn't know what he wanted.

"Are you going to scene tonight?" Patrick asked Michael. "We've got a fair number of masochists in the Lounge area tonight. I'm sure Andrew can point you in the right direction."

Well that got Adam's attention. For all he'd been standing here getting to know Michael a little better, somehow the topic of his preferred kinks hadn't come up yet. And that was a little bonus tidbit of information for Adam, because he knew Angel wasn't a painslut.

"No, I'm here so Angel can try a scene without feeling guilty about deserting Leigh," Michael said easily, clearly unaffected by the idea of Angel scening with someone else.

"You're not going to scene with Angel?" Andrew asked, with a side-long glance for Adam. He ignored both of them and looked over to see Leigh glancing at her watch and tapping it while Angel gave her a dirty look. More than one Dom was eyeing the two women like they were considering approaching, even though they weren't in the Lounge area.

Michael looked right at Adam, catching his attention and holding it.

"No, Angel and I like to flirt but nothing's ever going to happen between us. She's not ever going to be intimate with a guy who has been with one of her friends, and even if I managed to convince her to move past that, I know we're not compatible. The amount of pain which interests her is way too light for me and the amount I like to dole out would be nothing but punishment for her."

The words were said cleanly and succinctly, and he didn't look away from Adam once as he said them. Both Patrick and Andrew looked gleeful at Michael's bluntness. Adam kept his face impassive, not giving anything away. He didn't need everyone butting into his business when he hadn't even decided what he was going to do yet.

Yes, it was nice to have it confirmed by Michael that nothing was going on with him and Angel, and to get his take on why. Even better to know Michael was apparently actively encouraging her to find someone else to play with. But he wasn't going to let anyone manipulate or push him into something he wasn't ready for, and he wasn't ready to make up his mind about Angel.

Dammit.

"So you're a sadist?" he asked, casually. Andrew rolled his eyes. Patrick groaned. Michael smiled.

"It took me a while to come around to it, but yes."

He nodded. That was understandable. Movement caught the corner of his eye and he looked over to see Angel getting up from her seat. She half-turned to look back at the group of men at the bar, her eyes flicking over him for a moment before she gave Michael a stiff nod and started towards the Lounge area.

The lacy tiered skirt she was wearing flicked against the backs of her thighs, highlighting those long legs and the fact she had a well-rounded ass because there was so much space between the lacy edge and her skin. The top she was wearing was, for the first time, not a corset although it did lace up the back and was held closed in the front by hooks. It was made of suede and looked incredibly soft to the touch, as well as making her upper body easily accessible. The high heels she wore made her hips roll as she walked, emphasizing the aura of easy sensuality.

"Are you seriously going to let her get away?"

Adam cursed under his breath and he was moving before he could stop and think about it. Before he could stop and ask himself what the hell he was doing. Not because Michael goaded him, but because more than one Dom at the bar was watching her progress towards the Lounge. If she got there, she'd be followed and more than one of them would probably ask her to scene.

He didn't try to explain to himself why the thought bothered him so much.

With long, quick strides, he passed the distance easily and caught her by the elbow. Angel spun around in surprise, fast enough to break his grip, her body automatically settling back into a defensive posture.

Putting his hands up in front of him he took a step back. "Sorry." Dammit. He'd almost forgotten she taught self-defense and she'd probably be a little bit on edge right now.

Looking up at him, the startled, almost angry gaze softened and she relaxed. "It's okay. I'm just jumpy."

"I also want to apologize for how your Introduction Scene ended."

ANGEL

Studying Master Adam's face didn't give Angel much of a hint as to what he was thinking.

"Apology accepted."

When he'd first grabbed her arm she'd reacted instinctively, even as the thought went through her mind that no one was going to bother her here at Stronghold. She should have felt safe, but since she'd been on her way over to the Lounge area, cursing this man for not even glancing her way, she'd been bitten by an attack of nerves. Now that he was standing in front of her, looking down at her in a way which made her feel strangely vulnerable, she was feeling even more unsettled.

Maybe that was partially because she could still feel his fingers on her elbow. Damn he was hot. It wasn't fair she was so darn attracted to him when he seemed completely oblivious to her.

Leigh had bet he would follow her if she headed towards the Lounge area, but maybe he wanted to apologize where no one else could overhear? It would make sense.

"You're planning on scening tonight?" he asked, with a jerk of his head towards the Lounge area. The question sounded casual, but his blue eyes were looking at her with such intensity that she felt a wild hope springing up inside of her.

"Yes."

"I'd like to make up for the way your scene ended last time." He held out his hand, palm up. "Would you like to scene with me?"

Damn his impassive face. From the way he phrased the question it sounded like he was trying to set things right, to atone for his previous mistakes. Not because he wanted to scene with her again. The only hint there might be something more, that he felt as strong an attraction to her as she did to him, was in his eyes, which felt like they were boring into her.

She'd told herself she wanted to come to the club to experience scening, whether it was with him or with someone else. The truth was, she would have been willing to scene with someone else, but her first option had always been to try again with him.

"Yes, please." Her voice was breathy, which made her cringe inwardly as she put her hand in his. Good job Angel, go ahead and show him how much he affects you when he might only be asking out of professional courtesy.

Whatever, she'd take what she could get. If it was anything like last time, it was still going to be really hot. And maybe she wasn't totally crazy, maybe there would be something more than professionalism.

To her surprise he didn't immediately lead her away from where they stood. Instead he held her hand between them, his thumb rubbing over her knuckles. Who knew such a tiny gesture could feel so very intimate? Yet she knew if she tried to pull away, he would stop her. Control her. Even in heels it felt like he was towering over her and even though he hadn't moved an inch, it now felt like they were somehow standing closer to each other.

It was so pathetic how a little hand holding could make her pussy clench.

But it wasn't just his hand and the caress of his thumb, it was the way he was looking at her, the fact that he looked so damned hot in his button down white shirt and dark blue jeans, exuding the kind of dominant aura she'd always lusted after but never had entirely focused on her. Not until this man. The way he was holding her hand reminded her of the way he'd held it when she'd shaken hands with him at Chained, when she'd felt almost like he was testing her commitment to dominance.

This felt like a different kind of test entirely.

"The same limits as last time?"

All her hard limits, plus the no sex thing. Angel jerked her head yes. She knew she needed to confirm 'no sex' now, because during her Introduction Scene she would have done anything to have him fuck her properly. It was what her body craved, but her brain knew it wasn't a good idea. Especially if he was only scening with her again because it was a responsibility or a make-up session.

Maybe it would have been different if he'd approached her for no other reason than he'd wanted to, but even then, she wouldn't want him to think she was too easy. For whatever reason, she felt very comfortable with him. And was extremely attracted to him.

"Is there a particular room or piece of equipment you want to use? I don't believe the office is in use this evening, or we could wait for one of the other rooms. It shouldn't be long."

Possibilities whirled through her head from the tour she'd taken the last time. But when she had no idea what he was thinking or feeling or if he was even as attracted to her as she was to him, the last thing she wanted to do was give herself a false sense of intimacy by being alone with him. And there was another piece of equipment down in the Dungeon she'd always been wildly curious about.

"The Saint Andrews Cross," she said. "And um... not a whip but... something."

"Something." A little smile creased his lips for a moment before it disappeared again. "I can work with that." His thumb brushed over her knuckles again, this time with a little bit more pressure and he lowered his hand, although he didn't let go of hers, and started moving.

As she followed him down the stairs, she tried not to think about how nice it was to have her hand in his, or how warm his palm was, or how considerate he was as he made sure she didn't stumble on the stairs in her high heels.

He's trying to make things up to you from last time, she scolded herself. *He even told you so.* She couldn't take it personally that he was being so darn attentive to her this time around.

Last time it had gotten her kind of hot when he'd been pissy. This time it was making her all warm and tingly that he wasn't. So basically, according to her body, the man could do no wrong.

Delightful.

They were lucky, there were several Saint Andrew's crosses free, despite the number of people in the club. It was more crowded than it had been during her Introduction Scene. To Angel's surprise, a fair number of them were watching the scenes rather than participating.

She looked up at Master Adam as he led her towards one of the open crosses. "There's so many people here... don't they want to play?"

"Not always," he answered, glancing around the room at the various scenes and their audiences. "Sometimes watching a good scene can be as satisfying as being in one. Some people enjoy watching, period. And sometimes, if you don't feel like playing, you still want to be involved in some way."

"Do you ever watch?"

He paused for a moment and she wondered if she'd stepped over the line by asking him something personal. "Sometimes. Usually if I'm not here to scene I stay up at the bar."

Angel wondered how often he came to scene. Mostly it was curiosity, flavored with a tinge of jealousy. Not her business, so she didn't ask.

When they stopped in front of the St. Andrew's cross, Master Adam let go of her hand and stepped up to inspect the gleaming wood and the restraints screwed into it. Angel watched him silently. Apparently satisfied, he turned back toward her and she braced herself for the order to strip. It would be a lot scarier with so many people in the club, but she was ready to do it.

"Hands at your sides," he said instead, stepping towards her.

There was a little gleam in his eye as if he could see she was unsettled by the deviation from their previous scene's structure. But she put her hands at her side, tilting her head up at him almost defiantly until he raised an eyebrow at her, giving her a hard look. A blush spread across her cheeks and she dropped her gaze to his feet.

Peeking at him, he was too tall for her to see his face, but she could see him unbuttoning the cuffs of his shirt. He rolled them up to his elbows, the quick, brisk motions of a man getting ready for work. Why was it so damn sexy? It wasn't like revealing forearms was inherently hot, but waiting for him to roll up his shirt sleeves while she stood here, knowing she was going to be punished, pleasured, and who knows what else... well, she was drenching her panties to say the least.

"Stand still." His voice barked out and she stilled, realizing she'd been shifting her weight. Trying to peek at him from under her eyelashes again, she caught her breath at the hungry, almost predatory look that went across his face.

He didn't look at all grouchy or disinterested or any of the other emotions she'd seen him show before. She licked her lips to wet them and then followed it with a drag of her teeth across the lower one, her gaze flicked down, right to his crotch where he was starting to sport a bulge. It wasn't super obvious in jeans, but it was there.

He wasn't entirely immune to her. Unless he got hard every time he played, which also seemed possible. Might not have anything to do with her at all. But how to explain that look?

Then he moved forward to stand directly in front of her and began to unlatch her top. Angel's breathing stuttered and restarted as his fingers pulled apart each hook and eye, slowly revealing the curves of her breasts and then her stomach, until the entire top was gaping open. Her body was practically trembling with how much she wanted him to touch her, but despite how close he was standing and despite the fact he was undressing her, his fingers hadn't brushed her skin once.

It was unnerving. Exciting. Scary. Anxiety-inducing.

When he finally put a finger under her chin and tipped her head back to look at him, she barely managed to stifle a moan that he'd finally *touched* her.

ADAM

God she was beautiful. Her eyes were dark, her pupils fully dilated, and her breath was coming in soft pants that would have told him how aroused she was even if her nipples weren't drilling holes through the soft suede of her top. The fists clenched at her sides opened and closed again as she struggled to stay still, even though she obviously wanted to move, to touch him.

That turned him on too.

"Do you remember the color system from your Introduction Scene?"

"Red, yellow, and green, Sir."

"What color are you right now, Angel?"

"Green, Sir."

"Are you wet?"

A blush rose in her cheeks as her eyes flicked away for a moment in embarrassment. He tapped her under the chin with one finger and they refocused back on him.

"Answer me, sub."

"Yes, Sir," she whispered, her blush intensifying. Funny how she was perfectly comfortable having him begin to undress her in a club full of people, but admitting she was wet, just to him, made her blush. Funny and endearing.

"Keep your eyes on me."

Putting his hands on her shoulders, he began to push her top off, revealing her entire upper body. Angel sucked in a breath, practically vibrating beneath his hands as the suede slipped off and hit the floor. For her Introduction Scene he'd been too angry for anything but a punishment scene. This time he wanted to show her a softer, more seductive side of BDSM.

He ignored the small voice in his head taunting him, asking if it was because he now knew Michael was a sadist and he wanted to show Angel he enjoyed parts of BDSM which had nothing to do with pain and could give her something Michael couldn't.

The eye contact created an incredible amount of intimacy as she was bared to him, as he skimmed his hands over her shoulders and down her body, barely brushing the sides of her beautifully rounded breasts with his hands. Her rosy nipples were puckered up tight, hard and begging for attention. He ignored them and continued to skim his hands down to her waist before grabbing her hips and pulling her hard against him.

Angel squeaked as she fell into him, her hands trying to come up and not making it, trapped by his arms. She had very little control over her movement, and he could see the change in her expression as she realized it, as the amount of power he had over her came crashing down. It was different from being bound by restraints and yet it obviously affected her just as much.

He ignored how soft she felt against him, how warm, how inviting as her muscles relaxed and she looked up at him with trembling awe and anticipation. He hadn't done anything to earn the trust in her eyes, didn't deserve it, but it still made him hard as a rock to see it.

The constant eye contact allowed him to watch as hers began to glaze, his hands skimming down her back to the zipper on her skirt. He could have turned her around to do this, but he'd decided to have her pressed against him instead. It enhanced her vulnerability and allowed him a pleasure he otherwise might not have had.

His eyebrows raised. "No underwear?"

"No Sir."

"Why not?"

"I came to play."

Knowing she'd been walking around with no underwear under her short skirt, as well as the sudden image of her doing a scene with another man flashing through his head, sent conflicting reactions raging through his body. He tamped them down, struggling for his usual control. Reminding himself that she hadn't seemed eager to play with any other man and hadn't jumped right into the Lounge area, helped.

Reminding himself that she was here, with him, helped even more.

Maybe he couldn't completely sort out how he felt about Angel, but one emotion kept coming up almost as often as attraction, and that was possessiveness.

❦ 13 ❦

ADAM

Pressing Angel against the St. Andrew's, Adam secured her wrists to the restraints, adjusting them for her height. He'd chosen to position her facing outward, because he wanted to be able to see the expressions on her face. As well as seeing her fascination with the other scenes going on in the room. Also, her embarrassment and arousal from seeing the people watching them. It had been one thing, last Thursday, when there hadn't been as many viewers and she'd been bent over so she hadn't been able to see them for the most part.

Now every time she looked out into the crowd, she blushed.

"What's your color, Angel?"

"Green, Sir." She licked her lips and he resisted the urge to kiss them.

Kissing was for something more than a scene. He wasn't sure how she felt about him, but he didn't want their first kiss to be while she was bound and unable to move away.

"Can you hold your legs in place? Or should I restrain those too?"

He wanted to give her the choice of following an order or having some help with it, although his preference was bondage. Having her completely helpless, open and spread for him.

"Umm... I can try?"

He chuckled. "You don't sound very sure of yourself."

"I'm not sure I could have held myself in place last time, if it hadn't been for the restraints," she admitted.

There it was again, the honesty that made him want to trust her, despite her original deception. Since coming to Stronghold, as far as he could tell, she'd been completely honest the whole time. The least he could do was return the favor, so he grinned, wickedly, and saw her short, sharp intake of breath.

"Well then since my preference is for full restraints..."

Kneeling for a moment, he pulled her legs apart as far as he wanted them, cuffing her ankles so she was open but not entirely exposed. Even so, from his position at her feet he could see right up into the lips of her pretty pink pussy and he knew she was soaking wet.

ANGEL

The last cuff was pulled into place and Angel had to stifle another moan. Why was being completely helpless such a turn on? Not to mention, she'd never thought she had exhibitionist tendencies, but she was getting off on how many people were seeing her helpless and exposed at the hands of Master Adam.

In some ways, this was already so much more intense than her first scene with him. It felt more intimate, maybe because he wasn't so angry, but it also felt personal. Facing him, being able to see his expressions, being able to watch what he was doing made everything seem much more real. She couldn't focus inwards or lose herself in her head, because everything was happening right in front of her eyes.

Including how he was staring at her like he wanted to lick her from her toes up to her splayed open pussy. She hadn't been aware of the air circulation in the Dungeon before, but now she could clearly feel a slight cool draft of air on her wet, heated flesh. It only turned her on more.

"What's your color, Angel?"

"Green," she practically sang. Oh so very green.

"Good," he murmured. His hand caressed her calf, his touch so very light on her skin. It tickled but it didn't, because she didn't feel at all like laughing. It was gentle, like the brush of a butterfly's wing, and all the more teasing because of the very fragility of the touch.

Fingers traced up her calf to her knee, which she'd never thought of as a particularly erotic area, but as his fingers splayed out over the cap she felt an answering tingle in her pussy and she shivered. Looking down, she saw his blue eyes gazing intently up at her, studying her body's reactions.

"What are you doing?" she asked. This wasn't at all what she had expected it to be.

Master Adam's small smile grew larger, his gaze sharpening. "Whatever I want."

Another shiver went through her as he shifted, reaching out his hand to her opposite ankle, which put her pussy right in front of his face. Angel's breath caught in her throat. The boundaries which had been set down said he could touch her there, hell she *wanted* him to touch her there, but sex—including oral—was supposed to be off the table according to the limits they'd made for the Introduction Scene, which she'd agreed to continuing to abide by tonight. If he did break the agreement she could use her safe word and the Dungeon Monitors would come running, but would she want to?

She already knew the answer and it was embarrassingly revealing.

But he touched her ankle and calf, moving his hand slowly upwards the way he had on her other leg, his breath wafting across her shaven mound while his mouth didn't come any closer. It took a considerable amount of her willpower to keep from canting her hips toward him, her body wanting to beg for more contact. Fingers glided across the backs of her knees and to her inner thighs.

Please please please please please...

She had to bite her lip to keep from saying it out loud. To keep from begging. It felt like her legs were tingling and the sensation was moving up her entire body without him even having to touch her there. The throbbing ache of her nipples was repeated by the walls of her pussy, which clenched over and over again, trying to find relief from the tension building inside of her.

"You're very wet," he murmured, his voice appreciative as his fingers made little circles on her thighs, just below her pussy lips. Angel whimpered. When his hands gripped her thighs and then moved upwards, not even brushing the swollen lips between her legs, gripping her hips instead, she had reason to bless the restraints even as she cursed him.

If it hadn't been for the bondage she'd probably have sunk right down to the floor because her knees had gone too weak to hold her upright. On the other hand, if it hadn't been for the bondage she could have grabbed him and made him touch her the way she was aching to be touched. She could reach down to take care of things herself.

That she couldn't do any of those things made her hotter and wetter, which made her feel even more wild.

He'd barely done anything to her and she was ready to *beg*.

When his hands skimmed up her stomach to cup her breasts she whimpered again, half-choking on a pleading moan as he gently squeezed. Dazed, she looked straight into those bright blue eyes, writhing and automatically tugging at the restraints on her wrists as he squeezed and kneaded her soft flesh. He deliberately kept his fingers away from her nipples.

The bastard.

Thumbs brushed over the tips of her nipples, sending sparks sizzling down her spine, and Angel arched her back, trying to gain more contact. Instead he squeezed her breasts again, carefully avoiding any further contact with the budded tips.

"Oh, for God's sake, touch me!" she blurted out, too far gone to care if he laughed at her or that other people were hearing her desperate need.

But he didn't laugh. Instead, he looked directly and deeply into her eyes, maintaining a connection that was almost uncomfortable in its intensity.

"I am touching you."

As if to demonstrate he brushed his thumbs over her nipples again, as lightly as he had the last time and Angel's insides clenched as she yanked at her wrists. A little smile appeared on his face, but somehow she knew he wasn't laughing at her. No, he was smiling because he was *pleased.*

"More," she begged. Her backside smacked against the cross as she writhed for him again.

Rather than giving her what she wanted, he released her breasts and started stroking her sides in what should have been a calming manner but instead made her feel even more wildly needy. "That's not for you to say, Angel."

"Please? Sir?" It was on the tip of her tongue to call him all the names running through her head, but that wasn't going to help her situation. She'd say anything to get him to stop the throbbing that was consuming her from the inside out.

Master Adam pressed his body against hers, the hard ridge of his erection rubbing against her belly, her breasts crushed against his chest as he caught her between him and the Saint Andrew's cross. Her eyes nearly crossed at the wave of lust surging through her. Cradling her head in his hands, his fingers sliding into the back of her hair, he tilted her head back to look up at him, his mouth hovering over hers by mere inches.

She strained to reach his lips, but all that did was rub her against his body. The restraints held her too securely and he didn't seem inclined to help her.

Damn him. She wasn't going to beg for a kiss.

"You're all tied up, sweetheart," he murmured softly. While his big body blocked her sight to the rest of the dungeon, she knew people were watching, even if they could no longer see her. The deep rumble of his voice vibrated through his chest and into hers, the rhythm of his words almost hypnotic. "You can't make me go faster or slower, you have to wait for me to decide how and when I want to touch you. You won't come until I want you to." He leaned down to whisper directly in her ear, making her shiver convulsively as his lips brushed her sensitive earlobe. "And if you keep telling me what to do, I *will* gag you."

Oh fuck. His body rocked against hers and she went nearly mindless from the absolute thrill. It didn't even matter he was fully clothed and she was completely naked, somehow that made everything dirtier, hotter. As did his words.

ADAM

Reluctantly Adam pulled away from the soft curves of Angel's body, his eyes going to her hands and feet, reflexively, to check on them and make sure there was no discoloration. He'd restrained her securely and not too tightly, but she'd been tugging so much on them that he wanted to make sure she hadn't inadvertently tightened them somehow. It was a good thing he'd used cuffs on all four limbs, otherwise he was sure she'd be trying to use them to entice him into doing what she wanted.

Not that he needed much enticing, but drawing this out was a measure of his own self-control, as well as being a heady aphrodisiac. There was nothing hotter to him than seeing a woman's eyes glaze over with desire, and with Angel he found himself wanting to reduce her to a begging, lustful, hot mess.

It wasn't that she was dominant or that she was trying to top from the bottom; no, she was impatient. She didn't try to hide or temper her body's response. Eventually he knew she'd become better at controlling herself, as the newness of BDSM wore off and she had a better idea of what to expect in terms of the sensations and emotions scening engendered, but right now she was almost like a virgin, on the brink of sexual exploration.

It hadn't escaped his notice that she'd been surprised he hadn't immediately started laying into her after he'd gotten her tied up. This kind of scene was nothing like the one he'd done with her before. In fact, it wasn't the kind of scene he normally did at all. This was a slow seduction, an intimate introduction, the kind of building block which laid down a foundation for something much more than a simple scene or an exclusively club relationship.

Not that he had any kind of relationship with Angel yet, but he was starting to think it was a definite possibility. Their chemistry was through the roof. It took every ounce of his control not to put his mouth on her lips, on her body... but if he started then he wouldn't be able to stop.

The little noises she was making in the back of her throat were driving him absolutely wild, which was why he'd had to pull away or he would have completely lost his control. Stepping back, he maintained eye contact with her as he reached out and picked up the flogger he'd had at the ready. Angel eyed it with a mixture of trepidation and excitement, her breasts jiggling as she practically panted with need. He knew exactly how she felt.

"I'm going to start off slow and not too hard," he told her. "If you start to feel uncomfortable or like it's hurting too much or you get scared, say yellow and I'll stop and we can talk about it. Okay?"

Angel nodded her head.

"I need to hear you say it out loud, sweetheart."

"Okay, Sir." Her voice was husky, strained. Needy. He felt an answering surge in his cock. Was it possible to pass out from having too much blood pooling in one's groin? He was starting to feel almost light-headed, he was so hard.

Flexing his wrist, he gave a couple of experimental swings to make sure he had the weight and aim he wanted. Angel's eyes followed the strands of the flogger. It was lightweight, soft leather, about two feet long, and it could caress or it could sting depending on how hard he swung it.

Right now, he planned to caress.

She tensed as the strands came towards her and then shuddered as the soft leather wrapped around her hips, her body relaxing as the soft slap registered on her nerves. Just hard enough to be felt, not hard enough to be painful. Adam grinned and swung the backhand, catching her other hip, letting the strands wrap around to her back-side. Then he flicked his hand up and caught one breast... then the other... and back down to her hip.

It was a series of figure eight shapes made with his wrist, sensual and skilled. She didn't even notice when he began to swing the flogger a little harder, her body was moving with the strokes, her hips lifting to accept the kiss of the whip and then her back arching to present her breasts. The buds of her nipples turned darker and darker as her creamy skin began to pinken under the assault of the flogger.

Watching Angel was beautiful. He could feel the weight of the crowd at his back as it gathered and was surprised to find himself feeling jealous again. Adam knew he could be a bit of an exhibitionist. He enjoyed showing off his skill as well as garnering admiration, but for the first time he found himself almost wishing he could keep the sight of Angel in the throes of erotic ecstasy to himself. Because ecstasy was what was on her face, practically shining from it. She trusted him completely and it showed in her easy acceptance of her flogging, in the way her body moved to meet the strands as they came down, and the obvious pleasure she received from it.

Sometimes he could be involved in a scene like this and feel mental pleasure, something transcending the physical. This evening he felt that and more. Watching Angel aroused him almost painfully—even more so because he knew he wasn't going to find his own culmination tonight. He hadn't last time either, but he had been working out some of his own issues then. Tonight, he wanted to make this experience completely about her.

A low moan interrupted the almost hypnotic rhythm he'd established, and he glanced up at Angel's face. Her lips were parted, her golden eyes glazed and dark with pleasure, and her cheeks were flushed almost as pink as her breasts and hips now were. Appreciative murmurs behind him had him squashing another bout of unreasonable jealousy.

Experimentally he flicked the flogger at her inner thighs and watched her body arch as she processed the new sensation. He flicked the other thigh and then very gently directed the flogger right at her splayed pussy folds.

Angel moaned again, shuddering, and her fingers clenched and then opened.

"What's your color, sweetheart?" There was no response, just another shudder through her body. Adam stepped closer, letting the flogger droop downwards. "Angel, what's your color?"

She blinked and her eyes refocused on him. Not in subspace then, the elusive headspace a submissive could reach during a particularly intense scene. At that point the color and safe word systems ceased to work because a sub would accept almost anything done to them.

Adam was both relieved and disappointed Angel wasn't there, although he could tell she was close. Reminding himself he wanted her fully aware of who she was with, and what they were doing, he cleared his throat.

"Angel, what's your color sweetheart?"

For a moment she seemed to search for the words and then she smiled up at him, a beautiful smile of complete trust and bliss. "Green."

"Good girl."

And he rewarded her, and himself, by switching his flogger to his left hand and thrusting his right hand between her legs. She was so very wet, practically dripping, as he found her entrance and pressed two fingers inside of her. Heat convulsed around him as he stared into her eyes, filling her vision as he stretched her pussy.

Angel rocked against him with a whimper, her swollen, wet folds rubbing against his palm and the heel of his hand.

"Please..." Her voice was a thready, needy whisper.

"Please what, Angel?"

Her head fell back as she moaned. He worked his fingers inside of her, reveling in her abandoned sensuality, the way her body spasmed in response to his manipulations.

"I want you... please... more..."

Shit. Adam's cock pulsed as he realized what she was asking for, knowing it wasn't possible. During her Introduction Scene she hadn't given him permission for more than hands and toys and they'd established at the beginning of this scene they would continue to use those parameters. Just because she wanted it now when she was lost in an erotic haze of need, that didn't mean he could go about changing the scene. He *had* to honor the agreement they'd come to beforehand. It was the same as getting her drunk—right now she was blitzed on pleasure and she wasn't completely in her right mind.

He wouldn't take advantage of her, but he would give her a mind-blowing orgasm and maybe next time...

"Shhh," he murmured, leaning into her and allowing himself the titillation of feeling her body pressing against his, as much as he could with his hand between them. Their foreheads pressed together, lips only an inch or so apart, so he could look right into her eyes. He would find satisfaction in the incredible closeness of their bodies and the intimacy of the moment, and that was *all* the satisfaction he would find from her tonight. "I'm going to take care of you."

"More... please... Adam... I want to... oh God... please... fuck me..."

Even as she said the words it was as if the very idea propelled her over the edge and into glorious climax. Her entire body shivered as he leaned into her, pressing her against the cross as her pussy tightened around his fingers. Rubbing the heel of his hand over her wet flesh, he could feel the swollen nub of her clit pressing back and he worked it as relentlessly as his fingers did inside of her. Angel sobbed his name over and over again, making his knees weak with his desire to be inside of her as she came, to make her *scream* his name.

As her orgasm slowed and then subsided, Adam found himself leaning against her almost for support. The scene had taken more out of him than he'd realized, as the sounds of the Dungeon came flooding back. He'd almost forgotten where they were and that they had an audience. Ignoring the appreciative sounds behind him, Adam knelt down to hastily undo the ankle restraints, before holding her up with one of his arms as he released her wrists.

Mistress Lisa was working as a Dungeon Monitor and she was there to hand him a blanket to wrap Angel in, giving him an approving smile before she disappeared back into the crowd. Knowing she would send someone over to clean the equipment, Adam tenderly wrapped Angel up in the blanket and carried her over to the aftercare section.

Settling her onto his lap, she nuzzled right into his chest. Actually, she insisted on unbuttoning his shirt so she could stick her nose right into his chest hair. It tickled as she rubbed her face against his chest for a moment, and then subsided with a happy sigh.

She wasn't in subspace, but she wasn't quite coherent either. All she wanted to do right now was cuddle and he was happy to fulfill that desire for her. Aftercare was taking care of whatever the submissive's needs were following a scene, and while he knew he was going to need to get her a bottle of water in a bit, right now he was going to enjoy holding her in his arms.

Quietly hoping she'd want to repeat scening with him as desperately as he wanted to with her.

❧ 14 ❧

ANGEL

Music blared from Angel's speakers as she tried to concentrate on her latest project—a corset for Lexie. It was going to be the exact same shade of blue as Lexie's eyes, which would look electric against her black hair. A little smile flitted across Angel's face as she thought about how much it would piss off all of Lexie's "big brothers" to see her in such a garment, because she was pretty sure there was no way Lexie would want one of the high-necked shirts Angel had worn when she'd donned the same corset for a night at Stronghold.

Pissing off Lexie's 'big brothers' sounded pretty good right now.

Well, okay, really only one of them. The others were kind of innocent bystanders, but she didn't care if this drew their ire as well. Right now she was feeling a bit pissy.

It was Tuesday evening, *three days* since her visit to Stronghold, and all she could think about was Master Adam. Mostly she thought about how incredibly humiliating it was to have begged him to fuck her and be rejected, although logically she knew he couldn't have done anything else. She was more upset about her own loss of control and letting him know how much she wanted him when she didn't have any kind of idea as to his own feelings.

After their scene, their incredibly intense and soul-baring scene, he'd delivered her back upstairs to Mike without a single qualm. Hadn't seemed bothered when Mike had taken one look at her and declared he was driving them home. Hadn't said anything other than good night—although there had been a hot, intense look in his eyes when he'd said it—and then let her go!

The next morning she'd tormented herself wondering what he'd done after she'd left the club, because goodness knows he hadn't gotten off with her... and she'd been well aware while they were cuddling in the aftercare area he'd been hard as a rock. *What do you think he did?*

Shut up!

It wasn't something she wanted to think about. She wouldn't think about it. Because she had no claim on him and whatever he did once she left, he was perfectly within his rights to do so. They scened together. They hadn't kissed or anything. He hadn't asked for her phone number.

But some part of her mind insisted the scene had been more than a scene and she hadn't imagined the incredible intimacy that had sprung from it.

The door to her room opened and Angel glanced up, already knowing who it would be. None of her roommates would enter without knocking and Mike was out at a job interview, so that only left one person.

Musical notes clashed together before Angel reached over and turned off her speakers and a distressed looking Leigh held out her phone to Angel. It was playing Aerosmith's "I Don't Wanna Miss a Thing," which was Michael and Leigh's "song".

"He keeps calling and I can't... I'm not ready to talk to him yet," Leigh said, holding the phone out towards Angel beseechingly. "I don't know what to say to him. Please... answer it and tell him I'll call him soon. Just not yet. I don't know what I want from him so I don't know what to say to him."

Wow... that was new. Angel blinked, but reached out to take the phone from her friend. The fact that Leigh was even considering maybe she wanted to do something other than get back together with Michael... it killed her to think how much her friend must be hurting to come to such a conclusion, but at the same time she wanted to support that. Maybe this time things would be different.

She slid her finger over the little arrow to accept the call.

"Hey Michael, it's Angel."

"Oh... um. Is Leigh there?"

"Yeah, but she doesn't want to talk to you right now." Angel shrugged when Leigh glared at her. What else was she supposed to tell him? "She needs some time... she'll call you in a couple of days, okay?"

"What does she need time for?" Michael asked, sounding frustrated. "I told her I love her and I didn't realize she didn't want to take an actual break... I would have never suggested it if I didn't think it was something she wanted." Angel tried not to roll her eyes. Maybe he wouldn't have suggested it *this time*, but he sure as hell hadn't had a problem trying to take advantage of it to date other women. She wondered if he'd been shot down already or if he'd realized how much harder he was going to have to work to find someone to bang who wasn't Leigh.

"She needs the time and you need to give it to her," Angel said sharply, her temper rising. "If you don't want to then that's your decision, but at the very least stop calling her and give the girl some space."

"Is she seeing someone else? Is that what's going on? Because I thought she didn't want us to see anyone else!"

"No, she's not, she's not ready to talk to you, yet."

As much as Angel would have loved to have told Michael that yes, Leigh was considering dating other people, she knew it wasn't true and Leigh would be pretty pissed if Angel lied about it. It pissed Angel off how much antagonism and affront there was in Michael's voice when he'd asked if Leigh was seeing other people. It was okay for him to, but not for Leigh? Ugh, she wished she could reach through the phone and punch him in the balls.

"Give her a couple of days, she'll call you when she's ready to talk."

"Okay. Fine. Tell her I'm not going to wait around forever."

Angel bit her lip to stop herself from retorting Leigh shouldn't have to wait around forever for his proposal either. *Not my business.*

"Okay," she said instead. "Bye."

She ended the call without waiting to hear if he said anything else.

Leigh sagged in front of her eyes, going over to sit on her bed and looking pale and almost wraith-like. Immediately Angel folded the corset fabric and went to her, wrapping her arm around Leigh's slender shoulders as they started to shake.

"Hey baby... it's okay..." she murmured. "You know you don't have to get back together with him if you don't want to."

"But I do want to..." Leigh said, turning her head into Angel's welcoming shoulder, tears muffling her voice slightly. "I don't know if I should. What's the point of sitting around waiting for him to get to the perfect place in his life to propose to me if he's going to spend the rest of his life wanting to date other women?"

"Shh..." Angel hugged her. "You are the best damn thing that ever happened to him and you know it and he knows it. He sounded pretty impatient to talk to you. He said he loves you." Angel truly believed he did, at least inasmuch as he was capable of. Michael was kind of a narcissist, but as much as he could, she believed he cared for and loved Leigh. But he would never put her before himself, in any way.

At least from what Angel could see, but she was trying hard to be there for her friend and what she wanted. And she hated to see how Leigh's self-esteem rose and fell with her perception of how much Michael cared about her.

"I know he does. And I love him. I don't know if it's enough anymore."

There wasn't anything she could say to that, so Angel hugged her friend and thought about how much men sucked.

ADAM

"Knock knock."

Adam looked up from the papers spread out on his desk and tried to quell the immediate surge of bundled negative emotions clenching his gut. The man in the doorway hadn't done anything to deserve his animosity. Not really. It seemed to be an automatic reaction ever since he'd met him.

"Hey, how was the interview?" Adam asked, forcing his voice to remain casual.

Finding out Michael wanted to sign up for a temp agency while he waited for the usual D.C. cattle call of auditions had prompted Adam to offer some help. A way to prove to himself it didn't bother him how close this man was to Angel, that Adam didn't see him as a threat.

With an easy grin, Michael leaned on the door frame, hands in his pockets. He had the kind of confident nonchalance Adam had always envied. Michael looked like a man who could relax easily, even though he wasn't as playful as Chris. Maybe it was the way his hair fell in his eyes. Adam had a feeling that was the kind of thing a lot of women found attractive, and it had probably helped the man a lot in his career, but he knew such a look would never work for him.

"It went fine, I think they'll probably call you about taking me on. I wanted to stop by and say hi and thank you."

Adam waved his hand in acknowledgment. "No problem. It benefits my company to have plenty of people to place in jobs."

"And makes sure I won't end up back on Angel's couch in a month or two if I can't pay my rent, right?"

He felt his face freeze, an immediate reaction to covering up his emotions. "Sorry?"

Michael laughed and Adam had to squash another surge of emotion, mostly anger.

"You should call her. She's been pacing around the house and making her housemates nervous because she keeps muttering under her breath and they have no idea why."

"I didn't get her number." It wasn't a real excuse. He hadn't asked for it because he knew he could get it from Patrick any time he wanted. Of course, the day after scening with her it had occurred to him that calling her without having asked for her number made him kind of look like a creeper. "And I figured she'd be at Stronghold this weekend."

For a moment Michael looked at him with something akin to pity. "You know, most women don't like to be taken for granted."

"I'm not... I don't want to rush her." He didn't know why he was talking to this man. He barely knew him. Hell, he hadn't even told any of his friends this, and Justin had been in his office at lunch asking about Angel. "She's new to all of this," he muttered.

Looking amused, Michael shook his head and stood up straight. "Don't take too long. Angel's not the most patient person in the world, not once she knows what she wants." He chuckled, gave the door frame one last rap with his knuckles, and left.

Great. Now even people Adam *wasn't* friends with were butting in.

ANGEL

Leigh grabbed the dish of scalloped potatoes from the backseat while Angel was picking up the blueberry pie when her phone buzzed with a text message.

"Argh."

Juggling the still-warm dish with one hand while trying to dig her phone out of her purse with the other, slightly hampered by her bulky winter jacket, Angel gave it up for a lost cause. She'd check it inside. Leigh looked at her with amusement.

"Come on, let's go," Angel jerked her head at her parents' front door.

"Doesn't look like Mike's here yet."

"No, he said he might be late. He had a late coffee date with one of his former directors, trying to find out if there are any backstage jobs going on during the next couple of months."

"Do you ever regret not doing the theater thing?" Leigh asked as they headed up the walkway.

"No. It's a great hobby, but a shit job."

Trying to make a living at it would ruin the enjoyment of theater for her. Mike seemed to thrive on it. Then again, he was a sadist, so maybe he channeled the stress into beating some willing sub's ass.

Now that she'd spent a little time at Stronghold, Angel could believe it. Scenes could be great stress relief as long as you didn't get too emotionally involved.

Not that she was. She wouldn't let herself be until she knew what the heck was going on with a certain someone else's emotions. What game was he playing anyway?

"Are you going to keep standing there or are we going in?"

Oops. They'd not only reached the door, Angel had been standing in front of the side with the doorknob, staring off into space without paying any attention to her surroundings. Muttering a few choice words under her breath, she tested the door and was relieved to find it unlocked so she didn't have to go digging through her purse for her keys.

"Hello?"

"My babies are here!"

Both Angel and Leigh laughed as Angel's mother came bustling into the room, beaming with glee that her "girls" were home. Strangely, while Leigh and Angel's mothers had never become particularly close to each other, they had each basically adopted the other's offspring. In fact, Leigh got the first hug and kiss on the cheek from Angel's effusive mother.

She was a beautiful woman, shorter and curvier than either Leigh or Angel. Long black hair had been done up into a messy knot on the back of her head. Behind her was Angel's dad, standing a few inches taller than Angel and with a cheerful smile on his round face. Her mom was half-Korean and her dad was half-Chinese and they'd given Angel a mixed bag of genetic traits as well.

"So, how are things with you?" Angel's mom asked Leigh, taking the potatoes and ushering her into the other room. She couldn't hear Leigh's answer but she knew her friend would be saying something innocuous, despite the fact that all the parents knew there was something bad going down with her and Michael. Otherwise he would be here too.

"Hey Dad, good to see you," Angel said, dropping a kiss on his cheek.

"You too, Angel-Face," he said cheerfully, following the gaggle of women. "Have you heard from Captain lately? He's got his own ship now."

Angel groaned. "Oh my god... he's Captain Captain now?"

She hadn't heard from either of her big brothers lately. They tended to gather for the big holidays and otherwise there was an occasional e-mail back and forth but not much more contact than that. Percy (short for Percival) was out in Arizona and Captain was working on a private cruise line one of his college friends had started. Neither of her brothers were particularly good at keeping in touch over long distances, although they were incredibly affectionate and boisterous in person.

Captain, the oldest of the three siblings, had gotten the short-end of the stick when it came to names. His full name was Captain Glascock Jones; both Captain and Glascock were family names about to die out so her parents had somehow decided it would be a good idea to give him both. The poor guy couldn't even go by his middle name—although she knew he'd had a damned good time in school being addressed as "Captain" by his teachers. He'd grown into it and by the time he'd become Captain of the Varsity football team in high school no one was making fun of him anymore.

However, Captain Captain of an actual ship was a completely different story.

"Captain Captain of the Wandering Wreck," said her dad with a grin. "It's a pirate themed cruise ship."

She couldn't help it, she burst out laughing. "He's a real swash-buckler now!"

"He wants us to come out this summer and see his ship," said her dad proudly.

That was one thing she had to hand her parents, it didn't matter what their kids did, as long as they did it with enthusiasm then her parents were proud and happy. They absolutely supported Angel's endeavors with teaching self-defense and her Etsy store, as well as her enjoyment of community theater. They'd supported Captain when he dropped out of college and joined his friend Garrett in starting up the cruise ship line and they'd supported Percy when he'd finished college and gone on to be the only Jones child to get a normal nine to five job.

Percy didn't know what to do with his family a lot of the time. Maybe it was middle-child syndrome, but he'd always been one to quietly go his own way, and he was the only one who'd wanted a "normal" career.

"Sounds like fun, I may join you. Maybe we can even get Percy along and make it a family vacation."

They hadn't had one of those in years.

"That'd be wonderful," her dad said, his face brightening. "Honey, did you hear what Angel said? We're going to make the cruise on the Wandering Wreck a family vacation!"

With a small sigh, realizing she shouldn't have spoken up unless she was sure it was what she wanted to do since she should have known how her dad would take the thought, Angel followed him into the kitchen where her mom and Leigh were. Then again, her dad knew exactly how to twist all of his children into line when he wanted to and she knew she wouldn't be able to say no to him. Looked like they were going on a family vacation that summer.

Her phone buzzed on her hip again, reminding her of the text message she'd received when she was getting out of the car.

Turning on the screen, she saw she had two texts from Lexie.

Hey Angel! I was hoping maybe you'd have some free time tomorrow night...

If you do and you'd be up for helping me decorate Stronghold for the party this weekend, let me know!

Grinning, Angel texted Lexie back.

Sounds like fun! I'll be there.

ANGEL

"How's the job hunt going?" her mom asked Mike. He'd shown up about fifteen minutes late and now he was getting grilled. Which was good because it took attention off of Leigh, which she probably needed after the interrogation she'd gone through upon arrival. "Angel said you're going to stay in the area for a while?"

"That's the plan," Mike replied, giving her mother his most charming smile. "I had an interview today and got in touch with one of my old directors. I might have a small gig lined up, doing some prop-making for her upcoming show. I still have to meet the prop-designer."

"Wonderful," her mom gushed. She gave Angel a sly look. "And you're staying at our Angel's?"

"That's a temporary situation, Mom," she hastily inserted as her father scowled suspiciously at Michael. Dad wasn't exactly super talkative when in large groups, but she could tell he didn't entirely like what he was hearing. While her mom loved Mike and hoped for something between him and Angel, her dad was conservative enough not to want a man living in Angel's house without some kind of commitment prior to the living. Preferably commitment involving a ring. Housemates excepted, of course, although he hadn't been thrilled about *that* either. "He's got his own place to move into next week."

"And after that, hopefully I'll have a temporary job for the day time so I don't end up back on her couch," Mike said. He had the same easy-going grin on his face he always did when he was enjoying himself, but Angel knew he'd deliberately stated he was sleeping on the couch to both reassure her father and give a hint to her mom. Bless him. "I think the interview went well today. I have Angel to thank, she introduced me to the owner of the temp company."

I did?

"She's so helpful and thoughtful, isn't she?" Angel's mom beamed at her.

"Mmm hmm, Adam's a great guy and on top of finding a good, long-term temp job for me."

Angel choked on her green beans. "Adam?"

Beside her, Leigh giggled, and Angel kicked her in the ankle.

"Yes," Mike said, his tone of voice completely bland and so innocent he might as well have screamed he was in a trouble-making mood. "He seems awfully invested in making sure I don't find myself back on your couch once I'm off of it."

Both of Angel's parents blinked and then their heads swung around to look at her.

Oh. Oh, he was so dead.

❧

ANGEL

Knock knock knock.

"Come on, Angel, I said I was sorry! Let me in, it's cold out here!"

"You should have thought of that before you threw me to the wolves!" She glared at Leigh, who was sprawled out on the couch in the main room, rolling with laughter. Mark, Sam, and Q weren't much better. In fact, she'd already had to stop Sam from attempting to let Mike in the front door. They were all taking far too much amusement in her pain.

"I didn't realize they'd take it that way! I tried to stop them!"

"Ignorance is no excuse!"

Mike's one little comment, which he had made to tease her, had sparked a half hour long intensive interrogation of all three of them, but mostly Angel, as her parents' hopes sprang up wildly.

"Angel, seriously, I'm cold! I'm going to break down the door in a minute if you don't let me in."

"Let him in, he's big enough to do it," said Sam. "And it is really cold out there."

Grumbling, Angel yanked open the door and stared at Mike with all the aggravation she could summon. It was a little bit hard when he did look a bit blue around the edges and he was holding himself and jumping up and down a bit to try and keep himself warm.

"Are you going to behave from now on?"

Mike muttered something under his breath and then glared at her. "Yes."

She eyed him suspiciously, pretty sure she'd heard something about spanking her in that mutter, but she wasn't going to ask him to clarify in front of her housemates. Knowing Mike, he would, loudly and proudly, and that would open a whole new can of worms.

❦ 15 ❧

ADAM

It was silly to feel relieved when Angel showed up at Stronghold without Michael, but that was exactly how Adam felt. Silly because they could use another set of hands that belonged to someone tall. Lexie was being a little tyrant about how many decorations she wanted hung from the ceiling above the bar and pretty much anywhere else she could find to hang things. Mostly hearts. Pink and red hearts. He was pretty sure she'd chosen the cheesy decor with no other goal in mind than antagonizing Patrick, since Lexie was not a pink and red hearts kind of girl, but all of them were suffering for it.

Surprisingly, Patrick was taking the decor in stride, something which clearly riled Lexie up. He was the only one *not* grumbling under his breath, which had Lexie muttering and shooting him suspicious glances. Adam wondered if Patrick was relieved Lexie had only brought cheesy decorations and not her cheesy boyfriend.

"Angel! Oh good, you're here, did you bring the fabric?" Lexie sped over to give the other woman a hug, not even letting her strip off her coat. Angel hugged her back, her gaze flitting around the room, but even though he was only standing about five feet away she didn't look him in the eye. It wasn't exactly dismissive, it was more like being ignored. Either way he didn't like it.

"Yeah, but I need help bringing it in. There's a lot of it."

Fabric? Dear god, what had they gotten themselves into now?

"I'll help," he heard himself saying, and had the satisfaction of seeing Angel look up at him with a startled and wary expression on her face.

"Oh good, thank you Adam!" Lexie beamed at him before her eyes focused over his shoulder. "Andrew, no! The strings are supposed to be long!"

Adam turned around to see Andrew, scissors in hand, about to cut the strings of the hearts Lexie had given him to decorate the bar with.

"They're hitting me in the head."

"They're *supposed* to look like they're floating around your head, you ding dong."

"I'm not hanging them so I get smacked in the face every time I turn around."

"Come on," Adam said, taking Angel by the elbow and turning her around. She looked cute in a squashy purple jacket, matching earmuffs over her ears and a pair of jeans which looked like they'd been broken-in to the point of comfortable perfection. It was so unlike the outfits he'd seen her wear to the clubs, but it fit her personality in a completely different way. Soft. Warm. Touchable. "You brought fabric?"

She gave him a little smile that could best be described as nervous as they walked back out into the February chill. "Yeah, Lexie said she wanted some fabric to hang from the doorways."

Adam sighed. "Of course she did. Where'd you get fabric from?"

"I do a lot of sewing and I have a bunch of reds and pinks I thought might work. Since we're hanging it, I figured I can always wash it and make it into something later."

"That's nice of you. You're making a corset for her too, right?"

"I help where I can. And I like Lexie."

"Oh wow..." Adam was struck a little speechless when Angel's trunk popped open and he got a good look at her idea of suitable fabrics for doorway hangings. He'd been expecting pretty utilitarian pinks and reds, the kind of bright colors he associated with elementary school Valentine's Day parties and which Lexie was currently decorating the club with.

Instead, the trunk was filled with swathes of deep burgundy, dusky rose, and other hues he didn't have names for. They looked rich and inviting. In fact, they kind of reminded him of the decorations in the Arabian Fantasy private room on the second floor of Stronghold. He had a vision of entertaining Angel in that room, with her in one of the many harem girl outfits available, and suddenly he felt all too hot inside his skin, no matter the temperature of the air around him.

"Think she'll like them?" Angel asked.

"I think Patrick will, which is more to the point. Where did you get all these? You can't tell me you have all this fabric laying around the house."

"Oh, I tend to pick up fabric all the time when I see it on sale, even if I don't have something in mind for it yet. I know I'll use it eventually. Here."

Automatically Adam held out his arms to accept the bundle of variegated reds and pinks she thrust at him. Soft, velvety, silky... a myriad of sensations rubbed across his bare hands, which he buried in the fabric.

Bossy little thing when she wasn't in a scene, he thought with some amusement. She hadn't hesitated before loading him down with fabric.

"You didn't already have plans for tonight?" he asked as she held a much smaller bundle of fabric than his in one arm while closing her trunk. "Lexie said she asked you kind of last minute."

Angel gave him a look, as if wondering whether or not the question was somehow loaded. It wasn't, he was grasping at straws on how to talk with a woman whom he'd already been intimate with but that he wanted to get to know on a different level. "No. Originally, I was planning to hang out and do a bit of reading, but I can do it later."

"What are you reading?"

"I'm re-reading Anne McCaffrey's Pern series."

"That's the dragon-riders one, right?"

The blink of surprise he got in return made him grin at her.

"Yeah, have you read it?"

"I tried to a long time ago, when I was still in high school. I couldn't get into it."

"Oh, you should try it again! It's so good, it's one of my favorites," Angel said, her entire face brightening and the small hint of wariness she'd been looking at him with lifting completely. "The newer ones, by her son, aren't as good as the originals, but I still like some of them, and hers are fantastic."

"That's kind of how I feel about the Dune series."

"I love Dune!" Now she was looking at him with something like disbelieving awe. He grinned. Hers was pretty much the usual reaction when someone found out his reading preferences.

"What, didn't think I'd be a sci-fi book nerd?"

"Well you have to admit, you don't fit the image," she said teasingly. Strangely enough, he liked being teased by her. "Who are your favorite authors?"

The conversation continued as Lexie assigned them the task of hanging the fabric on the doorways, which Adam was happy to accept. For one, it got him out of climbing up and down the ladders to hang stuff on the ceiling of the main floor, and for two, it meant more time alone with Angel without him having to arrange it. He manfully ignored the wink Andrew gave him as they headed upstairs.

Angel read more of the newer sci-fi/fantasy series while he had mostly read the older classics, although there was a fair amount of crossover between them. She'd never read any of his favorite newer authors, Robin Hobb, and he hadn't read a lot of what she'd read, mostly because she'd read a great deal more than he had, period.

"I read kind of fast. Although not as fast as Leigh. She's a speed-reader like you wouldn't believe."

"I read kind of slow and I don't have a lot of time for it."

"That's too bad," she said sympathetically, holding up a swatch of glimmering dusky pink fabric for him to nail into place. They were putting two pieces of fabric on either side of the doorways, so people could part them to walk through. "I read as much as possible. My parents didn't encourage television when we were younger and they refused to buy us video game consoles, so it was either play with my brothers or read."

"And you chose to read?"

"I chose both, but a lot of the time reading was preferable. Big brothers are mean."

He chuckled, although a small pang hit him in his chest as he thought about his own big brother. "What'd they do?"

"What didn't they do?" Angel rolled her eyes. "Whenever we played any kind of good guys vs. bad guys game, I was always the damsel in distress."

Adam raised an eyebrow. "Think maybe that's why you like being tied up?"

"Ew, no!" Angel said laughing, trying to shove him and then throwing up her hands in frustration when her tiny push barely moved him. He couldn't help but grin at her obvious annoyance with the observation. "I hated it when they tied me up. Although..." She got the most wickedly mischievous expression on her face as she giggled. "There was one time when we were playing Pirates and my brother Captain—"

"Your brother's name is Captain?"

"Yeah, my parents chose uncommon names for all of us. Anyway, Captain was the pirate and he kidnapped me and tied me to the 'mast' of his ship—which was this big tree in our front yard—and then he and Percy were running around sword fighting and doing all the fun stuff. While they were doing that, I managed to get myself free, make the rope he'd used into a lasso, and I ended up being the one to 'get' the pirate that time." The triumphant smile on her face said her brothers hadn't seen it coming.

"And was Percy thankful for the help?"

"Alas... no. So I tied him up along with Captain and left them there. I told them if *I* could get out of being tied up then they could too."

Laughing with Angel made Adam feel as though tension was melting off of him. He couldn't remember the last time he'd felt this relaxed. Or that he'd enjoyed himself this much. Even though they'd chatted and talked while she'd been at Stronghold, their conversations had always been somewhat constrained. Maybe it had been because there were other people around or because they hadn't known each other well enough yet, but they'd never shared any personal stories like this. He'd liked talking to her but this... this was something more.

Wasn't it?

ANGEL

"What about you?" Angel asked. "Any siblings?"

It was amazing how fast his eyes could change, from the warm blue of a clear sky in summer to the crystal ice of winter in moments. He forced a smile, but Angel could tell it was forced because it didn't come anywhere near his eyes.

"An older brother. He's dead."

"Oh... I'm sorry." She felt absolutely wretched for bringing it up and she didn't know what to say to make it better. They'd been getting along so *well*. Dammit. She'd been surprised when he'd first offered to help and even more so when he'd been pleased they'd been paired together for work, but it had made her happy too.

Seeing another side of Master Adam had made her like him even more. Although he was dressed the same as always, in a white button-down shirt and a pair of dark jeans, he'd seemed more relaxed all around. They'd been having an actual conversation for once, instead of making small talk. And he hadn't seemed angry or grouchy one bit, until now.

"It was a long time ago," he said slowly, avoiding her eyes. "His name was Brian."

Angel bit her lip and then decided to ask the question anyway. Better now than to wonder about it and end up bringing it up later, right? "How did he die?... You don't have to answer if you don't want to."

"No, it's okay." But the way he was avoiding direct eye contact with her said otherwise. She wanted to hug him so hard, but everything about his body language said not to come any closer, not to touch. "It was a drug overdose when he was in high school."

There was a long moment of silence between them. Any pretense of work had stopped and they stood in the quiet hallway, facing each other. Tension was in every line of his body and his eyes seemed to be looking inward at something she couldn't see. Empathy surged.

"I had a friend who committed suicide in high school," she said softly. "I think the worst part about it, for me, wasn't her death. It was wondering why I hadn't been able to prevent it. Why I hadn't seen the road she was on and why I hadn't been able to do anything to stop it."

Finally, *finally*, he met her eyes again. The ice was still there, but it seemed like maybe it had thawed a bit. Angel looked back at him, her face calm even though the emotions roiling in her chest were not. She didn't talk about Hannah often. Ever, really. It was too painful. But he'd shared an integral part of himself and she couldn't not respond. Couldn't not try to reach out.

"Yes," he said, very softly. "That's exactly it."

He studied her face as if looking for the answers, but she didn't know what he saw. The muscles around her mouth and jaw felt stiff. But after a moment he smiled, and this time it did reach his eyes. A bit. And the ice thawed a little bit more.

"Let's go decorate the doors down in the Dungeon," he said, with a lightness neither of them felt.

"It'll be the fanciest jail and doctor's office in D.C.," she replied with cheerfulness that was only slightly forced.

ADAM

They did the Interrogation Room last, the easy camaraderie between them finally coming back after they'd both made a concerted effort to move away from depressing topics of conversation. Returning to their conversation about books had broken the tension completely when she told him about her first fantasy book by Tamora Pierce and he'd immediately known she was talking about the Lioness Quartet.

Angel had howled with laughter. "Those were written for girls!"

"Sexist," he retorted, although his cheeks turned a bit red. "They were good books."

"I know... I... the main character's a girl!"

"And you read the Hardy Boys."

"I know... I know..." she said between fits of giggles. "I have trouble picturing *you*..." And then she dissolved into laughter again.

Adam scowled at her, but she could tell it wasn't for real. There was none of the intensity she'd seen when he was angry with her.

"You're going the right way to get that sexism beaten out of you," he threatened, stepping closer to loom over her. "I've got all the equipment I need right here in this room."

And the atmosphere changed.

He hadn't meant it to. Not really. But she'd looked so beautiful flushed with laughter, so carefree, so different from the way she had upstairs when she hadn't shown him pity or judgment but instead had showed him that she understood. He'd found himself wanting to touch her, to kiss her.

They weren't in a scene now. He could kiss her without breaking the restrictions he'd put on himself.

Watching the laughter fade from her eyes to be replaced with a different kind of warmth, with the sparkle of anticipation and hope, Adam knew he was going to do it. Hell, maybe he'd known since the moment he'd seen her walk in the door.

Her lips parted slightly as he leaned down, slowly enough that she could move away if she wanted to. But she didn't.

Adam brushed his lips over hers gently, testing. A whimper sounded low in her throat at the slight touch and then he found himself cupping her chin in one hand, the other arm snaking around her back as the fabric she'd been holding dropped to the floor around their feet. Granted, they hadn't had much left after doing every doorway in the club, but up until now they'd been more careful with it. He hadn't wanted her to have to wash fabric she hadn't even used for decorations.

Now he simply couldn't care.

All he cared about was how she was responding to him, her mouth obediently opening beneath his, her hands clutching at his shirt as she pressed against him. She tasted sweet and minty and like a woman. Her kiss wasn't passive, like some submissives could be, but it wasn't aggressive either. She met every stroke of his tongue with one of her own, with an enthusiasm that had his already hard cock feeling like granite.

Deepening the kiss, he tightened his arm around her, sliding the hand on her chin to the back of her head so he could hold her securely in place. Somehow, he had to keep control over the situation.

ANGEL

No one had ever kissed her like this.

It wasn't the passion or the skill or even the taste of him... no one had ever kissed her so demandingly. Every muscle in his body was rock hard against hers, his erection digging into her stomach, and yet it was as if his entire focus was on her mouth. Taking her breath away.

Literally. She was getting a bit dizzy, but who cared? Air was overrated anyway.

She loved the way his hands felt on her—controlling, authoritative. There was no guesswork about whether or not he was enjoying the kiss or what he wanted her to do. Adam took what he wanted and it was all she could do to keep up with him. It was the hottest kiss of her life.

When he finally pulled his lips away, she realized exactly how starved for air she was, sucking it in as her chest heaved and she stared up at him. Blue eyes studied her. His gaze was hot but didn't look nearly as wild as she felt. That stung a bit. She wanted to ignite the same kind of uncontrollable heat and need in him that he did in her.

"We should go back upstairs," he said softly. "Before anyone comes looking for us."

"No." She said it automatically, without thinking, her hands bunching into the fabric of his shirt as if she could hold him there by sheer force. As if he didn't outweigh her in sheer muscle mass.

One blonde eyebrow lifted, questioning not only her no but also her judgment in saying it to him. Damn, she wished she could do that, but her eyebrows never cooperated.

"I want... I want more," she said, a little unsteadily but firmly.

The eyebrow lowered as he studied her expression. "You want a scene?"

Now it was her turn to hesitate. She licked her lips. "I want to... do something for you. The past two scenes have been all about me, I want to know you're enjoying yourself as well."

"Trust me, I enjoyed myself," he said, chuckling. Fingers pressed into her back, traveling up her spine and she would have melted against him if she hadn't been so set on getting her way with this.

The balance of their two times together had been sadly out of whack as far as she was concerned. After all, wasn't a Dom supposed to be the one taking his pleasure? And yet he hadn't once. Maybe it was because he wasn't interested in her in that way, although the stiff length still pressing against her body seemed to indicate otherwise.

Still, maybe she should give him an out. Maybe there was another reason.

"We don't have to if you don't want to," she muttered. "It was just an idea."

Perhaps a bad one, but Angel liked to be honest about what she wanted. Especially considering how her acquaintance with him had started off. And right now she wanted him. She'd wanted him the last two times they'd scened together but the last time she'd begged and he hadn't given in. Maybe this was a bad idea.

That conclusion seemed even more justified as he released her and stepped back. She immediately felt cold without him pressed against her.

"Take off your shirt."

"What?" Startled, she looked up at his face. She'd been steeling herself for pretending his rejection didn't matter, for acting like everything was okay even though he was turning her down. The last thing she'd expected was an order to remove her shirt.

A small smile played on his lips. Almost teasing. "We don't have to if you don't want to."

Having her own words thrown back at her so unexpectedly made Angel smile a little too. For a moment she hesitated... but it wasn't like he hadn't seen her butt naked before. She pulled her shirt over her head.

The bra she was wearing was one of her favorites, royal blue with a little bit of soft cotton sky blue lacy edging along the top of the cups. It wasn't the sexiest bra she owned, but she loved the way the blue looked against her skin tone, and it didn't look like he minded it wasn't lacy or see-through.

"Take off the bra and get on your knees."

That shouldn't make her as hot as it did. If any of her previous boyfriends had said something like that to her she probably would have found it derogatory or disrespectful. But when Master Adam said it, she felt desirable and eager to please.

As her shaky fingers unclipped the bra, she realized she'd very quickly and easily transitioned to thinking of him as Master Adam when she'd been thinking of him by his first name only for the entire evening before this moment. Was it because they were about to go into a scene? And was it something she did herself in her head, or had he influenced her thinking?

"Beautiful," he murmured as she carefully knelt down, trying to be as graceful as she could. It wasn't something she was practiced at, but her dance training helped a lot. "Play with those pretty breasts for me, Angel."

Heat flushed her entire body as she cupped her breasts and squeezed them, watching Master Adam watching her. This was not something she'd done before. It was uncomfortable, unnerving and so damned erotic she was creaming her panties.

"Pinch your nipples."

Holy hell. Angel mewled as the spike of pain and pleasure went straight down to her pussy. She sometimes played with her breasts before masturbating, but rarely, and it never felt like this when she did it. Was it because Master Adam was watching? Or because he'd told her to do so in the first place?

"What's your color, sweetheart?"

"Green... Green and impatient, Sir," she said, a little impudently. She knew she was risking being punished, but it was true. To her relief he chuckled again.

"We're not having sex tonight, Angel."

"We're not?" Dammit, she sounded almost wistful. If he didn't want to have sex with her then she wasn't going to beg for it. Of course, if he did want to maybe he wanted to hear her beg...

ADAM

Big hazel eyes gazed up at him and he wondered if she knew how pleasing and tempting she looked. Her breasts were gorgeous, filling her hands completely as she rolled her darkening nipples between her fingertips. Those pouty lips were slightly parted, her skin flushed with arousal and pleasure, and he knew very well that she would have sex with him right now if he wanted it.

And it wasn't that he didn't.

He wasn't going to rush things. Not between them when it came to furthering their relationship or the first time they had sex. Right now he had no idea what she wanted. It was possible that, like a good submissive, she wanted to know she had pleased the man who had Dommed her during two intense scenes. Or it was possible she was as attracted to him as he was to her and she was thinking along the same lines as he was when it came to furthering a relationship.

But no matter the reason, he wasn't going to rush into this. And when they did have sex, unless all she wanted was to play in the club, it wouldn't be when he was feeling rushed and worried someone might walk in on them. Although the latter did add to the erotic illicitness of the situation.

Adam had never played in Stronghold when it wasn't open, although he'd been here during non-Club hours before.

"I'm going to indulge in a little fantasy of mine," he said softly, undoing the front of his pants as he stepped up to her. Angel's almond shaped eyes grew even bigger, flicking back and forth between his face and the bulge in the front of his pants. "One I've had since the night I first met you. Open up, sweetheart. And don't stop playing with those pretty breasts."

Obediently, Angel's lips parted as he reached out and inserted one of his thumbs between them. Her tongue laved over the tip, her mouth closing around the digit eagerly. It did make getting his cock out of his pants slightly more difficult, but he wanted to give her a little time before he began, to make sure this was really what she wanted.

The little moan as her tongue swirled around his thumb said it was. She was eyeing his cock as he stroked it, her expression eager.

Deciding he'd waited long enough, Adam removed his thumb from between her lips and aimed his dick at her mouth. Angel leaned forward eagerly, her tongue snaking out to caress the tip. Catching her by her hair, Adam held her head at the perfect position for her to tongue him, not allowing her to take him in her mouth immediately.

It felt like heaven and hell all at once. He was teasing himself when he could already be enjoying her sweet mouth, but he liked the way she strained against his hand, trying to get to his cock. He liked seeing her tongue licking his cock and the way she kept looking up at him between her eyelashes, to see if she was pleasing him. No worries there.

"What's your color, Angel?"

"Green, Sir." She looked up at him. *And impatient,* her eyes seemed to say.

"Good girl."

Watching his cock slide between those little bow-shaped lips was as satisfying and erotic as he'd fantasized about. Angel didn't have a big mouth, but she stretched her jaw open to accommodate him eagerly. He felt the gentle scrape of her teeth along the underside of his cock, but he didn't chide her for it. Adam happened to be one of those men who liked a bit of teeth when he was getting head. Teeth, tongue, and suction... the best parts about getting a blow job.

She leaned forward, her hands starting to move off of her breasts and towards him and Adam growled at her.

"Keep touching yourself."

The little moaning whimper vibrated along his cock and his knees almost buckled.

"Pinch your nipples. Hard. And twist them," he said hoarsely.

As she followed his instructions she kept up the little noises, causing tiny changes in the sensations running along the surface of his cock. Holding her head securely in place, he began to gently pump his hips back and forth, watching as the shiny length slipped easily between her lips. Tilting her head back slightly so he could see her eyes, the vision was everything he'd fantasized about... and it felt incredible.

Even though he was holding her in place, she was actively participating rather than just providing a place for him to thrust his dick. Her tongue explored the bottom of his cock and the suction of her mouth was never-ending. If she'd been allowed to put her hands on him he was sure he wouldn't have lasted a minute—he'd told her to play with her breasts because he liked the visual, but it had turned out to be an inspired move.

ANGEL

This wasn't giving a blowjob, this was having her mouth *taken*. It was hot as hell too. As much as Angel wanted to try and take control of what was happening, because in her head that was how giving head worked, she loved it every time Master Adam denied her control. She'd never let a man take over her mouth like this, but if she didn't trust him after two scenes where she'd been tied up, how could she not trust him now?

There was something incredibly sexy about him having complete control, the way he was careful with how far into her mouth he thrust, the way he watched her to make sure she wasn't gagging or choking. Any time she did start to gag, he would pull back and thrust shallowly a few times before going in deep again. Enough time to allow her to get her breathing and gag reflex back under control. It was that kind of consideration which made it so easy for her to submit to him and allow him to do with her what he wanted.

A shudder went through his body.

"I'm going to cum, Angel," he rasped, and his hands loosened on her head. She realized he was giving her the opportunity to pull back in case she didn't want him to cum in her mouth.

Normally she didn't care one way or the other, but with him she found she really, really wanted to take this all the way through. She wanted to have him cum in her mouth and swallow him down. She leaned forward, sucking hard, and his fingers tightened in her hair as he groaned.

He pulsed between her lips, the head of his dick nestled against her throat so she couldn't even taste him, all she could feel was the warm fluid spurting into her as she swallowed convulsively. Something which felt remarkably like triumph sparked in her belly and her pussy clenched. It was the only time she'd ever become even more aroused when a guy came in her mouth. Her jaw ached a bit, her knees were getting sore, and her nipples were throbbing from the abuse she'd put them through while Master Adam used her mouth. Like everything else she'd done at the club with him, it had been one of the most intense sexual experiences she'd ever had.

The almost awed look he gave her as he slipped his softening cock from her mouth made her feel like a sex goddess. A warm glow suffused her body even though she hadn't come, because this time she'd given *him* pleasure instead of the other way around.

The salty, slightly sweet taste of him filled her mouth now, as he ran his thumb over her swollen lips. The expression on his face was almost tender, his touch gentle.

Noise outside of the room made them both look up and remember they were in the club, they weren't alone and they were supposed to be helping. Adam immediately stuffed himself back into his pants as Angel grabbed her bra and shirt and pulled them back on.

A rueful smile crossed Adam's face as he helped her back up to her feet. "That was wonderful, sweetheart." Brushing the hair back from her face, he placed a small kiss on her mouth and she thrilled to the touch. "You're going to be here tomorrow for the dance, right?"

"Of course," she said, smiling up at him as he placed his hand in the small of her back and propelled her back towards the door. This could have so easily been just a scene, but it was a good sign he was asking about tomorrow, right? That meant maybe he wanted to see her again.

Even if all he wanted to do was scene with her at the club, it wasn't like there were any other guys she was interested in at the moment. She could live with that until either he or she found someone else they were interested in.

"Good." His voice lowered as he pulled her close for a moment, his lips next to her ear. "I'm sorry we don't have time now, but I fully intend to take care of you later."

She had a stupid, silly grin she couldn't wipe off her face as they gathered up the fabric and went back upstairs to join the rest of the helpers.

16

ANGEL

The upstairs of the club had been completely transformed by the time Angel and Adam came back up from the Dungeon. Clearly, Lexie had focused most of her decorating efforts there. Hearts dangled from the ceiling of the bar, their ends brushing the top of Andrew's head as he moved around behind it, more hearts and streamers came down from the ceiling over the dance floor, and red and pink gels had been inserted into the lights to give the room a rosy glow. The stage was clear except for a spanking bench which had been set up in the middle of it.

"Patrick's doing a spanking demonstration tomorrow night for the party," Adam said, seeing where Angel was looking. He grinned, his fingers slowly massaging the small of her back in a way that made her want to melt. "Turning lots of heart-shaped objects nice and pink."

Angel laughed. "Sounds like fun."

"You won't need *him* to do that for you," Adam said firmly, steering her over to where the rest of the helpers had gathered.

Andrew was coming out from behind the bar to join them as well. Patrick and Lexie were standing on opposite sides of the table with

Olivia and several others, all chatting. Angel had met all of them, although she'd spent a lot more time with the friends who weren't there. While she would have gone to the side closest to them, which would have put her and Adam between Will and Rick, she was a little surprised to find herself led around to the opposite side of the table and placed between Olivia and Mistress Lisa instead, with Adam standing behind her.

Which of course meant she couldn't twist around to see his expression without being totally obvious. She knew Doms were supposed to be kind of possessive, so did that mean Adam considered her to be his? Or was it a post-scene kind of possessiveness? At some point she was going to have to let him know she would like to see him for more than club scenes, but this obviously wasn't the time.

"Just in time, we were about to have a celebration drink," Rick said, grinning as Andrew put a tray full of shot glasses down on the center of the table. His eyes flicked over Angel's flushed face and she wondered if he could tell what she and Adam had been doing down in the Dungeon. Immediately her face heated even more. Behind her Adam shifted closer, his hand on her hip and she *really* wished she could see his expression. "I got an official job offer at Westwood High School and as of this summer I'll be moving up to this area!"

Everyone cheered, although it was obvious they'd already heard this and it was being repeated for Adam and Angel's benefit. Angel chatted with Lexie and Karen, Mistress Lisa's submissive, while Rick and Adam talked about places Rick was thinking about living. Karen seemed interested in the self-defense classes too, which ended up pulling the mistresses into their conversation.

It ended up being a great way to finish the evening, with no awkwardness possible between her and Adam, because there were too many other people to talk to. Although she kind of wished they could have gotten a private word, she wasn't sure what she would say.

Hey, I like you, can we date outside the club?

After all, wasn't a Dom supposed to make the first move? From what she'd read, it seemed like the submissive always had the option to end the relationship if they didn't like the direction the Dom was headed in, but the Dom kind of led the way. Maybe she should wait and see what Adam said.

He walked both her and Lexie to their cars, which were next to each other in the parking lot, giving the younger woman a kiss on the forehead and Angel a kiss on the cheek right next to her mouth. If she'd turned her head a little bit their lips would have pressed together. But she wasn't going to push it.

"See you tomorrow," he murmured, and then he was gone. Angel sighed. Tomorrow couldn't come too soon.

ADAM

The club was packed. Adam kind of hated to say it, but it looked like Lexie's theme party was inspired. Truthfully, none of them had thought the club would be any busier than a normal Valentine's Day, but with it decorated and the party advertised to the members, it seemed like a lot of people had changed their plans from previous years. Lexie had been right, and Patrick had been wrong.

Maybe that was why the big man was looking so grumpy. Or maybe it was because he was watching Lexie and her boyfriend Trevor on the dance floor. Her boyfriend who was obviously staring at the other women in various states of undress. Either Lexie didn't notice, or she wasn't bothered by it, but Patrick and her other self-declared big brothers definitely had and definitely were.

Adam couldn't entirely blame the kid, these were obviously not the surroundings he was used to and there were a lot of things to stare at for a young man, but he didn't like how the kid was doing it while he was hanging all over Lexie. Or what ideas he might be getting. Yeah, he was going to be keeping an eye on that.

Olivia had volunteered to be Dungeon Monitor tonight so she was currently out of sight, but Hilary and Liam were on the dance floor nearby, and he could tell Liam was watching Trevor and Lexie too. Andrew was behind the bar, keeping an eye on the alcohol intake of everyone.

Adam grimaced. He wouldn't be able to leave the floor to go play with Angel either without feeling guilty and worrying in the back of his head about what might be happening up here. Not that Angel was here yet. It hadn't taken him very long to scan the room twice, to make sure, even though he'd asked Jared when he came in.

It didn't bode well that the big man was here rather than out with Marissa, especially since Jared hadn't been around at all last weekend. But the stoic, blank look on Jared's face had kept Adam from asking any questions. Adam felt bad. He'd been so wrapped up in what was going on with Angel, he hadn't even noticed until now that Jared hadn't been around the past couple of weeks.

He'd have to make it up to the big guy later.

"You know, you look like one of those things Lexie's always calling us," Adam said, coming up beside Patrick. The man's heavy arms were crossed over his chest and he was glaring at the dance floor. More specifically, at one particular couple on the dance floor. Adam hoped the submissives who offered up their bottoms for Patrick's spanking demonstration liked a good, hard spanking because it didn't look like the owner was in the mood to go gentle.

"Sentinels?"

"Yeah, that's the one."

"I can't believe I let her in the club."

There was a long silence as the pounding beat of the music throbbed. Lexie laughed, her head tipping backwards as Trevor spun her around. He wasn't a bad looking kid. Black hair, dark eyes, naturally tanned skin with a bit of an olive tint to it, the kind of muscles a guy who played sports would have, but Adam didn't miss the way Lexie's eyes still constantly veered over to where Patrick was standing. She might have been checking to see if she was still being watched, but it didn't look like she cared who else might be watching her other than Patrick.

"Has she tried to leave this floor with him yet?"

"No," Patrick said, sounding both relieved and disappointed at the same time. Probably disappointed because it meant he couldn't kick Trevor out and relieved because he didn't have to think about what reasons Lexie might have for such a move. He sighed. "Stay here for a bit, I need to check on something in the office."

Watching the dance floor was no hardship, especially because his current position also allowed him to watch the front door. There were a lot of couples and as many singles on the dance floor, the lounge area was basically deserted. Adam grinned a little bit as he saw a couple submissives outright flirting with Kris, a shy but competent Dom, on the opposite side of the dance floor. Maybe it was the party atmosphere, but it did seem like people were being more outrageous than usual.

Next to Lexie and Trevor, two female submissives were dancing with a Dom, and putting on a bit of a show for him and everyone else. Touching, snatching an occasional kiss. Every time he caught them touching each other inappropriately they earned a smack on the ass, but every time they managed a kiss—despite his maneuvering—they each received a kiss from him as well. It was a game and one all three of them were obviously enjoying, but Trevor was enjoying watching the two women touch and kiss each other just as much. Lexie was watching as closely, her body swaying in time with the music and her boyfriend.

"Master Adam," purred a voice to Adam's left. "I was hoping to see you here this evening." Laurie, a vivacious and curvy redhead shifted closer to him, almost touching. "Are you playing tonight?"

"I am, but I already have a scene set up, I'm waiting on my part-ner," he said, trying to shift away. Unfortunately, because the club was so crowded, he didn't have very far to go.

Laurie tilted her head as she looked up at him. While she was very attractive and they'd played before, months ago, the invitation didn't appeal to him at all. And it had nothing to do with her and everything to do with the woman he was waiting on.

"We could play while you wait... or dance."

Adam scowled down at her. "Shouldn't you be waiting in the Lounge for someone to come to you?"

"No one's doing that tonight," she said, sidling closer and pressing her breasts against his arm. "But if it bothers you, you can always punish me for it."

"Someone needs to spank you, but it's not going to be me," he said. "But if you keep this up, I'll make sure Patrick uses you for his demonstration." Laurie's cheeks paled. She was more than a bit of a brat, but she didn't have a very high pain tolerance; both of them knew Patrick's preferences would be way too rough for her.

Looking back over at the entrance of the club, Adam's breath caught in his throat.

What the hell is she wearing?!

Straps crisscrossed Angel's body, bright red leather, in the outline of a bathing suit, but there was nothing between the leather straps. Small rectangles covered her nipples and her pussy lips, but otherwise the entire 'outfit'—if it could be called that—was made up of those thin straps, crossing her creamy skin. Lust and possessive rage boiled through him and it was all he could do to keep from striding across the room and covering her up. Preferably with himself.

Looking up she caught his eye and her face brightened.

Next to him, Laurie sighed loudly. "Is she your partner for the evening?"

"Yes," he looked down at the attractive little sub and smiled apologetically. "Don't worry Laurie, there's going to be plenty of people here tonight." Breaking his eyes away from Angel had been difficult but necessary.

What was it about the woman that made him feel so out of control? So much like a barbarian? Maybe it was the leather, because his head was dancing with visions of hauling her over his shoulder and carrying her away like a prize. His brother had always joked they were descended from Vikings and right now he was feeling all too much like one. But he had to control his impulses—not only was there Lexie to look out for, but Patrick had specifically asked him to stay on this floor while he attended to whatever it was he needed to in the office.

He had the feeling a couple of minutes next to Angel, trying to keep his hands off all the skin she was showing, and he was going to forget both responsibilities.

ANGEL

Her fingernails bit into the skin of her palms.

I won't look over there again. I won't.

As if the image of the pretty, petite redhead pressing her breasts against Master Adam wasn't already burned into her brain. When she'd first walked in he'd looked up, seen her, and then turned right back to his conversation with the redhead. Smiling at the obviously flirting submissive. Encouraging her. Not that Angel could blame the woman for trying. Master Adam looked particularly good tonight. Not at all Valentinesy, but she hadn't expected him to. He was wearing leather pants with his usual button down shirt. Which had been unbuttoned about halfway down. Damn him for looking so casually sexy.

Had she misread his intentions last night?

Okay, so she didn't expect him to immediately break off mid-conversation just because she'd walked in the door, but she'd been here close to ten minutes now. Surely if he was interested in her, he could have wrapped up the conversation by now. Or did he plan on playing with more than one person tonight? The little ache beneath her chest which had started when she'd first seen him with the other sub was growing larger.

But it wasn't like she had any real claim on him. Heck, she had no idea what he'd done with himself on the two nights they'd scened together after she'd left. Maybe he'd gone and found himself a pretty redhead.

There was nothing between them, not really, and so no reason for her chest to feel so tight or like she was about to cry. Just because she'd had him in mind when she'd talked herself into wearing this ridiculous contraption.

Maybe it was a ridiculous outfit. Silly and not sexy. Or way too much. She felt silly right now, coming by herself, looking like this. Leigh was calling Michael tonight and had said Angel should go to Stronghold because it could be a long conversation and she didn't want to have to kick Angel out of her own room for so long. And Mike had a date with a submissive he'd met the week before, although they might show up later. Still, she wouldn't have come alone tonight, especially not dressed like this, if she didn't think she and Master Adam were going to do a scene.

"Hey there, beautiful." The deep familiar voice stopped her and Angel looked up, forcing herself to smile into warm blue eyes. Too bad those blue eyes didn't set her body tingling the way the ones across the room did.

"Hey Rick." He'd told her she could call him that, even in the club, rather than having to refer to him as Master Rick. "What's shaking?"

He studied her expression. "Are you okay?"

"Fine. Wonderful." Taking a deep breath, Angel made her eyes follow her lips. A lot of people couldn't smile from the eyes if they didn't mean it, but she could. She also didn't let her eyes stray over to where Master Jerkface was. "The club looks great doesn't it?"

"It does." Rick's eyes didn't move from her face and she had a feeling she wasn't fooling him. "I think everyone likes it, which should make Lexie happy."

"There's a lot more people here than I thought there would be."

He chuckled and she could feel herself relaxing now that she had someone to talk to, someone to focus on and distract her from the angry, jealous energy pulsing inside of her. "There's a lot more people than we all thought there would be. I'm sure Lexie's going to use that to try and convince Patrick to allow her to plan more themed events for the club."

Angel grinned. "Which will also mean allowing her in the doors again."

"But not past the main floor."

She shook her head and rolled her eyes. "Eventually you guys are going to have to give up on that you know."

Instead of responding, Rick held out his hand. "Wanna dance?"

This time she couldn't help it, her eyes flicked over to where Adam was standing. The redhead was still with him, her hand on his arm, gazing up at him with adoring eyes. Whatever. If he wanted to play with her first then Angel wasn't going to wait around for him. She'd dance with Rick and then she'd leave. As long as she did something before she left then it wouldn't look too pathetic, she wasn't going to wait around for Adam to ask her to be second in his line-up.

"I'd love that."

It took a lot of willpower not to look over at Adam again to see if he was watching as Rick pulled her out onto the dance floor. The music was what she'd once heard described as "industrial." It had a throbbing beat which was easy to dance to, not quite techno, not quite club and completely enthralling. The way the music flowed it encouraged movements that were fluid, sexy.

She didn't know if Rick did it on purpose, but she found herself positioned so Master Adam and the redhead were far enough out of her field of vision she would have to turn to see them. And there was no way she was going to do anything so obvious. It also meant she could relax and dance and enjoy Rick's company, because she couldn't see whether Adam was watching or what he was doing.

Dancing with Rick was fun. His movements were easy to follow, and although their bodies were occasionally pressed up against each other, it was usually because of how crowded the dance floor was. More than once he pulled her up against him to get her out of the way of someone about to step on her or who was moving a little too wildly and enthusiastically.

When the song started to change, signaling that whoever was DJing was blending it into the next song, hard hands came down on her hips and jerked her back. Angel automatically lashed out, her elbow digging into what felt like a rock-hard stomach.

"Ow!"

Her only consolation was that Adam hadn't been expecting it either, which left him gasping for breath as one hand immediately covered the place where she'd jabbed him. Rick burst out laughing. Putting her hands on her hips, Angel glared at Adam.

"What part of 'I teach self-defense' did not get through to you?" she shouted over the music.

Adam's lips thinned as he straightened, still rubbing his stomach. "Come over here where it's quieter."

Giving them both a salute, Rick melted into the crowd as Adam wrapped long fingers around her arm and steered her through the gyrating people and over toward the bar. The acoustics in the club were amazing and the music was still loud but you could still hold down a conversation away from the dance floor.

Yanking her arm out of Adam's grasp, she glared up at him, crossing her arms beneath her breasts. For a moment his eyes flitted down to the way her curves were hefted up by her position, but she ignored that. Well, not ignored, since it made her insides flush with warm pleasure, but she didn't let it distract her.

"What makes you think you can come up behind me and grab me whenever you want?" she demanded.

There was a long pause and she wondered if he was going to try to do the Dom thing on her—not that she was going to go along with it, at least not without a serious attempt at resisting—and reprimand her for her tone, but then his big body seemed to drain of tension.

"I'm sorry. I shouldn't have done that," he said, his hand straying back up to where she'd elbowed him. A little rueful smile crossed his face. "Although you got me pretty good."

Dammit, why couldn't he have stayed hard and mean? That little smile he was giving her made her want to smile back, and the apology sounded completely sincere. Plus she liked he was man enough to acknowledge she'd got him good instead of trying to play it off like the elbow to the gut hadn't affected him at all.

"I'd apologize, but you kinda deserved it for grabbing me." She scowled at him, but she knew she'd lost the edge and intensity to her anger. The little smile playing on his lips said he knew it too. Damn observant Dom.

ADAM

"Yes, I did."

He knew he'd grabbed her too hard the moment he'd done it. The only defense he had was how out of control she'd made him feel. Again. Watching her dance with Rick had been like exquisite torture, because she was beautiful to watch but he'd been roiling with jealousy the entire time. At first he'd been grateful his friend had given her someone to talk to, he'd been all too aware of the dominants eyeing her from the moment she'd walked in, but he'd needed a few minutes to control himself.

He'd taken the time to chat with Laurie for a few more minutes, pointing out some of the other Doms who might be to her liking—ironically Rick had been one of them.

That had taken care of Laurie, but by the time she'd trotted off to approach one of the Doms he'd pointed out, Angel and Rick were already on the dance floor and another submissive had come up to see if she could "serve" him. What was it with the submissives tonight? Normally that kind of thing wasn't the way interactions at the club were handled. The subs were supposed to wait for the Doms to come to them. They could show interest, of course, with looks or smiles or whatever, but they weren't supposed to be the first to approach. It had taken him another few minutes to let her down gently and by that time he'd already reached his limit when it came to watching another man dance with Angel.

Even if the other man was one of his friends.

"So why did you?"

"Why did I what?" Crap, his mind had completely wandered, he'd been looking over the straps covering Angel's body again. Although "covering" might be too strong of a term to use. They weren't covering a whole lot, but the caged look was hot as hell, especially now that he was close enough to see she was wearing matching red leather gladiator sandals. He didn't have a foot fetish, but he liked the way those looked.

"Why did you grab me?"

Not a question he wanted to answer. It made him feel too vulnerable. He decided to give her a partial truth.

"I wanted to arrange the scene we talked about last night."

Her mouth made a little 'o,' as if she was surprised. Which didn't make any sense, but that round little opening made the blood surge to his cock, as if it wasn't already hard enough from looking at her, remembering exactly how he'd used her sweet mouth last night.

"Excuse me, Master Adam?"

With a sigh he turned to see a leggy brunette standing next to him, looking up at him with obvious admiration. Although he'd seen her in the Lounge area before, he'd never talked to her and he didn't know her name. She'd shown up around the same time he'd met Angel, so right around the time he'd stopped playing. She was about the same height as Angel, dressed in nothing but a lacy red thong, black high heels, and dangling hearts from her nipple jewelry. Feeling decidedly impatient, especially as he sensed Angel start to turn away, he reached out and snagged her arm again. Too bad if she thought he was being grabby. At least this time he didn't get an elbow in the gut, she stilled and waited for him as he raised his eyebrow at the interrupting submissive.

To her credit, the brunette blushed, her eyes going back and forth between him and Angel as if realizing she was interrupting something. Then she ruined it by drawing herself up and tilting her head at him in an inviting manner.

"I heard Master Patrick was going to do a spanking demonstration this evening... I was hoping maybe you could give me a more intimate spanking demonstration?"

A low growl built in his chest, but no one would be able to hear it over the music. He didn't know why the subs were propositioning the Doms tonight or why they kept pestering him, but he didn't like it. Still, he wasn't about to be cruel.

"Not tonight," he said curtly. "I suggest you speak with Master Will over there." He nodded at the handsome Dom who was currently at the bar chatting with a few other tops. "He's very good at spanking scenes."

"Oh, thank you." The brunette looked disappointed, but that wasn't his problem. No, his problem was with the other brunette standing very stiffly next to him. Dammit, now what had he done wrong?

"Come on."

Doing his best not to drag Angel, he pulled her over to the wall, nearer the entrance and completely out of the crowd of people. She only resisted a little bit before obviously giving in, although she was still holding herself away from him. Her body language had completely changed again, going from wary but interested and now she was so reluctant she might as well have been holding a sign that said 'hands off.'

It was all very well and good to be able to read her emotions, but not if he didn't understand why she was feeling them or what she was reacting to. She couldn't possibly blame him for another woman hitting on him while she was there, could she?

ANGEL

This was so not happening. She might not have a right to be angry that he'd basically told another woman they could scene together some other time, right in front of her, but that didn't stop her from feeling pissed off anyway.

Not tonight.

The response echoed in her head. Before she heard him say that, she'd managed to convince her emotions she was basically okay with him possibly scening with other women since it's not like they'd talked about being exclusive or even dating. *Ha.* She was totally not okay with it and she should have realized it last night, the second she'd cared about giving him pleasure as much as she cared about getting hers. That he wanted to scene with her tonight and was willing to scene with other women on a different night, and to blatantly say so in front of her, hurt more than she had realized it would.

It was silly of her to think the first Dom she'd be attracted to would want the same things as she did. Sure, they got along, and they had a ton of chemistry, but he was obviously used to doing club scenes, with no emotional involvement.

Funny, but when she'd first gone to Chained, she'd been so worried about being physically hurt that she hadn't even considered the emotional dangers.

"You look incredible," he said, turning her to face him. Angel felt herself a little warmed by the compliment. After all, he was obviously a highly in demand Dom and he wanted to play with her.

For tonight anyway.

Yeah. She wasn't going to be one of those girls who took whatever crumbs were offered to them. That wasn't what she was looking for. Maybe if they hadn't already shared three incredibly intimate scenes that had felt like there was something more going on than sex... but she couldn't keep doing scenes like that when she knew he was scening with other women.

After tonight she could regroup and come back to Stronghold and she would stop scening with him and find someone who wanted the same things she did.

"Thank you," she said, and smiled back at him, but she was immediately aware that, while she'd been able to force the smile to her eyes for Rick, she couldn't do it now. And Master Adam's brow furrowed as he looked down at her, and she knew *he* knew everything was not okay.

When he touched her face, cupping her chin in one hand and running his thumb over her bottom lip, it was such an intimate, sweet gesture, it physically made her chest hurt around her heart. But she was an actress, she knew how easy it could be to make such a gesture seem real. Besides, he probably did care, in the way a Dom cared about a sub whom he'd taken under his wing, but that didn't mean he cared about her in the way she'd hoped for.

"Are you okay? I didn't hurt you when I grabbed you did I?"

"No." She shook her head to emphasize that point. Even though his fingers had been rough he hadn't hurt her. Not then and not physically.

He opened his mouth to say something back, when shouting on the dance floor made both of their heads turn. The words were indecipherable, but there was no mistaking the roar of sound, punctuated by much shriller yips. It was pretty easy to see where the focus of the uproar was, every head in the place was turned, looking at Patrick. And from the glimpses of black hair, bouncing around him, Angel knew whatever was going on must have to do with Lexie and Trevor.

Adam cursed. "I need to find out what's going on. Stay here for a few minutes and I'll come back and we can talk."

"Actually, I think I'm going to go home."

The look he gave her was so incredulous she almost laughed.

Geez... he thought he was something didn't he? Couldn't believe she was about to leave him high and dry when they had a scene arranged. But that wouldn't last long, she'd already witnessed how easy it would be for him to arrange another one.

"But you just got here."

"And now I feel like going home."

The muscle in his jaw tightened, his head swiveling back towards the commotion in the middle of the room before returning to her. "We planned to do a scene together tonight."

"I've changed my mind."

Cries spread out from the center of the room, filled with shock and something like glee. Lexie's shrill scream of "Stop!" was like the cherry on top of the noise sundae. Adam cursed again.

"Stay here. Don't leave." It was an order.

He turned and started to push his way through to the center of the crowd. As much as Angel wanted to stay and make sure Lexie was okay, she couldn't face Adam again tonight.

17

ADAM

It took longer than Adam expected to sort out the chaos which had exploded around Patrick, Lexie, and Trevor. Especially when he and his friends were having to get third hand accounts from the witnesses rather than any of the three who were involved. Patrick had shut down and gone stoic, Lexie was huddled in Hilary's arms crying, and Trevor was icing his jaw. And eye. And ribs.

And the kid was damned lucky it hadn't been more than that.

From what Adam understood, when Lexie had refused to try and sneak out with Trevor and head to one of the private rooms, her idiot boyfriend (and Adam hoped the kid was an ex-boyfriend now) had decided the middle of the dance floor was as good a spot to push things a little farther with their relationship. After all, wasn't everyone else around them doing the same thing? Lexie had told him no.

He bet Lexie had thought Trevor would take the no as it was meant to be. Instead, he'd kept pushing, and unfortunately for him 'no' was a pretty easy word to lip-read, which meant Patrick was there about two seconds later.

It probably would have all ended there, except Trevor had chosen to get in Patrick's face about it and had accidentally pushed Lexie hard enough she fell on the ground.

Exactly at what point and how Trevor had ended up with a black eye, swollen jaw, and bruised ribs, no one had been quite clear on. Justin was guarding the idiot with a grim look on his face, Patrick had shut himself in his office, Jessica was standing over Hilary and Lexie and not letting any of the Doms get close enough to question her, and to top everything off, Angel seemed to have disappeared.

Unfortunately, Adam wasn't able to do anything about that until they got everyone on the main floor calmed down, decided Andrew would do the spanking demonstration while Rick took over his bar duties, at which point Olivia came storming up the stairs practically breathing fire as she headed straight for Trevor.

Which meant Adam spent another twenty minutes playing "keep-away" with Olivia and calming *her* down.

So by the time he was finally able to go to the front desk and find out whether or not Angel was in the club, it had been over an hour since he'd left her by the wall with orders to stay put. Which, apparently, was exactly around the time she'd left.

Dammit.

He wouldn't have minded if she hadn't stayed in one spot for the time he'd been distracted. He did mind her leaving the club without talking to him, almost immediately after he'd told her not to do exactly that.

Trying to storm Patrick's office for her information proved unsuccessful, Lexie had already left with Jessica, Justin, and Chris, and Adam was reduced to texting Michael to ask for Angel's number. Which didn't help his mood any.

It was time to cut his losses and go home. The club was back on track and he didn't have to stick around for any further duties. Tomorrow he'd deal with Angel.

ADAM

This was such a bad idea.

Adam stared at the stairs leading up to the bright red door of the house in front of him.

Hell, calling Angel without asking for her phone number had seemed like a pretty bad idea, which is why he'd put it off last week. Then he'd gone and done it anyway this morning, calling her at least five times. But at least he'd gotten her number from Michael and not from the club, that was less creepy right?

Of course, now he'd gone way beyond the creeper factor by showing up at her house, uninvited. When Angel hadn't answered her phone or texted him back, he'd ended up getting a little panicky and had called Michael to make sure she'd gotten home okay the night before. She had, and was still at home, holed up in her room with the music turned up and her bedroom door locked.

He didn't like the idea that he'd done something to upset her enough she would react this way. On the other hand, she might be a crazy drama queen and acting like this to get his attention, but he didn't think so. A part of him was still pretty doubtful as to her intentions, leftover feelings from when he'd found out she'd been posing as a Domme, but he wanted to find out.

And if it did have to do with him, then he wanted to fix it.

Sitting around his house and waiting for her to call him back was not how he dealt with things. He was hands on and looking for immediate results. Which is how he'd ended up at the address Michael had texted to him. It looked like a pretty nice house. She'd mentioned housemates but she hadn't said how many. Several, probably, going by the size of it.

With a sigh, he picked up the book he'd left on the passenger seat and put it in his pocket. It was the first book in Robin Hobb's *Assassins* trilogy. He'd liked talking to Angel about books and she'd seemed interested in the authors he'd told her about which she hadn't read before. Robin Hobb being one of them. If it turned out she wasn't being a crazy drama queen and she had a reason for leaving the way she had last night and not answering any of his calls this morning, then he figured this was a pretty good peace offering.

Knocking on the door, he heard the low mutter of male voices. Was Michael here? Did he have friends over?

Adam didn't particularly like the idea of the other man feeling so comfortable in Angel's house that he had people over.

The door opened and Adam found himself looking eye to eye with a disheveled looking twenty-something wearing a Cthulu t-shirt. He looked Hispanic, with dark hair and eyes and slightly tanned skin. They weren't the same height, it was just that the man was standing up a step.

Crap. Had Michael given him the wrong address?

"Hey, are you here for the LAN? You're a couple hours early."

"Um... no." Whatever response Adam had expected, that wasn't it. "I'm looking for Angel Jones."

The man's eyes narrowed and swept up and down Adam's body, as if sizing him up. "She's upstairs. Come on in."

Adam stepped through the door, but the guy only backed away a few steps, obviously standing between Adam and the rest of the house. Because of the couch, which was on his immediate left, facing a gigantic television hanging on the wall, there was no way Adam could get by him without using brute force.

"Hey, who's this?"

There were two guys sitting on armchairs on opposite sides of the room, playing what looked like a first-person shooter game. One was like a mini-Jared, stocky and muscular, with a similar dark skin tone and a shaved head. The other one was a skinny, gawky looking white guy with glasses. They glanced over at Adam.

"Are you here for the LAN?"

Before he could answer the question, the guy who'd opened the door answered for him.

"He's here to see Angel."

The game immediately paused, and Adam found himself on the receiving end of three hostile stares. Great. With the game paused, he could hear the faint strains of music coming down from the second floor and he assumed that was where Angel was, which meant he had to get through these guys first. Maybe he could get some information from them, since they seemed to know something was up, before he decided whether or not it was worth it to try and get by them.

But before he could ask anything, the mini-Jared stood up to face him, still glaring. "Are you the Cowboy Casanova?"

"Excuse me?"

"The Cowboy Casanova," the guy repeated.

"He doesn't know what that means, Q." The white guy, who was still sitting in his armchair, groaned. "It's a song. She put it on repeat for two hours this morning. *Two hours.* I can deal with the angry-girl-country shit, but not the same song over and over again. I almost cried with relief when she finally switched over to the Dresden Dolls."

"So, are you?" Q demanded again. Adam might have taken offense except he suddenly realized he was facing what he and his friends would look like to Lexie's dates. Obviously, these guys cared about Angel and knew she was upset, which meant he had to soothe their ruffled feathers before he could get any useful information from them.

"I don't know," he said evenly. "I've never heard the song."

The guy in the armchair immediately launched into song, the twang vaguely country. Basically, sounded like the song was reviling liars and players. Great.

The guy stopped singing and looked at him expectantly, waiting for an answer. Adam's lips twitched. This was not at all how he'd imagined this visit going. He didn't think the translation of the song to the situation was literal, but he had to admit he liked the sound of 'feelings that you don't wanna fight.' The rest of it wasn't good though.

"I hope not," he said.

That made the guy in the armchair chuckle. "What'd you do to her anyway? She hasn't gotten pissed enough to play the Dresden Dolls for months. Normally we're only subjected to the country."

"At least she hasn't switched over to O-tep," muttered the guy next to him. "I never want to see her that pissed again." He sighed and looked Adam over again, some of the tension draining out of him. "I'm Mark. This is Q and Sam."

"Adam." He shook hands with Mark. "I don't know what she thinks I did, I came over hoping to find out. Any hints?"

"All we know is what the music tells us," said Sam. Q glared, first at Adam, then at Sam. Sam was obviously the chatty-Cathy, Q was the most protective and Mark fell somewhere in the middle. "This morning she was upset, something about *Cowboy Casanova* must have been cathartic or she wouldn't have put it on repeat for so long, and now she's moved on to being pissed. *Really* pissed. That's what the Dresden Dolls means."

Adam filed the information away for future consideration. Although, like her body language, knowing her emotional state didn't tell him how she'd gotten that way.

"Does she have any reason to be pissed?" Q asked, obviously not mollified.

"Not that I know of, but it doesn't mean I'm right," Adam said, earning a small smile from Mark. "We were kind of on a... date last night and it got interrupted by some drama going on with my friends." Which was partially true, although something had been going on in Angel's head even before that.

"How'd you get this address? You've never come by here before." Q's eyes narrowed suspiciously.

"Michael gave it to me."

"You're friends with Mike?" It didn't escape Adam's notice that Q also used the shortened name, even though Michael had stated his preference when he'd met the group at Stronghold. Because Q knew Michael through Angel and so that's what he knew him as, or because it would annoy Michael?

"Yeah." Close enough anyway. His turn for a question. "Ah... so which of you are Angel's housemate?"

Sam waved his hand around the room. "We're all Angel's house-mates. It's the three of us and her."

A hard knot seemed to form in Adam's stomach. Which he had no right to feel. It didn't mean anything that she was living with three guys. And had a close guy friend staying with her. But good God, didn't the woman have any female friends other than Leigh? He'd never considered himself a jealous person, but he didn't have any other label for the emotion surging through him right now.

"Didn't tell you she was living with three guys, did she?" Q asked, a little smugly. As if he expected Adam to turn tail and head out the door now, and that satisfied him.

"She'd mentioned her housemates, I assumed she'd be living with women." He cleared his throat, realizing they'd gotten off track. It didn't matter who her housemates were, he was there for *her*. "So, can you see if she'll come down here?"

"Nope." Mark grinned as Adam blinked. "We all know better than to bother her when she's listening to the Dresden Dolls. If she switches back to musicals or country, I'd be willing to try."

"Will you stop me from going up?" Maybe the element of surprise would help him.

Q didn't look happy with the idea, but he didn't answer either. Mark shrugged, a kind of disbelieving expression on his face.

"It's your life."

No wonder Adam hadn't been sure whether or not she was a Domme when he'd met her at Chained. It was obvious Angel had no problem pushing around her housemates when she wanted to, so she had plenty of practice at being in charge. Personally, Adam wasn't that patient. He wanted to know what was going on and if she reacted badly well, then, that would tell him something as well.

"Thanks."

"It's the last door on the right," Mark said as he moved aside so Adam could move past him towards the stairs. As if Adam couldn't follow the music.

Behind him, he could hear Sam chuckle.

"Bye bye boy. Have fun storming da castle."

"Think it'll work?"

"It would take a miracle."

The laughter that followed the *Princess Bride* quotes was not reassuring.

ANGEL

Music wasn't one of Angel's passions, but it was something she indulged in, especially when her emotions were feeling out of control. Maybe if she was a better singer then she'd be more passionate about it, but Leigh was the one with the gorgeous voice. Angel was the one who liked to belt out country or musicals or sometimes rock music as a way of venting her negative energy.

And she had plenty of that, she thought darkly, glaring at her phone.

Adam had called this morning. Five times. At first, she'd thought he must have gotten it from the club, but then Mike had texted her to let her know he'd given Adam her number. The stinker.

Of course, it wasn't Mike's fault since she knew he didn't know the way things had turned out at Stronghold last night. But she was mad at the world. Once she worked through that, she wouldn't be feeling so pissy at Mike anymore. Right now, she was enjoying a nice long wallow in being mad and once it was over she'd leave her room and be as cheerful and happy as ever.

She wondered what had happened to Lexie and the others. She hadn't called them because she knew Lexie would ask about Angel's night and she wasn't ready to talk about that yet. Especially since she knew she wouldn't be able to stop herself from asking what Adam had done after she'd gone home and she needed more emotional armor before she started asking those questions.

So she was sitting in her room, sewing, which kept her hands busy, and belting out the Dresden Dolls which was making her feel a lot better.

Her voice trailed off. Was that a knock at her door?

Worry, immediate and sharp, lanced through her. The guys knew not to bother her right now, which meant the only person who might be knocking on her door right now was Leigh.

When Angel had left the club last night, she'd discovered a disappointing voicemail from Leigh saying she and Michael had talked for a long time and she wasn't ready to give up on him yet. Leigh didn't want to feel like she'd wasted years on a relationship which hadn't gone anywhere. Personally, Angel didn't understand why Leigh would then want to waste more time, but she supposed that was because she didn't have Leigh's optimism about the relationship ending in happily ever after.

Seriously though, could the guy not hold his shit together for twenty-four hours?

Jumping up from her sewing machine, Angel crossed her room and yanked open the door, already ready to start comforting Leigh and call Michael every name in the book.

Angel tried to slam the door on the big, blonde jerk, but he put out his palm too fast. Bastard had reflexes, had to give him that.

Stomping over to her iPod, she hit the pause button and whirled around to see he'd already come into her room and was looking around. Angel scowled.

"What the hell are you doing here?" she asked, crossing her arms over her chest. "And how did you get up here?" She couldn't believe the guys hadn't warned him to stay away. Granted, she wouldn't pit her boys against Adam in a battle of wills... but then that begged the question, what did he want with her so badly?

"I came to see you," he said, peering at the pictures she had tucked into the sides of the vanity mirror on her dresser. There were a bunch, various shows she'd been in, trips with Leigh, hanging out with the boys, and several of her and her family. "Michael gave me the address. And then I followed the music."

Her lips twitched before she could stop it. Dammit, he wasn't going to make her smile. Especially since he wasn't even looking at her. Damn Michael too, for not giving her a heads up.

Having Adam looking at her personal things was unnerving, but she told herself she shouldn't care. After all, it wasn't like he meant anything to her. Angel went back to her sewing machine and picked up where she'd left off when she'd thought she was jumping up for something *important*.

"Are Lexie and Patrick okay?" That was good. Casual.

"Yeah, they're both fine," he said, with a subtle emphasis on the pronoun. Angel's lips twitched again. Trevor must not be. She wondered what he'd done, not that she thought much would have been needed to bring Patrick down on his head. "I don't think Lexie helped her quest to get into the club though."

"If Patrick would let her in with a Dom who knew what he was doing then things probably would have gone very differently," Angel said a little testily. Sometimes the way Adam and his friends reacted to Lexie was amusing, but only because she wasn't Lexie. If she were Lexie's shoes she'd be... well, she'd probably be doing a lot of the same things Lexie was if not more.

Adam sighed. "I didn't come here to talk about Patrick and Lexie."

She refused to look up as he moved away from her vanity and walked over to where she was sitting at her work desk. For a long moment neither of them spoke as she finished the seam she was working on. When she finally glanced up at him, Adam had seated himself in her armchair and was watching her, his expression somehow both blank and conveying his patience.

She turned the machine off and neatly folded up the fabric.

"So why did you come here?" It wasn't an idle question and not one she was asking because it was expected—although he obviously did expect her to. She truly wanted to know. Because it didn't make sense in her head.

"We didn't get to finish talking last night. I told you to stay put and you left." Those blue eyes managed to look hard and accusing without appearing cold. It was all she could do not to squirm in her seat guiltily, even though she knew she shouldn't feel guilty. Frightening how good he was at that.

After a night of contemplation and a morning of music, Angel knew how she felt and what had upset her. It wasn't his fault her perceptions of the situation had been different, and now she was confronted with him she felt her anger slide away. It said something good about him that he'd wanted to check up on her. He was a good guy. She hoped they could salvage a friendship after this and that, like Mike, her attraction to him would fade when she found someone else.

"I didn't feel like talking last night," she said. "I was kind of pissed, a little upset, and I needed some space." Adam shifted in the chair, looking like he was going to say something, but she kept going before he could interrupt her. "I liked you, not just as a Dom but I've liked spending time with you, and since we'd arranged for a... a scene... well, I didn't expect exclusivity because of that but I did think I'd have your attention for the night. So I came in and you saw me, but you didn't seem to care I was there because you were too busy talking with that other woman. And then, right in front of me, you told the other sub that you would play with her on another night ..." Hearing the bitterness creeping into her voice, Angel coughed and moderated it before continuing.

"I felt it was rude. Anyway, it hit me that individual scenes aren't what I'm looking for. I'm not cut out for scening with multiple people or for scening with someone who does. I appreciate the scenes we had and they were wonderful, but like I said, I really like you and I think we could be good friends, but only if things don't get all confused with the physical stuff." The way Adam was looking at her now didn't give Angel a clue as to what he was thinking. And she felt like she was babbling.

Nervously she flicked her tongue across her lower lip and then dragged her teeth across it, keeping any more words from spilling out of her mouth. She'd always been what her dad called a "straight-shoot-er," even when it made her uncomfortable. Maybe it was because she read so many books, but she always felt issues between people could easily be solved with telling the truth as they saw it, rather than hedging or trying to gloss over their feelings.

The silence stretched between her and Adam until she was starting to think maybe he was one of those guys who didn't appreciate blunt-ness either. Which would surprise her, but it wouldn't be the first time it happened.

Finally, he sat forward, resting his elbows on his thighs with his hands hanging between them.

"I think, perhaps, you're working from a misconception," he said. "I haven't scened with anyone but you since you came to Stronghold."

"Oh."

Angel didn't' know how to react to his straightforward and surprising statement. He was right, because if that was true then she'd been harboring a major misconception. The emotions rushing into her —surprise, guilt, hope—along with the quick review going on in her head of every interaction she'd had, and assumption she'd made, left her feeling surprisingly blank. Although an embarrassing heat rose in her cheeks as she realized some of the things she'd implied about him were obviously not true and, while they might not be deliberately insulting, could be considered unflattering.

"I'm sorry... I thought that because of the kind of club it was... I didn't want to assume one thing and so I ended up assuming something else and... I'm sorry," she finished a little lamely.

To her surprise, Adam gave her an encouraging smile. "I realize you're new to the club scene, and I can't blame you for some of your assumptions. But, to clear things up, I had no interest in Laurie last night. Patrick had asked me to stay out on the floor while he handled something in the office and when I saw you, I wanted to drag you off to a private room so I could be the only one to enjoy the delightful outfit you were wearing. Then I didn't want to interrupt your dance with Rick because I didn't have a claim on you for anything other than a scene. I stayed away for a bit longer than I probably should have. But I had no intention of scening with anyone other than you, nor do I have any interest in scening with Laurie or any of the other submissives who approached me last night."

At that, Angel couldn't help but giggle. He sounded so *affronted* the submissives had been approaching him last night rather than following the usual order of things. The look he gave her as she covered her mouth with her hands was both sardonic and slightly amused at her amusement.

"I did try to let them down easily, and when I told Amanda 'not tonight,' that's all I was doing. And as soon as everything from the Lexie-Trevor-Patrick situation was settled, I went home."

"Oh. So..." She couldn't quite bring herself to ask if that meant he wanted more from her than scening at the club, even though his actions and explanation seemed to indicate that. As brash and blunt as she could be, when it came to making the first move with a guy, she was terrible at it.

"I would like to take you out to lunch." He glanced at his watch. "A late lunch. Or an early dinner. Where we can talk and get to know each other some more. Because, while we might make good friends, that wasn't really my intention."

"And... you aren't going to scene with anyone else?" She hated the needy note in her voice, but that was something she didn't want to be making assumptions about.

Adam shook his head, standing up.

"No, and you aren't either." Go figure, any other guy in her life and the simple edict would have had her bristling. He said it and it made her feel all melty and special inside. The smile he gave her was pure temptation as he held out his hand. "So, food?"

⚘ 18 ⚘

ADAM

Adam was in a damned good mood and it had nothing to do with the fantastic food he was eating. Well, maybe something to do with it. But it had a lot more to do with his current company. Taking her out of the house for dinner while her housemates looked at him with something approaching awe—even Q—had done wonders for him.

They'd both made assumptions rather than talking things out, something he'd meant to fix even before they had their scene last night but they hadn't gotten the chance. Because he'd been dense enough to stay away and keep talking to Laurie without thinking about how Angel might interpret that, and because he hadn't clarified with Angel exactly what he wanted their relationship to be, she'd ended up feeling insecure and rejected.

He could fix that over dinner tonight because every minute he was spending with her was making him want to spend even more time with her.

Once they'd gotten to the restaurant it had been surprisingly full— surprising until he remembered it was Valentine's Day weekend. Fortunately, it was still early in the evening and Angel knew the hostess, so they'd managed to get a seat. Turned out she knew the waitress too, who had immediately come over with a plate of piping hot fresh bread, the kind which had obviously been made at the restaurant rather than ordered in. It was filled with herbs and spices and had a cheesy crust.

And the way he and Angel were both going at it, they were going to have to ask for some more.

"Did you use to work here or something?" he asked, after a third server stopped by their table to say hello.

"No, Q did. He was a bartender here. Eventually he cut back to weekends and now he comes in occasionally if he needs extra money or if someone needs a shift covered."

"Oh... I didn't realize restaurants allowed things like that."

"Normally they don't, but Q's uncle bought into the restaurant a couple of years ago and he's now married to one of the other owners," Angel said, grinning. "We still come here all the time."

Their server, a peppy blonde, appeared with a plate piled high with fried food in her hand, setting it down on the table even though they hadn't ordered anything.

"From Cara," she said, before briskly stepping off again.

"I love this place," Angel said with a dreamy sigh, reaching out to snatch one of the little morsels off the top of the pile and dunk it in the creamy looking sauce. She glanced at Adam. "Fried artichoke hearts. They know it's my favorite."

"They look good," Adam said a little cautiously. Fried food wasn't normally his favorite thing, but he'd never had fried artichokes before so he figured it couldn't hurt to try. Following Angel's lead he dipped it in the sauce.

Watching him, Angel smiled as he took a bite and then eyed the plate. Quickly he reached out and knocked over half the pile of fried hearts onto his bread plate.

"Hey!"

Laughing, Angel reached out to snatch some back, dragging the rest of the pile back onto her plate.

"What? They're good!" They were more than good. Crispy on the outside, creamy textured on the inside, and the dipping sauce gave them a tangy zing that had his taste buds singing.

"They're mine!"

"Sharing means caring," he intoned piously, causing another outburst of laughter from her.

"I've stabbed people for less," she threatened. "Mike had fork marks for a week."

"They're worth the risk," he told her, reaching for another. That she didn't do more than glare made him feel incredibly smug.

By the time they'd ordered and their food had come, at least half the servers and one of the managers in the restaurant had swung by their table to say hello. The rest had waved to Angel. It didn't make for the steadiest flow of conversation, but it did give Adam an opportunity to observe her with other people. It was obvious everyone at the restaurant liked her, she was friendly but not flirtatious with the guys, although more than one of them gave Adam a challenging look. From what he could tell, she was a friendly, tactile, outgoing person. Some of the guys might misinterpret a hug from her, but they couldn't miss the fact that she was obviously out on a date.

"Everyone here seems to like you, and not just because Q used to work here," he said, waving his fork in a little circle to indicate the workers in the restaurant who kept stopping by to say hello.

"I'm friendly with a lot of people," she said with a little shrug and another smile.

Friendly with, not *friends* with. It was a small but important distinction.

"Well, all of my friends like you," he said. "In fact, I'm pretty sure you'll be hearing from one of the girls soon. Jessica and Hilary are dying to spend more time with you."

Immediately Angel's face brightened.

ANGEL

"I like them too," she said. "And Lexie. And Olivia."

They were fun. She also didn't have any close girl friends anymore, other than Leigh. They'd all drifted apart over the years. But she liked the women at Stronghold. They were fun, and she knew they wouldn't judge her for the things she wanted in the bedroom. Jessica would be the last person to judge her, considering.

"Angel? Where'd you go?"

She blinked. "Sorry, I was thinking about your friends."

The look he gave her reminded her of Mr. Grouchy. As if her answer had disgruntled him somehow.

"What about my friends?"

"I was thinking Jessica seems incredibly secure... I'm not sure I could handle a relationship with two guys," Angel said, repeating her thoughts out loud for him. She trusted he knew she wasn't being judgmental. "I'd always be worried I wasn't keeping them both happy. It must be exhausting."

The expression on Adam's face lightened as he chuckled. "I think Jessica would agree with you about the exhausting part, but she doesn't seem to have any trouble keeping them both happy. As long as she's happy, they are."

Which seemed a little opposite to Angel. Wasn't it the submissive who was supposed to keep the dominant happy? Then again, she supposed in any relationship, if one person wasn't happy the other one wouldn't be either. Well, any good relationship.

The rest of dinner they ended up talking about each other's various interests. They had a lot in common, like their taste in books and movies, and as many things they were complete opposites on. While Adam was obviously athletic and spent time in Liam's dojo, he also loved to solve math problems for fun. Angel hadn't done math that wasn't necessary since her freshman year of college. When pushed, he admitted he was as likely to be playing his guitar as he was playing with numbers, but it still boggled her mind.

For his part, Adam seemed somewhat disturbed by her lack of desire for a nine to five job. He wasn't the first person to have that reaction, but he was the pushiest, despite how subtle he was. Once they got on the topic of jobs and careers she listened to a carefully worded spiel about how his company helped people find jobs. It wasn't until about ten minutes in that she realized he wanted to do the same for her.

And was disgruntled when she called him on it and when she told him she liked having part-time jobs.

"What about health insurance? And retirement?"

Angel shrugged, enjoying teasing him. "I'm pretty healthy and when I get arthritis and can't sew or teach self-defense anymore, I'll take over at my parents' dance studio."

"How are you going to do that if you have arthritis?" he asked, almost fiercely. It was kinda cute how concerned he obviously was, although she didn't know whether or not to be insulted he didn't seem to think she was capable of taking care of herself.

Then again, it's not like she was giving him any other kind of impression. Angel laughed.

"Relax, I have an IRA I put money into, I'm teasing you." She grinned at him, but Mr. Grouchy was not entirely appeased.

"What about health insurance?"

"I have basic insurance through the college I teach classes at."

Adam growled. "Then why are you torturing me?"

"Because it's fun? And you're so cute when you're grouchy?" She batted her eyelashes at him. The man wanted to smile, she could tell, but he didn't. Very impressive self-control. Instead he leaned forward, his eyes looking directly into hers.

"You, sweetheart, are going the right way for a—"

"Dessert?" Julia asked brightly, appearing at their table.

"I'm stuffed," Angel said, glancing at Adam. "But I could share something if you wanted..."

"No, if you're full then I'm not going to push more food on you," he said, a little blandly for someone who, she was pretty sure, had been about to threaten to spank her. Heck, she heard those words from Mike often enough, and they always gave her a little thrill when she could tell he meant it, but that wasn't anything like the shiver of excited apprehension that had trickled down her spine when Adam had pinned her in place with those bright blue eyes and started in with his deep, threatening tone.

It wasn't threatening in a way that made her feel frightened though. Well maybe a little. But that only added to the excitement it aroused.

Her response to him was a little unnerving. Sometimes initial attraction could fade, especially in the face of easy-going camaraderie, and she couldn't imagine any other guy saying something similar without her laughing at them. With Adam, she had absolutely no urge to laugh and she could feel her nipples hardening inside her bra.

"Okay then, here you go," Julia said, setting the check down on the table and clearing away the last of the dishes in front of them.

"Thanks, Jules," Angel said, automatically reaching for the little black book.

It disappeared from underneath her fingertips. Angel looked up and scowled at Adam to absolutely no effect.

"In case it was unclear, this is a date," he said, a little dryly, tucking a credit card into the book's pocket.

"I usually go Dutch on first dates," she replied stubbornly, resting her elbow on the table as she held out her hand.

"Usually, meaning not always, and this is one of those times."

She sighed, recognizing there was no way Adam was going to give in on this one. "Well, thank you for the lovely dinner."

"You're welcome," he said, looking pleased she wasn't going to argue even though his voice was firm. Arguing wouldn't have done her any good anyway. And now she knew she'd have to be sneakier if she wanted to pay for things in the future.

She liked the whole being paid for thing, it made her feel all warm and fuzzy inside and taken care of... but she also didn't think the guy should have to pay every time. She knew very well from her friendships that guys could get kind of fed up with always paying, especially if the girl they were dating had expensive tastes or took the gesture for granted. It was something to be appreciated, not expected.

"I brought you something," he said after Julia had picked up his card to run it. He reached into his pocket and set it down on the table.

Angel blinked and picked the book up, studying the gorgeously illustrated cover.

"Robin Hobb... the author you were telling me about."

"I thought you might like to borrow it. And if you like it, you can borrow the other two afterwards."

Strangely, her eyes ached a little bit, the way they did when she wanted to cry. Probably because this was one of the most insightful things a guy had ever done for her. Most of them understood she loved to read, but even if they shared her love they wouldn't have thought to bring by a book they thought she'd like. It was better than flowers or candy or... well... anything he could have brought her.

"Thank you... I... thank you."

Angel felt a little twinge of regret. Maybe she should have said she wanted dessert, even though she hadn't been hungry... just because she didn't want tonight to end. But Julia was already returning with the check and then Adam was helping her into her coat. As he captured her hand in his, she thought this was one of the nicest first dates she'd ever been on.

"What are you doing tomorrow?" he asked, once they were comfortably settled in his car with the heat blasting on them. They'd gotten a good parking space, near the entrance to the restaurant, but now that the sun had gone down there was even more of a bite to the air than usual.

"I usually spend Sunday hanging around the house, trying out recipes. I like to bake."

"A little domestic goddess, aren't you? Baking, sewing... do you crochet too?"

"Knit. Sort of." At his questioning look, Angel shrugged. "I can only do scarves. I haven't figured out how to do anything else yet."

He smiled at her as they pulled out of the parking lot. "My friends are coming over tomorrow if you'd like to join us. The girls should be there too."

"On Valentine's Day weekend?"

"This is the first year it's affected anyone other than Jared," he explained. "Normally we get together and hide out. This year it'll be a more like a party—but without Lexie's decorations."

"Yeah, I'd love to come," Angel said, enjoying the warm fluttering feeling in her stomach. She liked his friends, and it was always a good sign when a guy wanted to hang out with you right away, right?

Not that they hadn't been getting to know each other for a couple weeks now, even if things had gotten a little backwards and sideways since they'd gotten naked together before ever going out on a date. She took it as a good sign he wanted her there.

"Good."

When they got back to her house, Adam walked her up to the door even though she told him it wasn't necessary. He gave her another one of those looks that made her feel all hot and bothered inside and her knees get a little wobbly and she decided not to argue with him.

"Do you want to come inside?" she asked, feeling a little nervous despite the fact he'd already been in her house earlier in the day. She wasn't sure how he would take the invitation, all things considering.

"No, I've got to get home and make sure everything's ready for tomorrow."

"Oh, right," she said, smiling brightly. Her emotions felt a little jumbled, the weirdest mix of relief and disappointment flickering through her.

Before she could put her key in the lock, he put his hand over hers, stopping her. His other hand slid along her neck and cradled the back of her head, his skin a little cold but quickly heating as his fingers buried in her hair.

"Because I have a feeling your housemates are going to be right inside..."

Then his lips covered hers, and the faint sounds of a congregation of video-game-playing-males melted away. By God the man could kiss. He held her head, gently but firmly, as his tongue probed her mouth, gently but insistently. It was an extremely thorough kiss which made her feel like she was boiling from the inside out, barely aware of the freezing air around her.

When he finally pulled away, her back was now pressed up against the door and she was practically panting.

"I'll see you tomorrow," he said, looking extremely satisfied as she stared up at him. Another light pass of his lips over hers and then he was heading back to his car.

"Um... yes... see you tomorrow..." she called after him, awkwardly fumbling for words. "Thank you for dinner!"

He gave her a grin and a little wave as he got in his car. Although he started it up right away, she saw he was still looking at her, patiently waiting for her to go inside before he left. Now as a self-defense teacher, that was a sweet gesture she could approve of for more than one reason. She wished it didn't mean he got to watch her drop her keys as she fumbled to get them in the doorknob.

Twice.

❧ 19 ❧

ANGEL

"Crap... crap... crap... why is everything I have to wear crap?" Angel half-wailed, yanking off yet another shirt that had looked perfectly fine on the hanger and yet wasn't at all what she wanted once she put it on. The V-neck of her purple sweater seemed too low, the black jeans were too tight with her pink shirt, the blue cardigan made her look like she had ten extra pounds on her stomach, and it was too damn cold out to wear a skirt or dress. Which would probably be too fancy anyway.

When the phone rang it was a welcome relief, even though it was playing Wyclef Jean's *Take Me As I Am* which meant Leigh was finally calling her. Angel might not be super thrilled about Leigh and Michael getting back together, even if she'd expected it, but even listening to Leigh gush happily (like she always did when she and Michael worked something out) was preferable to trying on yet another fail outfit.

"Hey baby."

"Hey baby!" The happy, lilting note in Leigh's voice was always good to hear, even though Angel no longer trusted in Michael's ability to make it last. "How are you?"

"I'm good, although I think the more pertinent question is, how are you?"

"Good. Wonderful. Michael and I had a long talk and I think it helped. He's worried about being able to provide for me and provide for a family and I think he now realizes that a lot of his anxieties are in his head."

"Does this mean you're engaged?"

Leigh laughed. "No. Not yet. But we talked about it and he says when he proposes he wants it to be absolutely perfect."

The warm wistful tone made Angel want to smack Leigh on the back of the head. She knew very well that all Leigh wanted was to be engaged and married, she wouldn't care if Michael did some broad, sweeping gesture when he proposed. Which meant, once again, Leigh was setting aside what she wanted in favor of letting Michael put off proposing for even longer.

"So, what's your idea of a perfect proposal?"

"Oh, something small and sweet..." The wistfulness was back in full force. "I'd love it if he did it this spring during the cherry blossom festival. He knows how much I love cherry blossoms. Or, maybe at the restaurant when he first told me he loved me."

Yeah, Michael knew how much Leigh loved cherry blossoms, but it was Angel who went with her to see them every year. For Leigh, a perfect proposal would include Michael *going* to the festival at all. He'd been once, the entire time they were together, back when he and Leigh were in college.

Maybe he would prove her wrong and Leigh's optimism would be proven right. Either way, Angel had learned from experience that being negative would only make Leigh defensive.

"That would be sweet."

"Yeah... so what have you been up to this weekend? How was Stronghold and Master Adam?"

Angel filled Leigh in on the tumultuous events of the past forty-eight hours. It felt good to vent about her jealousy and her uncertainties, even though Adam had reassured her on that measure. Talking it through with a friend was always helpful. Especially when said friend was pretty sure the guy in question was wild for you.

"So now I have no idea what to wear. I'm looking for casual but sexy but not like I'm trying too hard... and everything I have is wrong."

"What about the purple sweater?"

"You don't think it's too low cut?"

"I mean, it's low cut but no I don't think it's *too* low cut. I think it's low cut enough. If you're that worried about it wear your teal scarf with the purple embroidery."

Angel nibbled on her thumbnail as she separated the two articles in question from the pile on her bed. "That looks good... see, I should have called you in the first place."

"I've told you not to try and get dressed for a date without me, you get all stressed out."

Wasn't that the truth.

"What do I wear with it? The black jeans are too low rise."

"Wear the medium blue ones with the bling on the butt. Adam's an ass man."

Angel laughed. "I knew that, but how did you know that?"

"Because every time I was at the club, I got to watch him staring at your fine ass," Leigh responded teasingly. Angel giggled. She'd always thought she had a pretty good butt, but it was nice to have it confirmed.

"He also likes touching it," she countered. "Which the bling doesn't exactly encourage."

"Do you want him to touch? Wait, did you guys..."

"No, of course not, I would have told you." Angel rolled her eyes. "Silly woman. But that doesn't mean we won't..."

"You haven't known him for very long."

"He brought me a book," her voice was still filled with the wonder of the moment. "Seriously, best peace offering ever. What about my dark blue jeans?"

"The ones that are frayed on the bottom? How many times have I told you to get rid of those?"

"They're comfortable. And soft. Hell, *I* want to touch my butt when I wear them."

"They're also so old they're going to fall apart at any second. Do you want to risk them splitting today?"

"You suck," Angel muttered, knowing she'd never be able to wear them around Adam now. At least, not anywhere but her own home where she'd be able to run and change if needed. The jeans were incredibly comfortable, but it wasn't just the bottoms that were frayed, the seams were becoming more and more worn. She hardly ever washed them for fear the fabric would fall apart in the machine.

"Wear the blingy ones. That way if he wants to touch your butt, he'll have to take them off."

"You're such a bad influence on me."

"Hey, you're the one who said you wanted to sleep with him. Besides, if he's not seeing anyone else and you're not seeing anyone else, then it sounds to me like he's your boyfriend, so what's not to encourage?"

"Well, we haven't talked about any labels yet, so I don't know about calling him my boyfriend."

"Then what would you call him?"

Silent, Angel pulled up the jeans with the bling on the butt and twisted to look at herself in the mirror. They did look good. Not only did the shiny draw attention to the shape of her bottom, this particular pair of jeans made her shape look spectacular. It hugged every curve and emphasized her bottom. It resembled a nice little bubble, perfect for curving fingers around.

"I would call him Adam, my exclusive date."

"Sounds like a boyfriend to me."

"Shut it. I'm going to put you down for a second so I can put on the sweater."

She pulled it over her head and then wrapped the scarf around her neck, letting the ends dangle down in front. It was still low cut, but paired with the scarf there was less skin showing and it somehow gave off the appearance of being more casual and less blatantly sexy.

"You're a genius, Leigh. If I ever become rich and famous, I'm hiring you as my personal dresser."

"I thought you didn't want to be famous."

"I don't. But if it ever happens on accident."

Leigh laughed. "Right. Alright baby. Go, have fun. Report back to me later."

"You know I will." Angel's voice softened. "I'm glad you're happy with Michael, but call me immediately if you need me. I don't care where I am. And if you know I'm at the club, call the desk and they'll come find me."

They both knew she was indicating a lack of confidence in Leigh's relationship, but Leigh knew she was only looking out for her.

"I'm hoping that won't be necessary."

"Me too."

"Have fun baby. Love you."

"I love you too."

Hanging up the phone, Angel glanced at the clock. Thank goodness Leigh had called or she would have been late. As it was, she'd be cutting it close. And that was so not the impression she wanted to give.

ADAM

It was a good thing Adam liked cleaning. He liked seeing dirt, dust, and grime being swept away to reveal a gleaming surface underneath. And knowing Angel was coming over to see his house for the first time, he'd been extra motivated. Not that his house ever resembled the stereotypical bachelor pad, but he'd be cleaning today anyway before people came over and he was making everything shine.

The date yesterday with Angel had gone even better than he'd hoped. Now he was more nervous than ever about having invited her over to hang out with his friends. Even though he already knew they liked her too.

The addition of submissives had shifted their group dynamic a bit, and he knew bringing in someone completely from the outside was going to shift it even more. But he hadn't lied when he said Jessica and Hilary both wanted to spend more time with her, he knew they had questions about the self-defense classes she was going to be teaching.

They seemed fascinated by Angel. The fact that she'd successfully disguised herself as a Domme, that she taught women's self-defense, and she managed to be quite successfully pushy with Michael, who was obviously a Dom intrigued them.

Adam hoped she didn't think she was going to get away with that kind of shit with him. Unlike Michael, who only muttered about spanking her ass red, he would follow through with it.

Making a face, Adam scrubbed harder at the toilet he was currently working on. He'd invited Michael over today too. It wasn't that he didn't like the guy, but he wasn't sure how he felt about the touchy-feely relationship Michael had with Angel. But it was something Adam would have to deal with.

He'd never considered himself a jealous or possessive person, but then again, he hadn't had a serious relationship in years. And when he'd been with Brooke, he'd never thought he'd marry her.

The hand holding the scrubber skidded off the toilet and he nearly face planted onto the ceramic before he caught himself.

Jesus... was that how he saw *Angel* already?

Get your shit together.

It made sense. What was the point in wasting time in a relationship he didn't think could work out in the long run? Which meant yes, he was already thinking of possible long-term with Angel.

As long as nothing happened to fuck it up and there were no more major surprises.

He couldn't deal with more surprises.

His phone buzzed and he glanced at the screen.

"Hey Olivia."

"My car won't start. I need you to come get me."

Adam groaned and glanced at his watch. "Can't you call someone else? People should be showing up any minute, I should be here."

"Justin's car is already packed because he picked up Hilary and Liam. Patrick's picking up Lexie, so you know he's going to be trapped there for a while catching up with her parents. Andrew's running late. Jared and Truckstop are making up again so he's probably not going to make it at all and Rick's coming from the complete opposite direction plus he's already been driving for two hours to get here. Now come get me."

She sounded a little annoyed, which he couldn't fault her for since she'd obviously called everyone else before she'd called him.

"Alright, I've gotta tape a note to the door and I'll come get you."

"Thanks."

Olivia lived about fifteen minutes away, so about half an hour round trip. Adam glanced at his watch again and sighed. Chances were, everyone but Andrew would make it here before him. He'd wanted to be here when Angel got here. Especially because he knew she was nervous about hanging out with his friends outside of the club.

Oh well. The sooner he left, the sooner he could get back.

ANGEL

When Angel pulled up to the driveway of the address Adam had given her, there was already a car in it with people piling out. It was a bigger house than she'd expected, bigger than the one she shared with the guys, and the lawn and garden were immaculate.

"You're here! Angel's here!" Jessica called out unnecessarily over her shoulder to the guys, who could obviously see. Angel giggled as she got out of the car. "I'm so glad you came!"

"Thanks, I'm glad I could," Angel said, warmed by Jessica and Hilary's exuberant greetings. Justin, Chris, and Liam were less expressive, but they all made her feel welcome as well. She helped them unload the trunk of various boxes and containers obviously holding food. "Good grief, are you guys catering or something?"

"Justin's an amaaaaaaazing cook," Hilary said. "Jessica lucked out with him."

"Hey," said Liam indignantly.

Hilary shot him an affectionate look. "I lucked out too, but I'm just saying. You could get Justin to teach you how to cook some stuff."

"Or I could have Justin cook it for me and take the credit," Liam muttered under his breath, putting an innocent expression on his face when Angel laughed and Hilary looked over her shoulder suspiciously.

"Huh, Adam's had to run out and get Olivia," Chris said, looking at a piece of paper taped to the front door. "He'll be back soon."

It felt a little weird to be going into his house without him there, but at the same time Angel was kind of glad to be able to look around and study her surroundings without Adam's presence. Get a feel for the man without him looking over her shoulder. The front door opened into a foyer with an immediate stairway. To her right she could see some kind of formal living room, but she couldn't get a good look at it because Jessica and Justin were behind her and she didn't want to hold them up.

As she followed Chris, Liam, and Hilary down the hall, there was a television room on her left; big with beige carpeting, a big TV, a comfortable looking brown leather couch with matching armchairs, and a fireplace. The others led her past that and into the kitchen, which was obviously completely updated with sleek granite counter-tops, a gas stove-top, a double oven, and a giant island in the middle.

"Good grief," she muttered.

"Ahhh," said Justin with an exaggerated sigh. "Heaven."

Jessica giggled. "Our kitchen isn't much smaller than this one."

"Yeah, but I don't have all his fun toys." Justin grinned. "Yet."

"Like what?" Angel wanted to know.

"If you can think of it and use it in a kitchen, Adam probably has it," Chris said, exchanging a knowing smile with Justin. "He's like a pack rat when it comes to his kitchen. A super organized pack rat, but still a pack rat. He's got three different kinds of coffee makers, a quesadilla maker, three different sized toaster ovens, two differently sized woks, a slow cooker, a garlic press—"

"And he never uses any of it," Justin said mournfully, cutting off Chris' recitation.

"Then why does he have it?"

"Lots of people gave him kitchen stuff when he first moved in here, because it was the only stuff he didn't have, and then he kind of started collecting it. He always says that if he uses it once, then it's worth having."

"And he uses three different kinds of coffee makers?" she asked, amused.

"Regular coffee maker, French press, and espresso. They all serve different needs," Chris said, winking at her. She giggled.

"Don't forget all his specialty spices," Liam said, throwing open one of the corner cupboards. Angel's jaw dropped. It had rotating circular shelves, five of them, and they were all filled with spices. Not only that, it was obvious they were *organized* by the little labels at intervals along each shelf. This wasn't a case of repeat spice buying like she did, he seriously had that many spices.

"Does he use all of those?"

"Nope, but I do," Justin said happily as he unwrapped aluminum foil from one of the dishes they'd brought. He was a lot less intimidating looking when he was cheerful and preparing food, Angel decided. It made him look a lot more like Chris in fact. "I'm going to sprinkle some of his truffle oil on this and stick it in the oven... I've got a couple other things to do and then I'll come join you guys."

She was going to ask where, but she followed the rest of the group out into the hall and down a staircase that had been hiding behind a door. Adam's basement was split into two rooms, the first of which was obviously a group entertainment room. If she'd thought the television upstairs had been big, this one was gigantic. There was a split section couch arranged in a U shape in front of it for people to sit on. Next to the television were several different gaming systems, to her surprise he still had the regular X-box and a PS2 rather than the more updated consoles.

The entertainment center was filled with DVDs, but there were also two rows of video games.

"Wanna play something?" a deep voice behind her asked, and she looked up into Chris' laughing brown eyes. "He's got a bunch of different kinds of games. Something for everyone, really."

"I noticed," she murmured. They were arranged in alphabetical order too, which she liked. It made things so much easier. There were a couple of her favorites, but she should choose a game more than one person could play...

Her finger lingered on one. Blinking innocently, she let her eyes go as wide as possible as she pulled it from the shelf and looked back up at Chris. "How about this one?"

ADAM

"No, no, no, no, no, no, no, NO, NooooOOOOOO!"

"Fuck! You little bitch!" Patrick's voice bellowed, drowning out Angel's 'no's.

It was the first thing Adam heard when he walked in the front door, echoing up from the basement and he bolted for the stairs, Olivia hot on his heels.

"Suck it, asshole!" Angel crowed.

"Damn it, not *again!*"

Adam came to a grinding halt halfway down the stairs when the room finally came into view and he realized why he wasn't hearing anyone but Angel and Patrick. The rest of them were in tears, gulping for air because they were laughing so hard. Chris was on the floor, holding his belly, while Lexie, Hilary, and Jessica were hugging each other on the couch, trying to keep from following Chris to the floor as they writhed with hilarity.

Liam and Angel were sitting next to each other on the couch with a space separating them from Patrick and Justin. She was flushed, the sleeves of her sweater pushed up, and he could see the curves of her breasts from the deep V of her neckline. She looked beautiful and excited, not frightened or angry.

"Yes!" Angel jumped into the air, pumping one fist.

"Watch out behind you," Liam warned. He was grinning, but most of his focus was on the screen and front of him and the controller in his hand.

"Don't help her, she doesn't need it," Justin snapped grimly as Angel, still standing, took the controller back in both hands, muttering under her breath.

"Your loss, she's on my team," Liam chortled.

Not one of them looked up to where Adam and Olivia stood, panting and gaping on the stairs.

Patrick growled and leaned forward, looking almost as grim as Justin. "I'm back in."

"Not for long..." Angel said tauntingly.

"I just got back—no...Crap! *Fuck!* How did you do that?!"

Angel laughed maniacally.

Making his way down the stairs, Adam could finally see what they were playing. Halo. And from the stats listed on Patrick's screen as it counted down the time until his character came back to life, Angel was dominating it by a large margin.

"You!" Adam looked over to see Patrick glaring at him. "This is all your fault!"

Lexie fell off the couch onto the floor, tears streaming down her face as Jessica and Hilary both made 'Oh no!' noises through their giggles and reached for her.

"I can't..." Lexie gasped, batting away their hands. "I can't... oh God, it's too good."

"Hi!" Angel said cheerfully, giving him a wave before turning her attention back to the screen. "Hey, Justin... I seeeeeeeee you... oh wait... no, come back here!"

ADAM

Later, gathered around the island in Adam's kitchen, Angel was surrounded by the rest of the women who all wanted her to teach them how to play video games. Jessica seemed especially interested, which wasn't too surprising considering how much Chris loved to play. Justin did too and was even more competitive.

Which was probably why he was still glowering at Angel from across the island. Kudos to her, she ignored the dark looks she was getting from both him and Patrick. Whenever she glanced at Adam, he grinned at her, and then she would glow as if lit up from some light within. He got the feeling that as long as he approved, and the girls approved, she didn't much care Justin and Patrick were being sore losers.

Not that he could blame them. She'd wiped the floor with them, with very little help from Liam. On top of that, she could smack talk with the best of them. Once he and Olivia had gotten downstairs, the Domme had soon joined the other giggling women at some of the creative insults Angel had come up with.

It was an entirely different facet to Angel which he hadn't seen before and it made him wonder how many other hidden sides she had. Sure, the gamer thing was kind of hot, but he'd barely heard her curse until today.

"She played us," Justin said darkly. "She's a... a... video game shark."

"Like a pool shark?" Chris snorted and then grinned at Adam. "You should have seen the innocence shining from her when she suggested Halo. It was practically pouring out of her and these guys fell for it like they'd been dropped off a cliff." He cackled. "Liam thought he was doing her a favor by offering to be on her team. I think these two idiots wanted to show off." He laughed again as Patrick and Justin switched their glowers from Angel to him.

"She said she'd played before with her housemates, what were we supposed to think?" Patrick said crossly. "I thought we could go easy on her, show her some things she could take back to show her house-mates... I was trying to be nice."

"Maybe you should ask *her* to show *you* the secret passageway she ambushed you from, what, three times?"

"Her housemates are all video game fanatics," Adam said. "I met them yesterday. Sam, Mark, and Q. They thought I was there for a LAN party."

"Three guys? She's got three guys for roommates? Unless Q's a woman..." Liam frowned as Adam shook his head. "And you're okay with that?"

"Wouldn't make a difference if I wasn't, so yeah." More so every day, in fact.

"Not sure I'd be," Liam muttered.

"What, you don't trust Hilary?" Chris teased, elbowing Liam.

"I do, but... it's..." Liam fumbled, knowing he'd walked into a verbal trap. He glanced over at the women, but fortunately they were too involved in their conversation for him to have to come up with a viable explanation for his girlfriend. "You know what I mean. I doubt you'd be thrilled if Jessica had been living with a guy instead of Hilary. It's just... semantics."

"Yeah, I know," Chris said cheerfully, popping one of the bacon-wrapped green bean bundles Justin had made into his mouth. "But we would have dealt with it."

"They seem like nice guys," Adam said.

As if to mock his determination to be completely jealousy-free, Michael chose that moment to show up, accompanied by Andrew. Since the girls were closer to the front door entrance, they were the first ones to greet the new arrivals as they appeared from the hall.

While he would have liked to say he didn't even notice Angel's greeting to Michael, it would have been a complete and utter lie. But what he did notice was almost shocking.

Leigh had been right. The tension, the flirtatious air which had always tinged the air around Angel and Michael had completely disappeared. They hugged, Angel called him 'Pretty Boy' again, he growled at her... but something was missing. Some connection between them that had been there before.

Was it as simple as Leigh had indicated? One of them becomes involved in an exclusive relationship and the attraction between them melted away? He'd been prepared to deal with it, knowing Angel and Michael wouldn't work in the long run—like he and Brooke hadn't—and they both knew that.

Instead, she now had the same air around Michael as she did around her roommates.

Angel looked over at him and smiled, her eyes bright. The space between them seemed to shimmer with far more intensity than the tension between her and Michael had ever had.

Moving over to the other side of the island, Adam led the way for the rest of the guys to mix things up, undoing the unintentional "boys vs. girls" separation that had occurred.

"Glad you could make it," he said to Andrew, slapping the other man's palm in greeting while he snaked out his other arm to put it around Angel's waist and pull her into him. It was the kind of physical declaration he hadn't made yet in front of his friends, and Andrew grinned in approval.

"Sorry I'm late. My sister seems to have changed tactics from ignoring my existence to trying to drive me completely insane." He rolled his eyes as Adam made a sympathetic noise, but he could tell Andrew was kind of relieved Iris was at least talking to him again. Even if she was being annoying.

"Well come on in, shockingly there's still food left. Although we ate all the cheddar puffs already."

ANGEL

Angel lingered as everyone else left. Adam hadn't asked her to, and she hadn't said she would, but she wanted to get a few moments alone with him. Not that she hadn't loved today and spending time with his friends. She'd especially appreciated that he'd invited Mike, who was already blending into the group. It was obvious he and Andrew got along well already, and the other guys seemed perfectly welcoming.

Which was kind of incredible, considering what a tightly knit group they were and how long they'd all known each other. But she guessed they were getting used to hanging out with new people, considering Jessica and Hilary had only started dating their men within the past year.

"So, do you have anywhere you need to be tonight?" Adam asked as he shut the door after Rick, Andrew, and Michael. The look he was giving her made her think of a large predator, pacing around prey he'd already caught and was deciding whether or not it was going to pounce.

"No, not really." She wound her hands in front of her, feeling both excited and uncomfortable. New relationships were always a little awkward. Especially when the other person was staring at you like you were a particularly delectable treat. And everything was made a million times more awkward by her acknowledgment to herself that she hoped sticking around meant getting naked and doing lots of naughty things.

She hated the whole insecurity thing over whether or not it was too soon to do *that* and would he respect her in the morning, blah, blah blah... but Leigh had been right about it sounding like Adam wanted to be her boyfriend. Even if he'd never said the word. And she didn't want to make more assumptions, but he'd flat out told her they were going to be seeing each other exclusively and that was good enough for her.

It had been months, maybe years, since she'd been with a guy she wanted that badly on such a visceral, sexual level.

"Good," Adam purred, stepping towards her. Looming over her in that uber sexy way he had. Angel's head tipped back, and she could feel her pulse fluttering in her throat as he leaned over and kissed her.

Not gently, but not roughly, he touched her with nothing but his mouth, a firm press of his lips against hers. They parted and she followed, her fingers locking together as his tongue delved in. While she wanted to put her hands up on his chest, she followed his lead and kept them to herself, making their only connection the kiss.

Then he pulled away, his blue eyes sparkling, looking almost mischievous. "So, want to go play some Halo? I want to see how I do against you."

Oh the jerk. The rotten, panty-wetting, pulse-pounding, pussy-teasing jerk. She'd thought he was going to suggest going to the bedroom. He was so going to pay.

"Bring it on."

20

ANGEL

Jerkface jerkface jerkface.

Mr. Grouchy had turned into Mr. Tease and her panties would have probably caught on fire by now if they weren't completely soaked through. It was the worst game of competitive Halo she'd played in years, even though she still beat him.

He'd decided the perfect place for her to sit was on the floor between his legs. Which wasn't so bad in and of itself; Angel preferred to sit on the floor when she was playing video games. More comfortable seating tended to make one want to sink into it and relax. On the floor she was forced to sit up straight which kept her pretty alert.

However, it was an entirely different experience being on the floor between Adam's legs when there was no one else in the room and she could feel him all around her. Every time she breathed in she could smell the subtle, spicy scent he was wearing. The heat from his body surrounded her. He was leaning forward so she could feel his breath across the top of her head and it made her skin tingle with goose bumps.

Still, she probably could have gotten past all that and kicked his ass no problem if it wasn't for all his damn little light touches.

Every time it looked like she was about to get the drop on him, he'd brush his fingers across the back of her neck, or on her collarbone, or down the V of her sweater, over the soft fabric covering her breast... and Angel's concentration would be shot for the one critical split second it took for him to get back under cover or duck out of her line of fire.

"Dammit all to hell!" she blurted out as he dodged again.

"We're going to need to work on your language," Adam murmured, his voice a deep rumble above her head. It took all of her willpower not to look up. His voice was kind of mesmerizing when he spoke low like that.

"There's nothing wrong with my language."

"Normally no, but when you're playing video games..."

"Are you threatening to spank me if I don't clean up my language?" she asked, only half teasing. At this point her nipples had been rubbing against the fabric of her bra for about half an hour, her panties were almost uncomfortably wet, and if she hadn't had the game controller in her hands she probably would have already tried to jump him.

The game paused and her fingers tightened around the controller. Now she didn't dare look up at him. Heat rose up in her cheeks. She bit her lip to keep from blurting out anything else stupid.

"Is that what you want?" he asked. She couldn't read his tone at all. Was he amused? Interested? Condemning? She could feel her shoulders hunching in, as if to get away from the male body surrounding her even though he wasn't touching her.

"No."

Angel squeaked as she was suddenly lifted by her waist and turned over, her controller still clutched uselessly in her hands.

"I said no!"

"And you were lying."

Smack!

"Ow!" He'd gotten her on her sit spot, right where she would be most sensitive and the sharp slap of his hand would hurt the most.

Although, considering the jeans she was wearing, it's not like she'd left him much of a choice. Damn Leigh and her insistence Angel wear the bling-y jeans! They hadn't thought about *this* aspect of it!

"It's interesting," Adam said, almost conversationally as he rubbed his hand over the spot he'd smacked. Angel tried not to moan. Or think about how close his hand was to her pussy. Didn't matter that she was still wearing jeans, she could still feel the heat of his palm. She pushed her face into the couch cushion and hugged the controller to her chest. "You're not a brat exactly, but you're not exactly well-behaved either."

"By whose standards?" Angel asked, taking a peek back at him through the curtain of her hair. But he wasn't looking at her, he was looking at her ass. And she became so interested in looking at him looking at her ass that she completely missed the raise of his hand.

Smack!

"Ouch!" He'd gotten her sit-spot on the other side.

Well at least each one was smarting equally now. She'd always hated asymmetry.

"That's what I mean," he said, chuckling, as he rubbed the new spot. "You didn't say that because you wanted me to spank you again, and you could have said something a lot more insulting or sarcastic, but you weren't exactly polite either."

Angel rolled her eyes. "By whose standards, *Sir?*"

She squealed as he smacked each side of her ass, equally hard.

"Now that *was* bratty," he said, sounding disapproving.

ADAM

"Sorry, Sir." Her voice was low but contrite.

While Adam didn't normally like being called Sir outside of Stronghold, he found he didn't mind it from Angel at all. He hadn't meant to start a scene with her, but it seemed she'd started one with him. Yet he couldn't even call it topping from the bottom. He'd heard the wistfulness in her voice when she'd asked if he was going to spank her, almost like a shy little request she wasn't sure she wanted him to hear, and he hadn't been able to resist.

Not that he'd been able to resist much with Angel. Sure, he'd been trying to distract her while they played, but he could have found any number of ways to do that. Instead he'd tormented them both by teasing her.

It had also been a test of his control. How much could he touch her, tease her, before he couldn't resist moving beyond that?

The view down her sweater had been very nice, although he had to admit he liked this view too. Her rounded ass was lifted by his thigh, her upper body laid out on the couch with her arms tucked underneath her chest. From the way her head was tilted he was pretty sure she was watching him, but he didn't meet her eyes. Everything about her body language said she was feeling shy and vulnerable and he didn't want her to retreat.

No, he wanted to coax his lovely, little submissive out to play.

Shy wasn't normally a word he would have associated with Angel, but that was the vibe he was getting from her. And it made sense, he thought, trailing his fingers across the lower curve of her bottom, enjoying the way she made little squirming movements as he did so. Shy about showing her true self, about exposing herself.

And the fact was, she was doing so for him... well it took his breath away. He would treasure her submission all the more, not because she was a strong woman and he loved it when a strong woman submitted, but because she was so sweetly, timidly hesitant about it. This wasn't about proving he was dominant to her, but about proving to her that he could be trusted with this revelation of herself, that he would protect and cherish her for it.

He leaned down and kissed her, under the curve of her bottom where he'd spanked her a moment before, and then pulled her up onto his lap, leaning back against the couch, adjusting her so his raging erection was caught between their bodies.

She burrowed into his shoulder, her arms still curled protectively around her chest, although she finally dropped the controller she'd been holding. The way she snuggled into his arms suggested more than a desire to cuddle, she was trying to hide her face against him. He resisted the urge to chuckle and enjoyed the fact that she obviously wanted to be held by him even though she felt vulnerable and embarrassed. That was always a good sign.

"Good girl," he murmured into her hair, taking a deep breath. She smelled like berries, and she relaxed against him.

Fingers touched his chest, stopped as if testing, and then slowly crept across towards his shoulder when he didn't say anything. The light touch, the hesitancy, was making his cock throb.

"Are we going to finish the game?" she asked in a little voice.

Funny to think that at one point in the past few weeks, he might have wondered if she was trying to play him. If she was pretending to have a little tremor in her voice and body. Now the thought didn't even cross his mind except as a relief that he'd moved past his suspicion about her.

"Would you like to?" he asked, shifting her so she was leaning back and he could look at her. Her face was flushed and her pupils were dilated, although she was having trouble looking him in the eye. Adorable. "Or would you like to play?"

Their eyes connected as heat flared between them and then her gaze skittered away again as her cheeks blushed even brighter. Adam chuckled.

"Your safe word is Uncle," he reminded her, leaning down to capture her lips before she could respond.

ANGEL

Hot and heavy, was the first thought through her mind as Adam shifted, his weight pressing her down onto the couch. She opened her mouth beneath his, fingers clutching at his shirt as he kissed her. Deeply. Thoroughly. Until she thought she might melt into the cushions.

He'd maneuvered himself so he was fully on top of her, one of his thighs between hers, and all his wonderful weight practically crushing her. Not that she wanted him to move. Who needed air anyway? She'd rather have all his hot male muscle pressed against her entire body.

It felt like her body was on fire. Sure, it had been great getting a kiss from him last night, but that had been quick and fleeting... not like this where she could feel his need pressing into her, his mouth demanding reciprocation. This was the kind of kissing which only came with real desire, that said she was far more than a body to scene with. Angel could kiss like this for hours.

Well, if she hadn't been so ridiculously primed and horny, then she could kiss like this for hours and be satisfied.

As it was, she felt like she might burst out of her skin, she was so needy, itching, burning up like a moth inside a bonfire...

When Adam pulled his mouth away she suddenly realized she was grinding against his thigh. She'd been completely unaware of it because she'd been so into the kissing. Immediately she went still, immediate embarrassment making itself known as her cheeks burst into flame—and not the good kind.

She tried to duck her head down away from his gaze, but he chuckled and then pulled her sweater up.

Oh... so that's why they'd stopped kissing.

But he only pulled the sweater over her head, not over her arms, leaving her pinned to the couch by her own clothing. The expression on his face as he looked down at her was pure masculine smugness, and even though she loved how he was looking at her, she still couldn't control the impulse to hide.

But he wouldn't let her.

As if the flames in her panties needed any more fanning.

How pathetic was it to be turned on by impromptu sweater bondage? It didn't even *sound* sexy. But being held immobile by the hot, dominating man who had one hand on her sweater above her head, pinning her arms in place, and was running the other hand down her bra strap? Yeah... that had her panting.

"So... how far do you want us to play tonight?" Adam asked—as if she was supposed to be capable of coherent thought and speech when his fingers were playing along the edge of her bra. Her nipples were so hard she was surprised they weren't drilling right through the undergarment. "Angel? How far do you want to go?"

Her face felt so red, she had to be blushing all the way to her roots. "You're the Dom, aren't you supposed to decide that?"

"That far, huh?"

Damn him for being able to read her so well. If she could have punched him for chuckling, she would have... but he'd already leaned down for another kiss, she could have bit him, but why bother?

Then his mouth pulled away again and she let out a little sound of protest.

"That's not how this works, Angel, I'm not going to take over and do whatever I want without some kind of acquiesce from you."

"Why not?"

Adam brushed his lips over hers again, but this time it truly was a brush, leaving her straining upwards for more. Tease. Jerkface.

"If that's how you want to play it... tell me we can go as far as I want to."

"We can go as far as you want to," she repeated obediently, a shiver of excitement zipping through her as she spoke the words.

He leaned closer, his thigh pressing hard between hers and her hips jerked upwards, grinding her clit against his long muscle. When he spoke, it was in a low voice, directly in her ear and her insides clenched. "Tell me I can do whatever I want to your body."

"You can do whatever you want to my body." Her voice was breathy, wispy. Then some semblance of self-preservation reared up again. "Within my hard limits."

This time his chuckle didn't bother her in the least.

ADAM

He loved this snippy little side of her. She'd gone boneless beneath him, only to remember herself and set down the ground rules again. It was those quick changes which kept him on his toes, kept him guessing—made him wonder what it would take for her to lose control completely when she was here, alone in his house with him rather than in the safety of the club. That kind of letting go would mean a great deal of trust on her part.

He sort of rolled off the couch while standing up at the same time, taking her with him so he could flip her up over his shoulder.

Kind of a caveman move, but he liked it. And there was no way their first time together was going to be on his couch when his bed was a couple floors away. Besides, he'd been fantasizing about having Angel in his bed, not on his couch. Although the reality of her on his couch was quite nice too.

"Hey! What are you doing?"

Adam smacked her ass as he turned towards the stairs. Dammit. The bling had dug into his hand, although it didn't hurt very much it was still annoying. When he got those pants off of her he was going to spank her for wearing them. "Whatever I want, remember?"

"Yeah, I thought you were going to do it down here..." The sexual frustration in her voice was obvious, and if he hadn't already been as hard as a rock that would have done it to him. Well, that and having her delectable ass right next to his face, his hand was wrapped around her thigh with his fingers between her legs.

He took a deep breath, grinning as he caught the faintest whiff of sweet, musky feminine arousal. Considering she was wearing jeans, her panties must be soaked for him to even get a hint of scent. He picked up the pace a little bit, ignoring her protests as she was bounced on his shoulder. Sure he felt a little caveman, but he kind of liked the Neanderthal scenario.

Capture woman, drag her back to his cave, and don't let her out or near any other Neanderthals.

When he reached his room, he kicked the door closed behind him. The muttering stopped and she pressed her hands against his butt as her body shifted, obviously doing her best to look around the room. Like the rest of his house, it was neat as a pin, the complete opposite of the messy chaos of her room, because he hated clutter. There were a couple of bookshelves filled with his guilty pleasures, namely a lot of young adult science fiction and fantasy the other guys would probably tease him about. The more respectable authors who wrote for adults were on a bookshelf in a room downstairs.

When he set Angel down on her feet, she was already done protesting, her eyes flashing around the room as she frowned. Inwardly he sighed. He was still hard and ready to go but obviously his curious kitten wanted a moment to look around. As she turned around the room, taking it all in, she stripped the sweater from her arms, but the movement wasn't at all sexual.

"Is this a guest room?"

His mouth quirked. "No, this is my bedroom."

"But there's nothing *in* it."

"Bed, dresser, desk, bookshelves... what more do I need?"

"Pictures, trinkets, *something* to personalize the space a little!" She walked over to the bed, her fingers trailing across the quilt on it. It was the only splash of color in the otherwise utilitarian space. "This is beautiful. Why don't you have more things like this here?"

"My mother made it for me." Yeah, because talking about his mom wasn't going to further kill the mood. "And because I don't like clutter."

"You can have something on the walls without it being clutter," she said, shaking her head. A little smirk crossed her face as she turned back to look at him. "My room must have driven you nuts."

"You have no idea," he murmured, stepping closer. He wasn't interested in examining his room—why would he be? "But I didn't bring you up here so you could tell me how to decorate my bedroom." The only decoration he wanted at the moment was Angel herself—and how pretty would she look secured to one of his walls?

Just like that, with one step toward her, Angel's eyes flared with heat and they were right back where he wanted them to be. Her tongue flicked out against her lower lip. Shit, he loved her mouth. Adam had always been an ass man and in the past hadn't put much thought into how attractive a woman's mouth could be. With Angel, he constantly fantasized about sliding his cock between those bow-shaped lips. He wanted to do it again.

So why shouldn't he?

"On your knees." His voice was harsh, deep, demanding. Angel dropped like a stone, almost looking surprised at how quickly she'd gone down. If he still doubted whether or not she was a true submissive, that would have told him right there. She'd obeyed without thinking about it, without having been trained for it. Some submissives still might have argued, but Angel already trusted him, already accepted his dominance of her, and she reacted accordingly. "Put your hands behind your back, I want you to hold onto your elbows."

The position thrust her breasts out. The bra she was wearing was nothing special, purple like her sweater and with a little heart dangling in the center between her breasts. He kind of wished he'd told her to take it off, but at the same time denying himself the sight was a delightful tease.

Keeping his eyes trained on hers, he began to unbutton his shirt.

❧

ANGEL

The man should work for Chippendales. *Hellooooo, hot body*. Although wasn't she supposed to be doing a sexy strip show for him? Not the other way around?

Not that she was going to complain if he wanted to strip down for her, but it did seem sort of backwards. Then again, she was going off based of what she thought a Dom would want... and she was demonstrably not a dominant. The whole point was Adam wanted her to kneel and watch him while he unbuttoned his shirt.

She wanted to run her tongue all over his stomach. Rub her face in his chest hair. Really wrap herself around him and touch every inch of him she could with every part of her body that could reach him. And instead she had to kneel here and watch him undress for her. She was proud of herself for not drooling.

He had a fantastic body. Muscular, defined, but not so cut his muscles looked like they'd be too hard to cuddle with. Fair hair, slightly darker than the hair on his head, centered on his chest, although there was also a thin line of it heading down from his belly button into the Promised Land. Angel had read that in a book, and the author had been talking about a woman, but she figured it was apt enough for Adam.

"You look hungry, Angel," he said softly, stepping closer as he shucked off his shirt and began undoing his belt. Her eyes raised back up to his, which were a bright, glittering blue. "Would you like something to fill your mouth?"

"Yes please, Sir."

Her mouth watered, her fingers tightening on her arms. Kneeling here in front of him like this, with her hands behind her back, it should have felt wrong. Every feminist bone in her body felt that way. But they'd also all completely melted under the heat. She liked being on her knees like this for him, liked the way his eyes slid over her face and down to her breasts, liked the approval she saw in his expression.

Would she do this for any man? Absolutely not. But Adam made her feel special. He made her feel like she could submit to him and he would only respect her more because of it, not less. They'd gotten off to a rocky start, but she was glad he'd been the one to do her Introduction Scene. Glad they'd been paired up right from the beginning. Because she didn't think she would have felt this with any of the other Doms. None of them held the same level of attraction. None of them had even guessed at Chained that she wasn't what she seemed to be.

But Adam saw right through her. He'd taken the time to get to know her even though her initial lie had offended him on some basic level. And she wanted him to see her, to know her. For the first time, she felt like maybe this was a man she could have a real future with.

And right now, in his bedroom, she felt like this was the most intimate, most *bare* thing she'd ever done—and she was still wearing most of her clothing. It wasn't about the physical stuff, although that was part of it, it was about the connection between them.

When he pulled his beautiful cock out of his pants, she didn't just give him head. She worshiped him with her mouth. Her tongue. Licking up and down the sides of his length, she put her whole body into it. And then she sucked him in between her lips and took him deep.

The groans, the fingers now sliding through her hair, only encouraged her. She felt fuzzy, warm, as all of her focus centered on the pleasure she was giving him.

"Hands back where they belong." His voice snapped out as he

pulled away, leaving her lips open, panting. Angel blinked and then almost jumped as she realized her hands had moved of their own volition. She hadn't even noticed, she'd been so wrapped up in wanting to take him in.

Immediately she put them back behind her, wrapping her fingers tightly around her elbows to keep them in place, before looking back up at him.

He stepped closer and the slick length of his cock slid easily back between her lips, making her hum in delight. He groaned again, obviously enjoying the vibrations of her mouth around him. Flicking her tongue against the underside, she explored the veins along his shaft as she moved her head back and forth, trying to take him a little bit deeper each time.

After a few moments she managed to get back into the rhythm she'd had before, into that same head space where everything seemed to melt away except for pleasuring him. It was almost hypnotic, the sucking, the moving, the taking... her jaw ached and yet she wanted to go on like this for hours. She loved the way his fingers felt, running through her hair, touching her forehead, her cheeks, in an almost reverent manner.

Every part of her body ached to be touched, and yet she was content as long as he was.

"Fuuuck... Angel... I'm gonna cum..."

She recognized it for the warning it was; he wasn't going to give her the option of pulling away this time, he wanted her to swallow him. And she wanted it too. His hips thrust, much less gently than they had been, and they were working in tandem now rather than it being her efforts alone. Tears sparked in her eyes as his cock pushed at the back of her throat and she pushed down the instinct to gag and did her best to accept him into that tight space.

Whimpers worked their way around his cock as she sucked hard, eagerly. His cock pulsed against her tongue and then hot fluid was coating the back of her throat. Swallowing convulsively, she closed her eyes and held on as she suckled his orgasm, milking him for every last drop.

Finally, his groans and heavy breathing slowed, his hands relaxing on her head as his cock began to slowly shrink inside of her mouth. She could breathe again, but she was reluctant to let him go.

A low chuckle made her open her eyes and look up at him, her lips still around his dick.

Adam tapped her hand. Oops. Both of her hands were wrapped around his legs again, nails digging into the backs of his thighs, as if she'd been trying to drag him deeper into her mouth.

"You are both a very good, and a very bad girl."

🦋 21 🦋

ADAM

The look on Angel's face was of conflicted desire as his cock finally fell from her lips. Immediately he missed the warmth, and at the same time, he loved seeing the turmoil in her full expression and the way she nervously flicked her tongue out along her lower lip.

"Sorry..." Her hands fluttered away from his thighs. "I don't know why... Sorry."

Hiding his smile, because he had enjoyed the way she'd clutched at him while she'd been swallowing him down, Adam shook his head. "You've built up a small pile of punishments already, sweetheart. Calling your Dom names, disobeying orders..."

"I didn't mean to! Well, okay, I did mean to call you names but I didn't know I wasn't supposed to. You never told me not to."

The best part was, she wasn't trying to be a brat and gain more punishment by arguing. He could tell. No, she was genuinely trying to talk him out of it, and from the way she was squirming, he was pretty sure it was because she wanted an orgasm.

"Stand up," he said, holding out his hand in case she needed assistance. She took it. "Take off your jeans."

As she was doing so, he finished taking off his as well, leaving him standing naked while he looked over her matching bra and panties. She'd been surprisingly graceful taking off her jeans, positioning herself to give him the best view of her butt. The firm curves were not entirely covered by the thin fabric of her underwear, which he had to admit was one of his favorite looks if a woman wasn't wearing a thong. Or nothing at all.

Sitting down on the edge of his bed, he held out his hand. "Come here, Angel."

Her face reddened as his eyes swept over her nearly bared body, but she reached out and took his hand. The little squeak she gave as he tugged her quickly down over his lap was too cute for words.

"Lovely," he murmured, running his hand over the purple fabric stretched over the cheeks of her ass. It was soft cotton, closely fitted to her skin without digging into it.

"Um... thanks." Angel peeked at him through the cloud of hair covering her face and he chuckled, rubbing the rounded curve of her butt a little harder with his hand, squeezing her cheeks. With a little moan, she wiggled her bottom at him, her body asking for more.

"So. Twenty for moving your hands after I told you not to, fourteen for the seven names you called me, and ten for trying to argue your way out of those fourteen."

"But!"

"You want more?" His hand tapped threateningly on her bottom and she immediately fell silent. "Respect is always important, and I shouldn't have to tell you not to call me names." Try as he might, he couldn't entirely keep the amusement out of his voice and he felt Angel relax over his lap. Which was good. He wasn't going to give her a very hard spanking, enough to heat her bottom to a nice bright pink. And he was quite sure she was going to enjoy it.

Mostly.

"So why are you getting a spanking, sweetheart?"

Angel groaned and wiggled her bottom, but he left his hand resting there, waiting for her answer. She sighed.

"For moving my hands, calling you names, and trying to avoid a spanking," she said softly. Her head twisted around, her bright amber eyes wide and innocent. "But I didn't mean to move my hands, I didn't even notice I had."

"It will be good for you to work on it," he said sternly. She let out another little huff of air and twisted her neck back around, laying quiescent over his lap. "You'd better keep them in place now, grip my quilt if you have to."

Waiting until she'd bunched the fabric into two tight little fists, Adam raised his hand as she tensed, anticipating the blow.

"Relax. And count each one."

A deep breath and she did as he commanded, a feeling of delighted power rushing through him.

Smack!

"Oh!" There was more surprise in her voice than anything else. He hadn't hit hard, just enough to sting. "One."

"Good girl."

Smack!

"Two."

By the time she got to ten, her voice was becoming a little more strained. Now that she was warmed up, the skin of her bottom slightly pinker than the rest of her, he felt able to begin to spank her a little harder, knowing it would still be enjoyable.

"What color are you at, Angel?" His fingers drifted down to where her panties were covering her bare pussy lips, teasing the outer lips of her labia through the wet fabric.

"Green, Sir." The breathy response was accompanied by a little wiggle of her bottom, seeking out more touch from his fingers. She whimpered a little as he pulled them away instead and returned his hand to the warmed skin of her ass.

Smack!

"Eleven!"

His cock was already swelling again, and she counted out each slap, her body rocking against him. Not because she wanted to get away from it, but because she desperately wanted to rub her clit against his thigh, and she wasn't in quite the right position to be able to do so.

Smack!

"Twelve!"

Smack! Smack! Smack!

"Thirteen, fourteen, fifteen!" She sounded almost breathless at the end of that little salvo. Adam rubbed his hand roughly over her bottom again. He loved watching her flesh jiggle and move.

When he reached twenty, Angel was squirming a lot more, moaning a little with every slap. He could tell the spanking was starting to hurt, but she was also more and more aroused by it.

"Good girl. That was the first set."

Admiring the rosy pink of her bottom and how it contrasted with the deep purple of her panties, Adam decided he wanted to do the next two sets on her bare bottom. Not that it would change the sensation level for her. That thin fabric was no protection from his palm, but he knew it would add a certain fillip to the second part of the spanking.

ANGEL

This was so much more intimate than the spanking bench, and not just because no one else was around and they were in Adam's bedroom. Angel had never been across a man's lap before, never felt a man's cock beginning to harden against her side as he spanked her, and never wondered how much of her body a man in Adam's position could see. She hoped it was only her bottom, because the idea that he could see how soaked through the crotch of her panties were was embarrassing.

Why? No idea. Innate modesty? Something which had never bothered her before, but she'd never felt this kind of vulnerability before either.

Then he pulled down her panties and she moaned, both embarrassed and aroused, as she knew there was no way he could miss how freaking turned on she was by this. And somehow, the embarrassment got her even hotter. She knew she wasn't into humiliation, but being embarrassed over Adam knowing he'd gotten her hot with a spanking?

Yeah, that revved her engine even more, despite it also making her want to sink into the floor.

The one nice thing about this position was that he couldn't see how beet red her face got when he chuckled and ran his finger up the lips of her sopping wet pussy.

"Hmmm... it seems as though you're enjoying this a little too much for it to be a punishment," he said, swirling his finger around her wet flesh. Angel moaned and clutched at his quilt even tighter, unable to stop herself from following the movements of his finger. She gasped when he squeezed her ass hard, igniting little sparks—not quite painful, it was more like little pleasurable, stinging bites against her skin. "I guess I'll have to make sure these next ones are harder."

Smack! Smack! Smack! Smack! Smack!

Angel cried out, her hips lifting up and down as if asking for more; every muscle in her legs tensed and relaxed, trying to ameliorate the painful slaps on already sensitized skin. In complete opposition to the painful spanking, her pussy got even wetter.

"Keep counting, Angel, or I'm going to start over."

"Twenty-one, twenty-two, twenty-three, twenty-four," she said quickly, her voice catching a bit.

The heat seemed like it was growing, both along the top of her skin and between her legs. Adam's dick was growing harder as well, pressing into her side, and she desperately wanted to turn and rub herself against it, to relieve some of the pressure building up inside of her.

The spanking hurt more than she'd imagined when she'd been reading and fantasizing about experiencing it, and unlike when she was over the bench at Stronghold, she was having trouble losing herself into a haze of lust. Maybe it was because Adam was pressed so close to her, maybe it was because he kept changing the rhythm of his slaps, or maybe it was because he was making her count, but she was completely present in the moment rather than losing herself in it.

He started a pattern down each of her buttocks, from the top of the curve down to her sensitive sit-spot, and as he got closer and closer to her pussy it hurt more and it made her want his touch more. The counting kept her focused, the heat made her want to writhe.

Trying to rub herself against his thigh didn't quite work because she didn't quite have the right angle.

Feverishly she wondered if she would have better luck at rubbing her clit against him if her head was towards the floor, rather than having her upper body laid across his bed. Had he done that on purpose? She wouldn't put him past him.

Tears sparked in her eyes, both of the mingled pleasure and pain and from her sexual frustration. The spanking hurt, wonderfully, horribly, and she was so confused as to whether she wanted him to stop or to keep going forever. Each blow made her butt tingle and sting, but it was followed by a warmth, a glow, heating up her insides until she was twisting her hands in his quilt to keep herself from going for her pussy.

It didn't help that her breasts were still covered by her bra either. Her nipples were aching for some kind of contact, but she couldn't even rub them against the nubby fabric of his quilt. Maybe the spanking wasn't the real punishment, maybe making her ready to climb walls in order to have an orgasm was.

"Thirty-three!"

Smack!

"Thirty-four!"

Only ten more to go, she thought, clinging to the quilt. Ten more and... he'd said she was a bad girl and a good girl. If this was what bad girls got, then hopefully she would get a good girl's just desserts afterwards.

"Last ten. What color are you at, Angel?"

"Green, Sir." Funny, that her color for feeling good was green, when her ass was being turned red. At least it felt red. Hot and red and making her insides oh so very needy.

Smack!

"Thirty-five!"

Adam began spanking her faster, as if working his way to a grand finale, each blow coming down a little bit harder and working its way towards her needy core. Her body throbbed, torn, wanting more and yet concerned about taking any serious pain... as if of their own volition her legs spread, giving him access to her pussy as his hand came closer and closer.

Would he spank her there? Or was he only teasing her again? And which did she want it to be?

"Forty!"

"Forty-one!"

"Forty-two!"

Angel cried out. His hand hadn't come down nearly as hard, but it had come down with absolutely precision, squarely onto her splayed pussy. Her body jerked, the spasm going through her was as much pleasure as it was pain. Fire... heat... and the strange revelation that if he kept it up she was going to cum.

"Forty-three!" she managed to gasp out when he cleared his throat and reminded her she was supposed to be counting.

Her head felt fuzzy. Like a radio station with too much static. Adrenaline, endorphins, and fifty different kinds of sexy crazy were running through her veins.

Thwap!

"Forty-four!"

It felt like everything inside of her tilted and strained, her inner muscles clenching as she approached orgasm and was left clawing for the edge of the cliff. The blow had landed directly where the last one had, leaving her pussy lips stinging and unfulfilled.

She let out a frustrated scream.

And ended up on her back in the center of Adam's bed, one of his hands underneath her, making her arch up her breasts... and then they were free. Since his other hand was firmly planted on the mattress next to her, she knew he'd undone her bra with one hand.

"Impressive," she said through her panting breaths. "Now fuck me." Her voice lilted upwards on the end of the sentence, making it a plea rather than an order. Undulating her body, she rubbed it against his, feeling a wet trail along her inner thigh as the head of his cock dragged along it. Her nails dragged along his sides, down to his hips, and he groaned as his body rocked against hers.

"You... are trouble," he growled, pulling her bra from her body and tossing it away. "Put your hands above your head and *keep them there.*"

With a little whimper, she obeyed. Just hearing him order her around in his deep voice made every inch of her skin tingle.

❦

ADAM

The tight, dark pink nipples pointed up at him were too tempting to resist. Lowering his head, Adam took one and then the other into his mouth, nibbling as Angel's body writhed and bucked beneath him. The little whimpers working their way out of her throat were delightful, as was the way she panted for breath in between.

Sliding his hand down her stomach, he found the cream-coated lips of her pussy and slid a finger in to the music of her moans.

"Oh please... please, please please..." Angel's hips bucked as he teased her clit, seeking out contact. The begging made the blood in his cock surge and he sucked hard on her nipple as he tempered his own response. She was so wet and silky against his fingers, her legs spread wide as if to invite him into her body.

Shit... why was he even waiting? Other than to prove himself he could maintain his control, but she wanted it and he wanted it... it was a Dom's privilege to be able to indulge himself and lose control on occasion, as long as he didn't hurt anyone. And he didn't think Angel was going to be complaining if he got inside her sooner rather than later.

He lay little kisses on stomach and then her breasts, working his way up her body. Her hands had moved, from being stretched up above her head to laying right beside it, but he decided it was close enough.

With an elbow planted on either side of her, the tip of his cock nudged between the wet fold of her pussy, immediately coating it in honey. He caught her eyes, the pupils huge pools of darkness in glowing amber, dark lashes fluttering wildly over them. Those perfect pink lips were parted slightly, ready to moan or cry out or scream his name.

"Don't move," he growled. Angel whimpered in reply as he began to push forward.

She was like hot silk, a wet glove gripping him as he pushed into her body. While the rest of her tensed, straining to follow his command, her inner muscles were fluctuating wildly, as if trying to suck him in deeper. Pulling out slightly, he thrust hard and buried himself within her on the second stroke. Unable to stop herself, Angel's body arched beneath his, her splayed pussy grinding against his body as she spasmed around him.

Hands were suddenly on his shoulders, the back of his neck and Adam shifted his weight to pinch her nipple.

"Hands back in place, Angel."

"Sorry, sorry," she muttered, although her heart wasn't in it, as she returned her hands to being stretched out above her head. He got the impression she, again, hadn't realized she'd moved them.

"Good girl."

He kissed her, long and slow, enjoying the way her muscles tightened around him and the small movements of her body as she tried to get him to move within her again. Invading her mouth with his tongue, he enjoyed his dominion over her body... so sweet and eager to be played with.

As he kissed her, he began to rock his hips, pulling out a few inches before slowly driving back into her. From the frantic, muffled sounds deep in her throat and the way she was lifting her hips up to his, he could tell he wasn't going fast enough for her and he enjoyed feeling her wriggling underneath him with all her pent-up sexual energy.

Then her hands found their way to his head again.

Grabbing her wrists, Adam pinned them down on either side of her head as he lifted his mouth away from hers.

"You can't stay in position, can you?"

"Sorry, sorry..."

Tightening his hands around those slender limbs, he leaned down to whisper in her ear. "Next time I'm going to tie you down so you can't move an inch."

Angel groaned, her legs coming up and around his body as if the idea of being held immobile made her unable to keep still. Giving up on the idea of having her hold position, Adam leaned his weight onto her wrists and began driving into her body with all the force she could desire.

With a loud cry, she arched up beneath him, her hips pumping as she tightened her legs around his waist. They were moving together, in a hard pounding rhythm, as her arms pushed against his hands, struggling to free herself. Holding her down beneath him as he easily slid in and out of her body made him even harder. His cock was throbbing inside of her as her muscles pulled and sucked at him, her cries becoming wilder and higher with every thrust.

"Adam... oh fuck... oh Adam!"

Her head thrashed back and forth in ecstasy as she let out a breathy scream of ecstasy, her body trembling as she clenched around him. Her tight sheath became even tighter, her muscles rippling as if to milk his cock, and he groaned. He'd wanted to hold out, to keep fucking her, but she was holding him so tightly he could barely move. The tingling at the base of his spine told him he was fast losing the battle for control over his body.

Rocking himself against her, he rubbed his groin roughly against her clit as she moaned his name over and over again, her body going into writhing spasms beneath him. Her pussy was like a vise, and he growled out her name as he felt his release in a burst of rapture, throbbing throughout his entire body as he spilled hot cum into her.

It felt like his orgasm went on forever, her muscles working the entire length of his cock until he collapsed, utterly wrung out, on top of her. The effort it took to release his fingers from around her slender wrists was almost too much for him. With his face buried in her shoulder, he tipped his head to kiss her neck, chuckling as she shivered and protested.

"That tickles!"

"Mmmm." Adam rubbed his nose against her sensitive skin and enjoyed the way she gasped and clenched again. "You smell nice."

Angel giggled, sliding her arms around him now that she could. "Sorry I kept moving..."

Adam laughed. "That's alright. Hilary, you are not."

He grinned into her hair, thinking about how he needed to get some restraints for his bed.

"What does that mean?" She poked his side, sounding a little perturbed.

"Ah, I'd forgotten, you wouldn't have seen Liam and Hilary playing yet."

"I *have* been kept pretty busy every time I've been at Stronghold."

"Liam prefers honor bondage, which is good because Hilary doesn't like to be restrained. They tend to scene in private, but from what we all have seen them do around us, he never needs to restrain her because she always stays in position for him."

"I can work on that..." Angel sounded worried.

With a stifled groan, Adam pushed himself up to look down at her. "I'm not Liam, sweetheart. I like real bondage. I'm looking forward to tying you up, especially now that I know how badly you want to move and touch me." The slightly doubtful look on her face faded into a shy smile. Leaning down, he kissed those slightly swollen lips, very gently and tenderly. "And when you do move from position, I get to punish you, which is also something I enjoy."

Laughing now, Angel slapped at his chest in playful reproach. Growling a little, Adam rolled, pulling her along with him so she ended up on top. Let her do the work to prop herself up and look down at him. Plus, he liked the way she felt on top of him, all soft curves and long limbs.

"That's good," she said ruefully. "Because I'm not sure I could stop, although I would try. I was already trying."

"I didn't mind... I liked holding you down too," he said with a grin, running his hands down her back to her delectable bottom. She winced a little bit as he squeezed, although he could tell the effects of her spanking were already wearing off a bit. "You've got such a fantastic ass."

A pleased little smile on her face, Angel fluttered her lashes at him a bit. "I've been told you're an ass man."

"And I saw on your survey for Stronghold that you enjoy anal play and sex," he said, grinning as he brushed his finger over her little crinkled hole. "We're well matched. But not tonight..." He glanced over at the clock and sighed reluctantly. "I have to go to work tomorrow."

"Oh, right," Angel started to push up and away from him.

Holding tightly onto her bottom cheeks, Adam frowned up at her. "Where do you think you're going?"

"Oh..." She settled back down a bit. "I thought that was my hint to leave."

"You can if you need to, but I'd rather you stay here."

She cocked her head to the side as she thought it over, very quickly, before looking back down at him with a brilliant smile on her face. "I'd like that."

"Good."

❧

ANGEL

When the alarm went off, Angel jumped, immediately awake. That was *not* her alarm. And that was not Michael or Leigh pressed up against her back. Her naked back, which is how she knew it wasn't Michael or Leigh.

The events of the previous evening came flooding back as the arm wrapped around her waist tightened.

"Good morning."

"Oh my God, turn it off," she moaned, trying to pull the pillow over her head to smother the annoying and overly loud beeping.

Adam's deep chuckle made her body tingle, even down between her legs which was a little bit sore from all the activity it wasn't quite used to. Last night he'd been rough. And wonderful. And so incredibly sexy and dominating. But her poor pussy wasn't used to that sort of treatment and it hadn't had any sort of treatment from the opposite sex for long enough she still felt a bit tender.

His arm moved away and the incessant, obnoxious beeping stopped. Pulling the pillow back away from her face, Angel turned over and snuggled up against him. Big, hot, hard man body first thing in the morning.

Yum.

Better than Wheaties.

She giggled.

"I sincerely hope you're not laughing at me," he said, pushing her onto her back so he could see her face. His fingers pressed down on the center of her chest, drawing little circles that made her skin tingle.

"I was thinking you're better than breakfast," she said truthfully.

Adam laughed and leaned down to kiss her, obviously not caring about anything like morning breath. Fortunately, her mouth didn't feel too disgusting since he'd made a toothbrush available to her last night. New and blue, which made her feel good since she could tell from looking at the brush he used that the one he'd given her was meant as a replacement for it. Not that it was a bad thing if a man was prepared with an extra toothbrush, but there were some connotations to being so prepared she wasn't a fan of.

Opening her mouth, she couldn't help but wince when he settled between her legs.

Immediately he pulled away. "Are you okay?"

"A little sore. It's um... been a while." The look on his face *now* was pure, smug male satisfaction and she couldn't help but laugh again.

Lifting his hips away from hers, Adam kissed her again. "Alright minx, time to get up then."

"Oh." She couldn't help the disappointment in her voice even if she wanted to.

Adam gave her a look as he sat on the edge of the bed, his erection bobbing heavily. "I can wait. Besides, this way I won't be late," he said, glancing at the clock.

"Aww, you were going to be late for me?"

"Yes," he said, dragging her over to him. "Now come take a shower with me so I can tease myself some more before I have to go to work."

Despite her obvious come-ons in the shower, Adam resisted anything past teasing each other. Which, as he carefully and gently washed her with a cloth, was probably a good thing because she was tender. If they had sex now, then she would need some extra time to recover.

They had a quick breakfast of cereal, while Adam grumbled about not being able to make her a proper breakfast because they'd taken so long in the shower, and some fantastic French press coffee before he walked her out to her car.

"I'll call you tonight," he said, kissing her soundly on the mouth.

"Okay." She smiled shyly up at him, feeling both pleased and surprised he was going to call her so soon. "I have class till eight."

"I'll call you at nine. Be good."

From someone else that might have sounded almost patronizing, from Adam it was teasing and not at all filled with any kind of expectation. Laughing, Angel pushed him toward his car and got into her own.

Her heart felt light, joyous and she turned up the Miley Cyrus song on the radio. If Adam hadn't been watching as she pulled away, she would have indulged in some serious happy dancing.

⚜ 22 ⚜

ANGEL

That night Adam called her, exactly when he said he would, and they ended up talking for hours. Angel wasn't always a phone person, and when she told him he confessed he rarely talked on the phone either unless it was to someone who lived far enough away he couldn't speak with them otherwise, but somehow it was easy to pass the time on the phone with each other.

He told her about his parents and their divorce. They talked about his mother's new husband and life in England and his father's long-term girlfriend, and a little bit about his brother. She got the impression he rarely talked about Brian, and never about his death. Instead, she heard about them as children, playing pranks and accidentally sending each other to the hospital while practicing their wrestling moves.

And in return she told him about her parents and their eclectic lifestyle growing up. Percy's impatience with his family, her brother Captain Captain and his ship, and the camping trips her dad used to take them on. Mom would come too, but she wasn't a camper, she just enjoyed being with her family, even if it was out in the middle of nowhere, but dad thrived on it. Adam laughed, sounding much more relaxed than she'd ever heard him.

By the time the phone call ended, they'd made plans for him to come over for dinner on Thursday. After she'd spent the night out, and considering the way things had gone down on Saturday, she wanted her roommates to be able to get to know him.

They ended up talking on the phone all evening Tuesday too, despite the muttered imprecations of her roommates outside her door. She knew they were a little worried, because she'd never spent quite this much time on a guy so quickly, but Adam made it easy. Fun. And a little sexy as he would send her flirtatious text messages throughout the day and tease her on the phone in the evening. She flirted right back, of course, and sent him a picture of her in the red leather outfit, which she was planning on wearing again the next time they went to Stronghold.

Which would hopefully be that weekend.

ADAM

When Adam's phone rang at eight thirty on Wednesday night, he picked it up without looking at the caller I.D., assuming it was Angel.

"Hey sweetheart."

A masculine chuckle greeted his response. "Well hello yourself, sweetheart."

Rolling his eyes, Adam went back to rolling out the dough he'd been working on. He'd told Angel he'd bring a dessert for dinner at her place tomorrow and he'd decided to make a pie using the recipe Justin had given him. Made from scratch, filled with peaches, and hopefully both delicious and impressive.

"Rick."

"I take it you're expecting a call from Angel? Don't worry, I won't take up too much of your time."

"What can I do for you?"

"I'm hoping you can put me up for a couple of days. I want to come up to your area in a couple of weeks and do some apartment hunting, I was thinking Thursday evening through Sunday morning if I can find a place to stay."

"Of course, not a problem." Adam was usually the first call on everyone's list when they needed a place to stay, for whatever reason. He'd put up most of his friends at one time or another. Hell, he liked doing it. Sometimes the house got a little lonely. He'd particularly liked having Angel overnight and in his bed, something he hoped to repeat again soon. Possibly as soon as the upcoming weekend. "Any weekend you'd like."

"Thanks." Rick paused. "So, ah... things are going well with Angel?"

"Yeah." Adam grinned. They'd talked on the phone for the past two nights, and even more surprisingly, it hadn't just been her talking. She'd insisted on an equal exchange of information, which was something that wasn't easy for him. He much preferred face to face conversation, but she was good at asking the right questions to get him going. "She stayed the night on Sunday. Surprised you hadn't heard already."

Especially since Adam had finally given in to Justin's probing questions and told him earlier today.

"Well... Nothing like hearing it from the source, anyway," Rick admitted. Adam laughed, for once not bothered that their friends were talking about him. "I don't want to interfere with any plans with her."

"No worries, she'll understand. We can always go play at Stronghold if we need to blow off some steam." His phone beeped at him and he glanced at the screen. "And that's my cue to go. Angel's calling. Let me know what weekend you want to come up and I'll have a guest room ready for you."

"Thanks man, tell your girl I say hi."

Hanging up on Rick, Adam switched over to Angel, feeling a little spurt of pleasure she'd called him even though she hadn't said she was going to. While he might be dominant, both in the bedroom and a fair amount in life, he could still appreciate being the one to receive a phone call instead of being the one to make it. It was nice to know she wanted to talk to him as much as he wanted to talk to her.

"Hey sweetheart, guess what I'm doing?"

"What?"

"Making pie."

Angel's delighted laugh burbled over the phone waves.

ANGEL

The doorbell rang and Angel dashed down the stairs. She'd purposefully prepared dinner to minimize the amount of things she would have to do now. Most of it was already done. The roast had been taken out of the oven ten minutes ago—as long as Sam had done the one task assigned to him and if he hadn't she would kick his butt—and was resting while the twice-cooked cauliflower baked. And when they were ready for dinner, she would need to take five minutes to do the asparagus.

When she opened the door she wasn't surprised at all to find him looking incredibly good in a long navy coat. She could already see from the collar that he was wearing one of his usual white button-down shirts. The man needed more color in his life.

"Hi, come on in."

A tremor of pleasure and surprise went through her when he stepped in the door, handed her the pie, and leaned down to kiss her, soundly, before he even took off his coat.

"And hello there to you, too," he said when he was done, blue eyes twinkling merrily. Sometimes, when he looked at her like this, she wondered how she'd ever thought him to be Mr. Grouchy. But that was part of him too.

"Hey man! Welcome back." Sam came sauntering into the room, looking quite pleased to see Adam, which surprised Angel a little bit. Out of her three roommates, Sam usually took the longest to warm up to new people. He wasn't unfriendly, just shy. Mark was the most outgoing and Q had a confidence that Sam couldn't match.

"Hey. Good to see you again," Adam said, grinning as their hands met. Which surprised Angel even more. She eyed both of them suspiciously.

Seeing the look, Adam's smile deepened as he slung his arm over her shoulder. "Sam gave me a new appreciation for country music last week."

Sam laughed and went to sit down in his favorite armchair, Angel gestured for Adam to sit on the couch as she put the pie he'd brought in the kitchen. The timer on the cauliflower had started beeping too. Time to put the finishing touches on dinner.

"Dinner will be ready in a few," she called back over her shoulder.

ADAM

As soon as Angel was out of the room, Q pounced.

"Where did you and Angel meet? She's never said."

"At a club."

"Really? Normally she never gives out her number to guys at clubs," Sam interjected, looking surprised.

"She didn't then. But she told me about the show she was in and I ended up going to see it and then we ran into each other again after that... and it seemed like fate." He deliberately didn't give them any details about exactly what club he'd met her at or where they ran into each other again because he didn't know how much information Angel had given to them.

"What do you do for a living?" Q asked, obviously not deterred from his questioning. Sam rolled his eyes sympathetically at Adam, while Mark chuckled but also waited for the answer.

"I own a head-hunting and temporary employment placement company."

All three of them look a little startled.

"You *own* it?" Mark asked.

"Yeah. What do you guys do?" Turnabout was fair play he figured, and if he was going to be spending time with Angel he was apparently going to be spending time with her housemates.

"Apple store, doing the repairs and stuff," said Sam.

"I've got the dream job, video game testing for Maxland Games," Mark said grinning.

"I write proposals for a contracting company," Q said. Adam raised his eyebrows, he'd been expecting another tech job quite honestly. To his surprise, he earned his first real smile from Q. "We can't all live the dream."

Just then the doorbell rang and the three men frowned at each other.

"Were we expecting someone else?"

"I didn't think so."

"Angel? Did you invite someone else over?"

She popped her head out of the kitchen. "No. Find out who it is, dinner will be ready in one minute." Flashing a brilliant smile at Adam, she disappeared again. Very faintly he could hear the sound of something sizzling.

With a slightly exasperated groan, Mark got up from his seat and went to the door. When it opened, Adam was a less than pleased to see Michael standing there.

All three housemates greeted him as if he had a standing invitation to be there and they were glad to see him. Q gave Adam a sidelong look, as if gauging his reaction to the other man, but Adam stood and smiled, giving Michael his hand. He'd lined up a job for the other man and had already received good feedback from the employer.

And he told himself he was *not* jealous about the welcome Michael could obviously always expect at Angel's house.

"Pretty boy!"

"Pest."

Adam sighed inwardly, but since things were more solid between him and Angel, he found their interaction easier to tolerate than he would have otherwise.

"Come on in, you're just in time for dinner."

"Thanks, I was hoping you might take pity on me. I've been eating my own cooking all week." Everyone chuckled. Looked like Michael was staying for dinner.

❦

ANGEL

Dinner started off a little awkward, but it got better as everyone relaxed. She understood why her friendship with Michael was occasionally hard for other guys to take. They were particularly close and at one point in her life she'd lusted after him. Hell, when she was single she still fantasized about him a bit, even though she knew it would never happen. The few times they'd gotten close to doing something post-Monica, her ex-best friend would always pop into her head and she had pulled away.

Besides, having been to Stronghold and playing with Adam now, she knew she was so not on Michael's level. She did like a little bit of pain with her pleasure, but Adam was much more to her speed.

She did what she could to show Adam she wanted to be with *him*. While she wasn't going to change how she interacted with her friends, she was perfectly happy to lean into Adam's shoulder, to keep their knees touching while they were eating, and to hold his hand whenever she wasn't eating. Since he was on her right that meant she kind of couldn't eat when they were holding hands, but that was okay. Being a pretty tactile person, she liked the constant touching.

After dinner Q offered to do the dishes while Adam's pie heated up in the oven.

"How 'bout a Halo match?" Sam asked, looking around the table. He grinned at Angel. "Adam told us about how you impressed his friends."

"Annihilated you mean," she retorted, grinning back at him. Adam's hand squeezed hers and she turned to see his eyes laughing. "Did he tell you about the game he played with me?"

"Ah no, I was trying to save myself the embarrassment," he said dryly.

"Nothing to be embarrassed about," Michael said, giving both Mark and Sam a look. They returned it smugly. "She's been trained by the best. You could lose hours of your life trying to get to either of these guys' level. Or Q's."

"Says the voice of experience." Adam chuckled.

"You didn't do too badly last time," Mark said reassuringly to Michael. "We could have a rematch... see if you've improved."

Michael groaned. "Adam? Angel? One of you want to be on the losing team with me?"

"I'm going to step into the kitchen and see if I can help Q out with the dishes," Adam said, surprising Angel. "He might need someone to dry."

"You don't have to do that," she said quickly, feeling a little awkward about having him do household chores. Even though she wouldn't mind playing Sam and Mark in Halo. It had been awhile since she and Michael teamed up and they always had fun even if they lost miserably.

"But I want to. Go play, I'll be there to watch in a bit," Adam said, dropping a kiss on her lips before standing.

"I'd almost rather you didn't," she grumbled, getting to her feet along with the rest of the group. "You don't need to learn their secrets."

ADAM

When Adam came into the kitchen, Q gave him a wary look. The arms of his shirt were rolled back to show off pretty muscular forearms and he'd finished loading the dishwasher and had started in on the pots and pans Angel had used. From the looks of it, she didn't follow the "clean as you go" adage.

Then again, he'd gotten the impression she did most of the cooking in the house and so the guys did the dishes in recompense. And the yard work. She had them well trained.

"Thought I'd help you dry," Adam said, picking up a towel. "They're going to play some Halo."

Q snorted. "You might want to watch that, it's pretty amusing."

Although his tone was bland, Adam still felt like maybe there was a little bit of a bite underneath. Q wouldn't be rude, but more and more over dinner, watching the interactions, he'd decided Q had a thing for Angel. Well hidden, granted, under the guise of brotherly vigilance, but there nonetheless.

"So they said, but I think I'll have plenty of opportunity to see that kind of thing," he said mildly, hinting to Q he was planning on being around quite a bit in the future.

"Maybe, but Michael won't always be here, and he and Angel are always entertaining as a team."

Even though Q didn't look at him, Adam was aware of the other man's regard. He was deliberately prodding Adam about Michael and Angel's relationship. Adam wondered how often Q had done that to some of Angel's exes. He bet it was a pretty effective tactic.

"I'm sure they are, they've been good friends for a while."

This time when Q glanced at him, it was with a glimmer of respect in his dark eyes. Adam began drying the pot Q handed him.

"You don't mind that most of Angel's friends are men?" This was said with a hint of challenge, as if daring Adam to try and make her choose between himself and her friends. Not a mistake Adam would make even if he hadn't like her friends—and fortunately for him he did. Feeling possessive was one thing, letting it ruin what he'd started with Angel was another.

"I wouldn't say I'm thrilled about it, but I can live with it. I like her," he stated baldly. "A lot." Q handed him another pan. It was good to keep their hands busy while they had this conversation, allowing them to talk without having to look at each other. The running water and the chatter of the others in the next room meant their words would go unheard except by each other. A safe place.

He'd noticed Sam and Mark tended to defer to Q, and even though they liked Adam they still looked to Q for a lead. Angel obviously cared a great deal for all of her housemates. While Adam wasn't used to being as open as he was with Q when it came to his relationships, he did want to get off on the right foot with all of her housemates. And being honest about how he felt for her was part of that.

"She's special," Q said finally. "A lot of guys like her. *A lot.* She's the kind of girl guys feel comfortable with, comfortable talking to and comfortable hanging out with. And she's beautiful. It's not the easiest combination to find, especially for guys who are a little bit more nerd than jock." A quick look confirmed to Adam that Q considered Adam to be in the latter category. Maybe he should tell Q about his sci-fi/fantasy book collection. "She deserves someone who can appreciate her."

"That's quite a recommendation." Adam paused and then decided to go for it. He picked up the next pot and watched Q closely. "I'm surprised you don't want her for herself."

For the briefest moment, Q froze. And then his hand went back to scrubbing again. He didn't look at Adam. "It doesn't matter what I, or any other guy wants. It matters what Angel wants."

Q was a good guy. Adam changed the subject and asked the poor guy about what kind of proposals he wrote for his job. He'd been right. Q did have feelings for Angel which went far beyond brotherly or friendly, but he would never act on them. Because he knew what Angel's answer would be.

And Q and any other guy could crush as hard on Angel as they wanted, if she didn't want them back then it didn't matter what their feelings were. Surprisingly, thinking over Q's words helped ease a lot of the jealousy and possessiveness Adam had been feeling. Angel had had plenty of time to get together with Michael before meeting Adam, but she was just friends with him. She'd chosen Adam to explore kink with, told Adam she liked him, and agreed to be exclusive with Adam.

When he and Q rejoined the others, he could look at them all with new eyes. Michael and Angel were seated side by side on the couch with almost no room between them and plenty of room on either side of them. It made him hesitate, for a moment, but then Angel glanced over at him and her eyes lit up. She tilted her head towards the space on her other side.

Did her eyes light up for others? Yes, but not the way they did for him. Because she was a vibrant, expressive person. And he liked her that way. He knew he had some trouble with being open emotionally, he'd been closed off ever since he was a kid. Even before Brian had died, Adam had been pretty controlled about expressing himself, especially with his parents always fighting over their kids' love and attention. After Brian overdosed he'd become even more so, because he'd seen how an excess of emotions had led Brian down the path to self-medication and eventually destruction. But he'd been overcompensating for years. Being around Angel made him feel like he was more open again, he couldn't help but reciprocate the incredible warmth she gave off.

And the moment he sat down, she snuggled closer to him. Grinning, he leaned back and watched the show.

The trash talking was epic. All of it coming from Michael and Angel, although Sam and Mark occasionally returned fire.

"Mother fucker... Goddamn it, how the fuck did you do that?"

"I have a straw here if you want to suck it up."

"Angel, you're too loud."

"Your mom's loud."

"Your mom was loud last night."

"I would fuck your mom, but she's a disease-ridden whore."

"Woah... woah guys, getting personal here."

"FUCK!"

"Your mom's a wet bandit."

"I'm the bandit that left your mom wet."

"Left her wet? What, you couldn't finish the job?!"

"Haha, take that! I raped you so hard your ancestors felt it!"

"Dude, too far."

"Right, right, sorry."

"You guys are idiots."

"Be quiet Q, people with hair are talking."

"Fuck you, man."

Eventually Adam stopped trying to hold in the laughter. On the other side of Michael, Q was chuckling despite the insults which occasionally got thrown his way. Wisely, Adam decided to stay out of it. Although apparently Angel didn't entirely approve of his plan.

"What's the matter, scared to open your mouth?" she taunted him, her eyes bright and teasing.

Adam gave her his best quelling look. "If I want to hear your lip, I'll scrape it off my zipper."

Dead. Silence.

And then an explosion as the guys started cheering and whooping for him. Angel's jaw had dropped, and she wasn't paying attention to the screen in front of her at all as Adam's stern look broke and he burst out laughing at her too. He'd never seen her look so thrown.

Then Sam started talking, his voice almost an intonation. *"And shepherds we shall be..."*

Angel's entire body jerked around to stare at the screen. "What? No!"

"For thee my Lord for thee," Mark joined in with Sam in a chant-like rhythm as both Angel and Michael cursed and started pushing buttons frantically. *"Power hath descended forth from Thy hand, our feet may swiftly carry out Thy commands."*

Adam recognized the quotation of the prayer from *Boondock Saints*, but he didn't understand Michael and Angel's reaction, since neither of them were dead yet or even under fire.

"Mother fucker... "

"So we shall flow a river forth to Thee..."

"Mike, Mike, run! FUCK, I hate you guys!"

"And teeming with souls shall it ever be...."

"No, no, no, No, NO NO!"

"In Nomeni Partri, et Fili, et Spiritus Sancti."

Both of Angel and Michael's screens went down and dark. Angel threw her hands up in the air. "Fuck you guys! I was distracted! That wasn't fair!"

Sam and Mark were laughing and sending each other long distance high fives from their armchairs.

"We haven't gotten to do that in ages!"

"Fuck yeah man!"

"Thanks, Adam!"

Adam blinked. "What just happened?"

Angel groaned and Michael chuckled, shaking his head. "If you're ever playing any game against these guys and they start chanting the Saint's prayer, know you're about to die."

ANGEL

After having the pie Adam had brought over, Mike left, then Sam, Mark, and Q had all suddenly decided they were going to go to their respective rooms to do... whatever. Not very discreetly, but Angel was still touched by the gesture.

She grinned at Adam. "I had a good time tonight. I'm glad you could come over."

"Me too." The smile he gave back in return was different than it had been earlier. More relaxed. Maybe it was because all the other guys were gone, but she'd noticed a very subtle change in him ever since he'd come back from helping Q out with the dishes. Normally whenever guys she'd dated had talked to Q they'd come back more tense than relaxed, which made her wonder what he and Q had talked about. She figured Q was the one to usually deliver the "hurt Angel and we'll hurt you" speech, but she couldn't imagine why that would make Adam so relaxed and cheerful. "Although I don't think I'll be playing Halo with any of your housemates any time soon."

"Worried you can't keep up?" she teased.

"Worried I'd be buried by the trash talk."

Angel laughed. She'd been so shocked when he'd lobbed the zipper comment back at her, it had been so utterly unlike Adam, but she'd been delighted. Maybe that made her weird, to be so impressed by the insult, but it was true. Especially because it had been so unexpected.

"You held your own."

"That I did."

They grinned at each other for a moment and his hand reached out to stroke the side of her cheek. Angel snuggled into the caress. She liked how tactile Adam was, and the fact that it seemed to be more than possessiveness or initiating sexual contact.

His hand dropped down to the collar of her sweater.

"I like this color on you."

"Thanks, me too." She glanced down at the sweater. "I like bright colors."

"I've noticed. I'm more of an earth-tones guy, myself."

"Really? All I ever see you wearing is white collared shirts."

Now it was Adam's turn to laugh. "I do wear other things on occasion. But white collared shirts are easy and they work for any occasion."

"Guys have it so much easier than girls," she complained snuggling closer. She was trying to work up the courage to ask him to go up to her room with her, but it wasn't easy prepping herself to make the first move. "We don't have any articles of clothing that do that."

"What about a little black dress?" Adam traced his finger down her nose to her lips as she tilted her head back at him. Being tucked under his arm was nice. Now if only she could get him to kiss her and then she could suggest they could go up to her room.

"That's still only appropriate for certain occasions. Besides, I don't think I own one."

"Somehow that doesn't surprise me." He brushed a soft kiss across her lips, not at all the kind she was looking for and then sighed as he glanced over at the clock. "I should head out."

"Oh..." She tried to keep the disappointment out of her voice but she knew she wasn't entirely successful. So much for being a good actress. "I was hoping that maybe..."

This time the look Adam gave her was amusement tempered with a sensual hunger that made her insides feel all jumpy. "Are we still going to Stronghold tomorrow night? We can play there... or you can come home with me afterwards. Or both."

"Yes," she purred, pressing her breasts against his side.

Adam chuckled and brought his mouth down on hers, much more roughly, stealing her breath away with the intensity of his kiss. When he finally released her, her body was throbbing. "I do have to go though. If you don't have any plans, I'd love to have you stay the weekend with me."

"I have to teach a dance class on Saturday for my parents..." she smiled hopefully up at him. "Want to come?"

"Sure."

This time the smile she gave him was nothing short of brilliant.

23

ANGEL

When Angel arrived at the club, she still felt the same amount of nervousness as last week as she pulled off her coat. Lexie gave her an approving once-over.

"Hot damn woman!"

Angel laughed. "If I'd seen you last weekend, you would've seen this outfit already."

The crisscrossing leather straps were surprisingly comfortable, or would be once she got in the club. The entryway was a little cold though. The low whistle by the door separating the lobby from the rest of the club made her glance over. Jared was on duty tonight and he gave her an encouraging wink.

Lexie groaned. "Yeah, I'm sorry about that. I heard you got here just in time for all the drama."

"Are you okay?"

"I'm fine," Lexie said stoutly. "People have been telling Patrick all week how much they enjoyed the Valentine's Day party. I think Stronghold needs to do more themed nights, so I'm going to try to convince Patrick of that tonight... which means not pissing him off with what I'm wearing."

Looking over Lexie's outfit of a baby blue corset and hot pants, which was incredibly sexy on her slim little body, Angel could only shake her head. "You think this won't piss him off?"

"Well in comparison to what he knows I *could* be wearing..."

They both giggled.

"Well, good luck," Angel said. "I love the idea."

"Thanks. Have a good night tonight—uh... where's Adam by the way?"

"He should be here soon," Angel said. They'd decided to take separate cars to Stronghold. Well, she had decided. She'd agreed to spend the entire weekend at his house, but for her that meant she also wanted to be able to leave when she needed to or go out and run an errand if she wanted to. Not that she thought there might be any negative reason to want that, but she liked the freedom of having her own car there.

"Great, well go on in. No one else is here yet except Andrew, he's behind the bar."

"Thanks!"

She stopped to chat with Jared for a couple of minutes on her way in. The big guy wasn't looking so good. His eyes looked tired and even though he smiled at her before waving her into the club, there was an exhausted resignation hanging about him which she didn't like. To be honest, it kind of reminded her of the way Leigh was when things weren't going well with Michael. Adam had told her about Jared's relationship with his submissive, Marissa, and to Angel it sounded like she was dragging the big Dom around on all sorts of strings. Kind of emotionally abusive, which was weird to think about when the victim was a big, hulking guy like Jared, but that was life.

It sucked that some bitch was taking advantage of him.

Seeing some of the looks she was getting from the few available Doms scattered around the tables at the bar, Angel decided she should head right to one of the barstools near where Andrew was tending bar and wait for Adam there.

As soon as he saw her, Andrew shook his head. She grinned at him as she sat down.

"Are you looking to start a fight tonight, little girl?" he asked, leaning on the bar. There weren't too many other people there yet, so he could pay the attention to her. "Adam's going to flip his shit when he sees you wearing that."

"Then he shouldn't have run late tonight. Besides, he already saw me wearing it at the party," she countered. "Not that he did anything about it then."

"Ah. Yeah, things got kind of messed up on Friday. What do you want to drink?"

"Just a water. Adam should be here soon and I think we're going to play."

Andrew laughed. "Dressed like that, you'd better believe you're going to play."

The big Dom flipped a glass off of its stack and grabbed the soda hose. Angel admired the economical grace of his movements. It was something she'd noticed a lot of Adam's friends had in common. They were large and in charge, but surprisingly graceful about it. Maybe it was the fact that most of them went to Liam's dojo. Angel knew Adam went there most Wednesday nights and he said the other guys would show up on a regular basis as well.

"What's doing, little girl?"

"I'm not exactly little, you know," she pointed out.

Andrew raised his eyebrow at her, those dark chocolate eyes looking rather reproving. "You'd better not be running yourself down."

She rolled her eyes and gestured to the leather straps crisscrossing her body. "Does it look like I've got body insecurities?" Okay, well that wasn't entirely true, she had some, but for the most part she liked her curves and her body and she wasn't afraid to wear something crazy. But it hadn't been what she was talking about. "I meant that just because you're a freaking giant, that doesn't make *me* little."

Staring at her for a moment, Andrew barked a laugh. He smiled, tilting his head as if he didn't quite know what to make of her.

"Oops... that was disrespectful, wasn't it?" She made a face as Andrew laughed again.

"You're fine, little girl, I can tell you didn't say it to be a brat. You aren't the type."

"Why do you make that sound like a bad thing?"

She'd surprised him, she could tell from the way his eyebrows jerked up when he looked at her before his gaze slid away. Then he smiled, a slow, hot, flirtatious smile and crossed his arms on the bar, leaning forward across the wood.

"Because I'm a sadist, little girl, and I like to hurt little brats."

Wow... her pulse was racing and not because she was turned on. Nope, because she wanted to run.

"You're kind of scary," she blurted out, falling back on an old tactic—whenever she was uncomfortable she would say the first thing that came to her head, because she'd found it usually broke the tension.

And, as usual, she was right. Andrew laughed, a deep-throated, full-bodied laugh that suddenly seemed to take years off his face. She stared, absolutely fascinated. While she'd seen him laughing and joking with his friends, she'd never seen him laughing like this, with complete abandon. It changed his face completely and she suddenly realized how often he looked almost angry; it was that before she assumed it was the natural shape of his face.

Turned out, it wasn't, and when he lost his air of tension, he looked a lot more approachable and open.

"So ah... what's with this song?" Angel asked, waving her hand up in the air, when he finally stopped laughing, although he hadn't lost the twinkle in his eye. The throbbing strange noises were kind of getting to her, she hadn't heard anything quite like it before.

"It's called 'Timestretch' by Bassnectar, why? Don't you like it?"

"I don't know... it kind of sounds like Transformers having sex."

Andrew lost it again. Around the bar, Angel could see people's conversations slowing or stopping as they stared at the big Dom. Good to know she wasn't the only one surprised by his unusual enjoyment of her quips. Then again, she'd never had a one-on-one conversation with him before. But she hadn't been trying to make him laugh, that was actually what it sounded like to her.

"Holy crap, Angel... no wonder Adam's finally starting to loosen

GOLDEN ANGEL

up," Andrew said, grinning at her. "The shit that comes out of your mouth, you kind of remind me of..."

His voice trailed off and the joy leeched from his face so fast Angel almost wondered if she'd imagined it. Most people would let it go. Most people would realize it was something he didn't want to talk about.

But Angel always liked to ask. Especially when she sensed the kind of pain she was feeling from Andrew right now. Sometimes talking about it helped.

"Remind you of..." She trailed off the same way he had. There was a long pause, one of his fingers drumming on the wooden expanse of the bar. "You don't have to tell me if you don't want to."

For some reason, those were so often the magic words. Andrew gave her a half-hearted smile which didn't make it up to his eyes. "I was going to say you kind of remind me of my ex."

He said it without heat or even anger. Angel reached out her hand and put it over top of his. Partly to comfort, and partly because the incessant tapping of his finger was starting to drive her crazy.

"Is that a good thing or a bad thing?"

There was another long moment of Andrew studying her again. She met his gaze calmly, sensing this was a strange moment for him. But she truly wanted to know. No one had been willing to talk much about Andrew's ex, although she knew enough to know the break-up had been bad. Bad enough he hadn't had a relationship since, nothing more than club play with submissives who understood the score. She didn't want to increase his pain by reminding him of his ex if it was a bad thing.

"You know... I think it might be a good thing," he said, his half-grin spreading a bit. "Kathy would always say ridiculous shit too, but she did it because she knew it would make me laugh. You say shit and it's ridiculous."

"Yeah, my verbal filter's kind of like Swiss cheese," she said a little ruefully, and was rewarded with another chuckle from Andrew.

It wasn't the same as his laughter before, but at least it was genuine.

302

Then his eyes flicked over her shoulder and he pulled his hand away. "Hey man."

Hands slid around Angel's waist, over skin and straps, and Angel twisted her head around to look up at the man whose heat was suddenly surrounding her. "Hey you."

ADAM

Adam hated the twist of jealousy he'd felt seeing Angel's hand on Andrew's. When he'd come in, they'd been in the middle of what looked like a serious conversation, with her hand over his, and Adam had felt some of his stupid doubts rising up again. After all, she'd wanted to experience BDSM and he'd taken over completely, not allowing her to try anything with anyone else.

Was she craving something rougher than Adam could give her?

Fortunately, he had enough brains to take a deep breath and stamp on his doubts before they welled up and overtook him completely. Angel wasn't that type. And Andrew would have been an extremely poor choice for her even if she was. Besides, if she wanted a session with a sadist, all she'd have to do is ask Michael. There was no doubt the man would oblige, with or without sex as part of the scene.

Looking down into those gorgeous, golden eyes, which were so obviously filled with pleasure at seeing him, he couldn't doubt she'd been nothing but friendly to Andrew. Angel was a tactile person and he would have to get used to that.

"You look stunning," he told her, lowering his head to hers for a searing and possessive kiss.

Kissing Angel in the bar, outside of a scene, let everyone know she was spoken for far beyond the Introduction and second scene Adam had done with her. He heard some of the surprised murmurs behind his back and when he came up for air again, Andrew's eyes were glinting in appreciation.

"You kids go have fun," he said, clearing away the glass of water Angel had been drinking. The look he gave Adam was indecipherable, something intense and complex enough Adam wasn't entirely sure what Andrew was feeling. "Hold onto this one Adam, she's a keeper."

It wasn't unlike Andrew to say something like that, but the tone in which he said it—there wasn't any laughter or teasing in his voice at all. Not quite a warning but... something.

Andrew turned his back and walked down the bar to a couple of Doms who were sitting down there, obviously deciding whether they wanted to drink and socialize or head over to the Lounge area where a couple of the submissives were gathering. Adam felt nothing but relief he no longer had to do that.

No, instead he got to spend his evening with the delightfully enchanting little submissive in front of him. Who was wearing her leather straps again. He stifled the impulse to take off his shirt and cover her up. In the past he would've said he liked it when a submissive showed off her body, that he enjoyed the spectacle, but Angel seemed to bring out the worst of his possessive qualities.

"What were you two talking about?" he asked, his curiosity aroused by Andrew's unusual intonation.

A little line appeared in the center of Angel's eyebrows, she swiveled around on the bar stool to face him, tilting her head back and to the side, somehow simultaneously being both cute and sexy. "He said I reminded him of his ex-girlfriend, Kathy."

Incredulous, Adam shot a look down the bar at Andrew, but the man was fully involved in the conversation he'd started up with the two Doms down there.

"He what?"

"He said it was a good thing," she offered up. Which only made Adam feel even more off kilter.

He muttered under his breath and Angel poked him in the stomach. "What?"

"I can't remember the last time Andrew said Kathy's name."

"Oh..." Angel seemed to think it over for a minute, chewing on her lower lip, while Adam tried to gather his thoughts. "He said it was because I made him laugh by saying silly shit, and she used to try to do that."

"Yeah, she did." He was shocked Andrew was willing to remember anything good about her. They'd all liked Kathy and the outrageous comments she'd made, right up until the day she'd ripped Andrew's heart out and made him out to be a monster. But no one talked about that, or her, anymore. Least of all Andrew.

"So... are we going to play?" Angel asked, almost wistfully, and Adam shook himself.

Now was not the time to get contemplative over Andrew's past relationship or his current issues with any kind of commitment. It was pretty obvious he had no intention of talking to Adam about it or he wouldn't have walked away the second Adam showed up. The poor guy was probably as shocked as Adam was that he'd even brought Kathy up.

Somehow, Adam wasn't entirely surprised though. Shocked, but not surprised. Angel seemed to have that effect on people, especially guys. Q was right—she made them feel relaxed. So relaxed that even the most stoic of them would end up dropping tidbits of their lives they didn't mean to. He remembered how he'd inadvertently brought up Brian and the issues he had with his parents and their divorce, something that normally would take him months to even mention to someone new.

Time to get her into a room to himself, before she ended up drawing out any more revelations from poor, unsuspecting Doms. Maybe he could set her on Olivia later for amusement's sake and see if Angel worked as well on her.

"Actually, sweetheart, I think you're going to jail." Adam grinned at Angel's sudden confusion, stroking his fingers along the bare expanses of skin her outfit made so readily available to him. "For public indecency."

ANGEL

Angel couldn't stop her giggling as Adam led her downstairs to the Dungeon. She was relieved he'd arranged for a private room this time. Not that she didn't like the Dungeon but considering this was their first time playing at Stronghold as a couple she was glad they were going to have some privacy because she was feeling a little nervous.

Excited too, though. Although some part of her brain was still pondering over Adam's reaction to her and Andrew's conversation. She was dying to know what had happened between Andrew and his ex. There was obviously a lot more to the story than a simple break up if Andrew hadn't even said her name for a long time. But she couldn't concentrate on that because Adam kept giving her the most wicked looks, making her belly fizz.

He looked delicious in the black leather pants and the white button down he was wearing. The outfit should have looked incongruous, but it fit him perfectly. Buttoned up, in control, and incredibly sexy. Yep, that pretty much described him.

The Dungeon wasn't very full yet, but Adam steered her right into jail. Closing the door behind him, he took the opportunity to shutter the view through the window as well, giving them complete privacy.

Turning, he looked her up and down, leering a little bit and she giggled again. Adam shook his head at her. "No laughing, ma'am, public indecency is a serious charge. Now get that exposed ass of yours behind those bars."

Feeling almost like a little kid, Angel practically skipped into the jail portion of the room and turned around as Adam closed the door behind her.

"Now what?" she asked, feeling a little confused since he was on one side of the bars and she was on the other.

Adam laughed. "Haven't done much role playing before, have you?"

"Nope. Never even thought about it." She twisted her hands in front of her and looked around the stark room as Adam settled down in the chair next to the desk. "So, are you the Sheriff or something?"

"Or something."

"So, uh... are you going to let me out of here? Or sit there staring at me?"

"I don't know, sweetheart. You're not giving me much of a reason to let you out of there. Can you think of anything you might be able to do to help motivate me?" The teasing grin Adam gave her was at complete odds with the stern tone of voice he was using.

Okay... she could do this... role play was basically acting, after all. Going up to the bars closest to his desk, she gripped one in each hand and rubbed her breasts against the cold steel. Behind the small patches of leather her nipples hardened as she licked her lips. Adam's eyes glowed, but he leaned back, putting his feet up on the desk as if he couldn't care less what she was doing.

"Come on officer... I bet I can think of a bunch of things you might want in exchange for letting me out of here." Unfortunately, she couldn't help but giggle again as she winked at him. It was too hard not to feel silly.

Adam shook his head at her, crossing his arms over his chest, but she could see the amusement in the quirk of his lips. "I don't know sweetheart, doesn't look like you have money on you... that outfit wouldn't allow it."

"I bet we could still come up with some kind of exchange." She licked her lips again and watched as Adam shifted, his eyes on her mouth. "I bet a big, strong Sheriff like you has a nice big cock that could use some kisses."

When Adam chuckled, it seemed like he was still in character, unlike her with the giggle bubbling up in her chest. "Don't see anything too special about a blow job, sweetheart. Lots of girls will get down on their knees to get out of jail. I think I'm pretty tired of those. Got anything else to offer?"

Angel made a face at him, but he grinned so she decided he was teasing and hadn't had too many girls in here begging to give him a blow job. It was just part of the character.

Taking one of her hands off the bars, she ran it over the leather straps, working her way down her body to the larger expanse of leather covering her pussy. Adam's eyes followed her hand down and she could tell he appreciated her teasing. Heck, it was making it a little bit easier to get into the role even though she still felt like giggling. She might like acting and improv, but this was so far outside her comfort zone she was caught between being kind of turned on and feeling silly.

"Walking around all publicly indecent has gotten me all wet," she said silkily, tracing the leather over her mound. The little cough Adam gave when she said 'publicly indecent' was obviously to cover up a laugh. Ha! Got him. "Would you like some nice, hot pussy, Sheriff?"

Appearing to think it over, Adam leaned back in the chair with his hand behind his head. Angel wondered if he was pulling her leg, trying to get her to make a jail break. She eyed the door. It's not like it was locked, she probably could... but the bargaining was fun too. Plus, she had a feeling that breaking out of jail would get her some kind of punishment and she didn't *want* to be bad unless he gave her no choice.

"As nice as that sounds, sweetheart, I think I'll pass. Pussy is easy to get when you're a man of the law." Now it was Angel's turn to laugh at his mock-stern tone. He sounded like a character from a bad Western. A bad, dirty Western. "I think you're going to have to offer me something more... interesting if you want out of that cell."

Anal sex. That's what he was after. And he wanted her to offer it up to him on a silver platter. Her other option was to jail break. And who says he wouldn't take what he wanted if she did that?

Angel licked her lips again. It had been a while since she'd had anal sex, but it was always something she'd liked. Probably because she felt incredibly submissive during anal, there was something wonderfully dirty and forbidden about it that made her feel like she was letting a man do something he wasn't supposed to. There was an intimacy to it, as well.

But yeah... she really, really wanted to do it with Adam.

Time to bargain her ass out of jail.

ADAM

This kind of foreplay was utter torment. Of course, keeping Angel caged up behind the bars was as fun as it was frustrating. Especially the expressions crossing her face as she slid back and forth between trying to role play and being amused. Granted, role play wasn't always his favorite thing in the world, but it was fun on occasion. And he was enjoying bargaining Angel down to entry into that luscious ass of hers.

Seeing her glance at the door to the jail again, he wondered if she was going to make a break for it. If so, he'd know she wasn't ready to do that with him yet. Although, of course, she could always say her safe word too, but he had a feeling Angel would rather make a jail break than say her safe word. Most submissives got a sense of pride out of never having to say it, and a good Dom never pushed so far that his submissive should feel the need to.

Angel licked her lips, dragging her teeth over the plump lower one, and he suddenly knew what her decision was going to be.

Those bright eyes almost glowed as she started unsnapping the straps of her outfit. *Holy shit.* If he'd known how easy it was to take that thing off of her, he would have ripped the damn, teasing thing off of her before shoving her in the jail. Although at that point she might not have made it in.

His cock was pulsing behind his zipper as he watched her little strip tease, her body swaying gently back and forth to the music which was always in the background, although he didn't think she realized she was doing so. The straps fell easily away to crumple onto the floor below her, leaving her completely naked except for those bright red heels on her feet... and separated from him by the bars.

Adam's arms tensed as he forced himself to remain still.

"You got something you want to offer, sweetheart?"

"Yes Sheriff," she said, cupping her breasts and pinching her nipples, which were already hard. At least he knew he wasn't the only one turned on. "Sounds to me like you need a good, tight ass for that cock of yours."

He had to stifle a groan as electricity seemed to shoot straight through his body. Angel was going to offer up her ass to him. Even though she'd marked it as something she had experience in on her survey, he knew it was still something that, for most women, required extra trust. A bit of extra intimacy beyond what regular sex needed.

Standing up, he went over to the door of the jail, keeping his eye on Angel as she trotted over to the entrance.

"Alright sweetheart, come on out, bend over my desk and show me what you have to offer."

She purposefully rubbed herself against him as she exited the jail, smiling happily although he could see she was nervous too. That little thrill of anticipation, of anxiety in her eyes with a hint of fear, was like an aphrodisiac for him. There was nothing sexier than a submissive who was aroused, excited, and apprehensive all at the same time.

Then Angel bent over the desk, resting her arms on its surface and exposing every inch of her gorgeous pussy. The heels she was wearing put her ass at the perfect height for him. Between the mounds of her ass cheeks, her tight, dusky little hole winked at him and Adam could feel his blood surging down to his cock. It was amazing he had enough running through the rest of him to keep his body moving.

Walking over to the desk, he opened the top drawer where he knew the lube was kept. Angel's head was turned slightly, watching his every move. He winked at her and moved back around so he was directly behind her.

Crouching down, he kissed the inside of her thigh, smiling a bit at her gasp of surprise. Working his way up her inner thighs, he eventually reached the wet heaven of her pussy. She was moving her hips up and down slightly, her legs spread far enough that he had easy access to her pink inner lips. Her little clit was poking out of its hood, swollen and eager. Adam flicked his tongue over it and enjoyed the way she moaned in response.

Lubing up his fingers, he continued to lick and suck on her pussy lips, getting her even more aroused. When he pressed one wet fingertip to the entrance of her asshole, circling it a little bit to tease the nerves, Angel groaned and pushed back against him. Damn that was hot. She obviously was more than ready to have something inside of her ass.

Obliging her, he sank his finger deep into her without any further ado. The taut ring of muscle at her entrance clenched down around him as he teased her clit with his tongue. Angel moaned, moving her hips with his finger as he began to slide it back and forth in her tight hole, loosening her up a little bit. When he added a second finger she gasped and shuddered a little bit. He could feel the strain in her body as she adjusted, and he realized she probably hadn't had anal sex in very long time.

Which only made his cock ache even more than it already was.

He sucked her clit into his mouth and felt the tremor shake her entire body. Fuck. Releasing her from his lips, he ignored her mewl of disappointment as he stood.

"Uh uh, sweetheart, you're not going to cum until I'm deep in that hot ass."

She whimpered again as her ass clenched around his fingers. Yeah, she liked that idea. Watching his fingers slickly gliding in and out of her ass, the tiny hole shiny with lube, he used his other hand to undo the front of his pants. There was something incredibly hot to him about taking Angel's ass for the first time while she was completely naked but for her fire engine heels and he was fully clothed.

Her tight little hole gaped slightly when he pulled his fingers out, giving him enough time to spread some lube over the length of his cock, line it up to her hot entrance and begin to press in.

Fuck.

Both of them gasped at the same time as the head of his cock was sucked into her, her body spasming around the intrusion. Adam rubbed her lower back soothingly, stopping his progression and giving her time to adjust to his cock, it was a hell of a lot thicker than his fingers. She had let her upper body slump onto the desk, her head turned to the side and her cheek pressed against the wood. He could see the fluttering of her lashes and her parted lips as she panted through the discomfort.

Watching her endure the discomfort, the slight flashes of pain, all for him was both humbling and wildly arousing. It was one of the biggest reasons anal sex was such a turn on for him. He loved watching the struggle, knowing she was doing so to please him, and it was going to eventually bring both of them incredible pleasure.

ANGEL

The stretch burned... fuck... she hadn't considered Adam's cock was a good bit thicker than anyone she'd ever had anal sex with. But it felt so good too. Toys didn't do the same thing. They were hard, more unyielding and they didn't pulse and throb inside of her the way he did. Angel moaned as he receded a bit then pushed in deeper.

Fuck yes... the burn expanded, making her insides clench and spasm as she whimpered. Feeling him sliding in was both uncomfortable and hot, it was the pull out that had her gasping and shuddering as nerve endings flared to life. The desk was cool beneath her cheek and breasts, her body pressing down onto it for support as he began to slowly rock back and forth, sliding a little deeper with every stroke.

Angel couldn't stop the moaning whimpers as the slow invasion continued. Her eyelids fluttered, but she couldn't focus on anything.

"What's your color, Angel?... Angel?"

"Green," she whispered throatily, her fingers curled as his hips surged and she cried out with the pain and pleasure of it.

The heat of his groin pressed against her buttocks and she realized he was all the way in. Her muscles rippled around him, adjusting, accommodating. That very involuntary act added to how passive and submissive she felt. It was wonderfully freeing. Anal had always turned her on, but this was more intense, more exciting than anything she'd ever experienced before.

"Good girl." Hands caressed her hips and then gripped and he began to fuck her ass, gently but firmly with long sure strokes which had her twisting as her insides writhed with the new sensations. She could feel the breath being sucked out of her as he pulled out, her cries muffled by lack of air when he shoved back in.

It was dizzying, wonderful pleasure, mixing with the sharp stinging bursts of discomfort heating her lower body. Every thrust had his cock pushing against some spot deep inside her, as if there was a g-spot in there or something. She was moaning and shuddering and unable to stop even if she wanted to. The sensations running riot through her were wildly out of control.

The ecstasy rolled through her, unlike any orgasm she'd ever experienced before. Her pussy to spasmed emptily even as the fullness of her ass had her writhing as the starbursts of sensation sparked and ignited inside of her. The rolling sensation of pleasure seemed to travel from her trembling legs all the way through to her fingertips, which were now wrapped around the edges of the desk.

"Oh fuck... Angel..."

The sensation of Adam expanding and then throbbing inside of her only made Angel wail harder as the storm of sensation became almost painful in its intensity. Her ass felt like it was on fire, in the most incredibly erotic way possible. She tightened around him, despite the fact that it made her burn even hotter, wanting to increase Adam's pleasure.

Suddenly his large frame was covering hers completely, practically crushing her between him and the desk. Heat surrounded her and she cried out as she felt him pulse inside of her, filling her bowels with hot cum.

She didn't know how long she lay underneath him, shuddering and completely content, before he pulled away from her. She moaned in surprise and a bit of arousal as the plug was pressed back into her bottom, keeping his cum inside of her, big enough she wouldn't have to work to keep it in without hurting as it was lodged inside of her.

When he helped her stand, wrapping a blanket around her, she put up her arms and wound them around her neck, helping him as he carried her out of the room and to the aftercare corner. The plug jostled a bit, making her wince and shiver as spasms of pleasure rippled through her; the aftermath of her intense orgasm.

"Mmmm, that was nice," she said, feeling all fuzzy and warm as she rubbed her face into his shoulder.

His chuckle seemed to vibrate through her. "That's an understatement sweetheart."

✣ 24 ✣

ANGEL

Shifting nervously by the door to Adam's house, Angel tapped
her foot impatiently. Not that they were late yet, but she was
feeling the build-up of nerves she always did before introducing her parents to a guy. Both of them were going to be at the
studio today; which she'd warned Adam about over breakfast this
morning.

Her cheeks warmed with pleasure when she thought about breakfast. Eaten naked. Last night he'd ended up getting her bag out of her
car so he could give her a ride from Stronghold to his house. She had
meant to take her own car, but after the intense scene she'd been all
too happy to let him talk her into coming in his instead. They were
going back to Stronghold tonight, after all, and she could take it over
to his place from there.

Waking up this morning, with her ass snuggled up to a pretty
prominent erection, had been rather nice. Although, to her surprise he
hadn't done anything with it before getting out of bed and cooking her
breakfast. French toast and scrambled eggs with diced fruit on the

side. Yum. She wasn't normally a breakfast person, but after last night she'd been *starving*.

After a nice, leisurely breakfast she'd glanced at the clock and realized she needed to get ready to go to the dance studio. Which was when the nerves had set in again. If they left now, they'd be there twenty minutes earlier than she needed to be, which she didn't want, but she wanted to get there and get this over with. Little bit of stage fright over her parents meeting Adam maybe?

Yeah. He wasn't the kind of guy she normally dated. He was bigger, badder and more in control and a lot more focused than any of her past boyfriends. Trying to figure out how her carefree and eccentric parents and he would react to each other was nerve-wracking to say the least.

"Hey, are you ready?" Adam came striding down the hall towards the front door. Angel grinned at his outfit.

"Oh my, getting fancy are we?"

"What are you talking about?" He looked down at the blue button-down shirt and jeans he was wearing.

"I didn't know you had shirts in any colors," she teased.

Adam made an exasperated sound, catching her waist with one arm and pulling her in for a kiss. She pressed herself against him, kissing him back with all the nerves and excited energy bundled up in her chest.

"Now I know why Michael calls you 'pest,'" he said wryly as he pushed her out the front door.

ANGEL

About five minutes into the class, Angel realized she'd been had. Any beginners' class tended to be easy to step into and many people were familiar with the waltz, but they didn't move with the smooth assurance Adam did. He hadn't mentioned he'd taken dance before but there was no other explanation.

"Okay, very good everyone! Ladies move to the next gentleman."

Her eyes narrowed as Leslie, one of the older women in the class, stepped up to dance with Adam. Leslie was sweet, but she was also terrible at following any kind of lead, except when she was dancing with the instructors. And yet, as the older woman chattered up at Adam, Angel could tell she was following his lead. Which meant it was particularly strong.

Like most ballroom dance classes there were more women than men enrolled, so Angel was dancing the man's part, which meant she didn't get to dance with Adam and she couldn't watch him the entire time, but from what she could see, this was not his first class. She didn't know whether to be impressed he knew how to dance or annoyed he hadn't told her. Show-off.

But that didn't stop his smile from flickering every time she looked at him.

Out of the corner of her eye, she saw her parents come in and check out the class. She'd given them the heads up that she was bringing her boyfriend by.

Since they were familiar with everyone else in the class, they picked him out immediately. Her dad sat down on one of the benches along the outside of the room to watch her teach while her mom started chatting with a couple who had finished a private class with one of the instructors. Even though it didn't look like her mom was paying attention, Angel knew nothing escaped that woman's notice.

ADAM

By the time the class finished, Adam's neck felt almost itchy from all the prickling. He'd seen Angel's parents come into the room—at least he assumed they were her parents because she faintly resembled both of them—and ever since then he had a creepy-crawly feeling of being watched. Her father was a lot more obvious about it than her mother was, but he could feel it coming from both directions. It was a little bit distracting, although overall he was pleased about how he'd acquitted himself.

Years ago, he'd taken some classes in waltz with Brooke. They hadn't gotten very far but he'd used it on other occasions as well and he'd always focused on making what he did know look good rather than trying to stomp his way through a bunch of fancy steps.

"You should come to class more often," the woman he'd been dancing with said. She patted him on the arm. "You're a good boy."

Adam managed to stifle his laugh. "Thank you, I might."

His gaze flicked over to Angel, who was showing one of the men part of the sequence she'd taught during the class, and the woman's smile broadened. Giving his arm a final pat, she walked over to the closet where everyone's coats were hanging, then sat down on one of the available benches to change her shoes.

"You've danced before?" The question had him turning to face the older man who had appeared beside him. It took all of Adam's self-control not to jump, he hadn't heard any movement next to him.

Bright hazel eyes studied him alertly, flecked with brighter speckles of gold that harkened to the unusual shade of Angel's irises. "Mr. Jones, I presume? I'm Adam Rawn."

He held out his hand, which got a very brief shake as the shorter man peered up at him. The very briefness of the handshake didn't give him much of an impression. If he'd met Mr. Jones in the business world he would have assumed the other man wasn't interested in what Adam had to say, but that completely contradicted the way the man was looking at him.

"She must like you, if she brought you here," Mr. Jones said. He slid his hands into his pocket, seemingly waiting on a response from Adam.

"Ah... I certainly hope she does."

"So, you've danced before?"

Adam was starting to understand where Angel got her occasionally abrupt turns of conversation from, although with her father it was obviously habitual rather than occasional.

"A little bit."

"You're very smooth. Do you foxtrot?"

"No, just waltz and a little bit of swing." Despite the haphazardness of the questions, Mr. Jones' eyes were very sharp as he studied Adam, not at all put off by Adam towering over him. When Angel's hand suddenly slid into his, Adam gave it a quick squeeze, feeling faintly relieved, despite the fact that he'd never been nervous about meeting parents. Mr. Jones' conversational style was a bit rattling.

"Hi Daddy, did you like the class?"

"It was very good. Mr. Rawn has danced before." It was said almost accusingly. Adam saw Angel's lips twitch.

"Yes, I noticed that as well," she said, turning her head to look up at him. "He didn't mention it before we came here."

"I wasn't sure how much I remembered," he said. "It's been years."

"Dancing is all muscle memory," Mr. Jones said sternly. "Do you like camping?"

"Uh, yes."

"Good." The older man started to turn and then stopped, eyeing Adam again. "It was nice to meet you. Have a good afternoon, Angel."

"You too, Sir."

"Bye Daddy."

Mr. Jones strode over to his wife, whispering something in her ear before heading out the door.

Angel squeezed Adam's hand, grinning up at him. "I think he liked you. Normally he doesn't make much effort to talk to someone new."

"That was talking?"

"For him, for a first-time introduction, yes. Don't worry, once he's more comfortable around you he'll talk more. Probably."

"Ah. Okay. Good."

While they waited for Angel's mother to finish her conversation with her students, Angel pestered him with questions about his previous dance experience. That led to her dancing with him, wanting to find out what he knew—which took less than three minutes to show her.

By the time they were done with that, Angel's mother was standing on the sidelines and she gave them a little smattering of applause. Mrs.

Jones was like effervescent bubbles of personality, although her conversational style was scattered. She approached every single sentence with the kind of enthusiasm most people reserved for their favorite topics.

Comparing her to Angel was entertaining. Angel was so obviously a mix between her high-speed and verbose mother and her more laid-back father. Mrs. Jones didn't physically bounce as she chattered, but she gave the impression she was a high-energy, bouncy person. Her hands fluttered in front of her as she spoke.

He also learned Angel could talk at extremely high speeds when she was conversing with her mother.

Somehow, in less than fifteen minutes, Mrs. Jones managed to learn everything Adam usually imparted to a new acquaintance over a full dinner. The rundown of his parents, job, schooling, friends, and as much as he could tell her about the beginning of his relationship with Angel had never been recounted so quickly.

They weren't able to tear themselves free until some of Mrs. Jones' students arrived for a private lesson. And he'd thought his mother was a talker. Good thing she lived in England. He had a feeling that when the two mothers met, he would want to find a place to hide. Mr. Jones would probably join him.

Then he realized, with a bit of a jerk, that he'd thought *when* the two mothers met, not *if*. Grinning, he took Angel's hand in his as they headed back out to his car.

"What are you so happy about?" she asked, looking at him a bit suspiciously.

"Just glad your parents seemed to like me."

Now when she smiled, he could see how much she resembled her mother. And if Angel aged anything like her mother, then he wasn't going to have any complaints. "They did, didn't they? Although I think you had it easy, it's been a while since I introduced a guy to them, so they were prepared to like anyone."

"Hey now, don't take away from my glory," he admonished her with a little glare.

Angel giggled. "Sorry."

"Pest."

"I will bite you if you call me that again."

ANGEL

"Hey guys!" Lexie was positively brimming with happiness, seated at one of the tables at the bar rather than out at the front desk. Angel grinned, thrilled to see her friend inside the main room of the club—and not because of her party. Obviously, she was making some progress on her determined inclusion in Stronghold, although Angel couldn't help but wonder how the young woman's campaign on the club's owner was faring. "Look where I am!"

Adam growled under his breath and Angel nudged him with her elbow. "They've finally let you through the door, huh?"

"Only into this room, and only when accompanied by one of my faithful Sentinels," Lexie said, rolling her eyes and gesturing at the grouchy looking men arrayed around her. Olivia was the only dominant at the table who didn't look out of sorts. Even Chris' expression was clouded. Surprisingly, Patrick was nowhere in sight. "But the party was so popular and so many people e-mailed Patrick this week asking if he was going to do another one and when, that he's agreed to let me do a Saint Patrick's Day party! And since he already let me in this room for one night, it'd be silly to try to keep me out now."

"Yeah, and look how that turned out, he ended up beating up your boyfriend," Andrew said, glaring at the diminutive pixie. She beamed at him, completely oblivious to the threatening looming stance he had over her.

"Not my boyfriend anymore. And good riddance!"

"Cheers to that," Chris said, his trademark grin flashing across his face. Then, as if remembering himself, he glanced around suspiciously at the various Doms scattered around the bar.

As if any of them were stupid enough to think about propositioning Lexie.

Poor Lexie. Even if she was ever allowed into the rest of the club, Angel didn't think anyone would ever go against the displeasure of this group of Doms. Looking around the club, she didn't see Mike. He had told her he might not be able to come to the club as often as he might want to right now. She had a feeling he'd be more sympathetic to Lexie's situation, and it wasn't like he would be in the position of seeing her as a little sister.

Not that she thought the two of them would make a good match or anything, but at least Lexie would get to play... if she was ever allowed on the other levels of the club, so it was a moot point right now anyway.

"Come sit with me, Angel, I need more estrogen around me to combat all this testosterone!"

"Hey!" said Olivia indignantly.

"I already asked you to sit next to me, and you moved," Lexie said, grinning.

"Only because I didn't want to sit so close to Truckstop."

"Truckstop?" Angel asked as she took Chris' place on the stool next to Lexie. Andrew was playing guard on her other side, two spaces were left between where he and Olivia were seated. Adam dragged a stool over from another table and pushed it in beside Angel's. "And where are Jessica and Hilary?"

"They're on their way with Justin and Liam," Chris informed her as he pulled up another stool. "Hmm. We may have to get another table over here."

"That's probably a good idea," Olivia said. "Quick, before Truck-stop comes back."

"Olivia, play nice."

"What's Truckstop?"

"Not what, who. And you're about to meet her." The unfriendly glint in Olivia's silver eyes was sharp enough to draw blood. Angel twisted around in her seat to see Jared walking towards them with an attractive submissive at his side. She was shaped similarly to Leigh, with a smaller upper body that flared out into "child birthing hips," as Angel's mom liked to call them. Long dark blonde hair was bobbing in a high pony-tail. The dismissive look she cast over the table of Jared's friends didn't endear her to Angel.

Then again, considering Olivia referred to her by a derogatory nickname, it was obvious she wasn't part of the 'big happy family' vibe this group sometimes gave off. Angel wondered why. Everyone had been perfectly nice to her when she showed up, except for Adam. She glanced at him, but the expression on his face was completely neutral.

"Hey Angel, good to see you again," Jared said, smiling down at her with pleasure as his eyes flicked over her and Adam. She was uncomfortably aware that all small conversations around the table had stopped and everyone was watching her, Adam, Jared, and the woman —Angel was so not going to call her 'Truckstop,' even in her head, when she didn't even know her. "This is my girlfriend, Marissa. Marissa, this is Angel."

"Hi."

Immediate dislike surged, but Angel tamped it down. She couldn't tell if it was her own reaction or just due to how everyone talked about Marissa.

"Hi, it's nice to meet you," Angel said, going for diplomacy. "Were you at the party here last weekend?"

"No, Jared was working and then he took me away for a romantic weekend." Marissa snuggled up to him with an adoring look, before glancing around the group of friends challengingly.

"Aw that's sweet, where'd you go?" Angel asked as Olivia bristled. She could sense the tension between everyone, and Marissa's answer had increased that. There were some major undercurrents going on which she was probably stepping all over, but what else was she supposed to do?

Marissa smiled at her. It was almost a friendly smile. Almost. "New York City. We saw *Once* on Broadway and had dinner at the Rainbow Room."

The answer took Angel a little bit by surprise, since she would have never expected that answer. She didn't know Jared very well, but he didn't seem like a big city guy. When Marissa had said a romantic weekend away, Angel had assumed a B&B or the beach or something. She looked at Jared, who was watching the interplay between her and his girlfriend with his broad shoulders slightly hunched in a defensive posture.

"That sounds nice. *Once* won a Tony last year didn't it?"

"Yeah. It was okay." As Angel coughed to cover her reaction to the lackluster review to a show she had heard was nothing short of brilliant, Marissa's dark hazel eyes lifted past Angel's shoulder. "Hey Adam."

Angel suddenly understood why the others might not like Marissa so much. She could feel Adam tense behind her, see Jared's expression close down, and the rest of the group was suddenly humming with animosity again. It wasn't that Marissa had greeted him, it was the *way* she had. Flirtatious. Intimate. Completely inappropriate considering her boyfriend's arm was still around her.

"Hi Marissa," he said evenly, and suddenly Angel felt herself being pulled back against him. His hand spread possessively over her belly and she was suddenly glad he'd put her in a lacy black shirt rather than a corset, she liked being able to feel his very warm palm against her stomach. "Angel does some theater."

"Just community, for fun."

"Don't sell yourself short, you're a fantastic actress," he said warmly. Angel twisted her head back to grin at him and he planted a kiss on her lips. He tasted like the whiskey he'd been drinking.

Yum.

When she turned back to Jared and Marissa, she was surprised to see Marissa had turned her back to them and was whispering up into Jared's ear. The big man sighed.

"I think we're gonna head out. I'll see you guys later."

As everyone said goodbye, the look Marissa gave her was unfriendly. What the hell? Angel noticed most of them directed their goodbyes to Jared, without acknowledging Marissa, although it didn't seem to bother the other woman. If she even noticed. She gave off the appearance of not being aware of the animosity directed at her.

"So that's Truckstop," Olivia said, waving her hand after the departing couple. "Delightful, isn't she?"

"I don't understand..." Angel turned to Adam. "Did you use to date her or something?"

He choked. "Oh God no..."

"She's the type of woman who firmly believes every man wants her," Chris said. "And that all she has to do is crook her little finger and they'll come running."

"If you look up narcissistic personality disorder, you'll have a good idea of her personality."

"You should have seen how she dismissed Hilary and Jessica," Chris said, shaking his head. "The only reason she didn't immediately snub you is because she thought you were friends with Lexie and not another submissive. As soon as she realized you were competition, she was done with you."

"She thinks *all* of you want her?" Angel asked, looking around the group.

"She used to think I wanted her too," Olivia said with a smirk. "I disabused her of that notion. Which is why she doesn't want Jared to be friends with me anymore. Fortunately, he's not that far gone."

"Ignore her," Adam said, wrapping his arm around Angel's waist and almost pulling her off of her stool before she shifted to accommodate for his extra weight. "We all do."

"As much as we can anyway."

The conversation circled around, mostly focusing on Marissa's various antics throughout her and Jared's relationship. Angel now realized exactly how discreet Adam had been when he'd told her about the couple. His friends had no problem talking about how Marissa had threatened to kill herself the last time Jared had tried to break up with her. Ugh. She couldn't imagine trying to force a man to be in a relationship with her like that. Why would you want a guy you could only keep around by such extreme measures?

Fortunately, such negative thoughts and conversation were circumvented by the arrival of Justin, Jessica, Hilary, and Liam. The only one missing was Rick, although they all talked about him and Adam told everyone Rick was going to be in town to look for some apartments next weekend. Angel was surprised to hear Rick was going to be staying with Adam. Not that she had a problem with it, because of course she didn't get a say in it, but should she be irked he hadn't mentioned Rick's visit at all?

What point were they at in their relationship?

"Oooo good!" Lexie said, brightening. "That means Angel's free to come to our Ladies' Night!"

Adam groaned as Angel perked up. "Ladies' Night?"

"She means 'trouble waiting to happen' night," he said, pulling Angel onto his lap. She went willingly enough, pleased his possessive display hadn't been solely for Marissa earlier. "Just because Rick is staying at my place over the weekend doesn't mean that Angel won't be spending time with me."

"Yeah, but we wanted to invite her to Ladies' Night anyway," said Jessica. "We hadn't gotten the chance to yet."

"It's on Saturday night," Lexie said brightly. "We're having it at my new place."

"You have a new place?" asked Patrick, suddenly appearing behind her. How did a man that big manage to sneak up on an entire group of people? Despite the greetings thrown his way, Patrick wasn't at all diverted from the question Lexie hadn't answered.

And Angel had thought *Adam* was Mr. Grouchy. Patrick more than beat him out for the title. The scar across his cheek looked particularly intimidating when he was glaring like that.

Intimidating to everyone except Lexie apparently. She eyed her brother's best friend with a peculiar mix of annoyance, resignation, and sexual frustration. "Yes, I have a new place, I wasn't going to live at my parents for the rest of my life."

Patrick ignored the obvious sarcasm in her tone. "Where?"

"None of your business."

"Well we can't help you move in without knowing where."

"I don't think I asked you to."

"Lexie," he said, his tone threatening. Angel glanced around the circle at all the fascinated watchers to the drama. Did they all see what she saw? A young woman with an infatuation and a man who was fighting his own attraction? Or did they see Lexie as Patrick's little sister, the way he was trying to treat her? Most of them looked either thoughtful or highly entertained, so it was up in the air.

"It's BYOC—bring your own chair," Lexie said, turning her back on the big Dom entirely. Unperturbed, she ignored the growling noise he made behind her. Justin's cough sounded suspiciously like a laugh and Olivia wasn't doing a damn thing to hide her amusement. "I don't have any furniture yet other than my TV."

"Good. A night *in* sounds perfect," Patrick said. "Every time you go out you wreak havoc."

Tilting her chin up, Lexie willfully ignored him as she kept her gaze on Angel. "I'll text you the details."

25

ADAM

Strolling into Liam's dojo, Adam was almost surprised how relaxed he felt. Life was good. Fantastic even. He greeted Justin and Chris who were already there and stretching out, waiting for Liam to finish whatever he was doing in the office. Sitting down on the mat beside them he started going through his own warm-up stretches, although he felt a lot less tense than he normally did.

"How's Angel doing?" Chris asked, when Adam settled down into horse stance once he was done warming up.

"She's good." A little smile stretched across Adam's face, which was what inevitably happened any time he thought about Angel. They'd had a great weekend together and then yesterday he'd gone to her parents' house for dinner, which had been both enlightening and entertaining. Just as she'd promised, her father had slowly opened up during the evening, although he still hadn't talked very much in comparison to her mother. Then again, as far as Adam could tell, not too many people talked very much in comparison to Mrs. Jones.

"Got you whipped already, huh?" Justin teased him. "I don't think I've ever seen you smile at the *mention* of a woman."

"Angel's special," Adam said, perfectly willing to admit it. More and more special to him every day.

He'd always considered himself a pretty decisive person, but he hadn't realized how much until he'd started dating Angel. When Justin and Chris had first started dating Jessica and then Liam had gotten involved with Hilary, he'd refrained from commenting on how fast their relationships had moved in his opinion. Adam was of the opinion that there were always surprises in a relationship and it was best to get to know everything about your partner before becoming as involved as his friends had.

Now he wondered if they had felt the same inevitable *rightness* to their relationships as he did right now with Angel. A more negative part of him wondered if that's what his parents had felt and look how it backfired on them. But so far his friends' relationships seemed to be going well, no major surprises or revelations from Hilary or Jessica. Could he have that with Angel?

Although he didn't tell her, he was already thinking in a very long-term kind of way. Wanting her at his house every weekend. Every night, but he'd take weekends for now. Wanting her to meet his parents. Wanting to impress hers. Wanting promises and assurances for a future.

And it shocked him that he wanted all of those things *now*. What had happened to his careful planning? His control over his emotions until he could be sure there weren't any more unpleasant surprises coming his way? Sometimes he wondered if he'd uncovered all of them. Angel was refreshingly blunt and honest, now they were past that first big lie, so he didn't think she was hiding anything from him, but what other things—like all male housemates—did she not consider relevant?

When she was around, these thoughts didn't even occur to him. When she wasn't, they would trickle through his head; insidious little doubts gnawing at him. He was self-aware enough to know those doubts didn't have anything to do with her though, they had to do with his mom. Once, a long time ago, he'd asked his mom why she'd up and left the way she had. Her answer had been about what he'd expected; she hadn't felt like she could talk to his father about what was wrong. Which was a combination of his dad having a strong personality while his mom was passive aggressive. Angel wasn't his mom, and he knew that intellectually, but the insecurity and the worries still plagued the back of his mind.

He nearly fell over from horse stance when he figured out why.

Holy hell. I think I'm in love with her. When had that happened? Dumbass. He should have realized it when he first started thinking about whether or not he might have a real future with her. Sure, that was something smart to think about at his age anyway, the possibility of a future, but it was more than that.

"Yeah he's got it bad," Chris said, snickering. He glanced over at Justin, sharing one of their knowing little looks which had a wealth of conversation packed into it. "Remember when we first looked like that?"

"So how serious are we talking?" Justin asked. "Cuz Jessica and Hilary like her a lot. Lexie and Olivia do too. You'd better do right by her or they're going to be in a snit."

Adam chuckled at the threat. "You've been spending too much time with Hilary. A snit?"

Justin shrugged. "It's descriptive."

"Well if you're going to be gossiping like a bunch of old ladies at least you're in horse stance while you do it," Liam said as he walked into the room. He cast amused looks over all three of them. "What are we talking about?"

"Adam and Angel."

"Ah. Rick's jealous as hell of you by the way," Liam said.

"Once he moves he'll have better luck finding someone. The way the submissives all jump to play with him at the club, it's not like he's going to have any trouble finding willing prospects." Adam frowned, remembering. "They're getting ballsier too, I had more than one of them coming to *me* at the party last week."

"You're not the only one," Liam said, looking amused. "Although Andrew didn't seem cut up about it."

"It felt wrong," said Adam grumpily.

"You can work it out here. Shake out your muscles and we can start forms."

After putting his friends through a grueling workout, Liam suggested they all go for a beer. Sending a text to Angel that he was going to be late in calling her, Adam was surprised at how disappointed he felt when she told him she was going to bed early and she'd talk to him tomorrow.

Did she feel this constant need for his company? While he liked that she was pretty independent, he couldn't help but feel a little put out when she took his absence so easily. Which was insane, because if she was clingy then he wouldn't have liked that either. Maybe a little clingy would be nice.

It occurred to Adam, when he sat down with Liam, Justin, and Chris at the nearby bar that the conversational topics among his friends had shifted drastically. Even more so now the three guys apparently felt he could be included on the relationship talk. Not that they didn't bring up sports or work or their friends or their usual inside jokes, but the talk about women was a lot more specific and a lot more serious. Especially for Chris and Justin.

"We aren't sure what to do," Chris said a little glumly, rounding up his explanation to Adam of the current struggle he and Justin were having with their relationship. Primarily, how to marry her when only one of them could do so legally.

"Have you talked to Jessica about it at all?"

"No."

"Don't you think maybe you should?"

"Thank you! Back up!" Liam said, tipping the mouth of his beer bottle accusingly at Chris and Justin. "I've been telling them that for days."

Justin glared at him. "We want to work it out between ourselves, find a solution we can present to her."

"She'd probably appreciate being able to help with the problem," Adam pointed out. "Isn't the whole point of a relationship being able to work through things together? Don't you think she's going to be pissed when she realizes she's been left out of some important decisions?"

The pair looked at each other, a little uneasily. Adam didn't envy them. This whole relationship business was hard enough when he was half of a couple and trying to find his way. Being part of a permanent threesome added a whole new set of issues, and it seemed like every time the trio worked through one, another one would pop up in their way.

"Besides," he added, "you've only been with her for what... nine months? Not even a year? Don't you think it's a little bit early to be talking about this anyway?"

"Not really," Chris said with a shrug. "We've been talking about it with each other for about two months now, trying to figure out a solution that won't leave either of us feeling left out. It's not like we're going to ask her the second we figure things out."

"We want to figure them out before we ask her," Justin finished.

"Hell, I'll probably end up asking Hilary to marry me before these two idiots figure out an equable scenario," Liam said with a snort. "I told 'em to flip a coin."

"You're already thinking along those lines too?" Adam asked, surprised. Liam and Hilary had been together even less time than Jessica, Justin, and Chris. Although, granted, their relationship dynamics were a lot easier in general.

Liam grinned at him. " I've known since... hell, probably from almost the beginning I wasn't going to let her go. Ever. And in Hilary's world, that means marriage. I want it all official and locked down too. We're working out some of the kinks now that I've finally convinced her to move in with me."

"Some of the kinks?" Chris waggled his eyebrows lasciviously, making all of them groan at the pun.

"You know what I mean," Liam said. "Bickering over how to put the dishes in the dishwasher, what we're going to watch on television every night, when we need our own space... that kind of thing. We might move to a new apartment though, I think she feels a little bit like an interloper in my place even though I made room for her." For someone who was describing the little issues in his relationship, Liam sounded almost smugly content.

Trying to picture Angel living in his house, Adam had to admit he liked the idea of having her there. All the time.

"Ah ha!" He blinked and looked up to see Justin pointing at him and grinning. "I know that look! See? You haven't known Angel for long, but you can't help thinking along the same lines, right?"

Shrugging, Adam shifted, feeling a bit exposed and uncomfortable. "Yeah, but I'd rather take it slow."

"Oh, I'm not asking Hilary to marry me anytime soon. But that doesn't mean it's not on my mind."

Later, home in his own bed, Adam realized Liam wasn't the only one thinking about marriage. If he and Angel continued down the road they were on now, he could see him thinking about it in the future. Sure, there were little things to work through first. Not the least of which was his own issues when it came to marriage and worrying about unhappy revelations.

As Adam knew, he hadn't done anything to piss Angel off or upset her. It was completely smooth sailing. Which was seemed ridiculous thing to worry about, but he didn't remember his parents' fighting much before the divorce. His mother would shove down all of her emotions until they came out in passive-aggressive little snippets his dad didn't notice, right up until the day she got fed up and left.

Angel hadn't said anything to him about the way he'd treated her when she'd first come to Stronghold and he'd realized who she was. In fact, she'd pretty much taken everything he'd dished out. Sure, he'd searched her out and apologized, but she hadn't insisted on it and she'd forgiven him immediately.

Had she not been that bothered by it? Or was she not the type to hold a grudge once she'd received an apology?

Or had she sat on her emotions, the way his mother always had, rather than standing up for herself?

The various scenarios whirled around his head, eventually dragging him down into an uneasy sleep where his dreams were filled with running through fog, a glass slipper in his hand, trying to find Angel, knowing she was nearby but refusing to answer when he yelled her name. It was not a restful night.

ANGEL

"And tonight's gonna be a GOOD GOOD niiiiight!" Angel sang, bouncing as she parked the car in front of the apartment building.

She could understand why Lexie hadn't wanted to share the address with Patrick or any of her other "sentinels." It wasn't a terrible neighborhood, but it wasn't the best either.

As much as she wanted to sit in her car and finish out the song, she also knew it wasn't the best idea. Sometimes the whole proactive self-defense thing could take all the fun away from simple things. Was it likely someone would come and car jack her while she was sitting and dancing in front of an apartment building? No. But she didn't want to be a statistic either.

Lexie had better be the first person enrolled in her self-defense class, Angel thought. Yesterday she'd talked on the phone with Patrick about it, they were going to start advertising soon. Monday and Wednesday nights. Which was good because it gave her something to do while Adam was at Liam's dojo on Wednesdays.

Silly, but she'd missed him this week even though she'd ended up seeing him yesterday. It was probably a good thing they'd had an evening completely apart. Things were moving fast. And by *things*, she meant her emotions. Yesterday it had seemed like he'd pulled away a bit. There was nothing she could put her finger on. But she didn't like feeling like she was falling in love with him—okay, was probably halfway there if not more—without knowing how he felt.

Not that she had any idea how to bring up the conversation.

Sighing, she grabbed the folding chair she'd brought from her backseat, along with the bottles of wine—one white, one red—and headed toward the front of the building.

Lexie hadn't been kidding when she said she didn't have any furniture. Since Jessica and Hilary had gotten there right before Angel, and Olivia ended up practically following her into the building, they all got the grand tour together. Which consisted of being shown the bathroom and the tiny kitchen, which kept the small space from being considered an efficiency.

There was a mattress in the corner for her to sleep on, a large television set up on what looked like a decrepit coffee table, and some cushions and blankets scattered in front of it. The tiny kitchen was fully stocked though, with the important things.

"Found it!" Lexie tossed the corkscrew to Olivia.

Angel shook her head. "This is why twist off tops are the best."

"Corks are classier."

"But ultimately useless now that most wines are made to be drunk within a couple of years rather than being stored for decades," Angel told her.

"I should have known! He's corrupted you already," Olivia accused, waving the wine key at her threateningly. Angel cracked up, because she couldn't deny her opinion came from Adam—heck, she hadn't known why some bottles came with twist offs and some came corked until him.

"Come on you guys, bring out the glasses!" Jessica called from the other room.

With the corkscrew in one hand, wine glass in the other, Olivia sauntered out of the tiny kitchen, Angel and Lexie following her.

"You don't have a couch, but you have wine glasses," Hilary said, giggling as she sat down on the chair she'd brought, accepting the glass Angel had brought her. "Thank you." The soft pink sweater she was wearing set off her blonde good looks; she might be one of the most sincerely nice people Angel had ever met.

"Priorities," Lexie responded cheerfully as she plopped herself down on the floor after handing Jessica a glass. Angel sat down next to her, feeling a little awkward about sitting in her chair when Lexie was on the floor; Jessica sat down too. Looking down at them, Olivia snorted and sat in her chair.

Even though she was relaxed, wearing blue jeans and a blue long-sleeved t-shirt, Olivia still couldn't be mistaken for anything but a take charge woman. Then again, Angel knew she appeared that way sometimes too. She didn't like taking charge in the bedroom or in a relationship. Pretty much anywhere else she was okay with it.

The redhead eyed the line of wine bottles they'd all brought. Since everyone had apparently decided to bring at least two bottles, it was quite a little array they'd gathered.

"There is more wine here than we could possibly drink in one night."

"Challenge accepted!" Jessica and Hilary's voices echoed through the apartment and they all cracked up.

"Are we going to make it out tonight if we do?" Angel asked, laughing. They'd all brought clothes to change into in case they decided to go out, but she didn't think she would make it if they were seriously going to drink all the wine.

"I guess we'll have to wait and see," Lexie said cheerfully. "I don't know about you guys, but I intend to get hammered tonight."

"At least if we go out, it can't possibly be as dramatic as last time," Jessica said. She looked at Angel and shook her head. "*Last* time we had a girls' night out, my asshole ex-boyfriend ended up at the same club as us and tried to get in my face. And then Lexie got in *his* face."

"And then the guys showed up and Olivia finally came back from paying the bar tab," Hilary added cheerfully. "It was a hot mess."

That led to a more in-depth recitation of how Jessica had ended up with Chris and Justin, and Hilary with Liam, than Angel had gotten to hear before. Which was fascinating. The Venus School sounded amazing, although Angel didn't feel the need to go there... although if things didn't work out between her and Adam...

What impressed her the most was how at ease everyone was with Jessica's decision to be with two men. Hilary admitted she hadn't been too sure about it at the beginning, but she'd supported her friend and now she could see how well the relationship worked. Not that they had everything worked out. Angel could tell Chris' estrangement from his family pained Jessica.

Hilary and Liam's story was a more conventional. And then it was Angel's turn to divulge the full story of how she and Adam met and got together, which included some revelations from Olivia.

"You should have seen him when you answered your phone with 'Pretty boy!'" Olivia cackled. "He *pouted*."

"I would give anything to see Adam pouting," Lexie said, giggling madly. Tipping the rest of her wine into her mouth, she looked mournfully at her empty glass. "All this talking is thirsty work. Should I open another bottle of wine?"

"Am I drunk yet?" Angel asked rhetorically, thrusting out her own empty glass.

All of them dissolved into laughter again.

"Should we order some food?" Jessica asked. "I could go for some pizza or Chinese or something to help soak up all this wine."

"That depends, are we staying here, or going out?"

They all looked at the line of wine bottles, of which they'd only worked through about a third so far.

"Staying in!"

Pizza arrived, they put on *Princess Diaries 2*, and no one paid attention to the movie because they were all too busy talking. Okay, they paid some attention to the movie whenever there was something worth watching on it. Like anytime Chris Pine was on screen. Even if he was ridiculously young in the movie, they all knew what he looked like now so it didn't matter he was practically a baby back when the movie had been made.

But mostly they talked. And Angel reveled in the girl gossip. Especially since she was getting all sorts of insights into the group of men Adam was friends with, and some insights into Adam himself. She was amused to find out Jessica and Hilary had both been intimidated by him, although she could understand why. Still, Justin was as intimidating and it's not like Chris and Liam were exactly pushovers. Lexie and Olivia, who had known him for longer, mostly seemed amused by Angel's effect on him.

"In a good way," Lexie reassured her. "It's nice to see him loosen up a little. Hell, he needed it."

"Poor Rick though," Olivia said with a laugh. "He got all of the guys to come down to Virginia with him and Adam was the one who walked away with the girl!"

"Yeah, we need to find Rick someone good once he moves up here," Jessica said. She looked at Angel, hazel eyes sparkling with interest. "What about your friend Leigh?"

"Back with her ex," Angel said a little glumly. "I wouldn't recommend her anyway, not until she and Michael finally finish their little carousel ride."

"That's a good way of putting it," Lexie said. "Reminds me of Jared and Marissa."

"Yeah, I had the same thought. I don't get their relationship. Or Leigh and Michael's."

"I try not to be too judgmental, since a lot of people don't get *my* relationship," Jessica said thoughtfully. Leaning back against a pile of cushions, her curls tumbled about her face, she looked extremely relaxed but a little sad. "Sometimes I don't get my relationship."

"What do you mean by that? I thought everything was going well." Lexie shifted over, putting her hand on Jessica's thigh and looking concerned. Next to them, Hilary sighed and stretched.

"It is... it's just..." Jessica threw up her hands in slightly drunken frustration. "They won't talk about the future. I get the feeling they don't want to even think about it. Sometimes one of them will say something about marriage or kids, but the second I try to turn it into a conversation they change the topic or... well... you know." The fact that she could still blush when talking about sex was pretty darn cute Angel thought. "They know it bothers me, but they still won't talk to me about it."

"Maybe they don't realize how much it bothers you."

"How can they not know it bothers me when we don't talk about the future? When we first got together, we always talked things out. Now they keep shutting me down every time I try. When I first seriously thought about being a threesome instead of a couple, I always worried about not being enough for them or coming between them. I didn't want them to feel like they had to compete over me or like I loved one of them more than the other. Now I feel like there's no way I need to worry about driving a wedge between them, because *I'm* the one getting left out!"

"Have you ever specifically told them it bothers you? Or do you let them shut you down."

The pretty brunette pursed her lips, looking both thoughtful and defensive. She sighed. "I let them distract me."

Lexie shook her head. "Okay, lesson number one for the night. Boys are not psychic."

"You know, you probably shouldn't give out advice you don't

follow," Olivia said mildly, swirling the red wine in her glass. She was looking up in the air, her tone as innocuous and innocent as possible.

"Shut it," Lexie said glaring. "I'm... I'm shy."

The tension in the air broke as everyone cracked up again. Except for Lexie, although even she was giggling, her pale skin splotched with pink. She didn't blush pretty at all, but there was still something endearing about that.

"Look," said Olivia finally, still chuckling every time she looked at Lexie. "Though we adore men individually, as a group, I'm sure we're all aware, they're kind of stupid. And Jess, you unfortunately always have to deal with them as a group, albeit a small one. Worse, they're a dominant group. Which means if something is bothering you, and you hide it, they're probably going to operate on the mentality everything is fine because *they're* taking care of it. At least, they think they are."

"That's what I was trying to say," Lexie complained.

"If they're not talking to you about something," Olivia continued, ignoring Lexie, "then it's probably because they think they have it covered. If that bothers you, then you need to let them know because otherwise they're going to keep doing it."

"But how am I supposed to force them to talk about it when every time I try to, they start kissing me and then... you know."

"You could always tie them to the bed while they're sleeping and then wake them up to start the conversation," Angel suggested. Everyone stared. Not at her, but at Olivia who had literally fallen off of her chair because she was laughing so hard—which of course started the rest of them laughing again.

"Oh God..." Olivia gasped out between burbles of hysterical laughter. "I can see it... tied up... side by side..."

"Stop... oh God, stop it hurts!" Jessica had tears streaming down her face. Angel couldn't even say anything she was laughing so hard at the picture in her mind—which she somehow hadn't even considered before she'd suggested the tactic. There was no doubt they would both be *furious*.

She wondered what Adam's reaction would be to something like that. Sure it'd be hot as hell to have him at her mercy, but she knew half the reason she'd be turned on by it would be because she'd be thinking about what he might do in retribution. Very, very bad things.

"I wonder what would happen if I tried that," Lexie said. Hilary half-screamed with drunken delight before she rolled back and forth, her hands on her stomach as she laughed. None of them could talk. While it hadn't been said outright tonight, they all knew exactly *who* Lexie would try it on.

Angel thought she had balls for even imagining it.

"If you ever do that, you *have* to take a picture of his face!"

"If any of us ever do that..."

"Well, except for Olivia, that's the norm for her."

"Ok, Olivia, if you ever have a sub and—"

"None of them would *dare*." The way Olivia drew herself up, regally disapproving, had all of them sucking in their breath for a moment, worried they'd gone too far. Then her eyes sparkled, and she burst out laughing again. "Oh my God, your faces..."

By the time Angel drunkenly slid into sleep, her head pillowed on Jessica's arm, she realized that for the first time she'd had a ladies' night with a group of girls where she truly liked every single one of them. It was a novel experience. She was sad Leigh hadn't been there to share it.

❧ 26 ❧

ADAM

A week later, Adam was sitting at the Stronghold bar, chatting with some of the Doms who were there while he waited impatiently for Angel. Not that she was late, he was feeling impatient because she'd spent the evening before and all of today with her friend Leigh. He'd gotten a lot done around his house but he'd missed her presence. It had only taken a couple of weeks for him to get used to having her with him all weekend.

They'd had another good week together. And he was still trying to convince himself all the smooth sailing wasn't a bad thing. Just because it reminded him of his parents and the way his dad had thought everything was fine when it wasn't, that didn't necessarily mean something was wrong. Maybe this was why he hadn't had a real relationship in a while, the risk to his heart was high. The more invested he became in her, the more worried he became something was going to go wrong.

"Hey Adam, can I talk to you for a second?"

Adam swiveled around on his stool to face Patrick. Excusing himself from the other Doms, he and Patrick moved away towards the less populated side of the bar, closer to the entrance. Since Andrew was running late, everyone was down on Mistress Lisa's side of the bar.

Just then, Angel came in through the entrance, her face lighting up when she saw him, followed by Liam, Hilary, and Michael. The latter hadn't been to Stronghold in a couple of weeks, Adam realized. Angel had mentioned he was busy most evenings.

He was pleased to realize it didn't bother him at all that Angel and Michael had shown up at the same time. Smiling back at Angel, he waved a hand at the others as his pretty little sub came and snuggled up under his arm. She was wearing a soft dark green velvet bustier, rather than one of her corsets, and a short black skirt. While he liked her corsets, if they were going to play then the bustier was a lot easier for him to get into. Last week when he'd chosen her outfit he'd known she was surprised he'd picked something almost modest. Not that he didn't like the blatantly sexy as well, but he knew she would choose that on her own, which made him want to see her in something slightly different. Today's outfit was almost a mix between the extremes.

"Hey sweetheart," he said, brushing his lips over her forehead before turning his attention back to Patrick. "So, what's up?"

The big man's dark eyes flickered over Angel and then back to Adam. He raised his eyebrow, pulling at the scar across his cheek. "This was the last week of you being out of the Introduction Scene rotation; I wanted to know if you needed to be taken off permanently."

Underneath Adam's arm, Angel stiffened. Adam inwardly cursed. He'd completely forgotten about the rotation.

"Give me a second," he said to Patrick, stepping away and pulling Angel around to face him. Her eyes were practically glowing with anger as she glared up at him. Dammit. "Look, I wanted to talk to you about this..."

"Oh really?"

"I'm sorry this is getting sprung on you like this—"

"Oh yeah, cuz *that's* the problem."

"I wanted to talk to you about how my friends are going to view this."

"I don't know what exclusive means to you..."

"When the other guys said they weren't doing Introduction Scenes anymore..." Adam continued

"But to *me* it means you aren't getting down with anyone else, period."

"Everyone knew it was because they were in serious relationships," Adam finished.

"Oh, so now our relationship isn't serious?"

Angel had pulled away completely, hands on her hips, eyes flashing, and her voice was getting louder. Grabbing her by her arm, Adam started to pull her in closer, but she wrenched them around, pulling her neatly out of his grasp. Dammit. He'd forgotten she'd know how to break a hold, not that he wanted to hurt her or anything, he wanted to touch her to reassure both of them this was not what she obviously thought it was. She was such a tactile person, it made him feel almost panicky that she didn't want him touching her.

"That's not what I meant!"

Crossing her arms, Angel's finger tapped against her bicep as her lips tightened. Behind him, he could see Liam, Patrick, and Michael all watching in amusement. Hilary was safely tucked into Liam's lap, her big eyes wide and incredulous. Frustrated, Adam focused on Angel dragging his fingers through his hair as he tried to order his thoughts.

"Maybe you should explain what you *meant* then."

He didn't know why he'd been so worried Angel might end up being like his mother and hiding away her problems. That was obviously not the case. Which was a good thing, although he wished she was less willing to have a fight right here, right now. It would be better if she'd let him explain right from the get-go, rather than providing entertainment for whoever wanted to watch. Sure, he could forcibly remove them both from their current location, but he didn't think that would go over well with her either. Better to explain first, then move them when she was willing to be touched again. Preferably somewhere he could spank her ass.

"I meant when Justin, Chris, and Liam stopped doing Intro Scenes, it meant... I mean..." Angel raised her eyebrow as he fumbled over his words. "Look, I think our relationship is serious. I do. But I hadn't talked to you about what my friends' expectations would be if I stopped doing Introduction Scenes, that's all I wanted to talk to you about right now. I didn't want to assume you would be okay with what ends up being a public gesture about our relationship."

"Well I am!" She put her hands on her hips and glared at him.

"Okay!"

"Fine!"

"If we agree, why are we yelling?" Adam threw his hands up in utter frustration. Liam and Michael were laughing at him. Out of the corner of his eye he could see several other people watching with interest. Thankfully the background music and conversations going on at the other end of the bar were loud enough they probably couldn't hear everything.

Angel glared at him again. "Because you didn't answer Patrick immediately and tell him to take you off of Introduction Scenes which made me think you didn't *want* to be taken off!"

"Dammit, that was a rhetorical question!"

"Well I decided to answer it," Angel snapped back. Making another sound of frustration, Adam dragged his hand through his hair again. She laughed.

Scowling, Adam took a threatening step towards her. "Don't laugh at me right now, sweetheart."

"You need to lighten up," Angel said, still laughing up at him. "How could you not have found all that funny?" The blaze in her eyes had simmered down, now they were sparkling with suppressed mirth. How the hell did she switch moods so suddenly? He was still feeling all ramped up and irritated.

"You need to let me give you an explanation before you get all pissy with me."

"Well I have a temper. You're lucky I didn't get Patrick and Jared to hold you down so I could paddle your ass."

Okay, now she was asking for it. Adam went for her, and even though she backed up quickly she wasn't fast enough to evade him. He hefted her up onto his shoulder, leaving her hanging down behind him with her ass up in the air. One of his hands wrapped around her thigh, settling between her legs, the other rested on the bare curve of her ass.

Somebody wasn't wearing panties, which meant everyone else was probably getting quite a show.

"*Adam!*" she shrieked, her hands coming up to uselessly tug at the hem of her skirt.

He ignored her, turning toward their friends. At least he could thank his lucky stars Olivia wasn't around to personally witness their little scene. Or Chris or Andrew. They'd hear about it, of course, but at least neither Patrick, Liam, nor Michael would be stupid enough to tease him right now. Hilary was smiling up at him approvingly.

"Patrick, I won't be doing Introduction Scenes anymore. And Angel and I are using the school room for the next hour." Adam spun around, heading for the stairs at the back of the club.

"Oh good," Angel's voice drifted up from behind him, full of sass. He could feel her push herself upwards with one hand on his waist, probably to look at his friends behind them. "I'm feeling hot for teacher."

Smack!

Adam snarled. She was so going to regret doing that. He resisted the temptation to give her ass a slap back immediately. He was going to wait until they got up to the school room where he could take his time. Laughter followed them out of the main room, not just his friends, but every single person who had seen her spank him. He wondered if Angel realized they were all laughing because they knew she was going to regret doing that.

Going by her giggles, he didn't think so.

ANGEL

Ooooooh she was in so much trouble.

And she didn't mind at all. Angel had to admit she liked the occasional caveman thing. Having Adam do it in front of everyone who was in the club, after telling everyone he was off the market, was even better. She'd stopped being mad once she realized that, in his own way, he had been trying to be respectful of her input into their relationship by not immediately telling Patrick he wasn't going to be doing Intro Scenes anymore. Even though she wished he had told Patrick immediately.

But, as Lexie had said last week, boys aren't psychic. And, as Olivia had said, sometimes they're kinda stupid.

Besides, Angel wasn't the type to stay angry for long or to hold a grudge. Their argument hadn't been the scary kind of angry. He'd been trying to placate her while he explained. Which she had been able to see the amusement in once she'd gotten over the initial flash of anger.

Stalking down the hallway, Adam took her to the last room on the left of the upper floor. When he set her down on the teacher's desk, seating her on the edge, she did a quick scan around the classroom. There were some student desks scattered around the room, which didn't look particularly comfortable, and a blackboard and what looked like a children's play area in the corner. She wondered if that was for the Daddy Doms and their subs.

When she finally focused on Adam again, he was waiting patiently, a wicked gleam in his blue eyes. With his arms crossed over his chest and his crisp, white collared shirt, he did look like a teacher. A hot teacher all the girls would have crushes on.

That kind of thing had grossed her out in high school, but right now it was a fun little fantasy to have.

"So, professor, what's up?" she asked impertinently, unable to keep from teasing him. Going by the hard gleam in his eye and the barely controlled energy simmering beneath the surface, Adam's temper didn't slide away the way hers often did. Which, perversely, made her want to poke at him more.

Watching him lose his usual amount of control had been satisfying, when she was angry, and once she'd stopped being so irritated it had been kind of hot.

He muttered something under his breath before he unbuttoned the cuffs of his shirt and began rolling them up, exposing the muscles of his forearm. Who knew a forearm could be so sexy. Pretending meekness, Angel tilted her head and waited for him.

"You are in a ridiculous amount of trouble," he said, once he had finished rolling up his sleeves, the action evidently having calmed him a bit. Looming over her, he planted a hand on either side of her thighs, leaning in so close they were almost kissing. "In fact, Miss Jones... I believe you are a discipline problem."

"Oh, well I'm never against a little discipline," she said teasingly, leaning back and away from him so his face was now in front of her breasts. Her nipples were hard little points thrusting through the fabric of her bustier. Normally she liked corsets better because they held in all the stuff she liked having hidden, but right now she was a bustier fan. Adam's eyes lingered over her nipples, something he would haven't been able to see if she'd been in a corset. "If you think it's necessary Mr. Rawn."

"I definitely think so," he said, a sexy little growl in his voice. Angel squealed as he suddenly flipped her over. Holy crap... the quickness of the spin had made her skirt lift up, completely exposing her backside to him. Not that it hadn't already been pretty exposed when he'd had her over his shoulder. She couldn't lie though, that little bit of exhibitionism had made her even wetter when he'd been carrying her off.

Fingers stroked over the bare skin of her butt and she moaned a little. The desk was hard and cold underneath her body, but who cared? She was all hot and wet and bothered.

"You have such a fantastic ass."

Smack! Angel squealed a little as the sting flared where his hand had landed.

"Nicely rounded."

Smack!

"I love watching it jiggle when I spank you."

Smack!

Angel bit her lip to keep back a comment about how a woman doesn't want to hear how her ass jiggles. She had a feeling she was already in for enough of a punishment without adding to it.

He chuckled, a pleased sound that made her insides heat up even more.

"And it turns so nice and pink so easily."

Smack! Smack! Smack! Smack!

Whimpering, Angel did a little dance as the burning made her squirm uncomfortably. This spanking had more of a bite to it than any of the recent ones he'd given to her, the crisp swats coming down hard and unforgiving on the unprotected cheeks of her ass. She pressed her palms hard into the desk to keep from reaching behind her and trying to cover them, but it wasn't easy.

Smack!

"Ow!"

He'd gotten her right on the tender area between her bottom and thighs, and Angel's hands moved of their own accord.

"Uh, uh," Adam said chidingly.

"I couldn't help it, that hurt!"

"It's supposed to." She heard him open one of the desk drawers and then warm fur was wrapped around her wrists. "This should help."

The cuffs tightened and then he pulled her wrists up so they rested in the small of her back. Angel bit her lip against a moan. There was something about being restrained, unable to even try to resist, that made her even hotter. Only because it was Adam, though, and she trusted him not to hurt her beyond what she could handle, no matter how annoyed he was with her at the moment.

But he might take her right up to the edge. And now there was nothing she could do about it. Her pussy clenched.

Smack!

Her wrists jerked against the cuffs, his hand easily holding them in place by the chain linking them together. His hand came down again and again.

Angel moaned and writhed, squealing whenever his hand came down hard on a particularly sensitive spot. And the more he spanked her, the wetter and needier she got.

ADAM

There was something immensely satisfying about delivering a hard spanking when Angel truly deserved it. He understood why she'd gotten upset, but she hadn't given him a chance to explain before she'd blown up at him. If she'd done so publicly elsewhere, he could have gone easier on her, but they'd already had the discussion that at Stronghold she was his submissive and would act accordingly.

Spanking him while he'd carried her away was going to have its *own* repercussions.

But not yet.

Squeezing the pink globes of her ass, he enjoyed the way she moaned and squirmed under his hands. Her wrists were crossed almost delicately, held firmly in place by the tooled leather cuffs with a short chain between them. He was going to need to start carrying around his own on a regular basis. He hadn't missed how much Angel liked being restrained—and to be perfectly honest, he'd be happy keeping her in cuffs every second they were in the club and for long periods of time outside of it.

"Alright, Miss Jones," he said, grasping her by the hips and pulling her off the desk. Turning her around to face him, he pushed her to her knees. The bright amber eyes looking up at him were glazed with arousal, her nipples practically drilling holes in her bustier. With her wrists locked behind her back, it thrust her breasts out even more, offering them up to his hands. "You're going to show me how sorry you are now."

Undoing his belt, he smiled as she licked her lips, tracing her perfect little mouth with her tongue. The second his cock was out, she was leaning forward, straining to taste him. He groaned with pleasure as her tongue swiped up the center of his head, collecting the drop of pre-cum gathered there. The sensation of her hot, wet tongue gliding over the head of his cock was teasingly blissful.

"That's it, sweetheart, take me in."

Angel hummed with pleasure as she let his cock slide between her lips, sending vibrations trickling up the shaft and his spine. As he moaned with pleasure, Adam dug his fingers into her hair, disarranging the messy up do she'd put it in even further. Pins fell to the floor, unheeded, as he wrapped his fingers around the back of her head and pushed her further onto his cock.

Wet warmth engulfed him, her tongue lashing against the under-side of his cock. He could feel her throat spasm as he pushed deep, and he retreated immediately to give her some time to get used to it. Without her hands she was a lot more vulnerable to him, unable to tap out if he became too rough, which meant he had to pay even closer attention than normal. Which was how he liked it, with him completely in control.

Looking down, he watched as his cock began to pump in and out of those gorgeous lips. Tilting her head back, he knew he was putting some strain on her neck, but he wanted to look into her eyes while he fucked her mouth. They were glowing, eager, staring up at him and he groaned before releasing his hold, allowing her head to slide forward into a more natural position.

He wanted as much stamina as possible for what he was going to be doing next, which was why he was going to get off in her mouth now. Then she'd have the taste of him on her tongue for the rest of the scene.

Moving his hips back and forth, he was gentle but firm as he began to take her mouth long, sure strokes. The length of his cock glistened as it pistoned between her lips, her hungry moans only encouraging him to move faster and harder. Every time she sucked him hard, her cheeks would hollow out, her tongue and throat working in tandem and wreaking havoc on his control.

"Fuck... Angel..." Gasping, he jerked forward, burying himself in her mouth. He could feel her pressing against him even though he was trying not to gag her, taking him into her throat as he started to cum. Every spurt made his knees feel weaker as she sucked and swallowed.

It was probably a good thing she did have her hands cuffed behind her back, she didn't need anything more than her mouth to drive him wild.

Shuddering, he let her milk every last drop from him before he pulled away. His cock, still half-hard, hung down in front of him.

"Thank you, sweetheart, that was very good," he said, caressing her head gently. Panting, Angel laid her head against his thigh, rubbing her cheek against his skin. "Now let's deal with the rest of your punishment."

Angel's head jerked back. "But—"

Curving his hand under her chin, Adam put his thumb on her lips.

He raised his eyebrow at her. "You thought if you spanked me, all you would get was a little spanking? No, the spanking was for not letting me talk to you and explain before you got all huffy in front of everyone. *Now* I'm going to punish you for being so insolent."

As he pulled her to her feet she didn't protest, but she was eyeing him warily, uncertainly, as if she wasn't sure what to expect from him now. Adam hid his grin from her, enjoying seeing her off balance. Sometimes his Angel was a little too sure of herself. And apparently he'd gotten predictable if she thought she was going to get off with just a little spanking.

❧ 27 ❧

ADAM

Adam unhooked the chain that kept Angel's cuffs together so he could help her take off the bustier, followed by the skirt. Getting her back up onto the desk, he reattached the cuffs to each other before laying her down flat on her back, moving around to the other side of the desk where there was a short chain under the lip of the desk in case anyone wanted to secure their submissive to the desk itself. Which is exactly what Adam did.

The desk was short enough lengthwise that Angel's bottom was only inches away from the end of it, her knees bent and pointed to the ceiling with her legs spread wide. He left enough give in the chain that he would be able to pull her to the edge of the desk itself once he was ready to. Right now, he was enjoying the view of her anxious face as he immobilized her upper body, as well as the slight jiggling of her breasts as she squirmed and the little cherry points of her nipples.

"What do you think, sweetheart?" he asked, leaning forward slightly to take each of her breasts in one hand, squeezing the luscious mounds roughly. "Do you feel vulnerable? Helpless?"

She squirmed some more as he pinched her nipples, moaning.

"Yes."

"Good. Because you are." He pinched her nipples harder, tugging them away from her body to emphasize his point. Angel cried out, arching her back as she tried to relieve the pressure on her sensitive tips. When he let them go, she flattened back down on the desk, her breath coming in short, excited pants.

"What color, Angel?"

"Green," she purred. Her cheeks were flushed and her eyes were glowing as she looked up at him, a banquet of feminine flesh for him to indulge in.

Grinning, Adam went back to the same drawer he'd gotten the cuffs from. Someone had left little samples of various oils in there, probably someone trying to convince Patrick to add them to the goodies regularly stocked around the club. Adam wasn't sure he liked the idea of communal oil bottles, but he was willing to use the samples available.

Hmm.... minty menthol. Perfect.

Opening the packet, he squeezed some directly onto Angel's nipples and began to rub it in. She eyed him suspiciously.

"What's that—oh... It's cold! And tingly!"

"Fun, isn't it?" he asked, letting his fingers glide down her body. There wasn't enough oil on them to give her more than flickers of the cool sensation against the skin of her stomach, but it let her know exactly where he was headed.

"Adam, I don't know—"

"Shhh... it's going to feel good. Besides, how are you going to stop me?" he asked, knowing the reminder she was at his mercy would only turn her on more. Angel groaned, but her pussy was leaking like a sieve. He ignored the way she was wriggling; the movement would make the air feel even colder against her nipples.

Parting her pussy lips with two fingers, he leaned down to suck her clit directly into his mouth, eliciting a shocked cry from her as warmth engulfed the little nubbin. He wondered how it felt, to have her nipples burning with icy fire while her clit was surrounded by his hot mouth. Flicking his tongue against it, he could feel the tiny bundle of nerves getting bigger.

She was going to both love and hate this.

Now that his tongue had completely teased her clit out from underneath its hood, Adam pulled back and put the packet next to the swollen nub.

"Oh, Adam, noooooo..."

"Oh, Angel, yes," he said tauntingly, grinning evilly as he coated her clit in the oil. Angel gasped, writhing as he rubbed it in with his fingers, trying to keep the oil centered on her clit rather than allowing it to spread to the surrounding areas.

"It's cold but it *burns.*"

Her legs started to close, an automatic reaction to protect her most sensitive areas, but Adam put his hands on her inner thighs, keeping them apart. Leaning forward, he blew directly onto her clit and then had to clamp his hands down as Angel writhed, moaning from the intense sensations he was creating. Fuck she was hot.

Standing back up, Adam pulled her legs up on his shoulders so her ass was at the edge of the table, lined his cock up with her pussy and shoved in, deep, fast, and hard. Angel screamed, her body arching as the walls of her tunnel clamped down around him in ecstasy. Her entire body jerked. Holding himself completely immobile, his hands pressing down on her hips, he didn't even allow her to rub her tormented clit against him, all she could do was pulse around him as her pussy muscles contracted and released.

Dragging in a ragged breath, Angel attempted to squirm against him and groaned when his hard grip didn't allow her even a centimeter of movement.

Feverish eyes fluttered open, looking up at him pleadingly.

"Adam, *please,*" she begged. That was all he needed.

ANGEL

Cold fire like she'd never felt before... her nipples were still tingling but the sensations there had faded in comparison to the way the oil was burning on her clit. It made her want to squeeze her legs together,

her body instinctively wanted pressure against her clit to help relieve the burning, but there was a big, hot, hard man between them who wouldn't let her. And when he finally pressed himself against her clit, she immediately wanted to rub and move and get some friction going to heat up the icy sensation, but he wasn't doing that either.

So, she begged.

And he began to move.

"Oh God... please... please... please... please..."

Her pleas became louder with every thrust of his hips, her sore bottom banging against the hard table. Jesus, she was burning all over. Her nipples, her butt, her clit, and inside her pussy where the friction of his rough fucking was driving her absolutely wild. She was stretched out before him like a pagan sacrifice, her legs hooked over his shoulders so he had full access to her pussy, and he was watching her like she was hotter than any porn star.

Was it any wonder she began to orgasm almost immediately once he started fucking her?

She screamed as the ecstasy shuddered through her, washing along her limbs as chaotic waves seemed to crackle and burst with electric pleasure. The echoes of her voice reverberating back to her sounded like she was sobbing. Adam's hands on her hips held her in place as he fucked her through the orgasm, keeping her from rubbing herself against him, prolonging the pleasure as he thrust over and over again. Her spasming muscles strained to hold him, the friction becoming almost uncomfortable as he plowed into her without pausing.

If her hands had been free she would be clawing at his back, trying to get him to cum so the intense sensations would finally peak and cease.

Instead, all she could do was cry out, writhe, and orgasm helplessly while his hard cock continued to pound into her.

When he pulled out, her entire body shuddered in relief for the momentary break. Then she felt the slick head press against her asshole, forcing its way forward. Angel gasped then groaned as he pushed in. This time he didn't work himself back and forth. It was a long, slow intrusion that made her muscles spasm and clench as he tunneled inward.

She was burning, inside and out. Every inch of her felt exquisitely sensitive. When she opened her eyes and looked up, she saw Adam's face, intense and serious, his own eyes glued to where their bodies were fusing together. She could only imagine how it must look, her pussy all wet and creamy with the results of her orgasm, while below her anus stretched tight around the thick girth of his cock. Fuck. She wished she could watch too.

That's if she could take any more of this at all. It felt like she was seconds away from cumming again and she almost didn't want to. Was the human body built to withstand this much stimulation? This much of a sensory overload? It felt like tingling, sizzling bubbles were popping against her nipples and clit, her pussy lips felt almost bruised from the hard fucking she'd just received, and the inside of her pussy would have been rubbed raw if she hadn't been so damn wet.

And now he was forcing her ass open and the discomfort was so wonderfully delicious, the burning stretch of muscles so damned exciting.

"Adam..." Her voice sounded hoarse. Distant. He met her gaze, his blue eyes blazing with lustful need. "Are you going to be gentle?"

His wonderful, wicked smile spread across his lips.

"No."

He pulled out and rammed in hard, not waiting for her response, and then did it again and again, fucking her ass as fast and hard as he had her pussy. And Angel screamed as the pain and pleasure rioted through her, her ass clenched down, pulling at him and he groaned. The tight ring of muscle burned even hotter as he thrust past it, over and over, until she felt like she was existing in a world of pure sensation.

Closing her eyes, her world narrowed down to the burn, the clench, the never-ending pulse of sensation that worked into her. She'd never trusted anyone with her body like this before, never let anyone push her past her limits, never given herself over to anyone the way she had with Adam.

The ecstasy seemed to have reached an incredible plateau. Her body was awash in pleasure, shot through with lightning bolts of painful rapture. She was floating on a sea of bliss, of rolling sensation, and when she finally felt him begin to throb and pulse inside of her, hot spurts of liquid filling her, the sea took her under.

ANGEL

When Angel blinked her way back to awareness, she was cuddled up in Adam's arms, sitting on a couch in what she recognized as the after-care corner. A warm blanket was wrapped snugly around her and her head was resting on his shoulder while he cradled her with one arm and stroked her hip with the other. Shifting slightly, she winced as her asshole squeezed and she realized he'd plugged her.

The man was obsessed with filling her asshole. Not that she had any real complaints about it. It was so dirty and hot, so very him to want to do something debauched when he gave off the vibe of being kind of uptight, that it made her enjoy it even more.

"Hey sweetheart, waking up?"

"Was I asleep?" she asked, tipping her head back. She felt all warm and muzzy and content. Especially when she saw the smile on his face. Tender. Sweet. And very smug.

"You were a little out of it." Dipping his head down, he gave her a long lingering kiss which had her sighing happily. "How are you feeling?"

"Very green, Sir."

Adam laughed and hugged her closer. "Good. Not so mad at me anymore?"

"I stopped being mad at you before you dragged me off like the caveman you are. Are you still mad at me?"

"No. Although next time we have a... ah... disagreement, we're going to handle it in private, not in public. And you're going to listen before getting mad."

"I'll try," she said, a little ruefully. "But just so you know, I do have a quick temper. I get over it quickly, too. But I'll try."

"That's all I can ask."

"And the next time someone asks, or otherwise inquires, whether or not you're in a serious relationship, what are you going to say?" She found the opening in the blanket and poked him in the chest. Hard.

"Ow! Cut that out. We're still in the club and I can still turn you over my knee if I need to." Angel giggled and he smiled down at her before his face became more serious again. "Angel, I know we haven't been together long, but you drive me absolutely up the wall and—"

"Hey!"

"Ouch! What did I say about poking me? And listening to my explanations before you get mad?"

"Fine. Finish." She scowled at him. "But the ending better be a lot better than the beginning."

Adam scowled back at her. "And this is exactly what I mean. You drive me crazy, you turn everything I think upside down and... you are not the woman I would have chosen to fall in love with." Angel froze. "At first I was worried you were a liar. Then I worried about your guy friends and how they all want you."

"No, they don't," she said automatically, before clamping her mouth shut again. She didn't want to interrupt him. Nope, she wanted to hear this explanation. Her heart was pounding faster than marching band's drum. Adam gave her bottom a little thwack.

"Stop interrupting, that's not my point." He said, and shifted her again, making it easier for them to look at each other directly. Those bright blue eyes were intensely sincere. "Then I worried you might be like my mom, that you might hide away your feelings when you're upset with me or don't like something I'm doing." Angel giggled and he gave her a wry smile. "Yes, thank you for proving me wrong about that tonight. The point is, you're scattered and unscheduled, you're constantly surprising me when I hate surprises, and I think, in the back of my mind, I kept looking for excuses about why this relation-ship wouldn't work. Even though every moment I was spending with you was making me incredibly happy. And then tonight when Patrick baited me and you almost walked out, all I could think about was how much I didn't want you to go. How it killed me to see I'd hurt you.

"I didn't know what my ideal woman would be like, but I never guessed she would kick my ass at video games, or make me laugh quite so much, or make me feel like being silly, or make me utterly lose my shit in front of my friends. I would have begged if you hadn't been willing to listen to me before walking out tonight, and I wouldn't have cared who knew it. I kept waiting for the other shoe to drop in our relationship and tonight I thought it had because of something stupid *I'd* done... and I hate that you felt insecure and unsure of me and I know that's my fault.

"So, what I'm saying is... you drive me crazy and I think I've fallen in love with you."

"Oh... Adam..." Angel's voice choked up and she launched herself at him. Well, as much as she could launch herself when she was already wrapped up in his arms and only inches away from his face. She kissed him. Desperately. Passionately. With all the emotion bubbling around inside of her since the day she met him.

Chuckling, he pulled away. "What, I give a long, involved speech and all I get back is 'oh Adam'?"

"How am I supposed to top everything you just said?" she asked, gurgling with laughter. "Or even match it?" She stroked her finger down his cheek before rubbing her hand through his facial hair, feeling almost awestruck that this controlled, closed-off man was hers and he had opened himself up to her in such an incredible, vulnerable way. "You aren't the kind of guy I thought I'd fall in love with either. Too controlled. Almost prissy sometimes."

"Watch it, brat," he growled.

Angel smiled at him, brilliantly. "I love you, Adam. Every grouchy, silly, demanding bit of you. And you drive me crazy too."

And grabbing his lapels, she gave into the little bit of Domme inside of her that he'd first met and been so intrigued by and pulled him in for another kiss.

EPILOGUE

RICK

I t would be amazing if he had any friends left by the end of today. Free beer and pizza did not make up for having to drag the endless line of boxes and furniture up two and a half flights of stairs. Especially since it was kind of unseasonably warm for June.

"Goddamn, Rick," Patrick groaned as he shouldered his way into the front door for the umpteenth time. "What the hell do you have in this box?"

Setting his own box down on the pile that had been started in the corner of the main room, Rick glanced at the label on the box Patrick was setting down and grinned.

"That's gotta go in the kitchen, it's got the stand mixer in it," he replied. Which also made it one of the heaviest boxes he had. Was it wrong to say a quick prayer of thanks he hadn't had to bring it up the stairs himself?

"Then you put it in the kitchen," Patrick grumbled. "I'm done with it."

"Thanks for bringing it all the way up."

The big man sighed. "This better show you how happy we all are to have you up here. I'm not sure we'd do this for anyone else."

"No one else would dare ask," Liam said as he came in through the door. His muscles bulged around the box he was carrying. Books, going by the orange label on the side. Probably some of the heavier ones going by the strain he was showing. "When Hilary and I move, I'm hiring movers."

"I'll do that next time," Rick muttered guiltily.

"Don't worry about," Liam said, adding his box to the pile in the corner. "We're glad you're up here. Plus, you've helped all of us move before. Turnabout's fair play."

Ever since Liam and Hilary had become a couple, Liam had started spouting off all sorts of weird old sayings, courtesy of his girlfriend and her father. Rick grinned. Being a high school English teacher, he had his own language quirks when it came to old words and phrases.

And it was true he'd helped the others move before, but to be fair, none of them had moved in a long time. They hadn't accumulated the amount of stuff he had at the time they'd moved. But every single one of them had shown up today to help him. Girlfriends in tow.

Speaking of which, Jessica came in the door carrying what was obviously one of the lighter boxes. "I think this is the last trip! Angel's got the other box that's going in the bedroom, Andrew and Chris have the couch, Jared and Adam have your mattress, Lexie and Olivia are handling the box spring, and Justin and Hilary have the last box."

"The heavy one?" Liam sprang up, but Jessica glared him back down.

"It's not that heavy and don't you dare insult her by insinuating she can't handle it!" Jessica said warningly before turning to go down the hall towards Rick's bedroom.

He couldn't help but sigh a little that the first five women in his bedroom weren't there for anything enjoyable.

Last summer, almost a year ago, he'd met Jessica for the first time. Unfortunately, Justin and Chris had already had dibs. All three of them had been working at the Venus School. Rick had decided to forego the school this summer. He didn't want more meaningless sex, even if he'd enjoyed being an Instructor there, he wanted a relationship. Had wanted a relationship for a while.

Then he'd watched Jessica fall in love with Chris and Justin and they'd moved in together. Not that everything was perfect with them of course, but he knew lately they'd been talking about what form their relationship might take in the future. For a while Chris and Justin had been trying to work it out between themselves, but Jessica had bulled right in there and said she had as much right as they did when it came to deciding who was going to marry who or whatever they were going to do. They hadn't worked it out completely yet, but they were well on their way.

Liam and Hilary had been next and they had already moved in together, although they were talking about moving to a new place since the apartment they were living in now had been Liam's for years and Hilary was feeling a bit like an intruder into his space. And, most recently, Adam and Angel had gotten together and he knew Adam was working his way towards getting Angel to move in with him. They'd been dating since almost the beginning of the year and Adam made it no secret he was head over heels serious about her. So far Angel had been ignoring his hints that he wanted her around on a 24/7 basis, but Adam had told Rick that more and more of her stuff was slowly finding its way into his house.

Even Lexie and Patrick's situation seemed to be coming to a head. He'd let her onto the main floor of the club twice now and it would be a third time in a couple of weeks. She was running the theme night parties at Stronghold that Patrick had decided to allow her to hold for holidays.

As the rest of Rick's friends came in the door, carrying the last of his possessions, he thanked each of them. Guiltily, he also felt better when he saw Jared and was reminded that having a relationship wasn't enough, he wanted a good relationship. Jared's submissive and girl-friend Marissa was off on another one of her overseas jaunts. She'd been thrilled to be offered a small modeling contract in Italy. Not surprisingly, she'd once again told Jared she wanted an open relation-ship while they were apart.

Man, he hated that bitch.

Jared was the only one of his friends who had the kind of relationship Rick *didn't* aspire to.

He was ready to settle down, find a submissive for the long haul. Hell, he'd been looking for months now. Knowing he wanted to move and then finding a new job and a new apartment had helped to relieve some of the impatience he'd felt about it, but now he was up in Maryland near his friends and near the club. Patrick had asked him if he wanted to be put on the Introduction Scene rotation, figuring it would be a good way for him to meet new submissives, but Rick had declined.

It wasn't that he was against newbies, but he'd be able to meet those subs eventually anyway. And he didn't want to have to deal with the whole, "when to stop doing the Intro Scenes" issue, the way Adam had with Angel.

Looking around at his amazing friends, who had all come together to help him move into his new apartment, he couldn't help but think about what an incredibly lucky guy he was in so many ways. It was the one thing he was missing that bothered him. Going into the kitchen to grab beers while they waited on the pizza, he glanced out the window. He had a fantastic view of the pool outside from both the kitchen window and his balcony.

There weren't too many people out there right now, surprisingly. He'd been told it was a pretty quiet neighborhood. A couple of skinny teenage boys, rough-housing in the pool itself, and a curvy brunette sunbathing by herself. Rick took a moment to appreciate the scenery, as she had very nice curves. It wasn't like he could enjoy any of the very nice curves currently in his apartment, so it was nice to have a bit of eye candy for a moment.

"Rick, are you getting the beer?" Olivia's voice came closer, as if she was heading for the kitchen, and he turned away from the window.

"Yeah, coming."

He grabbed the cooler filled with beer and ice that he'd set up earlier. They should be nicely chilled by now.

Putting a smile on his face, he returned to the main room. Everyone was sprawled out on either his couch or the various chairs that had been pulled over from the dining room area, looking sweaty but satisfied. Rick noticed all of the couples—and the trio—had ended up on his sectional so they could sit next to each other. Patrick, Olivia, Jared, and Andrew were all sitting in chairs. Although Lexie was sitting on the ground in front of Patrick, a pretty frequent position for her. He wondered when the big man was going to notice Lexie often set herself up in the position that would normally be reserved for his submissive.

"So... I wanted to thank you all for coming and helping me out today. It means a lot. Pizza is on the way, and here's the beer." With a grin, he set the cooler down in the center of the room as everyone cheered. The mood was relaxed and happy, but Rick couldn't help envying those on the couch as he sat down in one of the chairs.

He hated feeling jealous, but he had to wonder, when would it be his turn?

I HOPE YOU ENJOYED ANGEL AND MASTER ADAM. MASTER RICK FINDS his happily-ever-after next with his naughty new neighbor - CLICK HERE to pick up your copy of Taming the Tease.

Want a free Stronghold story - Liam and Hilary's engagement story is available exclusively to my newsletter! CLICK HERE to join the Golden Angel Legion!

THE END

ABOUT THE AUTHOR

Golden Angel is a USA Today best-selling author of heart and bottom warming romance.

She is happily married, old enough to know better but still too young to care, and a big fan of happily-ever-afters, strong heroes and heroines, and sizzling chemistry.

When she's not writing, she can often be found on the couch reading, in front of her sewing machine making a new cosplay, hanging out with her friends, or wandering the Maryland Renaissance Fair.

www.goldenangelromance.com

BB bookbub.com/authors/golden-angel
g goodreads.com/goldeniangel
f facebook.com/GoldenAngelAuthor
o instagram.com/goldeniangel

OTHER BOOKS BY GOLDEN ANGEL

CONTEMPORARY BDSM ROMANCE

Venus Rising Series (MFM Romance)

The Venus School

Venus Aspiring

Venus Desiring

Venus Transcendent

Venus Wedding

Venus Rising Box Set

Stronghold Doms Series

The Sassy Submissive

Taming the Tease

Mastering Lexie

Pieces of Stronghold

Breaking the Chain

Bound to the Past

Stripping the Sub

Tempting the Domme

Hardcore Vanilla

Steamy Stocking Stuffers

A Sassy Christmas

Entering Stronghold Box Set

Nights at Stronghold Box Set

Stronghold: Closing Time Box Set

Masters of Marquis Series

Bondage Buddies

Master Chef

Law & Disorder

Switch Play

Legally Bound

Shallow Submission

Hidden Away

Giant Tamer

Third Wheel

Dungeons & Doms Series

Dungeon Master

Dungeon Daddy

Dungeon Showdown

Daddies Everywhere

Chef Daddy

Foosball Daddies

Taco Daddy

Little Villain

HISTORICAL SPANKING ROMANCE

Domestic Discipline Quartet

Birching His Bride

Dealing With Discipline

Punishing His Ward

Claiming His Wife

The Domestic Discipline Quartet Box Set

Alien Tribute

Alien Abduction

Standalone

Mated on Hades

SHIFTER ROMANCE

Big Bad Bunnies Series

Chasing His Bunny

Chasing His Squirrel

Chasing His Puma

Chasing His Polar Bear

Chasing His Honey Badger

Chasing Her Lion

Night of the Wild Stags

Chasing Tail Box Set

Chasing Tail... Again Box Set

Made in the USA
Coppell, TX
14 March 2024

30107084R00217